SECOND CHANCE CIRCUS

Ryan Tang

Contents

Chapter One

The immortal soul industry was a seller's market. There were countless hungry demons and insufficient desperate humans.

That was what made Achille "Bones" Bonaparte unique. He'd tried to sell his soul a dozen times already, and it was only sheer numerology that gave him a tiny bit of hope for attempt number thirteen.

Although technically the only son of a minor noble, Bones dressed in tattered, black rags, as if to complement the unusually dark and unusually large shadows that doggedly followed him even on the sunniest of days. Due to a life spent secluded indoors, he had a blindingly pale face, the perfect contrast to the dark bags under his eyes.

Naturally intelligent, he'd spoken his first word at one year old. Even more naturally dour, he'd only smiled his first smile at age five, after a performance by the legendary Great Clown.

Both of Bones's parents were blond, but twenty-five years ago, Bones had been born with a shock of pitch-black hair that stubbornly stuck straight up above his head. Upon his birth, the midwife had nervously speculated it might have something to do with the heat, and Bones's mother,

Annabella, had furiously protested against any possibility of infidelity.

In reality, the pitch-black color was just a good, old-fashioned bad omen.

Bones's infernal customer was a particularly fancy demon by the name of Sir Francis Baskerville.

Despite his reptilian scales and the curled, goat-like horns that always forced their way through his precious plumed hats, Sir Francis struck a handsome and cultured figure. Before descending into demonhood, Sir Francis had been a highly successful merchant with exceptionally high wealth and exceptionally low scruples. His elegant, immaculately tailored, and ruffle-filled clothes perfectly fit the fashion from a hundred and fifty years ago.

A jeweled ceremonial sword hung at his waist—Sir Francis might have turned himself into a demon, but he'd paid for that knighthood with good money. He had no plans on dropping his "Sir," unless he received a full refund plus interest and a tidy fee for emotional damages.

Out of the thirteen who had attempted to purchase Bones's soul, Sir Francis was likely the most experienced and undoubtedly the most conceited. With his otherworldly knowledge of contract law and equal opportunity exploitation practices, Sir Francis owned a diverse portfolio of over two hundred and fifty souls.

The sight of their transaction was just outside Bones's cottage—an excellent location for Bones, who did not feel comfortable traveling.

The rustic evening countryside sprawled like a cat on a sofa, and the nearby field of wild green grass—taller than Bones himself—swayed rhythmically in the gentle breeze. It was the pleasant turn between spring and summer, and the sun was just beginning to set, basking the road in one final golden glow. A narrow dirt path wound its way through the grass, gradually descending a valley and connecting Bones's lonely cottage to the town of Golden Fields.

From afar, nobody would have suspected demonic dealings—the utterly cozy scene was not the slightest bit chthonian.

But Bones's exceptional life circumstances had resulted in exceptional experience with demons. The field of tall grass had been rustling a bit too much recently, and over the last week, he'd heard cackling accompanied by the faintest whiff of brimstone.

He knew that someone was waiting for him inside, and when he stepped up to the tall grass, Sir Francis's voice, oily enough for an instant heart attack, whispered back to him. "You…boy…your name is *Bones*, isn't it? It seems like you're *missing* something, Bones. A deal with me could solve all your problems, and I promise it will only cost you a tiny, little bit…"

Bones paused.

'Bones' was actually his childhood nickname. He was surprised that the demon knew it. What was next—guessing his mother's maiden name and the name of his first pet?

Then again, perhaps a demon who had conducted such thorough research could give him what he was looking for.

"I'm interested."

"Oh, excellent…excellent! What would you like? I promise short-term happiness. That's the Sir Francis Baskerville guarantee!"

"I'd like to make friends." At the mention of friends, Bones's voice took on a heart-wrenchingly resigned tone.

Sir Francis barely suppressed a cackle. Resignation, desperation, wits' end frustration—those were the perfect leading indicators of a soul bound for eternal damnation. "Friends? That's all you want?"

"Yeah. Other than Sofia, there's nobody else. Everyone I try to talk to gets way too scared. And it's not just humans. The last time I got into a carriage, the horse dragged us into the river to try to get away from me. Even ghosts and demons run away from me."

"Oh, they just don't see you for the treasure that you are..." Sir Francis chuckled. "And now...you are *my* treasure!"

Sir Francis lunged out of the grass, grabbing on to Bones's shoulder with a scaly claw—he'd always considered himself a master of the hard close. "Boy...your soul is mine! But don't worry... I have countless friends you can spend eternal servitude with, once you rid of me that pesky thorn Baron Angelo. He's been getting far too uppity, calling himself 'the Deathless Prince'—"

Suddenly, Sir Francis realized that his claws had splintered and crumbled into keratinous chalk. His whole body abruptly went frigid. This was far beyond a creeping chill—a breakneck blizzard rampaged up his spine. Goosebumps exploded on his arms and legs, threatening to dislodge his demonic scales.

Under normal circumstances, Sir Francis would have been wondering why in the hells he still had goosebumps, but sheer terror had overwhelmed all rational thinking. The shadows on the road lengthened and darkened, twisting into the shape of the guillotines he'd richly deserved during his mortal life.

Realizing his terrible mistake, Sir Francis let out a wail of terror, vanishing in a plume of scarlet flame. "What… What was… Angelo thinks he's the Deathless Prince…but…but it's you! You don't even need undead troops at your back. You're invincible on your own!"

"Wait! No! Come back!" Bones shouted.

He pushed his way into the tall grass, trying to find some hint of the demon. Their conversation had only lasted mere moments, but Francis had managed to talk to him for longer than anyone else except for his old maid, Sofia.

But as the grass continued burning, Bones had to accept that the demon was gone.

He sighed. It'd been rather rude of Sir Francis to scream at him, and even ruder to set the tall grass by his cottage on fire.

"Though I guess I feel pretty bad about what happened after he grabbed me…" Bones muttered.

Bones had been born with an apocalyptic amount of necromantic energy. Humans thought he had a civilization-ending case of bad vibes. Ghosts and demons were drawn to his power—but only to a point. Once they got too close, they fled in terror, like asteroids that realized they'd rather not fly straight into the sun. The unfortunate result was that Bones had a multigenerational and multidimensional sample size of beings who were terrified of him, and today, that unfortunate sample size had increased by one more.

Bones hurried over to the rough and simple well, little more than a cylindrical hole in the ground with a tiny brick wall around it. Bones had slowly and painfully dug it out for himself and Sofia after the old one had run dry two years ago. Despite the simplicity, he felt genuine pride as he heard the bucket hitting the water.

Slowly and steadily, Bones doused the flames. Then he patted himself down to try to remove the lingering smell of smoke and brimstone before returning to the cottage.

Just like Bones's clothes, the home was far more modest than his social class would have suggested—the entire building was smaller than most rooms in the Bonaparte family manor. While the cottage technically had three rooms, all of them were cramped and tiny.

The walls were made of rough-hewn slate, weathered by years of wind and rain. Moss crept up the walls and the roof was simple thatched straw. Smoke curled lazily from the crooked chimney. A small window, barely the size of a bread loaf, had been jammed into the left wall.

Bones knocked politely on the door.

Sofia's warm and welcoming voice shouted back at him. "Oh, come in already! Stop knocking—this is your home!"

Bones jiggled the perpetually stuck doorknob and braced his feet against the ground as he wrenched open the slightly misshapen door.

The door opened out into an exceptionally comfy scene. A warm beef and vegetable stew bubbled away inside the stone hearth. Sofia had already set out bowls and wooden spoons for dinner on one end of the beaten-up wooden dinner table, which rested beneath a tattered hand-drawn poster showing an enormous red-headed man landing a perfect somersault. On the other end of the table was a pile of very neatly stacked parchment next to fresh quills and an inkpot.

Sofia herself was leaning against one of the two red brick partitions that separated their tiny bedrooms.

She was Bones's maid and had taken care of him ever since he was a small baby. Even at seventy-five years old, Sofia remained tanned and muscular due to a lifetime of hard work, and despite her crooked back, she was still five and a half feet tall, only two inches shorter than Bones. During their rare arguments, she often liked to joke that perhaps she and Bones would have seen eye to eye if she had been younger.

Her hair was an even mix of brown and gray and her amber eyes shone with keen intelligence behind a pair of round, gold spectacles. Like Bones, she preferred wearing the same thing every day. In her case, it was a beige work shirt with brown trousers.

Set throughout the home were burning candles, which Sofia had lit to make up for the setting sun, but as soon as Bones entered, the flames guttered, then died. The air precipitously dropped by several degrees and the shadows lashed violently outwards, as if they wanted to join Bones and Sofia for dinner.

Sofia sighed. "Achille! Be careful when you close the door. You always slam it shut and create such an aggressive breeze. Professor Roman wrote a few weeks ago that our candles likely gutter out so easily because of environmental differences in air pressure. This cottage is at the top of a sloping hill, after all."

The maid hurriedly lit the candles again, muttering vague scientific formulas under her breath as she moved them to safer locations.

Sofia's dogged refusal to believe in the supernatural made her Bones's one and only companion. When she felt a strange chill in the air, she put on a warmer sweater. When ghosts ran screaming in fear of him, she checked for earwax. And no matter how many times the candles guttered away, she lit them again.

She firmly believed that there had to be a scientific explanation for everything, a belief she'd first gained when a traveling doctor had saved her father from the plague when she had just been a child. In gratitude for everything she'd done for him, Bones was constantly trying to lavish her with presents. She'd refused all of them, save for enrollment to correspondence courses at Islington University, the vaunted academy down the road from her hometown of Rustling.

Sofia finished lighting the candles and sat down with Bones for dinner. As she ladled stew into his bowl, she saw something in his eyes that she didn't like. "What's wrong?" she asked.

Bones didn't want to tell her that he'd tried to sell his soul to a demon. It was really rather embarrassing—he couldn't make a friend even if he offered to pay them with his eternal existence. And to make matters worse, Sofia didn't believe in demons in the first place. They'd had this conversation many times before, and he knew she'd gently recommend he create imaginary friends instead of imaginary enemies.

Bones ladled some of the stew into his mouth. The beef seemed to dissolve on his tongue. As always, Sofia's cooking was immaculate. It made him feel better, but only a little bit.

"Did someone run away from you again?" Sofia asked, her eyes narrowing.

"Yeah. That's basically what happened."

"Oh, Achille…" Sofia groaned. She was the only person who still called Bones by his given name. Back when she'd served his family, a surname-based nickname had been inherently confusing. "I know you think you're cursed to never have friends or some poppycock like that, but curses aren't real. There's always a rational explanation for everything. Let me ask you this. Why don't the dead tell any tales? If ghosts and zombies are real, why don't they ever accuse the people who killed them?"

Bones sighed. Every so often, Sofia came up with new arguments to debunk the supernatural.

Little did she know, ghosts *frequently* accused the people who killed them. The only problem was that nobody could see or hear them. In fact, their frustration with the justice system was what led to many hauntings to begin with. As for zombies, most of them had been reanimated without souls, leaving them unable to accuse anyone. If Bones had to guess, ensouled zombies *would* accuse their killers; they were just so rare that nobody had observed it yet.

But before Bones could launch into his lengthy explanation on necromantic taxonomy, Sofia shivered. "Hang on. Let me grab a sweater."

Bones opened his mouth, then shrugged and closed it again. In his mind, Sofia's superhuman ability to ignore the obvious evidence right in front of her was almost as impressive as his actual superhuman abilities. But out of respect for her ever-loving companionship, he'd dropped the argument many years ago.

Sofia came back with not only a new sweater, but a determined expression on her face. "I'm telling you, Achille. It's not just some curse. You need to get out there! Meet more people…you always just stay in the house and have me do all the shopping."

Bones smiled wryly. "Trying to get out of the shopping?"

Sofia laughed and rolled her eyes. "Maybe. But look, Achille, that was a great joke. If you made friends, they'd appreciate your humor as well. Before you worry about curses, how about fixing your posture and putting a brighter expression on your face? You're always slumped over with such a dour look in your eye. I bet things would be different if you laughed and smiled more."

The truth was that Bones couldn't argue with that. He didn't laugh and smile very often.

"You know what we should do?" Sofia asked. "Let's go to the Great Circus."

Bones almost gasped. "The Great Circus? They're performing again?" Over the years, Sofia had suggested many outings for Bones, but this was by far the most tempting. The Great Circus, led by the legendary Great Clown, hadn't performed since Bones had been a child.

"Yes. Word has it that the Great Clown has finally gotten over his depression—and his identity crisis. And they aren't just performing. They're looking for new troupe members. They're conducting tryouts after the show."

"New troupe members?" Bones's eyes widened and he gripped the table leg without realizing it.

"It certainly won't hurt to try out." Sofia smiled. "Best-case scenario, joining a troupe is a great way to make friends. And even if you don't get in, I'm sure the atmosphere and positivity will bring a smile to your face. I still remember how happy you were when you were a kid."

Bones still fondly remembered the joy of attending the Great Clown's show. The brightly lit celebratory atmosphere had nullified the eerie spiritual miasma that had followed him his whole life. It had even encouraged him to try tumbling, though he had never been particularly good at it. "You know what? Let's do it. I seriously doubt I'll get in, but at least I'll be able to refresh the old poster on the wall and see a great show. But let's make sure we sit far away from people. I wouldn't want to ruin it for them. Plus, we should walk to Golden Fields. I don't want to spook any horses again."

"Oh, you and your superstitions… I'm telling you, that was an unlucky streak of poorly trained horses. But very well, we'll walk. I'm just worried these old bones will regret it."

"Well, it beats fishing ourselves out of the river. Besides, if we need to, I can carry you back."

Sofia laughed, but Bones felt guilty. He knew he could do more than just carry Sofia home.

The vast stores of necromantic energy in his body could be used to heal people. Back when he'd been a child, he used to help people and animals, even plants. Even now, it leaked out from him sometimes, automatically healing his hounds.

He thought he could help Sofia, maybe even make her pain vanish. She'd worked for his family for decades, and he'd seen the toll that had taken on her. Sometimes, when he was by himself, he even dared to think of practicing.

But despite the swirling aura of energy around him, so great that it terrified demons and war heroes alike, Bones had desperately avoided using his magic ever since the terrible incident that had happened when he'd been only six years old.

Chapter Two

Bones and Sofia left their lonely cottage, slowly making their way to the winding road that led to Golden Fields. The weekly carriage Sofia chartered to conduct her shopping meant that the road wasn't completely disused, but it was still very poorly suited for walking, with gnarled plant roots and clunky stones poking out of the clumped and uneven dirt.

The tall grass growing along the side of the road, uncut and unmaintained, seemed to loom larger and larger with each step they took, the blades of grass ominously lurching outwards, like the swords of an advancing army.

Sofia *tsked* irritably as Bones pushed the grass aside, making sure it didn't get into their eyes. "If you insist on walking every time we go out, you should pay someone to clear off the roads, Bones. And watch out; you're about to trip over a hole."

Bones, who was still thinking about the demon that'd vanished earlier, gratefully adjusted his step. "I thought there were going to be clean and safe roads for all—one of the bards was singing about it the last time we went into town."

Sofia lowered her voice to a dark whisper. "It would be wise not to talk about this in town, but Baron Angelo has always promised much and delivered little. It feels like he spends more on bards than on builders."

Bones frowned, putting two and two together. The demon he'd met earlier had also talked about Baron Angelo. "Wait. We have a new baron now? Baron Matteo died?"

Sofia laughed in the unique way saved for the foibles of friends. "Over half a decade ago. Bones, that's the problem with being such a superstitious shut-in. Your news of the day is old information."

"That's a shame about Baron Matteo. I remember him being very kind to my father."

"He should have been. Your father saved him at the Siege of Trent. If the rebels had taken the castle, everything would have fallen apart for their House. You know, Angelo was supposed to keep on the tradition…but for some reason, he and your dad never got along."

"Really now?" Bones didn't remember much of his father, but every memory was of a warm and gentle man. It was hard to imagine him not getting along with anyone.

Sofia scoffed. "To be clear, because of Angelo, not because of Lord Gabriel. I don't remember much, but Angelo stormed out of the manor the first time we saw him. He was supposed to get a portrait done with you—you know, the son of the man who'd saved his father—but he rushed home instead clutching his hand and gibbering like a madman."

Bones frowned. Naturally, his mind went to his magical abilities, but he couldn't remember anything like that happening. "I wonder what happened?"

"I have no idea. You were only a baby back then—who has ever heard of a full-grown man running from a baby? But I've never liked him since, and I think time has proven me right."

But for all of Angelo's faults, he'd undeniably made a good investment not bothering to maintain the road outside of Bones's home. In the feudal system, all nobles benefited from passive incomes, but due to his aura of necromantic magic, Bones benefited from passive outcomes as well—without even meaning to, Bones was very good at taking care of himself.

Typically, an awkward and unathletic young nobleman and his elderly maid walking through the wilderness would have found themselves in some kind of danger, but Bones's civilizational case of bad vibes wasn't just restricted to civilization.

Though he didn't realize it, he and Sofia had indeed been spotted by a pack of hungry wolves. But upon getting close to him, the wolves had abruptly re-contextualized their understanding of predator-prey relationships, fleeing back to their den with a new appreciation for life and a desire to spend more time with their families.

Just before they arrived at Golden Fields, Bones's feet began aching, but as soon as the first trickles of pain tickled his mind, the necromantic energy surging through his body burst forth.

"No, it's fine…" Bones muttered. He clenched his teeth, trying to force the energy down. "Stop. Stop. Stop." But just as most people couldn't stop their fingernails from growing back or keep their blood from clotting, Bones had no say over his body's natural healing factor.

In the span of milliseconds, his aching muscles and tendons were consumed by eldritch flames before being instantly re-forged again.

Because Bones never used his necromantic abilities, he now had an absurd abundance of energy, to the point that his body automatically found ways to burn it off. This method of breaking his legs and re-forging them again was similar to a preposterously wealthy man purchasing a new carriage instead of waiting for a carpenter to replace the broken spoke of a wheel.

Bones abruptly stopped, shivering in place as Sofia bumped into him.

"Are you all right?" she asked.

"I…um…" Bones stammered, unable to speak.

He was terrified of going into town, and not because his legs had been shattered and forged anew—that had been so instant that it had felt like little more than a temporary itching. It was because they were going somewhere with a lot of people, and he didn't trust himself to control his abilities.

Sofia placed a firm hand on Bones's shoulder, as if trying to press the bad thoughts out of his body. "You're nervous about going into town, aren't you? You're worried about curses and nonsense like that."

"Well, yes."

"Look, Achille. I told you before and I'm telling you again. The biggest curse is a bad attitude. Your expression is *screaming* 'Get away from me or I'll kill you.' Of course, people are going to see it and get away from you!"

"Sofia…let's say you're right. The Great Clown is so talented that pays attention to me. But what if people are *supposed* to fear me?" Bones licked his lips nervously and asked a question he'd asked countless times before. "Sofia…what happened when you found me that night? In the family manor. What *really* happened?"

Sofia stifled a groan. She knew that this was an integral part of Achille's fears, some childhood trauma still buried deep within him. As his friend, she respected that too much to make light of it. But still, she had told this story countless times before, yet for some reason, Achille had never accepted it, even though it was the pure, unvarnished truth.

"You were out in the field beneath that big, twisted tree, the one your father always said was planted by your great-great-grandfather. There were a few crows in the nest above you. For some reason, they seemed very happy with you—I saw one move away just to avoid pooping on you. You must have fallen asleep or something. And good thing too because… Well, you don't need me to talk about that part. The manor burnt and the graves unearthed. The serfs' homes had been destroyed too and it seemed like even the animals were a little spooked, like they'd fled and come back. What a mess. I know what you think, but you didn't cause that… It was those bandits Baron Matteo brought in a few months later. The ones who dressed up as hyenas and robbed graves. They had a grudge against your father since they were on the losing side of the war."

Sofia saw Bones preparing to argue with her, so she hastily decided to strengthen her argument with an appeal to faith. "You know what? I swear it on the smile of Gon the Gut."

Bones raised an eyebrow. "Gon the Gut, huh? You really have spent a lot of time in Golden Fields."

She smiled. "Well, I've got to admit, their fondness for him is logical."

Sofia had never been particularly religious, but she'd always had a soft spot for Gon the Gut and his monastery of public servants. To her, religion had always seemed like another form of superstition. If she was going to believe in something, it better be someone with an actual historical record of great deeds.

"Come on, Bones. Let's go to the circus and have fun. I'm not scared of demons or ghosts... I'm scared of you wasting your life away."

With that, Sofia pulled Bones the last few steps into Golden Fields. Like with most people, the encouragement of a friend had emboldened him, though even if he'd wanted to physically resist, Bones's spaghetti arms and angel-hair legs meant he didn't have much of a chance against Sofia.

The village of Golden Fields was simple yet proud. A large sign proclaiming that the town was "A Breadbasket for the Barony" had been planted right before the entrance, and the fields of wheat, barley, and green bamboo stretched out far into the distance. Beside the bigger sign was a rickety one pointing the way to the Baron's Road, the eighty-mile route that connected all of the barony's major cities.

Numerous cottages, built from a mix of straw and bamboo and only a bit bigger than Bones and Sofia's home, clustered around the central town square, where a simple market sold meats, vegetables, and a few carefully carved wooden toys.

On either side of the market stood the town's two religious buildings. One was a stone chapel dedicated to the local God of Harvest. The stained-glass window showed a muscular man with a red beard wearing a sheepskin and carrying a scythe.

The other was a small temple with bamboo walls, dedicated to the legendary foreign monk known as Gon the

Gut, whose band of pilgrims had traveled from nation to nation, providing aid to all who needed it. The villages that he'd visited, sporadically dotted across the world, admired him to this very day. The stone figurine standing outside depicted an extremely rotund man with a peaceful expression and a very large stomach. Beneath the statue was a gleaming, constantly polished plaque from Gon's hometown of Lotus Fields.

Under normal circumstances, the most notable buildings would have been the granaries. The three towers loomed over the rest of Golden Fields, their weathered walls stained with the dust of countless harvests.

But today was different. The Great Circus was in town.

Bones's eyes widened as he gazed upon the massive red-and-gold tent. It felt like his feet were drawn automatically towards it, and a wide smile split his face. Though Bones was twenty-five years old, he'd spent so much time isolated that he'd missed out on many joys of childhood. Even something as simple as bright colors appealed to his neglected heart.

Most of the village was already inside, their voices echoing as they recapped the previous shows and debated which act was best. Perhaps the greatest testament to the Great Clown's skill was the fact that everyone was so eager to see second and third performances.

Sofia reached for her purse, but Bones shook his head, pulling a pair of silver coins from the pocket of his cloak. "Ah, I got it. As a thank you for convincing me to come here. Just looking at it, I feel like I'll have a good time."

When Bones stepped aside, all he got from the redheaded woman running the counter was a stray look. It was just like when he'd come as a child. The Great Circus was an almost absurdly positive and kind-hearted atmosphere, enough to nullify any creeping chills or lurking shadows.

A series of large, concentric wooden benches surrounded a central stage decorated in rainbow-colored polka dots. At the moment, the stage was empty, the Great Clown's troupe hidden behind a large, velvet curtain.

"Let's sit at the back," Bones said, pointing near the edge of the tent. Most of the village was seated near the front few rows, a sea of mostly redheads and smiling faces. About sixty percent of people in the Barony had red hair, an eccentricity that the Islington University scholars occasionally studied. It was the kind of question that normally would have interested Sofia, but for now, she was more concerned with Bones.

She smiled as the two sat in the far corner of the tent. Of course, she would have preferred sitting in the front row, but she wisely understood that convincing Achille to socialize was a step-by-step procedure.

As soon as they sat down, the brightly lit torch behind them guttered out.

Sofia raised a finger before Bones could speak. "I know what you're thinking…but let's go for a more action-oriented mindset. I wonder if they'll think I'm rude for relighting this torch for them."

"I think someone is coming to light it right now," Bones replied. Indeed, a muscular troupe member hustled urgently towards them, a fresh torch in hand, just in time for the first act to start.

A whole troupe of well-trained clowns cartwheeled onto the stage, spinning in increasingly complex patterns. "You know, Achille, that kind of training doesn't come naturally. I read a pamphlet that said some of these acrobats train as hard as warriors."

Indeed, the clowns' speed and coordination were almost unerringly nimble. As one clown did a handstand, sticking his feet high in the air, a second clown jumped on top of the upside-down clown's feet, using it as a platform to somersault through three other performers who'd joined their bodies into a ring.

"Just staring at them makes me dizzy." Bones laughed. "Just one look tells me I'm not making it very far at tryouts. There's a big difference between liking gymnastics as a kid and actually being good at it."

"Who knows, Achille? Maybe they have some kind of training squad you can join."

But as much fun as Bones was having, he couldn't fully lose himself in the show. Self-conscious as always, the young noble occasionally peeked away from the stage at the rest of the audience. However, nobody paid any mind to Bones. The skilled and talented performers even distracted the various spectral beings who'd been drawn to Bones's necromantic energies. Instead of fleeing in terror, the ghosts, demons, and spirits had all settled down to watch the circus as well—albeit a safe distance from him.

They formed a second layer in the audience, roughly equidistant between Bones and the villagers. Among them was a group of rotting clowns with pitch-black eyes; thin, needle-like teeth; and makeup so thick and congealed, it looked like sludge. They enjoyed the show more than anyone else, laughing and pointing at the stage while chittering amongst themselves.

"Sofia…" Bones murmured. "Can you see those people?"

Through long-standing experience, Bones knew that other people—whom he wistfully thought of as 'normal people'—couldn't see the supernatural beings drawn to him, but zombies, who had physical bodies, were an exception.

She glanced at the clowns and scowled. "So I'm definitely not a fan of those costumes…adding the zombie part seems awfully unprofessional. But, *Achille.* Don't you know it's rude to point and stare? Let them be. Maybe they want to try out for the show, same as you."

The reanimated clowns hooted and hollered with the best of them, their needle-like teeth clacking endlessly. They had been brought back to life sixty years ago by a necromancer with a love for petty revenge to terrify a rival with severe coulrophobia. After their job had been done, he'd let them loose to do whatever else they'd wanted—which had been to improve their craft. They'd spent decades traveling to find a show they'd thought could rival theirs, and their eager chittering, while terrifying to most, was simple excitement observing the Great Circus's superior craftsmanship.

The people sitting near the clowns did not seem quite so enthusiastic, but when the Great Clown himself took the stage, all eyes turned to him.

He was an older man, with flecks of gray in his burnt-red hair. While he'd physically gone to seed, he'd retrained himself over the years to focus on jokes and humor instead of displays of athletic skill.

"Thank you for coming here today." The Great Clown grinned. "You know, I'm getting pretty up in years and I don't move as fast as I used to. The other day, my wife was telling me that if the comeback tour doesn't work out, I might have to try to become a Gon the Gut impersonator."

The whole crowd laughed. The Great Clown had learned a long time ago that despite his greatness, the safest target for mean jokes was always himself.

Bones marveled at the man's quick wit and improvisation. In this particular barony, Gon the Gut was only well-known in Golden Fields. The bigger cities like Islington, Lorenzo, or Avaron Heights had no shrines dedicated to him. Little did Bones know that the Great Clown made a similar joke in every town with a rotund hero. If it wasn't Gon the Gut, it was Mario the Massive or Hugo the Hulk.

"It's amazing, Sofia. He was so good at gymnastics, but now he's great at telling jokes!"

"That stuff just takes practice, Achille. With enough work, you could entertain everybody too."

Bones was utterly captivated. "You know what, Sofia? I'm glad I came here. You're right. I can learn to make friends… I just need to crack a few jokes. I'm not saying I can become the Great Clown or anything like that, but if he can retrain, maybe so can I."

"Exactly!" Sofia beamed.

But right as hope blossomed in Bones's mind, disaster struck—not because of a curse, but because of a bunch of good old-fashioned assholes.

Chapter Three

As the sun slowly set outside, three dozen men in pitch-black cloaks rode up to the Great Clown's tent. Some were wiry and nimble. Others were stout and strong. A few carried crossbows, but the majority preferred clubs and daggers. All of them had sorely disappointed their mothers by turning to a life of crime and plunder.

Though their leather armor was decorated with black crow feathers, they called themselves "the Buzzard Boys." Their leader, Drustan the Dagger, had initially proposed "the Crow Crew," but he felt like the equally alliterative name just wasn't quite intimidating enough.

Drustan held up a hand for silence, then slid off his black horse—as the leader, he got the matching horse. The others were in whatever color was easiest to steal.

"They're inside the red-and-gold tent," he whispered. To most, his command would have seemed excessively obvious, but Drustan's recruiting procedure maximized strength and minimized intelligence.

Drustan, on the other hand, had both. The bandit lord was six and a half feet tall, with bulging muscles that seemed anatomically impossible. His hair was black, flecked with gray, and his face was rough yet jaggedly handsome. A massive crossbow was slung over his back and he carried three daggers at his belt plus two more hidden in his snakeskin boots.

A graduate of Islington University's military theory program, Drustan had been commissioned after graduation as an officer in Baron Angelo's army. The baron had been particularly attracted to his strong and handsome commander-like appearance. Typically, hiring underlings based on typecasting was a risky venture, but Drustan had served well, eventually becoming head of his personal guard. Unfortunately for Drustan, he'd lost his job to reanimation after Baron Angelo had acquired his zombie army nineteen years ago.

Afterward, Drustan had decided to cut out the middleman and do some freelance violence of his own. To his delight, he enjoyed banditry much more than soldiering—it was much easier to fight people who didn't have swords.

Drustan raised a finger, drawing a circle in the air. His men nodded, encircling the tent before abruptly bursting in.

At first, the audience and the performers had no idea what was going on. The Great Clown continued his skit about an irate monk who'd been cheated by an unscrupulous shopkeeper. "I'm sorry, my friend…but I'll be keeping all this gold. It was you who told me that change comes from within."

Then Drustan began shouting.

"Freeze! Freeze! Nobody needs to get hurt. Give us your gold, let us take a few women for the night, and we'll all consider this a safe and proper shakedown."

The Buzzard Boys had completely encircled the circus, but it just so happened that Drustan himself was right next to Bones and Sofia.

Bones whirled around, but Sofia tackled him to the ground, shielding him with her body. "It's the Buzzard Boys—they love preying on the weak, and their leader, Drustan, uses both green and purple poisons!" Sofia deeply enjoyed reading true crime pamphlets. Her hobby made her an expert at identifying when crimes were happening but had dubious benefits when it came to actually stopping crimes.

Bones clenched his teeth and bit back the magic surging through his body. The flickering torches in the side of the tent reminded him of the burning family manor. He had no idea what would happen if he unleashed his strength with so many people around him.

The rest of the crowd screamed in terror, throwing their bodies to the ground and cowering beneath their seats. Among them were the zombie clowns, who had left their butts on their seats in their haste to hide.

Drustan stared at them and cursed under his breath. "You! What are you freaky things?"

A few of his men shifted uneasily. They might not have been very bright, but they had a distinct feeling that they'd bitten off much more than they could chew.

"I don't know about this, boss…"

"Those guys look like bad news…"

For a moment, Bones dared to hope, but then the zombie clowns turned tail and ran, scooping up their butts and hastily jamming them back on. Despite their frightening appearances, they were clowns first and zombies second.

It was the performers who dared to fight back.

They yanked torches from the side of the tent, roaring like barbaric cavemen, their eyes lit with a deep, primal rage that until this moment, they hadn't known they'd had.

The lion tamer caught one of the bandits in the face with his whip, while a trio of acrobats tumbled their way through the threatening ring of robbers, sweeping them to the ground with wide, sweeping kicks. The jugglers threw balls at balls with castrating force and the fire-eater abruptly became a fire-feeder, slamming a torch straight in a bandit's face.

The Great Clown was the fiercest of all. He ripped a chair off the ground, carrying it like a battering ram, his muscles bulging under his tunic and his parted red hair bristling like twin bonfires.

"What are you doing?" Drustan roared. "Don't you realize what will happen if we get violent?"

Unfortunately for the Buzzard Boys, their careful target selection meant that they were a little rusty in the fighting department. The Great Clown viciously slammed the chair over a bandit's head and he slumped to the floor, his face a painful mess of splinters.

Drustan decided to take a tactical hostage. He grabbed Sofia off the ground with a vicious yank, pressing a dagger right at her neck. "Try anything and this woman gets it! Let me and my men go with some adequate payment, and there won't be any problem!"

The Great Clown and his troupe froze, their long-ingrained desire for a perfect audience safety record battling with their stout refusal to negotiate with brigands.

Unfortunately for Drustan, grabbing Sofia and revealing Bones was like picking up a stone and finding a terrible monster lurking underneath.

The young necromancer gulped, forcing the words out of his throat. "Back off. You…let her go!" His words were high-pitched and strained, filled with terror—not because of

Drustan, but because of the power rising in his body. The sight of Sofia being threatened had stirred Bones into an emotional frenzy. His magic reacted as if he himself had been attacked.

A faint bead of sweat trickled down Drustan's forehead.

His first instinct had been to laugh at the skinny kid trying to be a hero, but something was wrong. Every instinct in his body told him that he was about to die. The torch behind the boy guttered out, but just before it did, Drustan could have sworn the pitch-black shadows created by the flickering light had twisted into the shape of stocks and chains.

The rest of the circus, guests and performers alike, had fallen completely silent, their eyes drawn to Bones by a supernatural force they could not understand.

Over the years, Drustan had supplemented his formal military education by auditing courses at the school of hard knocks. Plenty of soldiers prized chivalric combat, but Drustan knew that the best strategy was killing his enemies before they revealed their secret abilities.

Drustan swiftly grabbed for his belt, his fingers wrapping around three daggers at once. He'd coated them with his very best purple poisons. With a vicious, whirling throw, Drustan pierced Bones's chest with all three daggers at once—one in each of his lungs and the last straight through his heart.

Drustan snarled. "So. Any other heroes? Or—"

He broke off.

His attack had been perfect, but he'd had imperfect information.

Bones's necromantic energy flared. His heart and lungs shriveled, then burst back into existence. The daggers flew back at Drustan with such speed that he didn't even have time to use Sofia as a shield. The three poisoned blades pierced his hand and he cried out in shock and pain, dropping her onto the ground as he staggered backward.

Unlike earlier, when Bones's magic had restored his damaged legs, replacing his heart and lungs while also eradicating the poisons from his body was a much more intensive task. Not only that, Bones's heightened mental state had his magic on full alert. As a result, the spurt of necromantic healing revealed Bones's true self, contaminating the tent with a frigid aura, the spiritual equivalent of absolute zero.

It was a truth of the world that every magical practitioner had a distinct color to their magic. It was the kind of thing that would have been very helpful to magical investigators, but unfortunately, magic was so rare that such a job was not easily available.

The color of Bones's magic was unknowable, on a spectrum that could not be processed by the human eye. And so, as the circus-goers perceived Bones, their minds automatically processed the unknowable color as whatever was personally most terrifying for them—scarlet blood, the void black of space, the glistening, white teeth of wolves, the list went on.

For the Great Clown, who had extremely bad allergies, it was the precise shade of spring grass.

For Drustan, it was the purple of the poison coursing through his body. If he'd been thinking rationally, he would have asked a henchman for a non-poisoned blade so he could cut his arm off, but the bandit lord had been terrified well past the point of irrational thought and into the realms of temporary insanity.

In the blink of an eye, it was over.

The fight was forgotten.

Weapons clattered to the ground and the torches guttered immediately, never to light again. The wood instantly rotted, tumbling to the circus floor with splintering finality.

Bandits, audience members, and performers alike shrieked in terror, fleeing the tent.

The spirits drawn to the audience by Bones had never been more grateful for their translucent nature and immunity to human social norms. They'd left the show early.

The Buzzard Boys dropped their weapons and fled, screaming and crying. They'd been scared straight of town. None of them would ever commit a crime again, nor would they ever forget to check under their beds at night.

The Golden Fields villagers considered not just running for the hills, but *moving* up the hills. After today's events, they thought it'd be safer to live on higher ground.

The Great Clown no longer had depression. It'd been replaced by PTSD.

As for Bones, he hadn't even actually used his magic. He gulped, forcing the latent energy back into his body and severing the invisible strands he'd instinctively placed on each of the Buzzard Boys.

Within mere moments, it was just him and Sofia inside the abandoned tent, accompanied only by a broken chair and a few dying embers.

"My word," Sofia muttered. "What just happened?"

"Oh, come on, Sofia. That was because of me. The... Well, I don't even know if I can call it a 'curse.' I guess it did save us."

Sofia frowned, genuinely confused. Unlike the rest of the audience, she'd missed seeing the daggers flying out of Bones's chest or the flood of indescribable color. For very understandable reasons, she'd had her eyes squeezed shut the entire time, on account of the dagger pressed to her neck.

"Achille...you can be really full of yourself sometimes. You think your 'bad luck' caused a bandit attack? That's nonsense. Bandits attack people because they don't want to get real jobs."

"No, I mean what happened after. How everyone ran away."

Sofia thought for a moment.

The scientific method taught in her correspondence courses told her to accept new evidence as it came. With her eyes squeezed shut, she'd had no way to observe new evidence and therefore no way to refute her young charge's claims. She decided to humor him, just in case he was right. "Well, Achille...if you did that, that makes you a hero. You singlehandedly stopped a bandit attack."

Bones sighed.

He supposed he felt some uneasy satisfaction. For the first time in almost two decades, his magic had actually helped other people. He just wished it weren't quite so terrifying.

Throughout history, there had been the occasional selfless hero who'd done the right thing even when nobody had thanked them for it. Bones did not mind thankless heroics—it was the thought of an entirely thankless life he had a problem with, and at this point, he'd come to accept that no amount of necromantic energy could revive his social life.

If only he could have sat and enjoyed the rest of the show, laughing and cheering with everyone else in the brightly lit circus environment. But now, there was no show and no possibility of a tryout.

But then a boisterous voice called out to Bones, slicing through his melancholy like a sword through cloth. "Hey, you! Kid!"

Bones turned, eager to explain to the voice that he wasn't a kid, but his words caught in his throat as a blazing skeletal arm pushed its way through the flap of the tent. The blazing skeleton it foreshadowed appeared shortly after.

"Who is *that?*" Sofia asked, practically spitting out the last word.

"Wait. You—you can see him?" Bones stammered.

Bones was no stranger to burning skeletons, but usually, they were ghosts of people who'd died in fires. Some of them hoped Bones could help them curse their arsonists, but they always ran away screaming before Bones could explain that his magic did not let him curse people.

But this skeleton was much stranger than any he'd seen before.

Not only could Sofia see it, but it was only five feet tall— perhaps even an inch shorter than that. Considering its height, Bones would have thought that this skeleton were a woman if it weren't for the flaming pompadour blazing above the skeleton's skull, which boosted the manifestation's height to five and a half feet.

Flames wrapped around the skeleton's entire body, but he seemed to control the fires, almost like how a porcupine could control its spines. The pure fire shifted beautifully as he walked forward, the full spectrum of heat completely represented: red, orange, yellow, blue, and white. Despite the intensity of the flames, his pearly-white bones were untouched by the head. The same could not be said for his cloak of stitched animal skins, but the material seemed unusually tough and durable, leaving only small flakes on the ground behind him.

The unusually short blazing skeleton waded through the tent, striding straight towards Bones with a confident grin on his face. Of course, all skeletons were anatomically forced to grin, but there was just something about this particular skeleton that radiated confidence.

Sofia scowled and stepped protectively in front of her young ward. "Bones. If that's a costume, that man has some kind of mental disease. And if it's real, it's probably some skin disease. Either way, you need to be careful."

Ignoring her concern, the skeleton walked right up to Bones and pointed at him, eagerly delivering the line that all egomaniacs considered the greatest compliment ever. "Kid…you remind me of me!"

Chapter Four

Bones knew just how important it was to make a good first impression, which was why he stared at the skeleton with his mouth agape as he considered every possibility. Evidently, this strange being wanted to be his friend. Not only was the skeleton unafraid of Bones, but he even seemed to think they had a good deal in common.

While Bones didn't have much experience in social situations, he had spent a great deal of time thinking about them. After nearly two decades of dedicated meditation—also known as beating himself up for no reason—he'd reached heavenly grandmaster rank in the immortal art of overthinking.

"Are you all right?" the skeleton asked, jerking him back into the mortal realm.

"Oh. Um. Sorry. Uh, who are you?" The words tumbled awkwardly out of his mouth as he responded on pure instinct. Of course, that was only the young necromancer's first question. As a general rule of thumb, extremely confident blazing skeletons led to a lot of questions. "Are you a ghost? If so, how can Sofia see you? And, um…all that fire…doesn't it hurt? Usually, the burning ghosts I run into are screaming in pain…"

It wasn't the most promising start to a conversation, but it was a start to a conversation.

In response to Bones's deluge of questions, the skeleton let out an indignant humph, accompanied by the clattering of the teeth and a slight puff of smoke. "You don't know who I am?"

"Um. No. Uh. I'm sorry, but I don't. I mean, you know, the fire… It kind of erases all recognizable features, and, um…" Bones staggered through his words with the telltale cadence of a man trying yet failing to be polite.

For some reason, Bones's innocent comment only made the skeleton even more upset. To add insult to insult, the kid had a zombie-like slouch, yet he still looked down on him. The skeleton had been relatively tall for his time, but his sterling genetics were powerless in the face of modern advances in nutrition. "I'm not just a skeleton on fire. I left my main body in my tomb a couple years ago. Have you ever heard of *traveling lightly*?" The skeleton spoke with such an utterly self-assured tone, it was as if everyone else would be abandoning their flesh and organs any day now.

The skeleton's absurd explanation only further entrenched Sofia's refusal to believe in the supernatural. But for some reason she couldn't understand, Sofia trusted this strange man. As a result, she withdrew from the conversation, standing a safe distance back. Despite her earlier misgivings, she felt it was time to let her baby bird spread his wings, though she kept a close watch to make sure he wasn't flying right into a window.

"As for who I am…just what *kind* of postmodern nonsense are they teaching at the schools these days? I managed to learn your language, even learned to speak like a modern man. But nobody knows that I'm Karn the Blazing Warrior, the greatest warrior in human history?!"

Bones, thanks to Sofia's insistence, had an exceptional education. The fact that he'd seen ghosts from such a diverse array of time periods only added to his unusually broad perspective, but he'd never heard of this man before. The name 'Karn' sounded like it was from a different country, maybe even a different century. "I'm sorry… I know a lot of legendary heroes, but I've never heard of you before. What was your signature weapon?" Through his study of history, Bones knew that signature weapons made for great ballads and even better marble statues.

"A blazing stick."

Karn spoke the words with such an authoritative tone that it was clear he thought Bones should throw himself to the ground in shock and awe. Much like his proclamation that everyone else should tear off their flesh and walk around as skeletons, Karn acted like carrying around a blazing stick was one of the most creative and mind-bending ideas of all time.

Once again, Bones retreated to his inner world as he desperately considered how to respond and make a good impression. Powered by his chronic overthinking, his mental sphere wasn't so much of a mind palace as it was a mind eldritch wasteland, his flimsy reasoning and constant logical leaps rivaling the bizarre shapes and forms of non-Euclidean geometry.

"Ha. I shocked you into silence, didn't I?" Karn boasted.

"I…uh…"

Karn didn't have eyes to narrow, but the flames seemed to crackle with greater intensity. "Look. Just say what you're thinking. I don't like people who are scared of speaking their minds."

"Well, um… I just… You know a blazing stick sounds pretty simple. Isn't it just a torch?"

"A 'torch'? What do you…?" This time, it was Karn's turn to break off.

Twin fireballs appeared in his eye sockets, spinning wildly in counter-rotating circles as smoke poured from his skull. Though he might have looked unintelligent from the outside, he had a lot of memories to scan through.

"Ah. I see. Torch. Another word for 'a burning stick.'" Karn nodded in self-appreciation. While conquering the world, he'd picked up a knack for languages in large part thanks to his unparalleled mastery of context clues. Of course, this had led to a very patchwork knowledge of languages, as he only tried to figure out what words meant when he found them interesting. "Look, kid. We only managed to steal fire from the gods when I was a teenager. Lighting a stick on fire so you could carry it around was so innovative, we didn't even have a word for it."

Bones's eyes widened as he put two and two together. "Oh. You're from *way* in the past. You're a caveman!"

"Well, back in my time, I was just a man. But yes. So, how did you send all those people scurrying away, kid? What's your power?"

"Necromancy."

"What kind?" Supernatural abilities were very uncommon—that was why people called them "supernatural." But Karn, who had conquered all the warriors in his time, was unusually experienced with them. "I fought a bunch of necromancers in my day. Do you make zombies? Skeletons? Maybe you manipulate blood? Poison people? Curse them?"

"I can move life energy around. I can take it or give it. Um… I, you know, I prefer giving it," Bones hurriedly added.

"Interesting." The flames around Karn seemed to crackle with greater intensity. "So that's that thing around you." To virtually everybody, Bones's aura of necromantic energy was only visible when he used his magic, but to Karn, it was a blazing bonfire of color, even more impressive than his own flames. He couldn't tell exactly what the color was, but he knew it was a color nonetheless.

"Wait…you can see it?" Bones asked.

"Oh, of course." A note of irritation entered Karn's voice. When the gods had made Karn, they'd created him with a double dose of stubbornness in place of his ability to feel fear. "In fact, I can tell that the color doesn't want me to understand it…so I'm working *extra* hard to comprehend it."

"Well, I'm glad you're not scared. When I healed myself, everyone else saw my magic and ran away."

To Bones's surprise, Karn threw his head back and laughed. "Impressive! Ha! They scurried off without you even having to attack them! Kid, you might be even stronger than me in my prime, back before I tore all my muscles off. It's a wonder you haven't conquered the world by now."

Bones kicked at the ground nervously, experiencing a risk that he'd never encountered before—the danger of opening up to someone he'd just met. But Karn had told him to be his genuine self, and he felt emboldened by those words. "Well, I don't like using my magic. I don't know why, but ever since I was a kid, I've just had a bad feeling about it. Something happened once…and I don't even know what, exactly, it was. And whenever I use it, everyone runs away terrified. I think instinctively, they know just how scary the backlash can be."

To Bones's surprise, Karn nodded, his neck rattling and his flaming haircut swaying wildly. "I know what you mean. Our abilities can be scary. The same thing happened when I was a child. The first time I fell into a fire and walked out fine, everyone started screaming. And don't let me get started on the time my brother and I were hunting a tiger."

"Um, what exactly is your power again?" Bones asked.

"Oh. Basically, I can't be killed." Karn laughed, his flames crackling merrily. He pointed at the blazing flames wrapped around his body. "People think it's the fires…but I just learned how to make them look cool after being on fire for so many years. It's all about walking with a certain swagger. They are especially useful without my face. I've realized it's hard to express emotion otherwise. You know how it is, moving the breeze and whatnot."

Bones didn't know how it was at all. It didn't sound like normal people could create aesthetic flame auras, but Karn was operating on a time scale unfathomable to Bones's level of experience. He thought of continental drift as the gods creating new content for him to experience.

The caveman went on. "Well, once people found out I couldn't be killed, they stopped trying to fight me. I thought I had everything. A huge fortune, any woman I wanted, lands as far as my eyes could see, and so much food, I started trying to figure out how to store it. The only problem was, I could tell nobody actually liked me. My immortality freaked people out. Once they found out how old I really was, my wives quailed when I approached, no matter how nice I tried to be. Even my children would shake and tremble. I passed on my fighting skills to some of them, but not my abilities."

Karn's voice took on a sorrowful tone that Bones knew well. Of course, Karn claimed that he wasn't a ghost, but most of the ghosts Bones had encountered lingered on because of past regrets. There was only one difference: this time, Karn had the same regret as Bones himself. "Yeah. That sounds like exactly what happens to me. And it's not even people, either. One time, a black cat spirit called me 'a bad omen'! It just feels like a curse sometimes."

Karn nodded. "Tell me about it. Even when the whole world belonged to me, I felt utterly alone. Our powers are great for keeping us alive, but they aren't very useful when it comes to real friendship. It took me a lot of years to get it, but I suppose it makes sense. It's hard to have an even relationship with someone when they're so much more powerful than you."

Despite the grim topic of conversation, a genuine smile split Bones's face. Receiving empathy and giving it back in turn was such a simple human experience, but it was one that the fates had robbed him of for his entire life. Sofia did her best to take care of him, and his parents before her, but they could never truly understand Bones's power. Even now, Sofia had no idea what Karn and Bones were blathering about— she was just glad that they were blathering about it.

Bones tentatively reached out a hand, and as he did, something miraculous happened. The necromantic energy swirling around Bones chilled Karn's ever-blazing fire.

The two shook hands.

Bones did his best to maintain a firm handshake, as his father had taught him all those years ago. Karn didn't really know what a handshake was, but he could tell it was important to Bones, so he shook vigorously.

"You know what's the real shame about all this?" Karn asked, pointing at the ruins of the circus. "Stuff like cave painting and dancing around the fire always seemed so much more fun to me. That was why I came here in the first place. I overheard people saying that the Great Circus was holding tryouts. I figured I might as well try to turn a new leaf, go from killing to entertaining."

Bones stared back at him in disbelief. Karn was more than just a kindred spirit—he could be a fellow troupe member!

Bones might have failed to join the Great Circus, but that didn't mean he couldn't start his own. In fact, it was probably for the best. Joining an elite circus would have been very difficult. Despite Bones's childhood interest in tumbling, his past work experience consisted entirely of sitting around and brooding in the corner of his cottage. Creating his own circus, especially with somebody equally inexperienced, sounded much more attainable.

There was only one problem. Asking Karn to join him. He'd never done anything so bold before.

"You know what? I…um… I think…" Bones repeatedly trailed off. Somehow, using his words was harder than using his magic, but he finally managed to force the sentence through. After all, Karn had already told him to speak his mind. "You know what? Let's start our own circus, Karn. I came to the show to try out too."

Karn grinned, the flames around him blazing excitedly. "Our own circus, huh? I like the sound of that. A circus for strong men like us! I don't want to be a strongman, though—that would be just a bit too stereotypical. I want some *spectacle*. Fire-eating would be more my thing."

Karn had always found the rising popularity of fire-eating rather irritating.

Everyone in his time had been terrified of his immunity to fire, but now it was considered exciting and entertaining. He could not possibly allow these fraudulent fire-eaters to take the social capital that was his birthright.

Of course, little did Karn know that it was technically their birthright too.

Over the years, Karn had sired countless children. Despite what one might have imagined about caveman mating habits, Karn was a serial monogamist, but due to his immortality, he nonetheless had wound up with countless wives. In some respects, he was a serial serial monogamist, having lived so many lives' worth of serial monogamy.

But despite his high reproduction rate, Karn had a pitifully low understanding of exponential growth. Over half the barony was descended from Karn, and while none of them had inherited his invincibility, plenty of them acted like they had. The Great Clown's performers weren't immune to flame, but they were reckless enough not to fear it.

Karn's prolific reproduction was the true reason for Sofia's inexplicable faith in him. On the surface, Sofia thought her desire for Bones's socialization outweighed her true-crime-induced suspicion. In reality, several of Sofia's children had successful and loving marriages with descendants of Karn, creating subconscious trickle-up trust.

She chose that moment to hurry back over and interject. All their mumbo-jumbo sounded like total nonsense, but maybe these two could put their creativity to work as performers. "That sounds like a great idea, Achille! Creating your own circus sounds like the perfect opportunity to adjust your attitude. However, I will say…a fire-eating skeleton isn't particularly impressive. I mean, anyone could just put a torch through a hollow body."

She eyed Karn pointedly, hoping that he would take that hideous costume off, but her attempt at adult normalcy backfired spectacularly.

"That's an excellent point," Karn agreed. "I need to get the rest of my body. You guys mind coming with me?"

Bones grinned as he received another basic human experience that everyone else had taken for granted, the simple joy of running errands with friends. "Yeah, let's do it."

Unfortunately, there was only one problem.

When the members of the newly forged circus—a mere trio at this point rather than a full-fledged troupe—poked their heads out of the tent, they found that it was getting rather late. The sun had set completely, and with the remaining Golden Fields villagers hurriedly leaving, even light from stray torches was rapidly fading away.

"Well, that's no problem," Karn declared. "I can provide all the light we need."

"I don't know about that…" Bones replied. Forest fires were a possible concern for even near-invincible necromancers and a definite concern for their maids.

"It would be best to wait until tomorrow," Sofia insisted.

"No worries. We can wait until tomorrow. Until then…we can sleep under the tent," Karn declared. Through his longstanding combat experience, Karn had created four hundred and sixty-seven different strategies of war. Scaring an enemy out of their home and then staying there was strategy eighty-two.

As the three drifted off to sleep in different corners of the tent, Sofia smiled.

She had no idea what was going on, but she knew that her beloved Achille had made his first friend. Sure, Karn might have seemed like a bit of a weirdo, but that wasn't too bad. After all, the boy himself was a bit of a weirdo too.

Chapter Five

Under normal circumstances, the tent's vibrant colors would have set the mood for comfortable and happy dreams. Not only that, Karn acted like a living fireplace, filling the large tent with the perfect amount of toasty bedtime heat.

But despite the relatively positive environment, Bones still felt lonely and guilty, having scared away the entire village. As excited as he was to retrieve Karn's body, he couldn't help but worry about the upcoming trip. Perhaps his necromantic magic would cause problems again—that worry was the very last thing Bones thought about before drifting to sleep.

On that night, Bones provided another point of evidence to the spiritual truth—above urban legend yet below concrete fact—that dreams were always about the dreamer's very last thoughts right before bed.

In his dream, Bones was a child again, sitting under a gnarled, old tree, the one that his father had said had been planted by his great-great-grandfather. The tree's roots were thick and twisted and it cast a dark shadow on the lush, green grass, but Bones was so familiar with it that its eccentricities had become comforting rather than intimidating.

Resting beneath the shade, he stared at a robust stone building, the Bonaparte family manor.

Built out of hearty red bricks with a roof made of dark-gray slate tiles, the manor looked a bit like a miniature castle. The fact that the grand walls of the barony's capital of Avaron Heights were visible several miles away in the background only made the manor seem smaller, but small and humble was just how the Bonaparte family liked it.

The main home was two stories tall, with many windows on both floors, perfect for gazing out at the beautiful rolling meadows surrounding the home. Though it was on the other side of the building, Bones fondly recalled the stained-glass window in his parents' bedroom, his father's only vanity. It showed him commanding the defense of Baron Matteo's fortress during the Siege of Trent. A tall watchtower stood on the left side of the home, blue-and-white flags flying proudly from its parapets.

Bones stared at the tower and gulped. He knew what this was. He'd had this dream before.

His father used to bring him up there to gaze at the former family lands. Well, technically, they were still the family lands, but with the house burnt down, the Bonaparte family gone, and the serfs having fled the area, there wasn't much left to own.

Bones had been back there once before with Sofia, but he didn't like to think about that.

Through the terrible implanted logic of bad dreams, Bones knew what was eventually going to happen. He'd dreamed this dream many times before, but he took a shaky breath as he tried to indulge in the nostalgia.

The sight of the family home was irresistible. It was the last time in his life where he'd felt like he'd belonged, where he'd had a legitimate place in society.

As soon as that thought had crossed his mind, a voice called out to him. Bones didn't recognize the tired and slightly exasperated-sounding girl, but there was something about her that seemed vaguely familiar. "Bones. That's not true. You always could find a place in society if you just left the cottage and looked for friends! I can't believe you're having this dream again. This is what happens when I let you wander off on your own."

Bones whirled around, trying to find the source of the voice. He had no idea who it could be. It certainly didn't sound like Sofia. But he couldn't see anyone out of place. He looked around for a moment longer but did not get up from under the tree. His mind was operating on pure dream logic; he stayed under the tree despite his curiosity because he knew he was supposed to be here.

The voice did not call him again, though he thought he might have heard an exasperated strangely fluffy sigh. It was so soft, he might have imagined it—then again, since this was a dream, Bones supposed he was technically imagining everything.

The family home was surrounded by a pleasant rose garden buzzing with bees. Rosebushes had been his mother's favorites. Wild rabbits chased each other around the estate's simple wooden gate—the low kind of gate that was really there for decoration rather than any genuine fear of any threats. A thoroughly retired soldier, Bones's father had often said how glad he'd been for lands located in the center of the Barony.

Gabriel Bonaparte was just as Bones remembered him: a muscular man with blond hair so shortly cropped, he was almost bald. At five feet and four inches tall, he was shorter than his relatively short son, but his proud posture and disciplined way of carrying himself demanded respect. Gabriel had always said that courage ran in their family instead of height.

The sight of his father made Bones's hands twitch. He wanted nothing more than to call out to his father, to have another conversation, maybe even show off with a cartwheel.

Back when Bones had been a child inspired by the Great Clown's show, he had eagerly practiced his tumbling and gymnastics, flipping and twirling on a padded mat in his room. His father had always encouraged him—the fact that his son had been able to adopt an eccentric hobby had been a great source of pride for Gabriel, a firm reminder that he'd cemented a place in the upper class.

And besides, Gabriel had hoped that gymnastics would teach Bones how to fight. He'd always said that with their shorter stature, there was no point fighting conventionally. They had to go for the knees, grapple foes, and bring them to the ground, where everyone's height was the same.

The thought of his father's advice brought a smile to Bones's face, but he stayed silent. He'd tried calling out many times before. No matter how loudly he'd shouted, his father could never hear him.

Gabriel Bonaparte was currently trimming the rosebushes, working alongside three of his men.

Before saving Baron Matteo, Gabriel had been among the lowest of low lords, little more than a random retainer in the shadow of Avaron Heights. Bones's father had often told him that people at the edges of society were always a bit better at seeing the cracks in the social order. Well aware of the precarious status that separated him from his men, Gabriel had done his best to treat them all like family. Meals had been boisterous group affairs with everyone in the manor.

Even all these years later, Bones remembered the men's names. They'd treated him kindly, their battlefield courage and loyalty to his father allowing them to ignore the looming unease they'd felt whenever Bones had drawn close.

Clyde had had a bushy mustache he'd carefully curled upwards each morning, Marvin had had clever eyes and a constant laugh, and Leo had been the strongest of them all, six feet tall with shoulders as broad as the horizon and an unruly shock of bright-red hair. Like his father, Gabriel's men had been extremely encouraging towards Bones's gymnastic endeavors, praising him to the high heavens for simple flips and tricks. Now that Bones was older, with a better understanding of how society worked, he realized that for Clyde, Marvin, and Leo, there hadn't been any upside to constructively criticizing their lord's five-year-old son.

Spirits wandered around the family cemetery, placed to the leftmost corner just inside the family's gate, drifting nonchalantly through the tombstones. After acquiring the funds to build the cemetery, Gabriel had spent a great deal of time tracking down his ancestor's remains and relocating them.

Even at that age, Bones had known that most people couldn't see ghosts, so he'd kept that fact to himself, though he'd felt a little awkward about the ghosts his father had erroneously relocated. There were a few ghosts who looked nothing like their family, as well as an ancient two-headed wolf whose remains must have decayed enough to be mistaken for a human's. Still, they—along with the actual members of his family—seemed happy enough to be at the Bonaparte lands.

Back then, the ghosts hadn't been afraid of Bones, but they would stare back at him if he'd looked at them for too long.

Bones talked to the ghosts when they talked to him, but he rarely spoke first. Most of the ghosts were old, and through a childlike extrapolation of logic, Bones had an extreme fear of disrespecting them. Bones respected his father, who in turn, had deeply respected his ancestors. Considering how far up the family tree some of these ghosts were, Bones figured he had to really make something of himself before trying to speak with them.

He played with the wolf, though, and if any passing spirits flew by, Bones would talk to them too—mostly because he was too polite to ignore anyone who talked to him first. Those spirits were more or less his childhood friends. They were the ones who had first nicknamed him "Bones." There were a few who visited him exceptionally often, spinning tall tales about their journeys around the world.

Bones felt another faint push from within his mind. "Bones, aren't you forgetting someone? I mean, I'm not mad or anything. You didn't forget me back when it mattered, even though I couldn't talk back then."

Before Bones could reply or even try to understand what the voice was talking about, the wind shifted and his heart plummeted so precipitously, it felt like it had gone six feet under.

"It's happening again…" Up until this very moment, he'd always hoped that this recurring dream could be a pleasant window into his past life, but it never was.

Something thumped to the ground beside him, letting out a painful wailing cry.

A voice called out to him. Perhaps it was the girl who had shouted at him before; perhaps it was just his subconscious. "You don't need to do this! It's just a dream!"

But Bones couldn't stop.

He knew how this dream went. He knew what would happen.

But he couldn't help himself.

He turned and found the baby crow that had fallen from its nest. It had hit the ground, shattering a delicate wing. Its pink, downy body stirred feebly. It was still alive, but barely.

When he looked up into the tree, he saw the other crows gazing down at them from a humble nest of straw and dirt. Six of them were tiny, pink with scruffy down, just like the chick. The mother was about three times the size of Bones's childlike fist.

As he stared back up at the birds, he could have sworn he saw concern in the mother crow's face, a silent plea for him to save her child. Bones remembered his mother once telling him that if he touched a baby bird, its mother wouldn't let it back into its nest, but he knew from his own experience that this wasn't true. Back when he'd been a kid, he'd helped wounded animals all the time, healing them before picking them up to safely bring them back home.

The bird let out a pitiful keening cry and Bones activated his magic instinctively, directing it with his thoughts alone. No matter how many times he had the dream, no matter how hard he tried to change things, he never could. Even now, at age twenty-five, he was still helpless not to help, just like he had been when he'd been a child.

Icy cold built in Bones's stomach as life energy trickled from him, gently wrapping around the bird's wounded body. Back then, he hadn't had the massive nimbus of necromantic energy he'd built up over the years.

Sometimes, when he healed others, it came at a cost to himself. Depending on how severe the other party's injuries were, he might be bedridden for a couple of days, but Bones thought that was far preferable to something dying.

The bird's wounds slowly vanished, but then a whole host of noises abruptly exploded in Bones's ears, colliding together in a cacophony of dread. A ferocious bestial growl, a high-pitched scream, and the echoing bangs of cannon fire.

In mere moments, the manor was burning, and a terrible, screaming howl emanated from deep within the earth. Necromantic energy swirled around Bones's body and he shouted. "No! I... No! Stop!"

Inside the manor, he could feel lives being snuffed out, their energy fading away into nothingness. He wanted to help somehow, but the fear and dread built further and further, his head pounding like someone had taken a sledgehammer to it.

He didn't know what was happening, even with the benefit of hindsight.

One moment, he had been healing the bird, and the next, this.

The rumbling and crying beneath the earth grew louder and louder, and then the scene immediately shifted.

In just the blink of an eye, Bones's beloved childhood home transformed into a desolate wasteland.

The manor had burnt down, the lush, green grass wilted into yellow dust before his very eyes. The gnarled and twisted tree that had sheltered the Bonaparte family for generations had splintered and cracked, shattering into countless scattered pieces of bark.

Bones's father was gone, as were the servants. The manor had burnt to the ground, but Bones couldn't feel any signs of life energy inside. When Sofia had found him days later, she'd said that there weren't any bodies. When he'd finally found the courage to come back years later, the two had picked through the burnt home, trying to find some faint sign of remains, but there was nothing to be found, not even a single stray bone.

The bird's nest tumbled onto Bones's lap, but the birds were gone. The bird Bones had tried to heal had vanished too, as had every other animal. The buzzing bees were silenced and the bounding rabbits were nowhere to be found.

Even the ghosts and spirits were gone. The graves in the cemetery had been completely unearthed, haphazard holes and shattered tombstones strewn throughout the once-peaceful dirt.

All that was left were the residuals of Bones's magical explosion, his almighty magic still clinging to the air.

Bones took it all in, tears welling in his eyes.

A few of the animals had returned by the time Sofia had found him, but the family manor still looked like this, all these years later. When Sofia had brought him back, she'd told him that his family would have wanted him to move forward, to repair all the damage that had been done, to manage the lands for himself, and to bring back the happiness that had once blessed the area.

But Bones knew he didn't deserve to come back. He'd still felt his lingering magic in the air when he'd visited, and the blight had extended all throughout the family lands, far from the manor and out to where the vanished serfs had once dwelled. Something terrible had happened, but even almost twenty years later, he still couldn't understand exactly what it had been.

The rumbling from within his mind cut through his grief. This time, it was almost painful. It was like someone banging on the door and shouting at him, only instead of a door, it was his subconscious.

"Bones! You are such an idiot! Don't you think this is strange? A random cut that skips through everything that happened? Don't you think you're missing something? Sure, your magic is in the air…but that doesn't mean you did all this yourself." As she continued speaking, the voice grew increasingly irritated. "King of the Jungle, I forgot just how stupid this dream was. I'm glad you're going out and doing stuff, but it seems like you really need me around if you're thinking about this crap as soon as you leave."

When Bones woke up, the dread of the dream was still heavy on his mind, a perpetual haunting weight. Across the room, Karn's blazing flames looked just like the fires that had consumed his home. The splintered torches from the release of his magic reminded him of he'd desiccated his great-great-grandfather's tree. He'd felt this way since he'd been a child.

After that dream, *everything* became a painful reminder.

But the dread slowly faded away as he heard that voice again, a faint call at the very edge of his consciousness. "Make sure you take me with you next time, Bones… It gets a little lonely without you."

Bones frowned as he tried to figure out who was talking to him.

His only hint was that the voice had called him "Bones" instead of Achille. Likely, it was someone from back then, but perhaps it was simply a demonic associate of Sir Francis trying to trick him. When he'd been younger, various demons, like succubi or incubi, had attempted to contact Bones through his dreams, though when they'd discovered just how miserable his dreams were, they'd vanished. It seemed like he'd been placed on some kind of demonic do-not-contact list.

So who could it be?

Bones's forehead wrinkled thoughtfully and with his hawk-like eyes, Karn saw the wrinkle of stress from across the room.

Filled with eagerness to comfort his new friend, he dashed to Bones with literal breakneck speed, vanishing from his corner and appearing above him in the blink of an eye, his skull spinning in wild circles due to sheer momentum. Karn cursed in his native tongue—a series of utterly unintelligible grunts—and turned his head back around to face Bones properly.

"What are you looking so stressed out for, kid?" Karn asked, speaking with caveman social graces. "You dream of some woman you're missing?"

Chapter Six

"What?" Bones stammered. "Uh…I…um… I mean, I wouldn't exactly say I was missing them. I have no idea who it was…but, uh…everything would suggest I knew them."

Bones had no idea where to begin responding. Karn's claim was so bizarrely accurate that he thought the caveman had somehow gained mind-reading powers. Instead, it was merely an example of a mind in the gutter being right twice a day.

"Ha, I knew it!" Karn chortled. "You're worried about your dream lady. I can't imagine what would have happened if you'd actually seen her."

Bones wanted to explain that his 'dream lady' was a lady he'd dreamed about, not a lady he dreamed of being with. On top of that, she'd sounded more like a girl than a full-grown woman, certainly more of a friend or neighbor than a love interest.

Unfortunately, Bones was stammering so hard, he couldn't get the words out.

After cutting through all the bizarre and tragic aspects of this story, Bones was just experiencing another common friendship moment—a friend ribbing him about a girl. However, Bones had experienced an utterly isolated adolescence. Since the young necromancer hadn't built up any immunity, Karn's cavern talk was a social superweapon.

It fell on Sofia to defend Bones. She got off the floor, stretching and yawning.

"Come on." She scoffed. "What would you know about women? Don't tell me that they *enjoy* that skeleton costume."

"Oh, I've known plenty of women. Maybe I can help Bones meet his dream lady."

Sofia, not knowing any better, judged Karn to be a typical tavern braggart, the kind of fellow who spent more time talking about meeting women than actually meeting women. "Really, Karn? Name one."

Karn's flames flickered. Until now, neither Bones nor Sofia hadn't realized that fire could be so condescending. "You wouldn't know any of them. They lived in a different time period."

Sofia was baffled into silence by the bizarre excuse, but she'd given Bones just enough time to recover from his embarrassment. His face returned from bright red to its usual pallor as he shook off the irritating status effect. "Let's talk about something else. Karn, you mentioned wanting to get your body back. How about we get going? Where, exactly, is your grave?"

"I don't have a grave. I have a tomb!" Karn protested. "Befitting of a great and legendary warrior!"

"Oh, right, sorry about that," Bones hastily replied.

For a moment, the two stared at each other silently. Karn was so indignant that he forgot to respond to the actual question.

"So where is this place, exactly?" Sofia asked. For the sake of everyone's sanity, she decided to assume that "tomb" was a mortally mangled mispronunciation of "home."

"Well, it's quite far from here."

"A city name would be helpful," Sofia replied.

"Well, I don't know how to read signs or anything like that. I've always been good at listening and speaking but never picked up the knack of reading and writing," Karn breezily replied.

"How about naming some nearby places?" Bones asked.

"It's on a towering mountain range. It used to be a new mountain when I built my tomb, but it's super old now. Huge, black stones with cracks all over them." Karn thought for a moment longer. "There was a huge fight outside a few years ago. One side massacred the other after they surrendered."

Bones turned to Sofia, an utterly baffled look on his face. He had only the faintest idea of what Karn was talking about. The caveman had lived under rocks at the top of a mountain, but Bones lived under a metaphorical rock. "Uh…tall mountains? I mean, that sounds like the Blackridge Mountain Range, but was there a war there recently?"

Sofia's eyes widened. "Wait. You live near the site of the One Day War? Are you a soldier for Baron Angelo?"

"*Who*?"

Orbs of flame spun in Karn's sockets again as he tried to comprehend Sofia's bizarre sentence. When he'd finished processing, he scoffed, filled with intense irritation at the absurd postmodern world. "'Barren Angelo'? What kind of nickname is that? Back in my day, we had *real* noms de guerre. The kind of thing that struck fear into the hearts all around us, like Karn the Blazing Warrior! People are far too taken with irony these days…"

"Um, no, *Baron* Angelo. He rules the lands around here."

"Well, that explains the poor state of things," Karn replied, talking right past her. "I was overjoyed to see that humanity had finally invented farming, but it seems like you lot are well on your way to un-inventing it."

Sofia sighed and shook her head, making a heroic attempt to turn the conversation towards saner pastures. "So your home is near the site of the One Day War and you were there when the massacre happened."

For the sake of *his* sanity, Karn had decided to interpret Sofia's use of "home" as her own mangled pronunciation of "tomb." He knew that old people without his immortality often lost teeth at her age. "That's right," he replied. "And ever since then, there have been a crazy number of ghosts, wailing and moaning about treachery and dishonorable combat. It totally ruined the ambiance, so I moved out, but I still kept all my stuff there."

Bones turned to Sofia. "So we're going to the Blackridge Mountain Range?"

"Blackridge Peak, to be precise. The tallest of them all. I mean, I don't know about all these *ghosts*, though. That sounds like superstitious nonsense. The thing is, Blackridge Peak is several days by carriage from here, almost on the other side of the barony. How did you get here, Karn?"

"Oh, I just ran…but neither of you looks like a good runner. I suppose we'll have to find someone to take us there." Despite being a caveman, Karn was well aware of carriages. He'd left many of them in his dust over the years.

"I guess that's what we'll have to do," Bones admitted. "But I think I scared everyone off yesterday."

He walked over to the flap of the tent, peeking outside.

The surroundings themselves looked just as calm and peaceful as yesterday, a rolling expanse of golden wheat that had forgotten last night's terrors. Only a few stray patches of decayed grass hinted at Bones's one-second explosion of necromantic energy.

Of course, the people themselves hadn't forgotten.

They all had hurriedly backed their bags, moving their possessions up the hills. Some had even begun dismantling their homes, pulling apart the straw-and-bamboo cottages and loading the component materials onto carts, peeking with fright back at the tent.

From the outside, all they'd heard were the trio's stray mutterings about strange dreams, forgotten tombs, and vicious massacres.

Most of the villagers already flinched at the sight of Bones. But after seeing the blazing skeleton who accompanied him, the few Golden Fields residents who had advocated staying in place promptly changed their minds.

"Wow. Yeah. They look pretty fearful, all right," Karn agreed, his teeth clattering in an inadvertently menacing manner. "Well. You know what? If there's a river nearby, I can go put out this fire. That might help."

"Um…yeah, I guess it would… Uh, probably not too many coachmen would want us to go inside their carriage on fire. I'm just worried it, um…you know, won't be enough with everything going on."

Sofia frowned. "Achille. I'm telling you. All you need to do is adopt a positive attitude. Without the flames, we won't spook any horses…that's all we need to worry about."

Belatedly, Karn realized he'd made another ego-centric mistake. He'd never actually asked the boy his name. Thankfully, Sofia was there to spare him the embarrassment. "Well, *Achille*…let me go put out this fire, then." He'd spoken the boy's name forcefully to make sure it seemed like he'd known it all along.

"Only Sofia calls me 'Achille,'" Bones replied. "I prefer…"

He broke off.

At first, Karn was busy remembering Sofia's name, but when he saw Bones's hesitation, he clacked his teeth disapprovingly. "Kid. You're overthinking again. Just tell me what you want me to call you." The man who'd dubbed himself "the Blazing Warrior" was predictably a big fan of nicknames.

"Well, uh, I prefer 'Bones.' You know, it's short for my surname, but, um, hopefully, that's not a slur for skeletons or anything like that."

Karn was caught between bafflement and frustration.

On one hand, Bones was being quite polite. Despite his invincible body, Karn's feelings could still be hurt—his ego was merely *nearly* invincible.

But as he'd explained many times before, he wasn't a skeleton. He was an invincible man who had simply peeled off his flesh to travel expediently. Yet for some reason, nobody understood that simple fact.

His flames cracked irritably, but then he shrugged.

The legendary warrior had used countless skills in combat, but here, he'd learned a new skill for friendship: dropping the argument and moving on. If Bones didn't understand after sleeping on it, he never would. "Nah, it's fine. I'm not offended. I'm going to go douse these flames."

Karn pushed up the flat of the tent, making his way to the river. Despite flashing his winningest smile at the villagers, they gave him an incredibly wide berth.

As he left the campsite to find a river, it fell on Bones and Sofia to find transportation.

"Achille, I'm glad you've made a friend, but is there any chance you can convince him to take off that hideous outfit?"

"From what he's said, it sounds like he needs to push his flesh back on."

Sofia rolled her eyes, deciding not to argue any further. "Well. Let's see if anyone in Golden Fields will take us." Before Bones could point out the obvious problems, Sofia pulled out the universal social lubricant, a clinking bag of gold coins.

"Well, I suppose that would do it," Bones reluctantly admitted, taking the purse from Sofia. "I'll try to find someone. It'll be easier if they see me from the start, I'd hate for them to bolt on us."

He pushed himself out of the tent, doing his best to look non-threatening. "I…um… We would like to hire someone to take us from the town," Bones stammered, sounding just as scared as the villagers.

The young necromancer felt very uncomfortable hiring servants.

For obvious reasons, most of the feudal nobility was happy to sit around collecting tithes from their serfs and living in luxury—it was a good and easy life. But as Bones's father had always said, people at the edges of society were good at seeing the cracks in the social order.

Nobles' wealth granted life through food and medicine, and they could order the death of any serf who displeased them. Bones's command over life and death was far more direct, and while the villagers of Golden Fields couldn't identify that outright, the fear they felt around him showed that they recognized it on a spiritual level.

A few of the villagers who saw the gold in Bones's hand hesitantly stepped forward, their desire for security battling their fear of an instant death they couldn't understand. At the end of the day, a large bag of gold was still a large bag of gold.

But before anyone on either side had taken more than a few slow and hesitant steps, a faint whistling sound wound out from the tall wheat fields. A carriage seemingly materialized out of thin air as it rode forth without disturbing the gently swaying wheat.

Bones gawked. "What just…?"

The carriage drew to a halt in front of him, far finer than the Bonaparte family carriage he remembered from his childhood. The exterior was gleaming white and decorated with finely etched filigree depicting animals from around the world, many of which Bones had only seen in books. Massive elephants capered with tigers and dogs frolicked with cats. The crimson chairs were so plush that they might as well have been sofas.

The carriage itself was pulled by zebras instead of horses. The lithe and muscular creature's bodies were covered with black and white stripes. Ever since he'd been a child, Bones had always found horses a little scary. Thick muscles rippled beneath their fur and their teeth were surprisingly sharp. Of course, horses were usually much more scared of him—but not this time.

The zebras stared back at him with calm and intelligent eyes.

The strangest thing of all—even stranger than the zebras—was the driver.

They were massive, at least six and a half feet tall, with muscles that rippled through their pitch-black cloak. They wore a black cloak with a low-hanging hood, complete with a veil that completely obscured their face.

They turned and stared right at Bones without flinching. Though Bones could not see their face, he knew that just like Karn, this was somebody who did not fear his power.

"Um, hello?" Bones asked. "Are you… Are you here to offer us a ride?"

"You intend to visit the gravesite of Karn the Blazing Warrior, correct?" To Bones's shock, it was a woman's voice despite the speaker's enormous size.

For a moment, he thought it might have been the strange voice from his dream, but they sounded nothing alike. The dream visitor had been young, almost girly. Although the coachwoman spoke in a subdued and professional manner, there was something about her voice that was naturally regal and commanding, like some kind of long-forgotten queen.

Hearing the commotion, Sofia poked out of the tent and gawked, just like Bones did. "What just…?" After living together for so long, the two had a habit of reacting similarly.

Bones's eyes went from Sofia to the carriage.

Unlike whatever Karn said he was, this woman was clearly a ghost. Bones could practically sniff the ectoplasm on her and the way she sank in and out of the seat was a classic tell of a ghost pretending to be human. "Um, excuse me, how can she see you? I, um…"

The coachwoman simply stared at him and repeated her earlier message. "You intend to visit the gravesite of Karn the Blazing Warrior, correct?" This time, she placed just a bit of emphasis on the last word and the zebras pawed the ground irritably, clearly interested in leaving.

"Um, well, I guess…"

Karn arrived mid-stammer, his flames doused.

His skeleton looked much less impressive without the blazing flames. An onlooker would have thought that he was a tragically killed child. "Oh, how lovely. A carriage just for us!" Since Karn had no real idea how the modern world worked, he didn't think this was suspicious at all. The not-a-skeleton simply marveled at the convenience. He hadn't known there was a way to call carriages on demand, but he was certainly glad of it.

"Well, I… Karn—"

"You know what, Bones? Maybe we should just take the carriage," Sofia muttered, making the executive decision.

From her extended study of true crime pamphlets, Sofia knew that it was a bad idea to accept rides from mysterious strangers, but the thought of walking for so long was simply too painful. Inadvertently, she'd fallen for the mental trap that caused kidnapping victims to accept rides from mysterious strangers.

"Excellent," the coachwoman said. "All aboard. The trip will cost one silver coin there and another back."

They got on. As the smallest of them, Karn sat in the middle seat.

Bones pulled out two silver coins from his bag, handing one to the coachwoman and placing the other in his robe. Then he turned to the villagers and threw the bag of gold coins at them. For most people, it would have been very difficult to throw a bag of gold without seeming condescending, but Bones's hesitation and nervousness made him perfect for the task. "Uh…sorry for ruining your show…um… Here. Have some gold…"

Even after the carriage had ridden away, it took a long time before one of the villagers was finally brave enough to pick up the bag. Once he did, he only took a single coin before handing the rest out, his face as pale as Bones's own. Even though Golden Fields was a strong and trusting community, the sheer amount of wealth meant that in normal circumstances, there might have been a desperate fight for the money.

But after seeing a burning skeleton, a ghostly carriage driven by a spectral figure in a hood, a pale-faced boy with a demonic aura, and an old lady who seemed to command all of them, the villagers wanted to make extra sure that they were living properly, just in case judgment was nigh.

Chapter Seven

As the zebras pulled the carriage down the road, Bones frowned to himself, trying to remember where he'd heard the vaguely familiar voice from his dream.

Unfortunately, Karn's constant fidgeting made it very difficult to think. He leaned out of the cab and into the driver's seat, his skeletal body rattling. "Are we there yet?"

"How could we possibly be there? We just left!" Sofia exclaimed.

"Oh, it'll be faster than you think," the coachwoman replied. A faint note of pride entered her voice, making her sound all the more majestic. "My friends and I know of many secret paths through the world."

Karn nodded. "Excellent. I'm excited to show my new friends my tomb… It's frustrating it's known for some other battle now, but I'm sure my legacy shall reign eternal. This is just a momentary blip."

"Well, I hate to say it, but you have a lot of catching up to do," Sofia said.

Right at that moment, the carriage rode by a physical demonstration of just how behind Karn was. A bard walked by the side of the road, wearing a fanciful black doublet and carrying a redwood lute in his hand as he sang a tale about Angelo's recent courtship of Duke Veras's daughter.

"Her hair was fair... His hair was fairer... A very beautiful woman...with the most beautiful man..." The bard had an elegant singing voice, but he swallowed his frown as the lackluster lyrics exited his mouth. Back when he'd been a young child dreaming of superstardom, he had never imagined becoming a professional propagandist.

"What was that man singing about?" Karn asked. "That song doesn't sound heroic at all."

Sofia side-eyed Karn with the accuracy of a master javelin thrower. She still couldn't tell if this was all some kind of preposterous act. "Baron Angelo has sent bards throughout the land to boast of his great victories and eternal kindness. I believe you would struggle to be better than known than him, especially with your seeming lack of resources."

"Bah. Bards. I don't care about music unless it's about me."

"Is that why you ripped off your ears?" Bones asked.

"What? No! Obviously, I can still hear without ears," Karn replied. "How else would I be responding to you?"

"Oh. I guess that's a good point," Bones admitted. He thought about asking Karn how he could listen without ears, but he decided not to, feeling embarrassed about his obvious mistake.

Of course, Sofia thought that Karn had his ears tucked under his skull costume, so she shrugged off the bizarre conversation.

As for Karn, he clenched his bony fist with irritation. He was rather tired of hearing about this Angelo. Barren or baron, he knew the man could not possibly rival his greatness, yet it seemed like this postmodern society enjoyed ironic jokes and catchy songs more than true great deeds. It was a real shame.

Bones had gone right back to thinking about the voice inside his head.

And so, just as all three members of the trio withdrew into themselves, the carriage rattled to a smooth and elegant halt.

"We're almost there," the spectral coachwoman declared.

Sofia blinked. "What? How?"

She stared outside the window, her eyes wide as she gazed upon a forest of thick, green bamboo, far thicker than anything near Golden Fields.

Bones was similarly shocked. He didn't know anything about geography—he just knew that aside from her supernatural blind spot, Sofia was usually right about how the world worked. He poked his head against his window, where he caught the briefest glimpse of a bridge, its planks painted every color of the rainbow, arcing over a calm, reflective lake nested between two valleys. Lotus flowers of every color glistened on the shimmering surface.

But then, their surroundings swirled and the carriage stood at the base of a tall, black mountain before the remains of an unmistakable battlefield.

Sofia gasped as she poked her head outside. "What…? How did you…?"

"Like I said, we have a different idea of how the world is connected. Good thing too, considering how terrible the roads are these days." the coachwoman replied. To her credit, her voice had only the faintest hint of arrogance after completing a multi-day trip in just a few minutes.

Bones eyed the coachwoman. He still didn't understand how Sofia could see her, but after this near-instantaneous carriage trip, he suspected it had something to do with the coachwoman's intense power—much like how normal people could see his necromantic aura when he used his magic.

"What an eyesore," Karn grumbled. "It's ridiculous arrogance to have a huge battle right in front of someone else's tomb…and even more ridiculous arrogance to put up a monument afterward. When I invented the idea of respecting elders, I'd expected it would turn out better for me."

Karn was right about one thing. The monument to the One Day War was a total eyesore.

A gleaming gold-gilded statue of Baron Angelo, an otherworldly handsome man with perfectly curled hair that trailed down to his shoulders, stood in front of the battlefield, a sword held commandingly in his right hand. Though the bodies of his victims had vanished, their rusted weapons and discarded armor remained, left as a grim reminder of what would happen to rebels.

Of course, Blackridge Peak, extending tall above the rest of the Blackridge Mountain Range, was a total eyesore as well. The distended mass of dark-gray stone resembled nothing more than a shoddily built roof. Splinters and cracks lacerated the weathered mountain, which was covered by unruly patches of un-melted snow.

"Can you make it up the rest of the way?" the coachwoman asked. She had been ordered to hide from the other people visiting the peak, and besides, the goats she would have normally hitched to the carriage for mountain trips were on vacation today.

"It should be fine," Sofia replied. "A short hike will be good for my health."

"It's not that short of a hike," Karn replied. Sofia's comment had been totally innocent, but Karn felt like his choice of tomb site had been subtly slighted. "Back in my day, this was the tallest mountain in the land."

"Really?" Bones frowned. "I mean, even in this barony, Lorenzo's Peak is taller… I remember climbing it with my dad. And I thought you said you ruled multiple nations."

Karn groaned. "Look, kid. I had a lot of stuff on me and I didn't want to waste time carrying it around. It was the tallest mountain in the land right in front of me."

The trio disembarked and slowly walked through the abandoned battlefield.

"I thought you said there were a bunch of ghosts here," Bones remarked.

Karn glanced around and shrugged. "Huh. I guess not. Well, it's a good thing I met you before I moved back in. Our circus sounds much more interesting than bumming around inside. Back in my tomb, all I had to do was try to break my record for longest nap."

"Maybe they wanted to move on. I suppose nobody wants to sit around and remember the time they were betrayed and killed. Only the angriest ghosts stay around to haunt places."

As they walked past Baron Angelo's statue, Karn stopped, staring into the man's golden eyes before clacking his teeth disapprovingly. "That man… He's holding a sword, but he doesn't have a warrior's eyes."

"Well, I mean, it's just a statue," Bones replied. "Though come to think of it, I remember that demon said Baron

Angelo had powers like mine. He's probably a magician of some kind, not a warrior."

Sofia, walking behind them, interpreted "demon" as "the man." Having raised many children and grandchildren, she knew that many young men around Bones's age were often frustrated by the man.

As for Karn, he looked deep into Bones's eyes, shifting his body to make the flames around him billow mysteriously. Unfortunately, he'd forgotten that he'd doused himself. "Well. Magicians can be warriors too, you know. It's not just about carrying a sword, and I can tell you now. You might *seem* like the shy and hesitant type, but I knew as soon as I met you that there was some real bark there."

"Um, 'real bark'?"

Fireballs once again appeared in Karn's eyes as he furiously worked to modernize his analogy. "Ah. I suppose with developments in weaponry, I should say, 'real steel.'"

"Oh. Thank you."

By then, they'd made it past the battlefield and towards the base of the mountain. The mountain itself was harsh and jagged, and the trail was equally challenging. A slow and painful chill—not from Bones's aura, but from nature itself—resonated through their bodies as they stared up at the peak. The top wasn't particularly far away, but the trail itself looked tough and hazardous.

"I can just go up there and grab everything," Karn said.

"No, I'd like to go with you," Bones replied. "It's just…"

"Oh, stuff it, Bones…" Sofia grumbled. "Don't underestimate me. I walk the terrible route outside of our home all the time. And look at that other group. There's no way they're stronger than I am."

"Huh. I never saw visitors too often," Karn muttered. "This is a little strange. Though I don't know which group you're talking about. Neither of them looks like they're in very good shape."

Bones nudged Karn, making a mental note that whatever allowed Sofia to see the coachwoman didn't apply to regular ghosts yet. "She can only see the powerful ones."

Indeed, there were two groups slowly making their way up the damaged and battered mountain.

The first was a group of scholars dressed in the exceptionally gaudy and cumbersome clothing of the Plumage Barony. Their heavy, cloth robes—shiny blue for the men and shinier pink for the women—were utterly drenched with sweat and their fanciful hats, covered with more feathers than a peacock's tail, looked like they'd been designed to overheat their skulls. The nobles were painfully overdressed for hiking, even when accounting for the chill of the Blackridge Mountain Range.

A man with a pair of silver spectacles seemed to be their leader. He jotted notes in a leatherbound tome as he walked, muttering something about a lack of archaeological funding.

Sofia sniffed irritably. "Bah. The nobles from Plumage always think they are better than everyone else."

"Plumage," Karn wondered aloud. "What's that?"

"Another barony. Quite far away from here, actually," Sofia replied.

"Oh. I see. What barony are we in?"

"The Sun Beam Barony, on account of the river that runs through it," Bones explained. "I don't travel much, though, so I just think of it as 'The Barony.'" He tilted his head to the side, staring at the nobles' outfits. "How did you meet Plumage nobles, Sofia? They seem kind of exotic."

"Islington University campus. There's a bunch of rich snobs who go there. These guys look like they might be from Islington too. Maybe I can ask them why there's been such a delay getting my last homework assignment graded."

Unfortunately, when they spotted the trio, the Plumage scholars wrinkled their noses and hurried up the mountain faster.

Suffocating in their outfits, the Plumage scholars would have appreciated a nice, bone-creeping chill, but the sight of Bones and Karn offended them so deeply that they couldn't spare another second in their presence.

Bones's tattered, black cloak was covered in holes and awkward gray patches, but Karn was even worse. Even leaving his excessively bony appearance aside, his ancient animal skins, so weathered that not even he knew what animals they'd come from, were the fashion equivalent of mystery meat.

Sofia could not see a second group. It was afraid of ghosts—four men and two women—muttering anxiously to each other, their bodies leaving a faint trail of ectoplasm as they made their way up the hill. They carried their heads tucked under their arms, a telltale symptom of execution.

Bones watched them cautiously. Executed ghosts usually bore grudges against the people who'd killed them, but the particularly upset ones extended their grudge to humanity in general. Bones knew he was safe; he just wanted to make sure they didn't mess with Sofia.

But as they drew closer, Bones realized that the ghosts looked distraught instead of angry. Their eyes peeked curiously at Bones as he walked by. Normally, he would have determinedly avoided making eye contact for fear of scaring them away, but then Bones thought back to his dream.

Once upon a time, Bones had greatly enjoyed talking to ghosts and spirits.

"Hang on a moment," he muttered. He left Sofia and Karn, veering off the trail a bit to head to the ghosts, taking slow and steady steps to let them acclimate to his necromantic energy. He didn't want to dash forward and spook them.

He stepped towards the ghosts. "Do you need something?"

They stared at him, shading their decapitated faces to avoid looking at him directly. All of them quivered in fear, and one even bowed down, falling into a white puddle on the floor as his body sank through the mountain.

"Um…it's okay," Bones said. "I…promise I won't hurt you…"

The beheaded ghosts had very soft and feeble voices that Bones strained to hear. In their defense, their vocal cords had some serious connectivity issues. To make up for it, they spoke as one, acting as a chorus to get their words out.

"You…boy… We heard that there were some executed ghosts here… We heard there was a great betrayal…and that many died after they'd laid down their arms to negotiate a peace…"

"Um, yeah, that's what I was told," Bones replied. "I don't really follow politics."

"Well…do you know…where we could find them?"

"No, sorry… Uh, my friend who lives here hasn't been back for a long time."

"Oh. Well…that's a shame… You see…we heard that they had been beheaded… We were hoping they might know what could be done about it…"

"'Done about it?'"

"Yes…it is very uncomfortable to talk like this…and when we don't carry our heads properly…we get very dizzy…"

Bones hadn't thought about that before. That was the thing about meeting new people—sometimes they had a very different way of looking at things. Fortunately, he thought he could help this time. "Um…you know, I think I might be able to help you out," he said. "Um…just let me…"

He turned back to Karn. "Can you come over here?"

"Sure," Karn replied. "Do they want something?"

Bones explained what was happening and Karn clacked his teeth in confusion. "So what do you need me for?"

"Well…I…um… Well, the last time I used my magic, something bad happened." He thought back to the irritated girl from his dream and hurriedly amended his statement. "Well. I don't know if it was *because* of me. But something bad definitely happened. And, uh, well, I was thinking with you here, you could make sure things don't go wrong."

"Oh. Well. Sure. You've got nothing to worry about with Karn the Blazing Warrior by your side!"

Having Karn by his side made Bones feel much more comfortable about using his magic. Karn was just as strong as he was—if anything happened, he could keep Sofia and everyone else safe.

Bones walked up to the ghosts, concentrating on his magic for the first time in many years. When he had been a child, he could heal with a mere gesture, even a thought, but now, just to be safe, he walked up and placed his hands on them, hoping to control his necromantic energy as much as possible.

Unlike what had happened at the tent, Bones remained calm, his heart beating steadily. His magic flowed into their ectoplasmic bodies and their heads flew from their hands, spinning through the air. With a final magical thrum, the heads reattached themselves to their proper places, a thoroughly successful re-necking the likes of which had never been seen before.

The ghosts gazed down at themselves—a simple motion that they nonetheless conducted with intense satisfaction.

"My word!" one of the men exclaimed. "You've done it!"

"That was a miracle!" one of the women added. "I haven't been able to talk properly in years!"

"Oh, I don't know if that's a good thing for us." The other woman laughed, earning herself an ectoplasmic smack.

"Thank you!" the ghosts exclaimed in unison before twisting and then vanishing off into the distance.

Bones watched them go with a satisfied smile on his face. "Second day in a row helping people with my powers…and they weren't even that scared that time."

Karn didn't get what the big fuss was. He helped people every single day with his powers, by keeping himself alive and blessing them with his presence. Still, he was glad that his new friend was happy.

The group made it up to the summit without any problems, with Sofia swallowing her irritation at the constant talk of ghosts she could not see.

"It's just inside there," Karn said, pointing straight forward into a cave. "It's past all the pillars."

The first chamber of the cave was a wide, circular area about fifty feet wide and long, held up by sturdy, stone pillars so thick, they looked a little like tree trunks. The cave itself was cool and dry. At the back of the chamber was a simple, roughly hewn corridor, the constant handprints making it painfully obvious it had been dug by human hands.

After a few steps into the cavern, they found the scholars from before, all slumped against a tall, stone pillar furiously wiping their sweaty foreheads and panting with exertion as they gulped down water. Their faces were flushed bright red—and not just because of the heat. They sounded angry and irritated.

"How are we supposed to get anything done with all the cuts to school funding?"

"Well, you heard what Baron Angelo's representative said. They said archaeology is a waste of time unless we bring back bodies."

"That's not archaeology; that's just graverobbing!"

The spectacled scholar scoffed. "Oh, next thing you know, that asshole Yesse Pennington is going to be campaigning for a graverobbing major."

"Good gods… Yesse is a suck-up's suck-up. It's a shock how pale he is, with how often he's brown-nosing."

"Well, we might as well make the best of what we have. Once we're ready, let's finish exploring. There's a legend about Blackridge Peak…that this used to be a sacred site where a legendary warrior was buried alive, and I bet it's past that corridor over there."

Karn was so excited, he almost tackled Bones in his haste to talk to the scholars, but he froze after just one clattering step.

"Bones…there's something there…" he said, pointing straight forward. "Something blocking the path to my tomb."

Bones stared forward. He didn't see anything with his eyes, but he still sensed a spike of eldritch energy. Karn was right. Something—or someone—was lying in wait for them.

After Karn took one more step forward, a voice roared at him, echoing through the entire chamber. "Leave! Leave this place if you want to live!" The deep, booming cry sounded like some kind of legendary warrior, a man who had faced down countless foes in his time.

The scholars screamed, their voices echoing through the cave as they bolted away as fast as they could, some even leaving their precious hats behind in their haste to escape.

Karn whirled back. "No, come back! I need to tell you about my legend!"

Unfortunately, his cries only frightened the Plumage scholars even more. They yelped and gasped, wailing in terror as they descended the peak as fast as they could.

Sofia stepped up to Bones, her jaw tight. "I don't know about this, Achille. It could be dangerous."

Karn stomped forward, every bone in his body rattling. Without his flames, he had to find another way to express his extreme disapproval. "I'll tell you what's dangerous: making me mad! Someone barged into my tomb and scared off my few remaining fans! Let's get them, Bones!"

Chapter Eight

Karn charged straight into the corridor.

Bones followed behind him, moving much more slowly while keeping an eye out for Sofia. In turn, Sofia was even more cautious, keeping an eye out for Bones. Due to this cycle of hypervigilance, they fell very far behind the utterly un-cautious Karn.

The voice hissed angrily again. "How dare you defy my orders? Do you realize what you are dealing with? There's no way an uncivilized brute like you could defeat me!"

Karn made it into the corridor, fiercely swinging his fists. "You! Get back here! Turn solid so I can hit you! Bones…this guy is immune to physical attacks. It's got to be some kind of spirit!"

"You moron! Why would I turn solid? I—"

The voice suddenly broke off mid-taunt, halting as soon as it had felt Bones's magic. Bones expected the spirit to cry out in fright, but instead, the voice was shockingly excited. "Bones? Is that you?"

Bones's eyes widened. This was a man's voice, so it wasn't the girl from his dream. Still, this spirit clearly recognized him. The only problem was that Bones had no idea who this was, nor could he see them. He decided to try to bluff his way out of it. "Yeah, it's me! I'm so glad to see you again! What are you doing in this cave?"

"Well, you remember how I was always looking for my wife?"

"Yeah, totally," Bones lied.

"I finally found her again! It was amazing! But then I got trapped here by this weird orb. My summoner wants me to guard this corridor forever and scare people off. But wait a second…I'm sure you could get rid of it no problem!"

"I probably could," Bones replied. When it came to a battle of magic, he was utterly confident.

"Awesome! I'll let you pass, but get rid of that thing for me. Do a favor for your old buddy Tycho!"

With a loud *whoosh* and a gust of wind, the spirit vanished, flying away without revealing itself.

"I knew it! An invisibility spirit!" Karn exclaimed. "Nice work getting it to leave."

"It seems like he knew me," Bones replied. "The name 'Tycho' sounds vaguely familiar…"

Sofia frowned. Before entering this cave, she'd been wondering if Islington University would accept a research thesis on mass delusion. But just like Bones and Karn, she'd heard that voice and she'd felt that strange *whoosh*.

If anything, an invisibility spirit was the *only* kind of spirit she considered believable—after all, she couldn't see the rest of them, anyway.

"Wait a second, Karn," Bones said. "How did you see the spirit if it was invisible? And come to think of it, how can you see ghosts in general?"

"Oh, I'm just good at paying attention. It's how I can see without eyes or listen without ears." After a brief pause, Karn thought of his father and amended his statement. "Ah. Well. That's not entirely true. I'm good at paying attention when I want to pay attention. Normally, I'm not paying attention at all. My dad was always getting on me about keeping constant vigilance, but it got hard to do that when I realized I couldn't die."

Bones smiled. "My dad was always teaching me that too. He was a soldier. He said that on the battlefield, the difference between life and death could be a single stray observation."

Karn grinned so widely that he inadvertently revealed that he was missing two teeth at the very back. "Ha! Sounds like our dads were similar. Man…my dad was a great guy. His only problem was he could be a little moody at times. Always yelled at me for taking unnecessary risks. Wish I could talk to him now."

Bones thought back to his dream and smiled sadly. "Me with mine too."

"Well, I'm sure both your fathers would just want you to be happy," Sofia eagerly chimed in. She felt much more comfortable dispensing generic life advice than trying to figure out what had happened with that alleged invisibility spirit.

Emboldened by Sofia's words, Karn and Bones walked through the dug-out corridor. "Made this tunnel myself," Karn boasted, proudly pointing out the handprints on the wall. "See?"

He placed his hand onto one of the prints, but it didn't quite fit. "Well. It will fit once I get my fingers back on," Karn assured them.

They made it to the end of the tunnel, and then he gestured dramatically. "And here we are: the tomb of the most legendary warrior in history. What do you think?"

Despite Karn's request for him to stop overthinking, Bones didn't know what to say. "Well. I'm, uh, thinking?" he replied.

Unimpressed didn't even begin to cover how Bones was feeling.

The Bonaparte family cemetery hadn't been particularly impressive, since they were merely minor nobility, but before the manor's destruction, it had at least been something—a well-kept area with orderly tombstones and plaques.

Karn's tomb looked like a cross between a homeless encampment and a natural disaster site.

The tiny crawlspace was smaller than Bones's room back at the cottage and even more disorganized.

Loosely strewn pieces of memorabilia—a bunch of burnt-out sticks from prior battles—lay across the floor, as well as the remains of an abandoned straw bed. At this point, there were only a few brittle sticks of yellow left; the rest had been consumed by waves of mold. A large, wooden chest rested by the side of the bed.

The walls were decorated with a scarlet substance that looked a lot like blood. At first, the haphazard trickles and drops seemed completely random, but as Bones stared at them, he thought he saw patterns in the chaos, perhaps a proud man carrying a sword.

At the very back of the room was a huge cave-in, an utter avalanche of cumbersome gray boulders that seemed to block off a farther path.

Seeing the squalor, Sofia felt a sense of relief.

The true crime pamphlet reading part of her had been worried that Karn had been trying to use Bones to steal something, but nobody would possibly try to steal from this total dump. Thieves, while not legitimate businesspeople, were usually still businesspeople of a sort, evaluating the risks and rewards of their heists. Robbing dusty holes at the top of mountains wasn't a viable business model.

"You two don't seem very impressed," Karn noted.

Bones, endeavoring to remain honest, stammered out an explanation. "Well, I, uh… When I think of grand tombs, I think of buildings and stuff like that."

Karn shrugged irritably. "We didn't have buildings in my time, all right? We took our caves and were happy with them. I had had to climb uphill both ways to put this thing together!"

"Well, has the place changed much since you left?"

"No, it was like this before…but my bed got a bit moldier over the last few years," Karn said.

Bones decided not to ask how moldy it had been before. "Uh…was the cave-in there too?"

"I made it myself," Karn replied. "Anyone who solves the puzzle will be able to acquire my fortune."

"Wow. A secret fortune?"

"Yes. The treasures of my age. Based on what I know of your society, I suspect everything is worth a lot more now. I got all the good stuff ahead of time." Karn didn't know much about modern society, but he liked what he'd heard about gold and fine wine. He had a keen interest in things that got better over time—they sounded like Karn himself, and he liked things that had a lot in common with him.

Bones slowly tilted his head to the side, studying the stones with keen interest. He deeply enjoyed puzzles—after all, they were excellent solo activities—but no matter where he tried to start, he couldn't make heads or tails of the stones.

He took another look at the overall cave, searching for other clues. "Does it have anything to do with these wall paintings?"

Karn whirled towards the walls. "What? No! They weren't there before! I have no idea what those are!"

His father would have been irritated, but in fairness to Karn, he'd been caught up in the excitement of getting his body back. Physiological needs like breathing, food, and water had ranked ahead of safety needs like keeping people from defacing his home.

"Oh. Um. Those aren't yours? I mean, I thought they looked a bit like cave paintings."

Karn scoffed. "What? No…just look at how random all these red splatters are. This is clearly postmodern nonsense. Let's clean this gunk off immediately!"

"Good idea. I can look for the orb Tycho mentioned too," Bones said.

"Well, I have some cloths in my bag," Sofia said, pulling them out and handing one each to Karn and Bones. Perhaps Karn was a good influence, after all. Bones had never cared about cleanliness before.

As the two men hurried across the cavern, wiping off the strangely artful blood splatters, Bones's right foot clunked against a small, glass orb filled with swirling, red mist. The strange device had been placed beside the bed and as soon as his foot had made contact with it, he felt a strange tug in his soul.

He bent over and picked it up, frowning.

The orb was swirling with necromantic energy, similar but different from his own. "This must have been what Tycho was talking about," Bones said. He felt a tug emanating from within the orb, anchoring the spirit to his task. Though Tycho had left temporarily, Bones felt the orb's power slowly forcing him back. Bones concentrated and the red mist vanished, the necromantic energy within the orb assimilating with the nimbus around his body.

"How did you do that?" Karn asked.

"I'm not sure," Bones replied. "I guess I can take in outside sources of necromantic energy too, not just life energy."

"At least it looks impressive," Karn said. "Did you get any stronger?"

"Not really," Bones replied, flexing his fingers. It felt like just adding a few more drops to the ocean. He'd barely even noticed it. "I don't think this necromancer is very strong. If they were, Tycho wouldn't have been able to leave at all."

"Well, at least all that random crap is gone," Karn said.

Then he walked up to the chest, popping it open and carefully counting out all his body parts, breathing a sigh of relief that everything was there.

He started with a hand, pulling the flesh over his bones. "It's a lot paler than before..." Karn muttered. "Haven't been out in the sun in a few years."

"It looks pretty tan to me," Bones remarked.

"Oh, I mean, it was out in the sun for a couple thousand years before I locked it up," Karn replied. Then he cursed—again uttering out an unintelligible string of harsh, grunting syllables—as the hand slipped limply onto the ground.

"Huh. For some reason, it's not staying…" Karn cursed again.

"Did you ever try to do this before?" Bones asked.

"What? No. It never occurred to me to try. I guess flesh doesn't stick back on again when you take it off."

"No, it usually doesn't," Bones agreed. He was beginning to understand exactly why Karn's father had been so moody. "Well. Maybe I can help."

He placed his hand on Karn, channeling his necromantic energy and sealing the hand back in place.

"Excellent." Karn grinned, flexing his hand. "Well, let me put everything else on before you zap me again."

He began digging into the chest, humming to himself as he slowly started putting everything back on.

"Wait a second," Bones said. "You had chests back in your day?"

"No. I stole this after I decided to peel my body off. Incidentally, I didn't even get all of it." As Karn spoke, his animal skin cloak swirled a bit, revealing parts still stuck to his back. "The good news is, I guess it makes it easier to get everything back on again."

"Um, yeah, I guess it kind of does," Bones replied, still not quite understanding what had driven Karn to tear away his flesh and organs. Lacking Karn's immortality privilege, he failed to see the benefit of constantly pursuing high-risk, minimal-reward ideas.

As he moved through the chest, Karn groaned. He was lucky Bones had fixed his hand. It was perfect for face-palming. "Look at this chest… I can't believe the bottle broke!"

Inside was a broken bottle, the shards stained bright red. At the base of the chest were a few more drops of blood.

"Well, there's no use crying over spilled blood, I suppose…" Bones nervously joked. "I think I should be able to fix it."

Sofia's judgment increased even further. "Karn. It feels like you might be living beyond your means spending so much money on props for pranks."

Karn saw her and raised his hand awkwardly. "Apologies, but do you mind turning around? I don't want to flash you when I'm putting my body back on." The social stigma against walking around naked hadn't quite existed when Karn had been born, but one of the under-discussed problems with immortality was it provided a lot more time to pick up new social neuroses.

Karn finished loosely putting everything on, then tossed on the additional skins at the bottom of the chest. A skeleton could walk around in nothing more than a cloak. A man, not so much.

"All right, Bones. I'm ready."

Bones's magic flowed forth once again. The damage was too extensive for him to heal completely. Instead, necromantic energy magically stitched Karn's awkwardly torn-off body parts together, sealing his body back into place. Seconds later, the magic jumpstarted his heart and bones, priming him to produce blood again. Moments later, Karn was whole, though thanks to the patchwork of glowing, magical stitches, he now looked like a zombie rather than a skeleton.

Bones watched the entire process with bated breath, again worried about some kind of magical backlash, but nothing happened. It was the first time in human history that helping a strange, old man get dressed turned out to be a good idea with no negative consequences.

Karn grinned, wiggling his fingers and toes and then taking on a few swaggering steps. "Ha. This is nice. It's surprisingly chilly being just a skeleton."

He poked at his face, feeling the strange mess of stitches. "Huh. I guess I probably shouldn't have ripped my face off. But nice work, Bones! You even fixed my two missing teeth— I'd misplaced them a few centuries back in a fight with a giant bear. Turned out it wasn't a good idea to let it get a few free hits in."

The legendary Blazing Warrior's real body had tan skin and a shock of messy, red hair. He wasn't unattractive, but he wasn't particularly handsome, either. His looks were definitionally average. With over half the barony descended from him, Karn's appearance had achieved the triple crown of averages: mean, median, and mode all at once. He had broad shoulders and muscular arms, but a fairly notable potbelly. Karn's motivation to train had dropped significantly after he found out that he couldn't be killed.

"All right, Sofia. You can turn around again," Karn declared.

Just as Sofia was wondering why a man who couldn't afford a home was spending so much of his money on highly realistic skeleton and zombie costumes, a feeble voice called out from the corridor.

"You... What... What are you doing here?"

A very thin and wiry man hurried into the chamber, walking so hurriedly, it appeared like he had three or even four bony elbows. He sounded like he was permanently short of breath, panting with every step, and his face was ghastly pale, even paler than Bones's own.

His brown hair was cut very short everywhere except for his bangs, which drooped over his manically darting, bloodshot eyes. A narrow, straggly mustache droopily framed lips that were so pale and thin, they were nearly invisible.

He wore a white tunic stained with scarlet blood. The sleeves had been torn off, revealing varicose veins that stuck out from his pale arms like glowing blue rivers.

The man stared at them, utterly shocked. "Where did Tycho go? I summoned him to keep my art secret so people wouldn't steal my ideas. Did you do something to him? Why did he let you find my studio?"

"What? Your studio?" Karn didn't know what a studio was. He just knew this place wasn't this man's anything. "This is my tomb—I am Karn, the Blazing Warrior, the most legendary fighter in human history!" Like always, Karn proclaimed this like it meant something, and like always, he was disappointed.

"Who? What?" If the man had gotten to "when," he would have realized why he'd never heard of Karn before, but the abrupt realization that his paintings had been destroyed obliterated all concept of intellectual curiosity.

"You… Do you realize… Do you realize what you have done? You have destroyed my beautiful works! Do you know the value of an original Jack Pillary?!" His eyes bulged with hatred and he clenched his fist. "You… Only your death can pay for this! Face the full might of my blood manipulation magic!"

"Oh, come on!" Karn groaned. "That's just my luck! I get my blood back one second before I fight a blood manipulation user? Let's end this quick, Bones!"

Chapter Nine

There were two kinds of blood manipulation, the normal kind and the overpowered kind.

The normal kind involved manipulating the user's own blood. The overpowered kind involved manipulating other people's blood, sometimes even when it was directly inside the other person's body.

Unfortunately for Jack Pillary, he had the normal kind, and not a very good version of the normal kind. Swaying and trembling, he pulled out a dagger and stabbed himself in the wrist. "Eat this: Jack Pillary's Crimson Wave!" Having fought for patrons and commissions in the cutthroat Avaron Heights art scene, Jack Pillary knew the importance of name recognition and branding.

A very pale, almost-white wave of very thin blood washed over Bones and Karn, doing absolutely nothing.

"What?" Jack stammered. "How? I—"

He broke off mid-sentence as Karn knocked him out with a precise punch to the temple. The pale-faced man slumped to the floor, unconscious, his thin and gangly body falling without a sound.

"Did you kill him?" Bones asked.

"What? No, of course not." To Bones's confusion, Karn sounded offended.

"Wait…haven't you killed a ton of people? That wasn't an unfair accusation!"

"Yes, it was. I'm an entertainer now! I'm done with killing, and when I decide something, I stick with it. I just knocked him out."

"Well, that's good," Bones said.

"Very good," Sofia hurriedly agreed.

Bones mused to himself as he stared at the unconscious body.

From the looks of it, this Jack Pillary had been another necromancer. When Jack had stabbed himself, Bones had felt the flare of necromantic energy. There was only one problem: the man was nothing like Bones.

"He didn't seem very strong," Bones said. "I wanted to ask him if our powers could hurt someone on accident, but it seems like he can't even hurt people on purpose."

"Well, in my experience," Karn replied, "magic isn't just very rare. Most people with it are also very weak. A man like you only comes around once every few centuries, Bones."

As for Sofia, her eyes darted from Jack's body to the corridor where she'd heard the invisibility spirit. Jack's extremely dramatic declaration that he had blood manipulation magic coupled with the exceedingly unimpressive result had caused her mental pendulum to swing back the other way.

"This guy is just like you guys," Sofia said. "Very strong imagination."

"What? There's nothing strong about this man!" Karn complained. "We're on totally different levels!"

"She's just like that," Bones said.

"Yeah, just sane…" Sofia grumbled.

"Well, as I was saying before I was so rudely interrupted, this is my hidden fortune," Karn said, walking over to the back wall. He started at the cave-in, grunting as he moved the boulders aside. "This is the key to the puzzle—people don't realize this so-called landslide is actually a secret wall. I'm not surprised it stumped you too."

"It looks like you're just digging into the landslide," Bones protested.

"Well, of course. What's better than a puzzle that only I am strong enough to solve? And just so you know, this isn't a landslide. I went all over the mountain finding just the right large boulders. I had to make sure they were the size of small boulders."

"What?"

But Karn was too focused to amend Bones's confusion.

With a few more wrenching heaves of stone, Karn opened up his makeshift vault, revealing a cave much bigger than his original tomb. It was floor-to-ceiling with gleaming, golden stones and the ground was covered in dust. "Behold! My fortune: shiny stones and flowers from all around the world!"

"Um…Karn…I think the plants and flowers died," Bones replied, gesturing at the dust. "I mean, it's been a very long time. And, uh, there's no water or sunlight here."

"Oh. Well. Erm. I still got all these shiny rocks at least," Karn insisted.

Unfortunately, things were only going to get worse.

Bones walked through the much-larger backend of the cave, touching each of the pieces of stone and turning them over in his hand. "Uh…it looks nice, but I think I recognize this from Sofia's textbook."

Sofia walked in, took one look at the rocks, and sighed. "Bones, I hate to say it, but you're right. Well, Karn. I don't know how to tell you this, but I don't think this is worth very much."

"What? Why?" Karn indignantly replied. "This stuff is shiny—way shinier than the coins you gave the coachwoman. If that's gold, this has to be super gold!"

Sofia paused for a moment. She was much more socially skilled than Bones, but there was no way to explain this without being insulting. "Sorry, but this is actually called 'fool's gold.'"

"*What?*"

"Yeah, it looks like gold, but it's not very valuable…" Bones sighed. But then he caught a glimpse of a tiny, golden fleck and carefully picked it off a stone. The tiny sliver of actual gold glistened on his finger as he showed it to Karn. "This is gold. There might be more here. Maybe we can, uh, gather it up and make a coin or something…"

By himself, Bones already had enough gold, but he didn't want to hurt Karn's feelings.

"I just don't understand." Karn groaned. "Back in my day, shiny rocks were good enough on their own."

"Well, I hate to say this, but it's kind of like inflation," Sofia replied. "Humans have gotten a lot better at mining shiny rocks, so the old ones aren't as valuable anymore."

"Well, um…you couldn't have known that, Karn. It's, uh, not your fault…" Bones unhelpfully added. "I mean, it could have been called 'genius gold' or something, you know, it's, uh… It's hard to project out in the future."

Karn's newly regained eyes whirled from Bones to Sofia, then back at his depreciated fortune. He'd seen plenty of slivers of gold, but he'd grabbed all the pyrite because it had been bigger—and he'd thought that that had been better.

At this point, Karn was more of a Depressed Warrior than a Blazing Warrior. If he knew what banks were, he would have considered declaring bankruptcy.

Throwing his hands over his head, he let out a cry of shock, rage, and despair, the loud noise undoing the mental damage caused by his fist. Back in the previous room, Jack Pillary groaned, clutching his temples as his vision swirled in and out of focus. At first, he hoped that the empty walls were remnants of his terrible nightmare, where a pair of vicious barbarians had destroyed the art he'd made with his literal life's blood. But then he realized that this was reality and not some bad dream.

He let out his own cry of grief, much softer and weaker than Karn's.

Karn whirled around. "Hey. That guy's awake again. He seems like an idiot, stumbling into my tomb and thinking it's his. Maybe we can sell him my fortune. Nothing wrong with fool's gold if you can find a greater fool to buy it."

Bones stammered, encountering another classic friendship moment—the pros and cons of calling out a friend for blatantly unethical behavior. But before he could return to his meditative overthinking realm, Jack staggered into the back vault.

Every step seemed to take a strenuous effort. He panted for breath and wobbled from side to side like a top running out of spin. Even though he could barely move, his eyes were filled with hatred. "You… You ruined my life's work. I was supposed to return to Baron Angelo's good graces. Now I am doomed to die forgotten! I put my blood into my work, sacrificed my health—all for you to destroy it!"

He began crying faint and wispy tears that slowly oozed off his face onto the ground.

Karn put two and two together and his scowl deepened. "Wait a second. You're a blood artist? Did you use that bottle of blood in the chest?"

Jack froze. "Um…I…um… I was desperate! My blood…so thin…"

"You know what? I can forgive you, on one condition. You can make it up for me by buying all this fool's gold for twice the price of real gold!"

"I have no money. Don't rob me… You destroyed everything I had of value. I don't even have the blood left to make more art…" The pale-faced man covered his face as he sobbed. "Please, just leave me alone to die in disgrace…"

Karn threw up his hands. "What? Don't you die in *my* tomb… Find your own!"

"Um, Karn, uh…maybe I can talk to him for a bit," Bones said.

Karn was understandably very annoyed at someone stealing his blood to deface his tomb. It was a particularly macabre case of insult to injury. But Bones felt bad for Jack. It was obvious he had a horrific case of anemia and Bones knew he could help the man restore his blood.

Of course, he didn't want to restore the very weapon that might be used to attack them. The blood wave was utterly ineffectual against Bones and Karn, but it might be able to hurt Sofia.

"Um. I can heal you and, uh, make sure you can do your art again, but I need you to guarantee that you won't use your powers against us."

"Okay!" Jack eagerly agreed. Because he'd been defeated in seconds last time, Jack thought this was the deal of the century.

With a gesture, Bones poured a trickle of necromantic energy into Jack, restoring the blood that was missing from his body.

The man stood up a little straighter, a faint flush returned to his pale skin, and he smiled brightly. "Wow! I feel great!"

Since Bones's energy was nowhere near its maximum level, Sofia was unable to see it. To her eyes, Jack had simply decided to sit up a little straighter. She made a mental note to remind Bones to do that too.

Jack waved his arms and blinked. "Wow. You really don't realize what you're missing when you don't have enough blood."

"Yeah, you don't," Karn pointedly agreed.

"Um. Well. Sorry about that, but I was truly desperate!"

"Yeah, uh, how did you end up here?" Bones asked. He didn't really know how the world worked, but generally, well-adjusted people didn't end up in caves decorating the walls with their own blood.

"Well. I used to be an artist. At Avaron Heights. It was all I ever wanted, even after I'd discovered I had magical powers. At first, things went well. I worked for Angelo's father as a sculptor. And I thought my work would continue with the son." Jack jerked his head at the entrance to the cave. "After the One Day War, he told me to make the sculpture for him down there, but I was betrayed, just like how he betrayed the rebels. He kicked me out of court instead of paying me. He's been kicking everyone out; he even sent Baroness Willow away, calling her 'a mere starter wife.'"

"Wait. If you were a sculptor, why did you do paintings instead?" Bones asked. The whole story sounded like a sordid mess. He just still didn't understand why Jack was painting with his blood.

"Well. Baron Angelo is obsessed with necromancy, so I developed a new technique I call 'drip painting.' I cut my veins and then control it with my blood manipulation to make patterns."

"So you used your blood to go along with the fad?" Sofia asked. The longer Sofia listened to his exceptionally weak magic user, the less she believed in magic. However, Jack's words confirmed the rumors she'd heard that Baron Angelo was obsessed with the occult. Having worked as a servant for so long, she knew all about nobles and their bizarre fads.

"Yes," Jack replied. "I was hoping I could return to prominence, be welcomed back into court, regain my commissions, and perhaps even find new patrons. And now that I have my blood back, I have an even better chance of success!"

Sofia raised an eyebrow. Jack's whole speech sounded like utter lunacy, but she felt like nobody, not even a pompous lunatic, deserved to work themselves to death over false pretenses. "Has Baron Angelo offered patronage to anybody?"

"Um. No. I don't believe so. The only people left are bards, financiers, and, for some reason, seamstresses. But my art is special. It's made with necromantic magic. I'm sure you all saw how artful it was before you destroyed it. Did you see that proud figure with a sword leading his zombie workers in the field?"

"I did not," Karn replied. "I just saw blood splatters on my wall."

"I don't mean to be discouraging, but it just looked like a mess," Sofia agreed.

"I saw the man with the sword," Bones replied. "And, I mean, I didn't *exactly* see the zombies in the fields, but now that you mention it, I can see what you were going for."

Jack clung on to Bones's acknowledgment like a drowning man clutching a piece of driftwood—though in his case, he was trying to avoid ego death rather than literal death. "Ah, yes, that was the best piece of art I had created yet. Baron Angelo in the field, directing his zombie servants to work in our place, letting the entire realm live in necromantic luxury. I call it 'The Deathless Prince,' after Baron Angelo's favorite prophecy!"

"What, exactly, is the prophecy of the Deathless Prince?" Bones asked. Sir Francis had mentioned the same phrase.

"It's some scrap of doggerel the baron found in an ancient tomb. 'The Deathless Prince shall sweep through the world, invincible with his undead troops at his back.'"

"I see," Bones replied. "It doesn't say anything about farming."

"Well, yes, that's true. But that's the power of art. I will implant the lovely idea of a fair and just Deathless Prince straight into the baron's mind!"

"Uh, I don't think you can count on that," Bones replied. He felt rather bad for Jack Pillary. The man seemed beyond delusional. "You know what? Why don't I be your patron instead? I can give you fifty gold coins for one year of work. Make some good art for me. I'm starting a circus. Maybe you can sell your wares outside or draw some posters for us."

Jack's delight with Bones grew even further. After all, the next-best thing after blood in his body was food in his stomach. "Oh, well, I won't say *no* to fifty gold coins a year! I'll create countless grand works of art for you, something to honor your immensely generous spirit."

Bones pulled out another purse from his robe, counted out the gold, and then handed it to Jack, who hungrily clutched the gold coins, his face infused with relief and gratitude.

Karn was quick to anger but also quick to forgive. Having heard Jack's story, he developed a newfound respect for him. The man was an artist—just like what Karn wanted to be. And besides, painting with his own blood required some small measure of bravery. "Well. Do you promise not to steal my blood again?" he asked.

"Um…yes, definitely!" Jack replied. "I mean, I didn't even know it was yours."

"Well, I'll also be your patron, then. You can keep working in my tomb. And don't worry about the naysayers! A lot of greats aren't appreciated in their time. Maybe your son or maybe some other descendant will popularize this drip painting. The way I see it, people are into all kinds of weird, postmodern nonsense these days."

"Oh, well, thank you very much," Jack replied. "It would have been a pain to head back to Avaron Heights, and even if I did, I don't think I have lodgings there, anyway."

"I would suggest getting a new bed, though," Sofia noted. "You don't want to get mold poisoning."

"And, uh, don't overdo it with your painting," Bones hurriedly added. "I'd rather get one really good painting a year than a bunch of bad ones. And I don't mind sculptures, either, if that's what you're feeling."

"Oh, I'll do my best," Jack replied. "Sculptures, paintings, and posters! You shall have them all. Jack Pillary is at your service as a circus artist. You three have given me a second lease on life!"

Karn smiled with his re-attached mouth as they backed out of the cave. "Well, that went about as well as a home invasion could go."

With that, the group descended from Blackridge Peak, where the coachwoman was waiting for them beyond the battlefield.

She knew that something must have happened because the scholars from Plumage had practically hurled themselves off the mountain in their haste to escape. Behind her veil, she smiled when she saw that Karn had gotten his body back. This was the exact intervention her master had hoped for—it would have been disastrous if Baron Angelo had somehow discovered Karn's body. "Ah, excellent. It's good to see you back in the flesh, Karn."

"Thank you!" Karn blithely replied.

The zebras snorted and pawed irritably at the ground. Normally, when the coachwoman brought them out, they got a lot of comments about how strong and exotic they were. They'd never thought they liked the attention, but now that everyone was paying attention to Karn instead, they felt a little miffed.

"Well, it's about time to return," the coachwoman said. "Would you like me to take you directly to your cottage?"

Bones's eyes narrowed. "How did you know about our cottage?"

The coachwoman stayed quiet.

Bones and Sofia eyed each other for a moment, but then Sofia shrugged. "You know what? We came all the way here without a problem and it beats walking for a month. Let's just do it."

Chapter Ten

As the zebras trotted away from the Blackridge Mountain Range, the trio kept their eyes keenly peeled, hoping to understand how they had somehow completed the trip so quickly.

But for some reason, the zebras had no interest in displaying the trick again.

They moved slowly and leisurely, far more leisurely than any trained horses ever would, repeatedly stopping to graze on nearby plants. When Karn leaned over to comment, the coachwoman waved him off. "Don't doubt us. We made it here with plenty of time to spare."

Karn wanted to reply, but as he stared at the destroyed forest range that had once surrounded the battlefield, he found something else to complain about instead. He scowled, putting his reconstructed facial muscles to good use. "I forgot about this. Fighting outside my tomb was bad enough. I forgot they remodeled my garden too. They have no idea how long it took for those trees to grow proud and strong."

Once cutting through a lush and bustling forest, the path away was now quiet and lonely, a testament to the tragedy of war. Thanks to all the trees Karn had planted, the base of the mountain range had once been a lush forest dotted with lakes, with the greenery even creeping up into the stone of the cold mountain.

But during preparation for the One Day War, the forests had been cut down for war machines, leaving nothing but barren stumps.

Now that Karn had a heart again, it began pounding wildly in his chest, driven by his mounting rage. He hadn't thought about these trees in years, but the longer he stared at the stumps, the angrier he got and the quicker his heart beat, a frenzied thumping that echoed in his ears, like his own personal war drum.

Most people with long lives had to learn how to let things go. Karn, thanks to his immortality, just took the heart attack and moved on without any problems. Eventually, his heart, as hyperactive as every other fiber of his being, would get bored and start pumping blood again, and even if it didn't, it wasn't like he needed it, anyway.

Sofia, unaware of Karn's impending medical issues and even more unaware of how little they mattered, stared out the window, determined to see the zebra's trick. "Karn…isn't this weird to you? How did we not see this route on the way here?"

Karn didn't reply. He was far too enraged for a brainteaser.

But as they continued slowly down the path and saw only a boring, repetitive scene of stump after stump, a new thought entered Sofia's mind: worries about Achille's spending habits. A working woman herself, she knew the precarity of a noble employer debating whether or not to pay, and she hadn't wanted to inflict those same worries on Jack Pillary, so she hadn't said anything in front of him.

Now, though, she wanted to make sure that Achille didn't take on any other starving artists in caves.

"Achille."

"Huh?" Bones turned, no longer staring out the other window. "What is it?"

"That artist earlier. You promised him fifty gold coins for a year of patronage. Do you realize how much fifty gold coins is?"

Overhearing that, Karn began mourning the sheer number of gold coins *he* could have had if only he'd picked the right kind of gold. His heart abruptly switched gears. Once pounding because of the destroyed forest, it now began pounding because of his lost fortune, all while maintaining the perilous momentum from before.

Bones blinked. He tried to think about how much fifty gold coins was worth, but he had absolutely no idea.

The young noble didn't think much about money at all, save for occasionally noticing that he had a lot of it. Gabriel and Annabella Bonaparte had been extremely frugal, living more modestly than any noble in the land, only spending money to fulfill the bare minimum of social obligations.

"Um, no. I don't know how much that is."

"A gold coin is a month's wage for an ordinary person!"

Bones blinked in surprise. Not only was he a noble, but he was also a social outcast. He didn't have a very good idea of what an ordinary person's life was like, either. Every so often, he would try to double or triple Sofia's wages, but she would say it was too much and refuse to take more. "Oh. I see. Uh. I guess that was my mistake. But, I mean, he seems like a pretty good artist. Look at the sculpture on the battlefield. Karn was even able to tell that Baron Angelo wasn't a real warrior."

"What are you going to do with a sculpture?" Sofia hissed back.

"Well, I mean, what am I going to do with gold coins?" Bones asked. "I wasn't spending them, anyway."

Sofia paused.

The boy had a good point there.

Most nobles burned through their money very quickly throwing huge balls or hosting convoluted hunts to entertain other nobles. Bones didn't do any of that. He didn't even buy new clothes. As a result, despite not maintaining any lands at the moment, he was the second-richest noble in the barony, second only to Baron Angelo himself.

But still, acting like he had unlimited money was a very good way to end up with no money at all.

"Look, Achille. If you want to be this generous, you're going to need to find new sources of income. Sure. You're *pay a few artists* wealthy. But you're not *keep the whole realm afloat by yourself* wealthy."

The mention of money temporarily stalled Karn's self-enragement process. "Well, we'll be able to make plenty of money with our circus. Why, I'll rebuild my fortune in no time, and Bones will have two fortunes!"

"Yeah, maybe we can do that," Bones agreed. "I mean, the Great Clown certainly seemed rich enough. Everyone was paying him for tickets."

Karn quickly moved on from fantasizing about his future success to fantasizing about what he would wear during his future success. Even cavemen weren't immune to the joys of retail therapy. "We need great costumes, greater than the Great Clown's. And a great tent too, greater than the Great Circus's. And Bones, I might not be able to pay for the circus stuff yet, but you can, right? And I can pay you back after. How much does a tent cost, anyway? Ten gold?"

"Uh…I don't know how much it costs," Bones admitted. "Sofia usually does the shopping. Do you know how much it would cost to make a tent like the Great Clown's?"

Karn hurriedly interjected. "Wait. That's not what I said. We need a tent *bigger* than the Great Clown's. How are people going to know we're better than him if our tent is the same size?"

"Uh…I mean…I don't know if we're *going* to be better than him…"

"Not with that attitude we're not," Karn retorted.

Sofia chuckled and shook her head.

These two lacked business sense in addition to common sense.

Running a circus would be much more difficult than either of them envisioned, but the potential was undeniable, especially with Karn's immense speed and athleticism. He was objectively superior to any of the Great Circus's performers, and while she didn't know exactly how Achille would perform, founder and owner were excellent roles for people with lesser technical skills yet greater access to start-up capital.

"Tents and costumes are specialty items," she explained. "You can't just go into your local store and ask for one circus costume."

"Where do you think we can find them?" Bones asked.

"When I visited Islington University, I remember their drama club had some particularly grand costumes."

"So we can get them made at Islington?"

"Well, Islington usually doesn't make things. The school places a big focus on theory. I suspect the costumes were made in my hometown of Rustling, just down the road, but it'll be worth checking just to be sure. Besides, it'll be good to go to the school. For some reason, my homework hasn't been graded yet."

"I like the sound of that." Bones turned to the coachwoman. "Can you take us to Islington instead?"

The coachwoman immediately replied. "No, I'm sorry. I can only take you back to your cottage." Normally, she would have been glad to extend the trip, but she'd been told to avoid drawing attention to Islington University.

"Oh. Well. We can just go there from our cottage, then," Bones said.

Karn nodded. "Yeah. That sounds good. It'll be a bit boring, though. I'm sure it'll be a slow trip and it will be a while before we can perform."

Sofia shook her head. "That's ridiculous. You should start performing right away. Islington is a major city, one that goes along the Baron's Road. There will be inns and taverns on the way there. It's a two-day trip, but we can stop at my favorite inn on the first night."

"W-Wait, w-what?" Bones stammered. The circus had sounded a lot more fun when it had just been a hypothetical. "I…uh… I mean, I don't even know what I'll perform yet!"

"It's just practice!" Sofia groaned. "You can try a bunch of different things. If people boo you or get mad, just go to a different inn or tavern where nobody recognizes you. I'm telling you—there's always an excuse to avoid getting started. If you have a dream, the best thing to do is to throw yourself into it wholeheartedly. That's how I always felt about my correspondence courses. Some Islington students look down on people from Rustling. It was hard not to feel inferior when I first got started."

"Wait, really? It was so obvious to me you'd be good at the classes." Bones laughed.

"Oh, thank you, I—" Sofia broke off as she stared out the window. The carriage had rattled to a sudden halt and the surroundings had completely shifted. "What in the world? How did…?"

Bones groaned. "It must have happened while we were talking."

The carriage was suddenly in the middle of a lush forest, one unlike any Bones had seen before. Ludicrously tall trees, taller than any in the barony, created a massive, looming canopy that blocked off most of the sun, leaving only a few faint rays. All around them, brightly colored birds, frogs, and insects darted across exotic plants—miniature trees the sizes of bushes and twisting vines with flowers that looked like snapping jaws.

High above them, the sound of endless rain echoed through the forest.

"The zebras are tired," the coachwoman explained. "We're going to switch here."

"Isn't this a rainforest?" Sofia asked.

"Yes!" the coachwoman replied. She sounded genuinely excited. "Have you been to one before?"

"No, I just read about them in my geography textbook. But I didn't know there was a rainforest in the barony."

"Oh, there isn't," the coachwoman replied. "We're not quite back at your cottage yet. I took a shortcut."

"A shortcut *out* of the barony?"

"Well, yeah. Like I said, the zebras were tired."

"Your zebras live in a rainforest?"

"No, their replacements do. The zebras can find their way home. All my friends are super smart—probably smarter than me, if we're being honest. I've always been the kind to act without thinking too deeply."

As the coachwoman spoke, the zebras walked off, wading into tall, green ferns, which rustled loudly with every step of the zebra's hooves. Yet moments later, they vanished completely and the ferns grew still.

The coachwoman whistled and then a pair of big, black cats, so swift and graceful that they were like living shadows, descended from the trees. They stared back at the coachwoman with brightly glowing yellow eyes filled with respect and adoration.

She smiled, patting them on their heads and whispering a thank you.

The coachwoman hitched the reins back onto the panthers' heads, and then they surged into the ferns, bringing the carriage right along the path where the zebras had finished.

This time, Bones and Sofia kept their eyes closely peeled, but it didn't do them any good.

One moment, the lush green of the rainforest had surrounded them, and then the next, they re-emerged in the tall grass just outside the main road, at an intersection that included the road between Bones's cottage and Golden Fields.

After all the day's events, it was now nearly evening.

The sun slowly set, basking the swaying grass with a gentle, orange glow. Another carriage rustled down the main road, the fine clothes of its occupants marking them as nobles. The sturdy and well-maintained vehicle looked out of place so close to Bones's isolated cottage. As the driver searched for a way back to the Baron's Road, a man with a mustache and monocle scowled in the back seat. "A death tax…how utterly ludicrous. We must pay the baron to avoid giving them my father's body?"

The woman next to him, a short lady with a white dress, tittered nervously. "I believe he wants us to call it a 'corpse tax,' though I'm not sure his chosen name is any more charming." She suddenly broke off. "My word. Like at *that*!"

The man was so surprised, his monocle fell to his lap and he hurriedly asked the coachman to pull near. "What are *those*?" he asked.

"Panthers," the coachwoman proudly replied. "But most of them are very dangerous. I would strongly suggest not getting one for yourselves."

"Unbelievable," the man replied. A faint tone of nervousness entered his voice and he nodded for his coach to leave again.

Sofia had no idea why the panthers weren't savagely mauling everyone in sight, but she supposed this was nothing good training couldn't handle. As for the fact that they seemingly could teleport from one area to another, she planned on consulting her physics textbook.

But as always, she was primarily concerned with encouraging her young charge. "Look, Achille. On the way here, you had your britches in a knot about people running away from you, but now people are running *to* us. If they hadn't been warned about the panthers, who knows how long they would have stayed here?"

Bones blinked in surprise.

Sofia was right.

Normally, people wouldn't have gone anywhere near their carriage, but now, plenty of people were stopping to point at them. It wasn't just the noble and his wife, either. A few stray travelers peered at them as they walked home for the night, and various spirits stared at the carriage with keen interest, floating shyly at the periphery of Bones's vision.

Perhaps his usual aura of bad vibes had diminished. It was likely because he'd burnt off some of his necromantic energy, but then again, he'd also absorbed some energy from Jack's control orb. Bones glanced down at the street. The shadows were still twisting eerily.

So why were people less afraid than they had been before?

Sofia snorted. "Oh, Achille. I can see what you're thinking clean on your face. You're too stubborn to admit it, but the truth is that you've just been smiling all day! There's nothing more helpful than a good attitude."

The carriage pulled up right in front of their cottage, the panthers stopping gracefully on a dime. The small, wooden cottage with its cramped windows and bricks looked the same as always, but with everything that had happened, he had a hard time believing he'd left just yesterday.

"Here we are," the coachwoman said.

"You're welcome to stay with us, by the way," Bones said. "Though it'll have to be in the main room. We don't have anywhere else for you."

"Oh, that'll be fine," Karn replied, grinning. "You know what, Bones? This was still a good trip. The real fortune was the friends we made along the way."

Bones smiled. "You're right, Karn. You know, it's funny. People don't say that earnestly very often, but that was the perfect time for it."

Karn's grin transformed into a scowl in world record time. He'd thought that he'd been extraordinarily creative coming up with that saying himself—but not only had people already come up with it, they'd begun twisting it into postmodern sarcasm.

As far as he was concerned, this had been far too much newfangled nonsense for one day. Karn hopped off the carriage and swaggered into Bones's house like he owned the place. Technically, he probably had once owned the very plot of land that Bones's tiny, little cottage rested on.

As for Bones, he stopped before disembarking, suddenly realizing where they could find another performer. The Great Clown's animal tamer was nothing compared to this lady.

"Hey. Would you be interested in working for our circus? I know we're, um…you know, just two random guys, but I think we could…um…you know, be amazing and all that, and uh…" This was Bones's first time trying to convince a woman that he was going to make it big, and like most men who attempted that difficult task, he had absolutely zero evidence.

"Thank you for your offer, but not now. I have made other commitments." The coachwoman sat in her seat like she wasn't planning on leaving it anytime soon.

"Oh. Um. Maybe another time? I mean… I, uh…don't think we could find anyone as good as you elsewhere. Maybe after your other commitments?" Bones's voice trailed off. He was on that awkward verge of pleading, and he knew it.

The coachwoman remained silent. She was contractually forbidden from providing any clues as to her other arrangements. After Bones disembarked, she pulled at the stirrups and her panthers led the carriage back into the tall grass, disappearing with a rustle.

"Well, it was a good idea to ask her," Sofia said, giving him an encouraging pat on the back. "The worst thing that can happen is they say 'no'."

Bones sighed and shook his head.

He might have been an all-powerful necromancer, but he wasn't immune to getting ghosted.

Chapter Eleven

That night, Bones did not dream about the great disaster of his childhood.

Instead, he found himself inside a massive tent. As Karn had demanded, it was far larger than the Great Clown's, perhaps even a bit *too* large. The great tent seemed to be at least as big as a city, a cavernous red-and-gold canvas that stretched out in every direction. The small clasps holding the roof together were so distant, they might as well have been stars.

He heard a polite cough and his focus shifted to the crowd.

As Bones stared at the countless faces, his feet quivered, and not just because of nerves.

He was standing on some substance of dubious and unknown nature, but he could not look down at it. His eyes were locked straight on to the crowd. The scene followed the strange dream logic where certain aspects were held in much greater focus than others.

All he could see was the audience—the very unhappy audience.

It felt like he could see every disapproving wrinkle on their forehead, every irritated scowl, every speck of contempt in their eyes. As soon as Bones wondered why they were unhappy, the explanation appeared in his mind, immediately taking on the same ironclad unchangeability as gravity.

Sofia might have said that he was funny, but there was a big difference between being socially funny and being professionally funny. Somehow, he'd managed to stumble into a joke that simultaneously offended every single person in the audience.

The first row was filled with beautiful women—twelve in total. The one on the far left was already exceedingly beautiful, with a strange glow around her face that Bones had never seen before in life. Yet the one next to her was just slightly more attractive, and the third one in line even more so. The slight increase in attractiveness went on and on, a gradient of stunning beauty.

Just as Bones began wondering to himself how this was even possible, their faces began morphing, turning ever more beautiful before his very eyes.

But their contempt remained.

"I'm sorry!" Bones exclaimed. For some reason, his voice sounded way higher-pitched than he remembered. He was talking almost like a baby. "I, uh, I'm sorry for that joke… I just…um…"

Bones trailed off, unable to remember what he'd even said.

"Are you really sorry?" one of the women asked.

"Yes. I mean, I was hoping to make everyone laugh. I would never try to, uh…offend anyone. I, um…"

"Okay. Then apologize specifically for what you said. I don't want some generic, nonsense, made-up apology."

But no matter how hard Bones tried, he could not remember what he'd said. His brain felt as smooth as a marble. As Bones stammered ineffective apologies, the women's faces abruptly turned bright orange. Their clothes were shredded to pieces as they spontaneously evolved into crabs, their eyes still filled with disdain.

The entire row of former women walked out of the show, clicking and clacking their claws. "Disgusting," they chirped. "It's a good thing we're not human anymore. Now we don't have to pretend to like his terrible show."

As soon as the crabs had skittered away, a tiny figure stood up in her seat. For some reason, Bones couldn't get a good look at her, but he saw a flash of orange and a tattered rainbow cloak that seemed to be made of a thousand pieces of salvaged cloth. "Bones, what in the world are you dreaming of this time? This is even worse than what you came up with before!"

Bones immediately recognized her voice. It was the girl from his other dream.

He wanted to call out to her, but no matter how hard he tried, he couldn't form a word. His throat scrabbled ineffectively, like a man trying to pull himself up from a collapsing cliff.

"No wonder you keep waking me up with these energy flares. Bones, I need you to remember me! Take me with you. It'll be lonely without you, Bones!"

Before she could say anything else, one of the crab women grabbed her, yanking her right out of her seat. "Get out of here. Trust me, you don't want to hear *anything* this guy has to say."

The second row consisted entirely of men with faces just like his father's—stern eyes and a blond mustache. They spoke as one, their voices building into a terrible wave of condemnation. "Terrible. Just terrible. Son, I thought I taught you how to be funny."

"Um…sorry. You see, I, uh…must have forgotten my routine or something. I…"

As they shook their heads disapprovingly, the ghosts from outside Karn's tomb wafted in through the ceiling. Their heads had fallen right off their necks again, and their expressions were twisted by pity and loathing. "You… You said that we would be fine…that our heads would stay on our necks… We should have asked you for a warranty…"

"I, um, I… I'm sorry about that…"

This was not going well for Bones at all. Sure, he wasn't confident in his performing skills, but his magic had always succeeded before.

A tremendous scuffling from the back of the tent interrupted the cascading groans and insults. It was the figure from before, her face still obscured by orange mist. "Bones! Listen to me! You have some serious self-esteem problems. Just make sure to bring me with you! I'm—"

But before she could say anything else, the crab women yanked her away again.

This time, Bones found he could talk. "Wait! Who are you? How do you know me? How can I find you?"

A cavernous, echoing howl cut straight through Bones's disjointed questions. "You suck!"

The entire tent seemed to collapse on him at once, bloodstained teeth ripping out from the folds of the red-and-gold tent. Bones, finally able to look down on his feet, realized that he wasn't standing on a stage at all. Beneath him was a pulsating mottled purple tongue.

This was no tent. It was the mouth of some great tent-mimicking beast!

Bones tried to call forth his necromantic energy, but it had completely abandoned him. For the first time in his life, he was just an ordinary person—and moments later, he was dinner.

Bones's eyes jerked open. He threw off his blankets, terrified that pincers were grabbing at his legs. "What in the world just happened?"

"King of the Jungle Bones, you have the worst subconscious in human history," the voice groaned, echoing in Bones's mind. *"I can't believe I'm putting in so much effort to reach you. Just make sure you remember to grab me at…"*

The voice faded away, and Bones couldn't reply. The last vestiges of the dream vanished, and he was back in his humble room inside their little cottage.

The cramped triangle-shaped space only had room for a narrow, wooden bed and a thin dresser filled with a variety of tattered, black clothes. The bed and dresser were each on one leg of the triangle, with the bed directly beneath a glass window. The final wall of the room was occupied by the door and a second, smaller poster of the Great Clown.

A faint ray of sunlight washed over Bones's face. It was the very crack of dawn and the rest of the cottage remained asleep.

In the other room, he could hear Sofia's loud snoring, and when he peeked out into the kitchen, he saw Karn sleeping by the fireplace. Last night, the caveman had been very impressed by the burning logs, marveling over how technology had advanced to the point that his signature weapon had become a household decoration.

Bones wasn't surprised that Karn had also decided to sleep there. It was somewhat akin to paranoid nobles sleeping with knives under their pillows.

After a loud yawn that threatened to unhinge his jaw, Bones debated ignoring the faint remnants of dream fear and going back to sleep. Not only was he tired, he still didn't know what the voice was trying to tell him.

But then a voice called out to him. "Hey! Bones! Thanks for freeing me yesterday! That orb was a real nasty piece of business. Had never seen anything like it before."

Bones glanced around, hearing the familiar voice but not seeing anyone. "Uh…Tycho, right? Where are you?"

"Yeah! It's me! Thought I'd pay you a visit, considering the favor you did for me. It's been a long time. How are you?"

After his dream, Bones had realized that there was a significant risk in trying to bluff his way through this conversation. "To be honest, Tycho, I don't remember you. It's been a long time since I was back at the manor."

Tycho sounded disappointed. Though he was invisible, Bones could almost imagine him drooping. "Well. I mean. I suppose it's been a while…" Tycho admitted. "This blasted power is a lot more trouble than it's worth. You know, I was extremely handsome in life. I'm sure you'd remember my face if you saw me."

Funnily enough, it was the familiar complaining that tickled the back of Bones's mind. Tycho had been a frequent visitor, the spirit constantly traveling the world searching for his lost wife. "Actually, I do remember you now, Tycho."

"Ha! Well, I suppose my personality is as memorable as my looks once were. Is there anything I can help you with? After the favor yesterday, Tycho Beauregard is perpetually at your service!"

Bones thought back to his devastated family home. Maybe Tycho could help him get to the bottom of it all. "Tycho…did you ever go back to my home after everyone left?"

Though Tycho was invisible, Bones felt him shudder. "Oh. Yes. I don't know what happened…but it seemed frightening. Were you in some grand fight, perhaps? I felt your magic lingering there."

"I don't know what happened," Bones admitted. "I was hoping you could give me a clue."

"Well, I can't." Tycho sighed. "I guess the one good thing is that after I fled, I found Ophelia…only for that contemptible orb to separate us again. What a shame. Finally found her after two decades apart, only to be wrenched apart by fate's cruel grip."

"Wow. Almost two decades. That's intense." It was hard for Bones to imagine loving someone for that long—he'd barely been *alive* for that long.

"Well, it's what true love can do," Tycho said, the smile evident in his voice.

"Is there anything I can do to reunite you two?"

"Wait, you want to help me find Ophelia?" Tycho asked. "I mean, you already granted me my freedom."

"Of course I want to help!" Bones replied.

"Why, that's delightful! First things first, I figure it would be best for me to stay still at some kind of agreed-upon meeting point. When I talked to Jack about my problems, he felt bad and suggested bringing her to the cavern with me. I thought it was a great idea. Unfortunately, I had no way to communicate my location to her."

"Staying in one place does sound like a good idea," Bones agreed. In a way, Jack's wise advice made him glad to be the man's patron. If the sculpting and drip painting didn't work out, perhaps he could retrain the man as an advisor.

"Do you know of any landmarks around here where she might be able to find me?"

Unaware that he was only adding to the rural legends swirling around the Great Circus's abandoned tent, Bones nodded. "Well, there's a huge, abandoned tent in Golden Fields that's pretty close to my cottage. You can't miss it."

"Oh. That sounds quite good," Tycho mused. "I think I will go there. And now for the bigger favor. Considering where you were yesterday, it seems like you travel a great deal."

"Funnily enough, it was my first time leaving this place in a long time…but from now on, I think I'm going to be on the road all the time."

"Excellent! Do you mind leaving some posts on bulletin boards wherever you go telling her where to find me?"

"Of course. Shouldn't be too hard."

"Well, there is a caveat. Unfortunately, neither Ophelia nor I can read. It just wasn't common in our day. Honestly, that's part of the reason we get lost so often. Thankfully, we have a motif that was important to us during our courtship, a cat doing a backflip. If she sees it, she'll know it's from me. Do you think you could draw that? A cat doing a flip, along with a drawing of the big tent in Golden Fields."

"I can do that," Bones replied. Due to his childhood passion for tumbling, he thought he could draw a particularly good backflip.

"Thank you very much, good sir. Just so you know, I'm bowing deeply right now. You've always been far too kind, Bones. You make an invisibility spirit like me feel seen! Well, I'm off, then. I'll be in the Golden Fields tent. If you're ever in the area, shout when you need me.

Just then, Sofia knocked on his door, yawning. "Achille. What's going on? Why are you staring at that window?"

Bones turned around and let out an abashed laugh. "Um. Well, you're not going to believe this…but the invisibility spirit from yesterday showed up. He asked me to do it a favor."

"I see," Sofia replied.

She had been trying to keep an open mind about all this supernatural stuff. After all, while she knew that Achille was prone to superstition and flights of fancy, he wasn't utterly insane. But still, the invisibility spirit from yesterday was the most evidence of the supernatural she'd encountered thus far—which was a rather polite way of saying that she hadn't encountered much evidence at all yet.

"Well, either way, let's wait for Karn to wake up, then we can figure out where we're going."

Bones glanced around the room. "If we're heading to Islington, it might be a while until we come back."

"Yeah, it's hard to believe, but I think leaving this place will be good for you, Achille. I'll make us a huge breakfast this morning, give us plenty of energy for the road. Does that sound good?"

"Oh, yeah. I'd love that."

As the two walked outside the room, something shifted underneath his bed. There was a loud clunk, followed by the rattle of the wooden bedframe.

Bones frowned. "What was that?"

He peeked under the bed, but all he saw was an old, cloth bag, the one he'd used to bring his prized possessions from the Bonaparte Family Manor to the cottage all those years ago. He shrugged, then went out to the main room, unaware that there was something under his bed that very badly did not want to be left behind.

Chapter Twelve

As Bones and Sofia walked into the cramped living room, Karn bolted upright, almost knocking over the logs on the fireplace. "Bones!" he cried. "I just had the most terrible dream!"

"You too?" Bones asked. It was hard to believe that Karn could ever have stage fright, but Bones supposed that was a very relatable fear, even if Karn came from a stage before stages.

"Yeah. It sucked. Everyone was cheering and applauding, but it wasn't loud enough."

"What?"

"Yeah. The battle cries of war as people charged at me, the screams of terror as people fled…those were *way* louder." Karn furrowed his brow like he wanted to form trenches in his skull. "Is this something innate in the human heart? That love and joy are weaker than fear and hatred? Bones! We *must* prove them wrong!"

"You know, Karn, it's hard to philosophize on an empty stomach. Why don't you sit down so we can have some breakfast?" Sofia suggested.

Karn bound to the table, his stomach grumbling. "Great. I haven't eaten in years!"

The cottage was already cramped for two, but the addition of Karn just emphasized how small the place was. Despite Karn's short stature, his broad shoulders and even broader enthusiasm caused him to knock a lot of objects over, and his strength led to those objects flying very far.

He shifted and sent a chair barreling straight into the wall, the force of the impact disturbing Sofia's completed homework. Bones leaned over, hastily catching the papers before they fell, then shuffling through them to make sure they were still in the proper order. The few sentences he saw just made his head hurt.

"How does this make sense?" Bones muttered. "Obviously, a ton of feathers would weigh less than a ton of bricks…" When he flipped back to the first page, he felt even more discouraged. "How is this possibly just an *Introduction to Physics*?"

Meanwhile, Karn had grabbed the chair, placing it back at the table. "Sorry about that."

"Oh, no worries," Sofia replied. "This place is a bit cramped for all of us. The good news is we'll be hitting the road soon, anyway."

She placed three wooden plates on the table, each with generous slices of wheat bread, hunks of white cheese, and globules of strawberry jam. "And don't forget this, either," she added. She placed cups of watered-down ale in front of Bones's and her own plates, then hesitated a moment before placing a third in front of Karn.

"Let me know what you think," she said.

Karn sipped it, then placed the cup back down, a quizzical look on his face. "There's some alcohol in this, isn't there? Look, you might be surprised, but we drank back in the day too."

"Really?" Bones asked.

"Oh, of course," Karn replied. "You can just make it from wild fruit or chewed-up roots. It helps everyone have a great time. Why, I remember a great celebration after my little brother's first successful hunt!"

As Karn went deep into drunken caveman lore, Sofia frowned thoughtfully.

If Karn really were some kind of invincible caveman, perhaps the history and archaeology departments at Islington would know something about him. After all, the Plumage scholars *had* mentioned a legendary warrior buried in Karn's tomb.

However, his stories were so outlandish that she couldn't help but doubt him. Shaking her head, she decided to wait for more evidence.

While Sofia was pondering history, Karn was enjoying modernity. He took a generous bite out of the bread, beaming from ear to ear. It seemed like food had gotten a lot better since the last time he'd had it.

"Delicious…" He let out a long sigh as he broke his very long fast. "I forgot how nice it feels to eat. If I'd known what I would be missing out on, I never would have tossed my stomach!"

"Do you even need to eat now?" Bones asked.

"No, probably not. I went a bunch of years without eating when I was sleeping in my tomb. But it tastes so good!"

With his invincible body, Karn didn't eat for nourishment. He ate for the love of the game. This particular game went into multiple overtimes, as Karn requested several extra helpings.

"So, where do you think we should go?" Karn asked. "You said that place Isleton has costumes, right?"

"Islington," Sofia corrected. "It's where our barony's university is located. I don't know if they can make costumes there, but their drama department has them. I think we should go there and check for ourselves." She pointed at the stack of papers on the table. "Not only that, the last few times I sent in homework, it wasn't graded and returned. I thought I would deliver it in person and see what's going on. Bones is generously paying a handsome tuition fee, after all."

Under normal circumstances, Sofia would have checked in at the school after her first missed assignment. But eight months ago, she'd been late completing her homework due to a visit from some of her grandchildren, and instead of admitting it, she'd backdated her envelope to imply that the couriers had made a mistake. Since she felt guilty about that, she thought it was appropriate to let Islington be late on three other assignments in exchange.

"And maybe after, we can stop by and see my family in Rustling. They've all been very eager to meet Achille. And perhaps you'll want to see them this time?" she asked, turning towards him.

"Yeah. That would be nice." Bones smiled. "Islington works for me. Rustling too. Most places are fine." Bones had always been wary of meeting Sofia's family, to the point that he'd stayed elsewhere when her grandchildren visited. But with Karn there, he felt much safer about any possible magical downsides.

"The Baron's Road isn't what it used to be, but it's still fairly safe with several inns along the way," Sofia said. "I think that could be a good path."

"It sounds like we need to go to Islington for our costumes, but I don't think our first show should be there," Karn said.

"Why not?" Bones asked.

"Well, isn't Avaron Heights the biggest city around these parts? I remember walking by the place when it was first getting constructed."

"I don't want to go to Avaron Heights," Bones immediately replied. His abandoned family lands were just below the elevated city, and he didn't want to return.

Karn instantly knew to change the subject. Bones had reacted like he'd dropped a viper on the table. "Well, Islington it is, then," he replied.

"Thank you." Bones smiled. It felt good knowing his new friend would support him without pressing for details. "Oh, Sofia. Do you mind if I grab some of your school supplies? I need a parchment and quill too, before we go out of the house. I promised someone a favor."

"Not at all."

He picked up a few rolls of the parchment, plus a quill and inkpot, then jammed them unceremoniously into the pocket of his robes.

"Achille, what are you doing? Get a traveling bag," Sofia protested. "What if the ink spills?"

"Ah, come on, Sofia." Bones grinned. "You always complain that my clothes are old and faded. Now I'm trying to dye them back again and you complain?"

She half-laughed and half-groaned. "Speaking of which…you're going to want more than just the rags on your back. Pack some clothes and get ready for traveling. Islington is almost two full days of walking on the Baron's Road. Your clothes are going to be utterly drenched."

"Point taken," Bones conceded.

When he went back to his room, he found his bed trembling, cracks spreading rapidly across the wood as if it were decaying from within. Without any warning, the bed crumpled before his eyes, followed by his mattress tumbling awkwardly to the floor. As it fell, it seemed to dissolve from within just like the bed had, the feathers stuffed inside rotting away into nothing, leaving only the deflated linen case.

"What just happened?" Bones muttered. "Well. I know Sofia would doubt it, but this, if anything, is an omen to leave this place… That was probably the creaking I heard earlier too."

He glanced behind him, but the bed had broken down so quietly that Karn and Sofia, making their preparations for the trip, hadn't even noticed. Rummaging underneath his bed, Bones pulled out his old traveling pack, still thickly coated with dust despite getting caught in the collapse.

The fine leather pack was old, weary, and covered with various burns. Bones had found it in the far corner of the destroyed home, away from most of the fire. Although the pack was very large—meant for an adult—the straps had been tied in almost comically small loops. Bones had brought the pack here as a child and hadn't touched it in years.

As Bones adjusted the straps, the bag abruptly trembled.

He jolted back in surprise, dropping the bag to the floor. Even though he had amazing magical powers, even though he'd seen spirits and ghosts, he wasn't used to bags moving.

"Achille?" Sofia called out. "What's going on?"

"Um…nothing," Bones replied. Bones's mind immediately settled on the worst-case scenario, and if there was something dangerous in the bag, he didn't want Sofia to be involved.

The bag trembled again and this time, he heard a strange, floppy noise coming in inside, like a padded arm whacking at the interior.

Bones was wary, but he also couldn't stop himself from helping out. As soon as he'd opened the bag, he found something inside that he hadn't thought about for a very long time: a tattered stuffed cat. He pulled her out of the pack, his fingers automatically caressing the makeshift cloth.

Her arms and legs were floppy, with no stuffing at all, but she had a big and soft almost-pillowlike stomach. Only the simply designed head—three buttons for its eyes and nose plus a stitched-on smile—had been properly proportioned. Otherwise, the stuffed animal looked much more like a giant balloon than an actual cat. She'd stitched and mended countless times, with so many different colors of cloth that the once-orange cat was now every color of the rainbow.

"Patches," Bones murmured. Patches had once belonged to his mother—she'd given her to him when he'd been two because he'd been so scared of the ghosts he'd seen at night. "Huh. I'm sorry. I forgot you were there."

He remembered hurriedly bringing her along, scooping her up from the rubble of the destroyed home. But once he'd made it to the cottage, Bones had left her in the bag. The reminder of his once safe and peaceful home had been far scarier than any ghosts.

A sudden swell of emotion, nostalgia, grief, and guilt all mixed up together, so powerful that he completely forgot why he'd opened the bag in the first place. As his fingers grew loose, a voice echoed in his head.

"It's okay, Bones." Patches's voice echoed directly in his mind, sounding shockingly familiar. Just like the girl from the dream.

Bones blinked, suddenly wrenched back to reality. "What?"

"It's okay. I get why you left me in the bag. Thank you for saving me from the fire. I was only able to come alive because you kept me with you for so long. I'm glad we can finally speak face to face... Your dreams are weird, Bones."

As Bones held Patches in his hands, he sensed the ember of magic inside her plump, plushy stomach and realized what had happened. She'd been animated by Bones's latent necromantic energy. Brimming in his body, held back by his reluctance to use it, the magic leaked out into a safe and familiar vessel.

Back when Bones had been a kid, he had often wished that Patches could come alive.

"Oh. Well. Um. Wow. Well, um... Hopefully, you weren't stuck in the bag for too long. I mean, I don't know when you woke up or anything like that."

"I was happy to watch over you, across the years. But I knew it would be lonely without you. I gathered up the energy to say something so you wouldn't leave me behind."

"No, I *definitely* wouldn't want to leave you behind," Bones replied.

"That's good to hear. Now, let me try walking. I've always wanted to see what that was like."

Slowly and hesitantly, Patches waddled across the room, doing her best despite her disproportionate body and floppy legs. Though she was a cat, her stuffed animal body was designed to walk upright, and she managed for a while.

"Sofia! Come in here!" Bones explained.

If anything would convince her magic existed, this would.

Sofia hurried in as Bones excitedly cried. "Look! Patches was moving!"

Patches promptly fell to the floor.

Bones blinked in surprise. "What? Patches? Come on. Say something to her."

But nothing happened.

"Achille…knock it off with the pranks and get packed," Sofia replied.

Bones shook his head and picked up Patches again, frowning in confusion. At this point, he was wondering if he *had* been imagining things. "Well. That was unfortunate. But still, come along, Patches. Though I guess now I'm worried you'll get hit by the inkpot."

He screwed the lid extra tight to be safe, then grabbed a few rags and put them in the bag too.

Patches remained silent throughout, having discovered that moving around in real life was much harder than moving around in dreams.

But more importantly, she enjoyed a good practical joke. As Bones sealed the bag shut, a mischievous chuckle echoed in his mind.

Laughing and shaking his head, he slung the pack over his shoulder and walked out of the home, to where Karn and Sofia were already waiting for him.

The sun shone brightly in the sky and the road itself seemed to glow, suffused, like Bones, with the optimism of a new journey. Karn was particularly joyful, cheering that the hunt for circus costumes was even more delightful than actual hunts.

As the trio walked down the winding path, the tall grass swayed around them, and Bones found himself thinking not of the coachwoman, but of the demon who'd tried to steal his soul. Bones was the kind of person whose heart went out even to the heartless, and he remembered that the demon had been very frightened of Angelo.

Hopefully, Sir Francis wasn't in *too* much trouble.

Chapter Thirteen

The sun had been high in the sky when the trio had left their cottage on their quest for circus costumes, but after a full day of walking, it was finally starting to set. As nature's light slowly dimmed around the intrepid travelers, Karn groaned. Civilization wasn't all it was cracked up to be.

The Baron's Road had once been the pride of the barony, but like everything else, it had slowly and steadily decayed under Baron Angelo's rule. Unfortunately for the people of the Sun Beam Barony, everyone else's *decay* was a master necromancer's definition of *progress*.

The wide streets had once been meant for pedestrians and carriage drivers alike, but neither fared particularly well in the worn-down conditions. Wheels rolled awkwardly over the mismatched and damaged cobblestones and passengers cursed at the unexpected turbulence. Weeds stubbornly encroached on either side of the battered and chipped stones, as if determined to trip anyone walking by. The faded, blue-painted guard stations were understaffed or completely abandoned.

"I still can't believe the baron put his name on this road… The whole place is a dump!"

"Technically, it was just his title," Bones quipped.

A very harried serf ran past, hastily scooping stones off the Baron's Road and dropping them in a straw bucket. The trio had been walking all day, and this was the only man they'd seen trying to clean the place.

"Here's an extra one for you," Karn said, pulling an embedded stone out of his foot and tossing it inside.

"Karn…are you sure you don't need to get shoes?" Sofia asked. "I don't know if there's a cobbler in Islington. They aren't very good at crafts, but there's certainly one in Rustling."

"This is worse than just walking around in the forest!" Karn exclaimed, stepping on yet another sharp rock. "I'll probably have to think about it!"

Bones was very glad for his own shoes, which were sturdy enough that he didn't notice any dramatic issues. Patches bounced along in his pack, the animated doll remaining mostly silent save for occasional mental words of encouragement about Bones's necromantic powers. *"Look, Bones. You can't just rely on putting your hands on people. When you were a kid, you could heal with gestures or even just a thought. I know you're scared about what happened, but with Karn here, this is the perfect time to practice. Plus, I'm kind of hungry."*

Whenever Patches spoke up, Bones chuckled, gesturing and feeding her a small trickle of his necromantic energy, which she accepted with a gentle purr.

A new bard walked by, wearing the same black doublet and carrying the same standard-issue redwood lute as the one from yesterday, singing at the top of his lungs. It was the end of the day, but he had a song quota to meet. "Angelo, Angelo, he struck them down in the dead of night. Angelo, Angelo, it was hardly a fair fight!"

Karn frowned as the bard walked by. "That song doesn't make any sense. Is killing people at night even worth anything? If you're bragging about midnight ambushes, you probably don't have too many real feats."

"Well, I suppose ill repute is still repute," Sofia replied. "Besides, he probably thinks it makes him sound strategic and intelligent."

"I know it's a one-day sample size, but your comment about too many bards and too few builders is proving correct," Bones said. "It seems to be a ten-to-one ratio."

"Even a single one of these bards is too many," Karn grumbled. He didn't have a particular reason for disliking bards; he was mostly just jealous that they weren't singing about him.

But despite the dilapidated road, the difficult walk, and the dipshit bards, Sofia felt strangely relaxed. "This is strange…" she muttered, glancing down at her feet.

"What is it?" Bones asked, hiding a smile.

"Well, we've been walking most of the day now."

"And?"

"Well, I take this route whenever I visit my family in Rustling. Normally, my feet would be aching so badly that I could hardly move. I would have given up and hitched a carriage ride ages ago, but for some reason, I feel fresh."

Sofia smiled and skipped a few steps.

Karn shot Bones a grin and Patches's tinkly laugh echoed in his mind.

Bones had been surreptitiously healing Sofia's feet all day, letting out a faint trickle of his power to mend her wounds. With his friends' encouragement, Bones felt safe not just testing his power, but doing something he'd wanted to do for a very long time.

Unfortunately, he still didn't know what he would do for his act.

Healing arthritis was an exceedingly useful skill and a service that Bones was happy to provide. He just wasn't sure if it could entertain the general public. He frowned, scrunching up his pale face as he plumbed the depths of his brain for ideas. "By the way…what do you guys think my act should be? I don't want to just sit around and watch Karn, no offense."

"Oh, none taken! With a legendary warrior like me around, it's hard not to be overshadowed. But, Bones, your power is equal to mine! You just need to find the right thing to do!"

"Didn't you say you liked the Great Clown's jokes?" Sofia asked. "That could be a start."

Bones trembled and a shiver went down his spine as he thought of his dream. "Uh…maybe. I don't know about that. I just don't feel very funny today for some reason."

"Maybe you don't feel funny now, but when you're in the mood, come up with something and write it down. Every time you do a new performance, your audience won't have heard the joke before. They'll just think you're a comedic genius with a ton of new material." Sofia chuckled. "Whenever I meet a new group of friends, I have a few jokes I re-use too. Always a good way to make a good first impression."

Unfortunately, before Bones could come up with a single joke, life decided to play a joke on him.

A carriage hurried past them, its wheels screeching awkwardly against the cobblestone, jerking so haphazardly, it looked like a dog shaking off water after a bath.

The driver hastily lashed the horses, hurrying them forward.

A young girl bawled from inside the cabin. "What's wrong with that man? There are stitches all over him!"

The driver called back. "Look at that boy in the hideous rags…he's a practitioner of the dark arts! Just look at the hideous scowl on his face. That's his zombie! But don't worry, lass, we'll be out of here soon."

"Hey, come on!" Bones complained. "I wasn't scowling… I was trying to think of a joke!"

But by then, the carriage was so far gone, nobody could hear the soft-spoken necromancer.

Karn, however, had no such problem. "Hey! I'm not a zombie! I just made some bad life decisions with my body and my finances! You wouldn't know a zombie if it smacked you in the face!"

Karn looked like he wanted to dart after the carriage and smack the driver in the face to show him the difference, but Bones hastily pulled him back. An alleged zombie was scary enough for normal people to deal with, but an alleged zombie that could outrun carriages was a far more terrifying problem.

"Karn…speaking of which…is there any possible way you can take those stitches off? It won't play well in the tavern," Sofia scolded.

Karn shrugged. "Sure, let me try." He grabbed one of the brightly glowing magical stitches and pulled. As the magical thread loosened, his cheek sloughed off his face. "Nah. It hurts. And it'll probably make me look weirder." He put it back on and Bones's magic did its work, tying the cheek back together.

Sofia stared at him, the mental pendulum in her mind swinging back to belief in the supernatural. It could have been some trick or optical illusion, but Karn seemed rather guileless. She resolved to keep an eye out for any other strange occurrences, but the rest of the trip was uneventful.

By the time the sun had completely set, the trio had arrived at Sofia's favorite inn. "The same family has run the Stone Hearth Inn since I was a little girl."

Bones smiled. "Yeah, you mentioned it before. I'm excited to stay for myself. I remember you said their sausages were delicious."

Karn licked his lips. "Meat for the first time in years... I can hardly wait!"

The Stone Hearth Inn was a large and roomy two-story building built from continually replaced wood. Most of the building was made from oak, but redwood and fir planks had replaced the particularly damaged portions. Thanks to an aggressive expansion during Baron Matteo's reign, a few of the premium rooms had balconies, but most remained small and simple.

At the front of the inn was a stone façade, decorated by a chipped and weathered yet colorful mosaic showing beaming travelers around a hearth. Attached to the right-hand side of the inn was a makeshift stable for the horses, protected from the weather by a frayed cloth tarp. Two carriages had been parked next to the inn, along the side of the road.

When the trio stepped inside, they found that the inside matched the exterior—beaten down yet cozy. The red carpet was threadbare in some places and outright non-existent in others, and the chairs and tables were mismatched, but the innkeeper had done his best to spruce the place up. Everything was very clean and through some olfactory miracle, the smell of crackling meat seemed to suffuse the entire inn. Several leafy trees dotted the room in big, stone pots, and jars of picked wildflowers sat on every table.

The patrons were dressed in heavy cloaks and various other traveling attire—a very reasonable thing to do for a trip, but a step that Karn and Bones had neglected.

Karn scoured the crowd, his eyes narrowing. "I was hoping the people from before would be here. I was going to give them a bit of a lesson in zombie identification."

"Funny, I was hoping they wouldn't," Bones replied.

The innkeeper stepped up to them, trying his best to look professional despite his doubts about this strangely dressed party. He was short and well-built, with a wide nose, bald head, and black beard that remained unruly despite his constant trimming.

"How can I help you?" he asked.

Sofia brought out her purse to pay, but Karn didn't back off. "How much is it? I'm trying to learn more about the economy… Did you know I lost everything because of a bad bet?"

The innkeeper frowned. "Um, no, I didn't know that."

"By any chance, do you know who I am?" Karn asked, completely ignoring Sofia's attempts to pay and forestall a possible eviction.

"No…I don't… Are you famous?"

"Oh, I should be," Karn replied.

To Bones's and Sofia's shock, the innkeeper smiled, scratching his black beard. "Well. Are you some kind of entertainer?" He tilted his head to the side. "Maybe a…zombie imitation act? Some kind of necromantic burlesque? I heard a rumor that necromancy is growing increasingly popular at Avaron Heights. It's even spreading to places like Lorenzo and Islington."

"Fire-eating, but close," Karn replied.

"Fire-eating, eh?" the innkeeper mused. "Well. It just so happens that our entertainment for the night canceled at the last second." He shook his head irritably. "We've booked him for a few performances, but he's utterly unreliable. Calls himself 'the Replacement Level Clown.' Name like that, you can tell he's got a real reverse-ego problem."

Bones, who had a real-reverse ego problem of his own, chewed his lip nervously. "Uh, quick question. If Karn performs, do we need to perform too? We can just pay and stay here, right?"

Sofia didn't even have time to roll her eyes before the innkeeper shook his head. "No, we're desperate for some entertainment tonight. If, uh, Karn, over here does well, you can all stay for free. But be warned, if he gets booed, you're paying double."

"Ha! Some pressure, I like it." Karn grinned. "But that won't be a problem. Just give me a torch and I'll have the whole audience cheering. How about that one on the wall over there?"

Before the innkeeper could even reply, Karn swaggered past him and yanked a torch from a sconce, waving it above his head in his typical manner—that is to say, in a manner disturbingly reminiscent of a man going to battle.

Karn let out a bellowing shout—half *war cry* and half *call to attention*. "Look here!"

The entire tavern seemed to freeze in place. Then a tall woman with brown hair dove under the table, shrieking for cover, and several travelers hastened to grab their weapons. A particularly prepared man with a drooping mustache seemed to produce a hand crossbow out of thin air.

"No, wait!" the innkeeper replied. "This is our entertainment!" He eyed Karn dubiously, his hand slowly reaching for a sword he'd hidden behind a loose panel of the wall. "You are…aren't you?"

"Yeah." Karn blinked. "I don't know what's wrong with everyone. I'm Karn, the Blazing…um…Performer!"

"I don't know about this…" Sofia muttered.

"I mean, I know Karn has the skills, but…uh…has he even p-practiced before?" Bones stammered.

Their questions were answered as soon as Karn began to perform. His fire-eating was most generously described as "brutalist."

"Watch this!" Karn shouted. He held the torch in his right hand, then stuck his left hand straight into the flames.

Some of the audience cried out, and others gasped in shock.

"Ha. That's just warming up." Karn chuckled.

He began randomly stabbing the torch into his body, laughing maniacally. "I bet you've never met anyone who could do this before!"

The audience had, indeed, never met anyone who could stab themselves with a torch before. They quickly decided that they didn't like it.

"What is wrong with him? Is that zombie costume part of the act?"

"I think he might just *be* a zombie… He just roasted his nuts!"

"I thought zombies were weak to fire!"

"Karn! Don't just stab yourself! Try to put on a show!" Sofia shouted. "People like it when performers do tricks with the fire!"

"Got it!" Karn replied. "Look here, audience!"

He hurled the torch into the air with all his might, throwing it with such speed that the torch simply disappeared from his hands. He leaped into the air after it, catching it in both hands and doing a seven-hundred-and-twenty-degree spin midair. Then he threw the torch into the air again. He leaped to join it, jumping with so much force, he wound up higher than the torch itself. With a single fluid motion, Karn twisted in midair, performing a somersault and kicking off the ceiling, finishing with a diving save before the torch hit the ground.

He landed right in front of the audience, lying on his back and holding the torch above him. It would have been a truly amazing show—the problem was that Karn had moved so quickly that nobody's eyes could follow his absurdly athletic movements.

To everyone else in the tavern, it looked like he'd just fallen over onto his back.

A disturbed murmur passed through the crowd again as they hastily backed away from him.

"Is he even a real performer?"

"He could hurt someone being that clumsy…"

Only the most keen-eyed viewer noticed that something strange had happened. "Wait…I think he made the torch disappear for a moment. Is this a magic show?"

"What? This isn't magic; this is fire-eating!" Karn indignantly retorted.

Sofia groaned. "He has no idea how to put on a show at all. Where did he get his education?" She raised her voice to a shout. "Karn! They can't see what you're doing! Take it slower. The whole point of a show is to entertain people!"

Karn's eyes widened as he took in Sofia's words. In battle, the most efficient route to victory was killing an enemy before they even realized they were dead. The opposite was true of performing. Audience members needed to be alive and cognizant. "Ah! I understand it now! Everyone…watch this!"

With a smooth and elegant toss, he twirled the torch through the air. For Karn, it was just a light underhanded throw, barely more than a flick of his wrist, but for everyone else in the inn, the flame danced and spun before their eyes as it twirled up to the roof and back again.

Karn caught it effortlessly, then pointed the torch at a lady with blonde hair sitting in the back.

"You!"

She jerked up in surprise, staring at him. "Uh…yes?"

He pointed to a torch in the sconce behind her. "Throw that torch at me. Anywhere is fine. Just get it close."

All eyes in the tavern turned to her.

Blinking her eyes rapidly, as if to convince herself she wasn't in a dream, the blonde lady shakily grabbed the torch and hurled it at Karn, missing him by about four feet. He dove and caught it before it hit the ground, then flicked it into the air. As he danced backward with dramatic, exaggerated steps, he tossed the other torch into the air to join it, and soon, he was juggling two blazing torches, twirling his body between the blazing flames with unerring precision.

"You!" Karn grinned. This time, he pointed at a man in a black cloak with an excessively paranoid gleam in his eye—the man who'd drawn his hand crossbow at the first sign of trouble.

For a brief moment, their eyes met, and they nodded, two warriors recognizing each other on sight. Keeping one hand hidden in his cloak, he threw the other torch at Karn, lofting it high and forcing him to make a difficult catch—which was just what Karn had wanted.

A high leap later, and Karn was juggling three torches.

"You next!" This time, he pointed at an elderly gentleman with white hair and an even whiter beard, who was wondering exactly how he could explain this amazing story to his grandkids.

Karn's performance carried on until he was juggling nearly every torch in the inn. The entire room was soon blanketed by darkness, leaving Karn's spinning torches the only source of light, like a more playful version of the sun in the sky. With his left hand, he snapped his fingers and pointed at the audience members, all while keeping the other torches twirling elegantly in the air with only his right hand.

It was a display of dexterity nobody in the tavern had ever seen before, but it was nothing to a warrior with thousands of years of practice.

Unfortunately, the show ended on a dubious note.

"You!" Karn grinned, inadvertently pointing at the man who would ruin his show.

Gary Michaelson III was a parchment merchant traveling to Islington. The city of education had a rich need for parchment, and he always returned home with a handsome profit. He was very successful in his field and lived a fulfilling life, but he'd always fancied himself a bit of a warrior, particularly a javelin thrower.

Unfortunately, he was about to discover why he needed to stick to sales.

"I've been waiting my whole life for a moment like this!" he exclaimed. He haphazardly ripped the torch off the sconce, accidentally sending the metal ornament tumbling to the ground with his fit of excessive enthusiasm.

Then he hurled the torch at Karn with all his might.

The torch flew only two feet—Michaelson's strength wasn't the problem.

It was his accuracy.

The haymaker throw slammed right into the wildflower bottle on his table, sending glass shards flying chaotically through the room while igniting the cloth and flowers alike.

"I've got it!" Karn cried.

In the blink of an eye, Karn hurled the torches he'd been juggling through the room, his accuracy so great that they landed perfectly back in their sconces. Then, before the fire could spread any farther, he snuffed it out with a flawless execution of the stop, drop, and roll protocol.

Michaelson blinked in disbelief. "I. Um. Sorry. Bad throw."

"Not a problem," Karn replied. He reached over and picked out the flowers that had fallen out of the jar. "These flowers are a bit burnt, though."

"Um. Yeah. I guess they are…" Michaelson muttered.

Karn smirked as an idea blossomed in his mind, his knack for self-aggrandizement turning into a knack for friend-aggrandizement. "Bones, you mind coming here to fix this?"

"'Fix it'?" Sofia muttered. "What is he talking about?"

Indeed, Karn's claim that the flowers were just a bit burnt was a grievous understatement. The petals had seared right off, and all that was left after Karn's rescue attempt were a few blackened stems.

Bones's traveling bag rustled as he stepped forward and Patches called out to him. *"Don't worry, Bones. Just like on the road. It will be fine… Your magic is safer when you slowly channel it through a medium, just like you did with me. Your aura won't scare people if you do it gently. Make that plant bloom until there's a flower for everyone in the inn."*

The entire inn seemed to hold its breath as Bones walked up to Karn. His heart beat nervously in his chest, and he couldn't help but fear that his magic would suddenly abandon him. Bones could feel his accompanying chill slowly infecting the room, but Michaelson's accident had set the stage perfectly.

After a close call with fiery death, the audience badly wanted to cool down again.

And when Karn had handed the flowers over, Bones instinctively knew what to do. After all, he had always liked healing.

"This time, don't point. It'll look more dramatic if you grab it."

As he grasped the blackened stems, he poured in his gathered necromantic energy. Green grew from the black and petals bloomed back into existence, the small wildflower transforming into a vine that slowly wound through the dining room.

The crowd stared in disbelief, then began to cheer.

"What is that boy doing?"

"It's magic!"

"Look at those flowers... I've never seen those colors before!"

Bones's smile grew wider, craving the crowd's cheers just like how a plant craved sunlight.

In his excitement, he poured in even more energy than he'd meant to.

He let out a cry of surprise, fearing the worst for a brief moment, but he kept his hands carefully on the stem, making sure his magic didn't go anywhere else.

And soon, every visitor had an entire bouquet blooming in front of them. Empowered by Bones's necromantic energy, the petals had adopted shockingly bright colors—violet, magenta, and dark blue, decorated with swirling patterns and glowing rings. Through sheer magical might, the flowers had evolved to the point that humans could now see the colors normally reserved for pollinating insects.

After a shocked pause, the crowd burst into cheering and applause.

"That was amazing!" the innkeeper exclaimed, hustling up to them. "The two of you can stay here free of charge any night you put on a performance like that! Is there anything else we can do for you?"

"Just the cheers of the audience are enough for me." Karn grinned. "My terrible dream proved false. In life, it was louder than the screams of the battlefield."

"Um…all right," the innkeeper replied, hurriedly turning to Bones. "Anything for you?"

Bones glanced across the inn. There was no noticeboard, but plenty of space on the walls.

"Yeah, do you mind if I put a picture up on the wall over there?"

"Um…may I ask of what?" the innkeeper replied, well aware of the dangers of crude graffiti.

"A cat doing a backflip over a tent in a golden field."

The innkeeper blinked, trying and failing to process the image. "You know what? Sure."

As Bones reached into his bag for his supplies, giving Patches an affecting pat on the head as he did so, the innkeeper shook his head and chuckled. As utterly bizarre as Bones's request sounded, he'd learned over the years that all geniuses had their eccentricities.

Chapter Fourteen

The next morning, the trio left the inn with faces full of smiles and stomachs full of delicious food.

Karn cackled, throwing back his head of blazing-red hair. "Ha. It went just how I thought it would go. All eyes on us, Bones! Soon, we'll be performing in the biggest tent in all the land! I thought I'd experienced everything, but this is the best! I guess it just goes to show—it's never too late to start living your best life!" Karn was so jubilant, he didn't even care about all the stray stones he stepped on. Instead, he walked over to the side of the road, picking up a decently-sized stick and twirling it in his hands. "All I have to do is practice throwing things slowly."

Bones nodded eagerly. "I was worried for a moment, but I can't believe it went so well!"

"That's because you're always thinking of the worst-case mentality, kid. Just performing in some building is nothing! We need a tent way bigger than the Great Clown's—and way more colorful too."

"Well, as long as it doesn't eat us…" Bones muttered.

"What? Why would a tent eat us?" Sofia asked. "Karn is right, Achille. You're *far* too negative."

But despite Bones's innate negativity, he felt happier than he could ever remember. As they walked down the battered Baron's Road to Islington, Bones practiced imbuing the flowers and plants on the side of the road with his necromantic energy.

When the plants were close, he reached out, gently stroking them as he passed. He gestured for the farther ones, pointing carefully and feeling the magic slowly trickling out of him. Occasionally, Patches encouraged him to direct his magic with his mind alone, but Bones didn't feel quite ready for that yet.

Flowers bloomed all around them, their petals tinged with mysterious colors as they blew through the air. The side of the Baron's Road gradually transformed into a beautiful kaleidoscope of foliage as the trio continued on their way their path. Even the once-dying grass grew taller and taller, creating a sea of shockingly vivid green swaying peacefully in the wind.

Faint yet admiring whispers echoed out of the corner of Bones's ears.

"What is that boy doing?"

"Beautiful… Those flowers are beautiful."

"It's even better than the ones in the underworld."

Spirits swirled at the edge of Bones's field of vision. Though they still kept a safe distance from the mysteriously powerful boy, they were utterly captivated by the flowers.

Bones smiled, increasing the flow of his magic further. The petals billowed higher and higher, twinkling and flashing until they'd built into an otherworldly storm of glimmering, exotic light.

"Achille. You're causing all that, aren't you?" Sofia asked.

Bones turned to her. Confusion and disbelief engaged in a civil war on his face. "Um…what? I, uh…"

He hadn't expected Sofia to ask such a direct question. Completely unaware of the scientific method, Bones had ignorantly believed that Sofia's refusal to believe in the supernatural stemmed from a strange form of reverse superstition.

His tendency to overthink and overanalyze promptly kicked in as he performed an instantaneous deep dive into Sofia's disbelief in magic, countless possibilities flashing through his mind as they raced at speeds far swifter than Karn could ever move his body. Perhaps she was a magician or even a secret magic-user herself. Maybe she'd been dumped by a magician.

All of the reasons told him to lie or risk losing his friend, so he stammered out an unconvincing excuse. "Uh, no, it's, a…um…spring bloom."

"It's summer," Sofia replied, cocking her right eyebrow like it were a crossbow.

"Um. Well, I, uh…"

Sofia laughed. "Look, Achille. All that strange stuff you were always worried about—candles blinking out or the room suddenly getting cold—well, I ignored all that stuff because there was no proof. But science is about changing your view based on what you're seeing. Here."

She stopped and pointed at a small dandelion at the side of the road. "Can you make that bloom?"

Bones nodded and gestured. The plant grew up to Bones's knee before sending its glistening seeds—shimmering violet entwined with the usual white—billowing down the road.

Sofia smiled. "Well. Seems like you have the beginnings of an act, at least…and I have a very good reason to change my mind. I'll have to show you to Professor Roman, though only *after* he tells me what's going on with my homework."

"So you'll believe me when I tell you magic is happening now?" Bones asked. As someone who did not like changing his mind, he was shocked that Sofia had changed hers so quickly.

"I'll have to evaluate everything on a case-by-case basis, but I'll certainly be more amenable to it, especially when you show me irrefutable evidence like this. But, Bones…you also need to remember the times I proved you wrong. You thought that you were cursed to never make friends. You thought you would be a bad performer. But look at you now. You're traveling the road with friends and starting your own circus troupe. You even had the whole inn cheering for you!"

Bones smiled shyly. "Well, Sofia, I suppose that's irrefutable evidence of your own. Maybe I *was* too worried before. My powers really can be used for good."

"That's the spirit," Sofia replied. She eyed Bones carefully. Now that she understood that his magic was real, she also understood why he'd been so worried all the time. "Achille. I'm sorry I didn't believe you earlier."

"Oh, it's okay."

"I know I'm a latecomer, but do you mind if I give you some advice?"

"Your advice is *always* welcome," Bones earnestly replied.

"If you're worried that you might lose control of your powers, you need to learn more about them. Obviously, I don't know much about magic. But now that I'm thinking about it, it sounds a bit like carrying an unsheathed sword around."

"It kind of is," Bones replied. "And, you know, I'm worried about cutting someone."

"I'm not surprised you're afraid of hurting people, Achille. You're a fine young man. But if you don't learn about your powers, you won't know how to control them. That's what will lead to accidents. Like I said, I don't really know what I'm talking about, but my thinking is that if you practice using your magic, if you gain total control over it, *that*'s when you won't worry about hurting anyone."

"Patches has been telling me the same thing," Bones said.

"Patches," Sofia hesitantly replied. "So she really can move."

"Yes…but she doesn't when you ask her to." Bones laughed. Patches laughed with him. "But you're right, Sofia. I will practice. And I'm glad you believe in magic now. I've always wanted your advice. Karn's just isn't quite as accurate."

"I have no idea how to control powers." Karn laughed. "My immortality is just a passive ability. Honestly, I don't even know how it works. Maybe Death is afraid of me. Wants to avoid a near-Karn experience."

A sudden clopping noise echoed from behind them, precise and clipped sounds that suggested disciplined and careful hoof steps. Bones, Karn, and Sofia all whirled around, abruptly on guard. The Baron's Road had been empty just moments ago.

"Bandits!" Sofia hissed.

"It's Death himself! I'm about to scare him off for another couple thousand years!" Karn exclaimed.

Bones shook his head as he noticed a shaking and rustling from the tall grass he'd just grown. "No, it's them…from before. They moved the same way back then!"

Moments later, the trio saw two striped muzzles slowly emerging from the tall grass that Bones had just grown. The zebras from the carriage seemingly clopped into existence, closely followed by four strapping goats with curled horns and long, white beards beneath their chins. The hardy beasts moved very slowly, their heads constantly glancing at the ground as if surprised to be on such flat terrain.

"Goats?" Karn asked. "Aren't these guys more common in the mountains?"

"I mean, I don't think this is the natural environment for zebras, either," Sofia replied.

Suddenly, the shadows shifted and with a faint growl, two panthers bound out from the grass. The smooth shadows moved so quickly that Bones instinctively called forth his magic, just in case they were pouncing at him, but they landed peacefully and elegantly in front of the group, briefly bowing their heads in a strangely supplicant gesture.

The animals, eight in total, all began making noises at the trio, clearly trying to talk to them. The zebras brayed, the goats bleated, and the panthers chirped and purred, almost like bigger versions of housecats.

Unfortunately, none of them had any vague idea of what they were trying to say.

Bones peeked into the grass, hoping to see the spectral coachwoman's carriage. Her ability to communicate with the creatures solely by touch was unrivaled.

But the grass was still.

"Um…I'm sorry," Bones said. "I…uh…don't understand what you're saying."

"We can't talk to animals," Karn added. Unfortunately, because they couldn't talk to animals, the animals didn't understand what he was saying.

"Is there anything we can do?" Sofia asked, her forehead wrinkling with concern. "I mean, they sound pretty upset."

"Maybe the coachwoman went missing," Karn suggested. "I mean, I don't see why else they would come looking for us. But how could anyone capture her?"

Bones nodded warily. He knew it was possible to capture spirits with contracts or other magical items. He'd seen it happen with Tycho. But someone as powerful as the coachwoman, with access to all of her animal friends, shouldn't have been captured so easily.

Something felt off.

But then, Bones felt a pulse in his mind, accompanied by a calm and gentle voice. *"I can talk to them."*

"Oh. Let me get you out, Patches."

Bones slung his bag out in front of his shoulder, pulling the stuffed animal out from inside.

"Give me some more energy. This might be a longer conversation," Patches said. As she spoke, Karn and Sofia reacted with surprise, staring at the stuffed doll as her voice echoed in their heads. *"Yes. Normally, I just talk to Bones, but I think it would be easier if he doesn't translate."*

"You know, you might be a stuffed animal, but charging you up so you can move makes you seem more like a wind-up toy," Bones remarked as he charged her. "Come to think of it, I could probably give you enough energy so that you could move around all the time if you liked."

"No thanks. Consciousness, like most things, is best in small doses. Speaking of which… do you mind holding me? My legs don't support me too well."

Bones laughed, holding her up to the animals, who stared at her with a mix of confusion and horror. From the animals' perspective, Patches was a terrifying shredded mannequin wearing skin from over a dozen different species with plenty of added artificial parts.

However, they were desperate.

They spoke to her, and then Patches nodded, her floppy neck sending her head bouncing haphazardly from side to side.

"Bones, they want your help freeing someone who is trapped in Islington. But it's not the coachwoman. It's her boss."

"What?" Sofia cut in. "What kind of pet wants to free their owner's boss? My cats and dogs were always overjoyed when I went back home."

"Would you like me to ask them that?" Patches asked.

"Um, sure," Sofia replied, wincing and holding a hand to her head as Patches's voice reverberated through her mind. She caught Bones's eye and shook her head in disbelief. In the last few days, it felt like she'd been brought into an entirely new world.

"They said they aren't exactly pets but are close enough to it. Leisure pets usually want their owners at home, but working pets want their owners to go back to work."

"Well. Fair enough. Maybe I should have gotten a working pet. Then I could have spent more time with them."

"Will you help them?" Patches asked.

"Yeah. We can help," Bones immediately replied.

Sofia frowned worriedly. "I don't know about that, Bones. Someone trapped in Islington? It might be dangerous." She turned to Patches. "Do they have any idea where this person might be?"

Patches turned back to the animals, relaying her question into their minds before replying. *"He's being held by a tall man with curly, blond hair, very pale skin, and an extremely strange costume."*

"Well, it shouldn't be too hard to find him. Plus, if his costume is any good, we can just save money and take it for our circus!" Karn declared.

"You say that like it'll be easy," Sofia replied.

"Of course it will be. Just one of me or Bones is enough. With two, it's over for anyone who tries to stand against us."

"Well, I mean, we should do the right thing, right?" Bones asked. "I mean, if someone is trapped, I think we should free them on principle."

"I suppose you're right," Sofia grudgingly replied. After all, she'd been the person to tell Bones to always do the right thing. "And perhaps something strange is happening at Islington in general. I mean, Professor Roman has never been late returning our assignments before… All right. Let's go, then," Sofia agreed. The thought of the mystery behind her missing homework motivated Sofia significantly, but the grateful look of the animals motivated her even further.

They bowed their heads in appreciation. From the goats, the gesture was somewhat menacing due to their curled horns yet still appreciated. Then Patches spoke again, broadcasting her calm and slow voice in everyone's mind. *"They said they can take us to the crossroads."*

The group glanced at each other. Thanks to Bones's necromantic healing, nobody was tired, but they wouldn't say 'no' to a shortcut.

"They said it will only take a moment. Sofia has a good idea of where Rustling and Islington split," Patches added.

"So they can do that weird world-spinning trick just by themselves?" Sofia asked. "Well, I would like to see that."

Karn and Sofia got onto the zebras, leaving one of the panthers for Bones. The muscular cat leaned low in front of him, allowing Bones to clamber onto its back, which made for an impressive yet awkward seat. Ridged and muscular, the panther's back pressed into Bones, the fur bristling uncomfortably against his legs.

Yet the trip only lasted a short moment.

With a mighty pounce, the panther leaped into the tall grass, which swirled hypnotically, moving in patterns that were somehow simultaneously chaotic yet orderly, a mishmash perceived not with Bones's eyes, but with his subconscious.

For a brief moment, he thought he'd seized upon the hidden connection that the coachwoman and her animals used, but then, it was gone again.

The world spun for one last time, and the group had emerged before a battered, wooden signpost planted at a curve on the Baron's Road. A narrow path, ill-maintained even in comparison to the decaying Baron's Road, wound off into the distance, snaking through the tall grass in a manner surprisingly reminiscent of the road to and from Bones and Sofia's isolated cottage.

The path leading farther down the Baron's Road was labeled 'Islington' and the much more neglected path was marked for 'Rustling.' The Baron's Road connected the region's major cities, without much more focus for towns or villages.

The panther nudged Bones with its head, a clear gesture that told him to get off.

When the trio had all dismounted, the animals leaped back into the brush, fading into the distance.

Sofia frowned and shook her head, feeling a little dizzy after the sudden move. "You know, even after experiencing this three times, I still don't understand how their strange magic works."

Karn scoffed. "Bah. Trying to figure out how someone else's powers work is always a waste of time. Let's just get going."

As the trio followed the path down to Islington, Bones noticed Sofia frowning as she stared at the sign. "Something on your mind?"

"I've never liked the separation between Islington and Rustling," she explained. "Even when I was a kid, the town did a lot for the university. I think the school does very important work, but they can be such snobs about it."

Bones was surprised. Simply because he'd never asked her about it, he'd previously imagined her love of Islington University to be absolute. "Did going to the school change how you felt about things?"

"Well, I've only been on campus a few times before... There are some truly brilliant and amazing people there, but I don't think I would want to stay there full-time. Correspondence learning is best for me. The Plumage scholars we met on the mountain were only a single standard deviation of snobbery above the rest of the student body. I don't remember their names, but the school had some truly generational egomaniacs."

"Maybe this man in the weird costume is one of them," Bones said.

From the crossroads, it was only a ten-minute walk to Islington, a sprawling city built along the rushing Sun Beam River and flanked on both sides by two walls.

The front-facing side, the alleged city gates, was little more than a low-hanging fence, almost identical to the simple planks that had encased the Bonaparte family manor. Built for more peaceful times, the fence was now much too low, considering the preponderance of banditry, but Islington didn't offer a carpentry course.

Behind the city was an enormous dam, built from massive, black stones. It loomed over the entire city, holding back the rushing tide of the Sun Beam River and modulating the water levels for the various rice-farming villages in the area, including Rustling.

Karn walked up to the fence. "We can just go in?" he asked.

"Yeah," Sofia replied. She opened up a panel, but by then, Karn had already leaped right over.

Bones walked in behind them, frowning deeply. "What's going on? It's so quiet."

All they could hear was the river burbling against the dam, but there were neither voices nor footsteps.

Karn called out. "Hello? Is anyone here?"

If anyone was there, they didn't reply.

Chapter Fifteen

The trio moved slowly moved into the quiet city—Karn in the front and Bones in the back, with Sofia protected in the middle. The situation was so bizarre that even Karn knew that it was best to proceed with caution and protect the vulnerable members of the group.

The gate creaked eerily shut behind them.

It wasn't because of anything supernatural—it was merely a poorly maintained hinge, but the group whirled around like a dragon had roared behind them.

Bones chuckled nervously. "I guess when you're worried, everything sounds scary."

Karn scowled. He didn't like feeling worried. "Hold on. If anything bad is happening, they won't mind if I do this. And if nothing bad is happening, well, there probably won't be anyone who can make me pay for this fence."

He wrenched a plank of the fence out of the ground, turning it around in his hands and then nodding when he judged the weight to be suitable. Then he started swiftly rubbing it with his hand, moving so quickly that the wood burst into flame. "There. Now we're ready in case anything happens."

But nothing happened.

They moved deeper into the city, a haphazard collection of buildings sprawled along the Sun Beam River, each with increasingly eccentric designs. Most of the occupants lived in two clusters of homes, one in the city's northeast and the other in the southeast.

The homes alone were nearly unrecognizable, a mishmash of bizarre bunkers, dirt huts, and buildings that looked like they were made from children's building blocks. Islington had engineers interested in designing the sturdiest home possible, historians who wanted to live as people had back in the old days, and child development specialists who wanted to create the ideal conditions for their young children.

They did not have city planners who could keep anyone in line, and the builders from Rustling they'd hired were more interested in receiving payment than dispensing advice.

Sofia frowned. "It's like a ghost town in here. All the homes are empty."

"Well, I can't guarantee if they are safe…but I don't think too many people were killed," Bones replied.

"How can you know?"

"If it was something that happened recently, you'd figure that at least some ghosts would linger for a while."

"It usually takes a bit before they leave," Karn agreed.

"Well, if anyone is around, it'll probably be at the main university campus. So let's check that out first."

Sofia nodded in the direction of the university's tall bell tower and multi-story barrack dormitories. The buildings, built from handsome red brick, could be seen from miles away.

As they headed towards the university, all they saw were increasingly abandoned streets. Some corners of the city seemed almost dusty, as if nobody had been there for a very long time.

After another twenty minutes of walking, they found themselves before a bizarre building. Karn raised his burning plank, Bones called forth his magic, and even Patches popped her head out of the bag. *"Do we need me to talk to that?"* she asked.

The building's utterly bizarre shape automatically suggested conspiracy, perhaps even some kind of invasion by merfolk.

Sofia, however, knew that the shape was simply due to human laziness and eccentricity. "No. This is the post office."

"What?"

"Yeah. Um. It was built by Professor Arial. He started the first correspondence course. Very nice man, but his passion for teaching is rivaled only by his hatred of the outdoors."

Professor Arial's post office was a sprawling, starfish-shaped building built from brightly painted blue stones with porthole-like windows and a wooden roof whose circular tiles looked a little like scales.

Located near the center of Islington, its prime position and unusual shape were the result of Professor Arial's complex calculations to maximize the amount of time he could stay indoors. Factors like distance from his home, the university, and the town gates were all accounted for in the post office's sprawling starfish-like arms.

Of course, the sheer amount of time he'd spent on the calculations had taken far more work than if he'd just built an ordinary post office and delivered the mail like a normal person, but as brilliant as the Islington Professors were, they were just as vulnerable as everyone else to the logical lapses of laziness.

At the front of the post office was a large, green canopy, which shaded a square, metal mailbox jammed to the brim with letters, so stuffed that it looked like it was vomiting. It was clear that deliverers had continued jamming letters inside until it had been physically impossible to continue, at which point an unruly pile of bonus mail had grown next to it.

Sofia frowned, tentatively approaching the pile. "What's going on here?"

She leafed through a few of the letters and her frown grew deeper. "Look. This is my physics assignment from two weeks ago. And it's not just Professor Roman…the other professors are listed too. Something must have happened."

"Let's stay careful." Bones kept his magic primed, brimming just beneath the surface, so he could protect Sofia in case they were ambushed.

Karn tilted his head to the side, trying and failing to read the letters. "Do you think there are any costume orders there? Maybe we could get rid of them, make sure we're first in line."

"It seems like too much effort to go through everything," Sofia said. "Besides, I've read that mail fraud is a serious crime."

The trio left the post office, continuing down the empty streets, passing through the looming university clock tower and dormitories and entering the main campus through an archway built from red and gray stones.

The walkway was one of four, each pointing to one of the cardinal directions. The eastern archway led to the university clocktower and barracks and the western exit led out to the Sun Beam River. The northern and southern exits pointed back out to the broader town.

All of the buildings on campus had a similar structure—three-story buildings built from red brick with sturdy, cedar roofs. Every floor had very wide windows, allowing plenty of sun to shine on neatly arranged desks and unruly stacks of books and quills. The wooden doors were emblazoned with golden plaques designating their respective academic specialties. The door directly in front of Bones displayed two crossed quills over an open book, and the one next to it showed planets spinning through a starry sky.

The adjoined buildings created a rectangular shape surrounding a warm and pleasant—but nonetheless abandoned—courtyard filled with marble statues commemorating previous professors.

But Sofia had seen all the statues before. Her eyes were instead drawn to a series of gleaming notices in golden parchment plastered along the first-floor windows. "Look at this, Achille. It looks like it came from the barony…"

Bones frowned, doing his best to read the handwriting. It was excessively elegant and fanciful, with so many extraneous loops, it looked like the letters were trying to metamorphose into butterflies.

Notice from the Sun Beam Barony: Educational Modernization Program

Due to the dire financial situation in the Barony, Baron Angelo will be adjusting funding to Islington University effective immediately. Henceforth, Islington will receive funding based on student performance in the following subjects.

> Medicine: Embalming Specialty
> Archaeology: Graverobbing Specialty
> Economics: Short-Term Financial Speculation Specialty

The Barony will also grant a scholarship to anyone who can make corpses stop stinking.

A few additional posters plastered on the wall, written in the same fanciful handwriting, seemed to support these educational initiatives.

Academia is useless—leave the ivory tower for the tombs and become a graverobber today!

We spend too much time and energy keeping people alive—embalming is a cheaper and more efficient way to spend time with family!

If the end times come, at least you won't have to repay your student loans!

"These are weirdly optimistic slogans," Bones remarked. "I can't imagine most of the students are all that happy about this."

Sofia frowned. "What is this nonsense? It sounds like they are trying to transition to some kind of zombie-based curriculum. I know Baron Angelo is into this necromancy fad, but Islington teaches scholars from around the world."

"We'll probably find out more if we keep going," Bones said, continuing forward and peering through the windows. Most of the classrooms were abandoned and dusty with disuse, until he walked by the medical building. The golden insignia on the door depicted vines curled gently around a heart.

Based on the list of grades plastered to the door, the student body was in terminal health. Almost everyone was failing their classes.

As he peered through the window, Bones found putrefied bodies, desk after desk of failed experiments. The students did not seem very good at embalming, and Bones couldn't blame them. In his experience, medical professionals generally preferred living bodies to dead ones.

The definitively un-embalmed corpse directly in front of the window had flies crawling all over it. Bones felt bad for whoever's body it had been. Getting killed was bad enough; having their corpse mangled by a botched embalming felt like adding libel to lethality.

Bones considered using his necromantic magic on the corpses but thought better of it.

While he could bring back the dead in a literal sense, he couldn't bring them back to life—they would only be undead, complete with the accompanying unfortunate ailments like a bad smell, a pallid body, and an inability to have children. On top of that, he could not imbue a reanimated body with a soul. Unless the deceased's spirit was present, Bones's magic would only create a mindless zombie, and it seemed like Islington already had enough problems.

They continued past medicine to the archaeology department building, indicated by a shovel next to a pile of gold.

Angry, red notes had been scrawled beneath this list of grades. "Artifacts are no longer wanted…the Baron wants body parts!" Beneath it was a further addendum. "To get an A, find body parts with unusual abilities!"

"Body parts with unusual abilities?" Sofia muttered.

"They probably want people like Karn. You know, whose flesh can't burn."

"Wow, it's very lucky we got to my body just before those kids from Islington," Karn said. "They might have turned me in to get a good grade!"

"Or maybe Jack would have sold your parts to the Baron if he got desperate," Bones replied.

The timing had indeed been suspiciously beneficial, but the trio was too focused on the mystery of the abandoned school to ponder any further. It was only after making it to the western archway that they found some hint of where everyone had gone. An additional notice in finely embossed gold had been placed right beside the archway, written in the same dramatically curling script as before.

Sir Yesse Pennington has been appointed as Baron Angelo's special educational representative.

Islington students must report to his practical research course held beside the Sun Beam River or face expulsion.

All other classes have been canceled indefinitely.

"Pennington…I remember that name. The other scholars were talking about him at Karn's tomb," Sofia muttered, shaking in disbelief at the note.

"Did you know him?" Bones asked.

"He was never on campus the few times I arrived in person, but the other students always said he was annoying. He's just a student…but this note makes him sound like he's higher up than the professors. A course by the river is even stranger. We've always been told to stay away."

Now it was Karn's turn to frown. "Why do they want you to stay away from the river? Does a monster live there?"

"What? No. It's because it's dangerous. You can fall in and get smashed against the dam, or if you somehow fit through the spillway, you'll just get carried out to sea."

"Oh. That's a shame," Karn replied.

"A shame there's no monster?" Bones asked.

"Well, yeah. I was thinking if there were one, we could beat it up and add it to our circus. We need a few more acts."

Sofia turned first to Karn, then to Bones, then sighed and shook her head, fearing that even *trying* to comprehend his logic would require a permanent downshift in brain function. "Let's just keep moving."

The trio walked through the western stone archway and out into a stone garden, decorated with small pools of brightly colored gravel and abstract statues made of rocks artfully piled on top of each other.

"It's through here and then past the wooden gate at the end," Sofia explained.

Just before making it to the wooden gate on the other side, they found a stack of battered, handheld signs made from snapped poles and dirty sheets of paper, dumped in an unceremonious pile beside a particularly tall rock formation.

"What do those say?" Karn asked.

Bones craned his head to the side, reading the words and frowning. "Keep Education Alive."

He licked his lips nervously, his innate guilty conscience creeping to the forefront. Even though he logically knew this had to be about the posted notes, this anti-necromantic propaganda felt awfully targeted.

Karn didn't feel the same way. "Hey, that's pretty good. If you know anything about me, it's that I love staying alive." He pushed through the wooden gate, revealing a rarely tread and poorly maintained dirt path, covered with stray stones and unruly grass.

There, they saw all the students and professors of Islington, doing something Sofia never could have imagined them doing: manual labor.

Chapter Sixteen

About a hundred feet from the gate, row after row of Islington University students and professors worked beside the river, sweating through their clothes as they awkwardly knelt before an absurdly long wooden table in front of a hastily built rickety wooden shack.

To Bones's eyes, the students looked painfully unaccustomed to manual labor. Of course, Bones was unaccustomed to manual labor too, but he was very accustomed to being unaccustomed to things. He recognized their telltale miserable slouches right away.

"I'm guessing they don't build things normally?" Karn asked.

"Definitely not. The Islington motto is *theory over practice*," Sofia replied. "I have no idea what's happening."

"Well, let's find out more."

As the trio walked forward, the wind howled in their faces, the earthy scent of the river mixing with a harsh medicinal scent that seemed to invade Bones's nostrils. "What is *that?*"

"I think it's embalming fluid…"

But as they drew closer, they realized this went far beyond a mere practical lesson. It was a necromantic assembly line. The students grabbed body parts from a series of black buckets, stitching them together before handing them off.

They slowly passed the body parts down the line, the stitched corpses growing larger and larger with every stop. The professors stood at the very end, tying everything together with clumsy and awkward stitches that most closely resembled an infant's attempt to tie shoes.

Islington's medical program focused on medical theory—they had not filtered people out for squeamishness. But for obvious reasons, working with stinking corpses in the burning summer heat was an unpleasant experience for even the most intrepid stitcher.

Not only that, the project looked like a total failure. The hideously misshapen hulks of flesh produced by the end of the assembly line lay flat on the ground, still and unmoving. Bones couldn't detect a single spark of necromantic energy in their bodies.

The trio continued their slow walk, their bafflement growing with every step.

"I don't think they could have found anyone worse to do this job…" Bones muttered.

"I don't think they could have found a worse job for anyone to do," Sofia replied. "This looks disgusting. Even Professor Roman is having a bad time, and he loves trying new things."

"Didn't you say he taught physics?" Karn asked. "Why do they have him tying up corpses?"

"No clue. That's him over there," Sofia said, nodding her head.

"Who? The weird man in the wig and makeup?"

The man at the very edge of the table seemed strangely familiar to Bones, though he had no idea why.

He wore a long, black coat that went all the way down to his knees, buttoned up despite the sweltering sun in the sky. A white ruffle poked out from above the top button, perhaps from a scarf or some old-fashioned doublet. His curly, white hair was arranged in a tall beehive that stood over half a foot into the air and his face was plastered with an absurd amount of makeup, more than any performer from the Great Circus.

"No, that's the economics professor," Sofia replied. "His name escapes me at the moment. But look… None of this matters. They are being forced to work. And if I had to guess, the person forcing them is inside that shack over there."

Though Sofia didn't have any battle experience, she had a great deal of experience with the psychology of malevolent nobles.

Indeed, Yesse Pennington was hiding inside the shaded shack, watching the rest of the school toil away in the sun. He had ordered them to build the shack for him first before commencing work.

Like the overall concept of making clumsy students and elderly professors work at an assembly line, the order to build a personal surveillance shack before starting work had been inefficient, but Pennington did not care about efficiency.

In fact, the entire assembly line was a case of extreme mission creep.

Pennington had only been ordered to identify students potentially interested in the baron's cause, skilled designers who could improve his zombie construction factories hidden beneath Avaron Heights. Forcing a whole line of nobles, including powerful and well-connected individuals from foreign lands, into sweatshop working conditions hadn't been part of the plan, but the pleasure of lording over people he knew had been too much for Pennington to resist.

Born to a life of immense privilege, Pennington had never hungered for food, so he hungered for power instead. If anything, he was somewhat excited to see his professors and classmates fail. It gave him an excuse to punish them later.

But in an irony of ironies, the mess of corpses was Pennington's own fault. He didn't have enough necromantic energy to animate all these behemoths.

Karn flex his muscles. "Well, that's probably the person the animals were complaining about. Let's go kick his ass. If it's an accidental ass-kicking, you can just heal him up after, Bones."

Bones's eyes narrowed. "I'm not sure if it'll be easy. There's something strange about the shack."

Despite Bones's general inexperience with magic users, he once again instantly recognized his necromantic kin. A vibrant, purple aura emanated from the shack and when Bones concentrated, he thought he could hear guttural growling echoing from within.

"Oh, don't worry about it." Karn scoffed. "Sofia, you should make sure to stay back, but we'll deal with it, no problem, Bones. Compared to ordinary men like him, we're a different breed. Sabretooth tigers among regular tigers."

As Bones pondered the difference in lethality between sabretooth tigers and regular tigers, a man stepped out of the shack.

With his well-groomed curly, blond hair; high cheekbones; and aristocratic nose, Yesse Pennington normally would have been handsome, but there was something just slightly off about his appearance. His blue eyes were a little too large and set just a touch too wide, just enough to make him look like a gecko.

At six and a half feet tall, Pennington towered over almost everyone else on campus, but neither his height nor his disturbingly reptilian appearance was the strangest thing about him.

His outfit was absurdly ostentatious, enough to put a whole flock of peacocks to shame. His swirling, black cloak, decorated with skulls and tombstones, trailed down to the floor. The scarlet carapace-like armor beneath it had a roaring dragon skull emblazoned across the chest. Unusually long, spider-like fingers clutched a tome with a freshly embossed leather cover of silver arcane signals.

Though the book was purely decorative, the orb he held in his right hand was extremely effective: a necromantic control orb, just like what Jack Pillary had used. The swirling, palm-sized device was filled with Pennington's purple necromantic magic, which glowed far brighter than Jack's ever had.

When the rest of campus had criticized Baron Angelo's reforms, Pennington had been the only one brave enough to come out as pro-establishment.

Baron Angelo had been drawn to Yesse Pennington not only due to his supplicant nature, but also his first name. The baron was always looking for more yes men and he was a big believer in normative determinism, a theory that Pennington now *also* agreed with.

After being granted his necromantic control orb, Pennington had thrown himself wholeheartedly into the necromancy industry. Never one for rising and grinding, he loved the idea of making someone else *arise* and grind for him.

Pennington's eyes widened as he saw Bones, then widened even further as he saw Karn's hunched-over, zombie-like body.

Karn's body abruptly vanished before appearing right in front of Pennington with equal abruptness.

But Pennington was much more skilled than Jack Pillary.

The aura of necromantic magic around his body swelled. Like Bones, Pennington's appearance subtly shifted when he used his magic. His body became gaunter and more skeletal, violet flames briefly flickering through his eyes as his necromantic aura expanded.

The orb glowed brightly and Karn suddenly froze in place, crashing to the ground as gleaming, purple chains abruptly wrapped around him. He let out a cry of shock, slamming to the ground. His powerful muscles battled against the purple chains, but he was completely unable to break free. "Hey! Let me go! Don't you know who I am? I'm a famous fire-eater! This is going to ruin my tour!"

Pennington didn't even deign to respond. He glanced at Bones instead, snickering. "That's funny. You made yours small."

"He didn't make me anything!" Karn howled. "Don't you dare think I'm just some zombie! What is this thing? What have you done to me?"

Pennington wasn't used to such a mouthy zombie, but as his dramatic costume made clear, he had a penchant for showing off. He wasn't going to pass up this natural chance to explain his magic. "The orb takes time adjusting to different targets, but soon these chains will sink deep into your mind and you shall be under my command!" At the end of his sentence, Pennington cleared his voice to better enunciate his sponsor shout-out. "My magic was granted to me by the Deathless Prince, Baron Angelo."

"What? It shouldn't work on me, then! I'm not a zombie! Bones! There's been some horrible mistake! Tell him I'm not a zombie!"

Bones had no idea how to reply. "Um…don't tell *me* that, Karn. Tell the magic that!"

Bones eyed Pennington nervously.

He could tell at a glance that Pennington was stronger than Jack Pillary or Drustan. Almost everyone, save for the strange figure with the wig and makeup, had stopped their work at the assembly line to instead stare at the necromantic confrontation, and Bones didn't want anyone staring at him.

This went far beyond mere stage fright. There was an actual danger here—at such a close distance, Bones feared the horrifying aura of his magic would drive everyone mad.

But if Karn couldn't free himself, he might not have a choice.

Karn struggled furiously, straining his muscles against the purple chain. "Hey! Magic! Let me go! You've got the wrong guy!" Somehow, the chains rattled and he finally managed to wrench them off. "Ha! You shouldn't have stereotyped me because of my stitches."

Pennington staggered back in shock, hurriedly reaching into his pocket.

Clearly, Karn was unbound by magical law, so Pennington turned back to his next option—the actual law, pulling a crumpled letter from his pocket. Following the instincts of generations of government bureaucrats before and after him, he brandished the crumpled note like a shield, waving it defensively before the irate Karn.

"Halt! Halt in the name of Baron Angelo!"

Considering Karn's absurd strength, the paper shield was much more effective than an actual shield. He stared at the note, his brow furrowing. "Bones…help me out here…what does this say?"

"Karn…don't read in the middle of the fight!"

"Wait…is that what the sheet says? Or is that what you're telling me?'

Before Bones could reply, a monstrous zombie burst from the shed, its four eyes locked straight on Karn.

With four eyes and four arms, the hulking, gray-skinned monstrosity had been necromantically designed for close combat. Made of several different bodies stitched together, the zombified goliath was over seven and a half feet tall, his rippling muscles so absurd and bulging that he had abs on his pecs. He was bare-chested, but he wore olive-green pants and had an additional cloak tied around his waist. His bulging upper left arm carried a massive sheet of metal, which it swung as if it were a piece of paper.

This massive zombie was Pennington's only successful creation; the other failed bodies at the assembly line a particularly grisly case of second-product syndrome.

The monster let out a triumphant battle cry. "I…am…Pennington!"

He looked at the master hopefully, but Pennington spat disgustedly on the ground. Pennington had only created the zombie yesterday, and it hadn't known a life free of the control orb's mental shackles.

Unfortunately, having Pennington's thoughts relayed directly to his mind had the unfortunate side effect of confusing the zombie on his real name. "For the umpteenth time, you're not Pennington. That's my name, the name of the necromancer who created you! Now, let's grab these two and…"

Pennington the Necromancer trailed off, scratching his chin thoughtfully as the scholars and professors fled into the distance, screaming in fear and disbelief at the necromantic violence. Just like before, only the economics professor remained, continuing to work at the table, even though nobody was passing any new parts to him.

"Hang on. Give me a moment…I'll come up with a suitable punishment." With reanimation claiming more and more jobs, Pennington sought to make himself irreplaceable to the baron, providing value that no zombie could match. As of late, he'd placed a particular focus on torturous punishments, figuring that he could probably specialize in inventing cruelties that no zombie could manage. Not seeing Bones or Karn as threats anymore, Pennington thought he had the time for a brainstorming session.

But seconds later, Pennington the Necromancer's carriage of thought was viciously derailed by Pennington the Zombie slamming straight through the rickety overseer shack. The attack had inflicted massive property damage and even greater bodily injury. Pennington the Zombie hit the ground in a crumpled tangle of excessive limbs and muscles.

Karn leaned over the unconscious body, a wide grin on his face. Pennington the Zombie's four eyes swirled with such randomness that if the students hadn't fled, some might have been inspired to study probability.

"Hey. Uh…you there…do you want to be our strongman?" Karn asked. He tilted his head to the side, trying to figure out if he'd accidentally killed him. "You look pretty strong, and you've got a pretty nice build there. Um, I guess that's kind of a literal build for you. Oh, and don't worry about being stronger than me, I actually want to be our fire—"

Karn was still offering his condolences when Pennington the Zombie offered him a knuckle sandwich. Two muscular arms slammed into the side of Karn's head, sending the caveman's eyes spinning. Then Pennington the Zombie used his other two arms to punch Karn in the gut, blasting him into the dirt.

"What is going on?" Karn cried, scrambling back to his feet. "This guy needs even less brain to fight than I do! Bones…you deal with the skinny guy. I've got the big guy!"

Karn and the massive zombie charged each other again, a clash of muscle against more muscle. Though Karn had crumpled one of the zombie's brains, Pennington the Zombie had been created with multiple brains stitched together, providing backups for this very situation.

As the two zombies tumbled off into the distance, Pennington the Necromancer raised his hand at Bones, his mouth curled into a sneer. "You know…the Deathless Prince Baron Angelo told me that these orbs operate by resonating with necromantic energy. They can control necromancers too."

Purple chains burst from his orb, wrapping around Bones's body. For a brief moment, Bones felt the chains pulling tightly around him and a lingering malevolent presence trying to worm its way into his mind. But then his magic flared and the chains rusted, falling to the ground and shattering into a putrid, purple dust.

Pennington scowled. Deep down, part of him knew what had happened, but his ego wouldn't let him process the information in front of him. "I must not have put enough energy into that one."

He clenched his fist, his veins popping out of his arm as he marshaled forth even more magic.

A voice echoed in Bones's mind. Patches wasn't very useful for fights, but she was much more observant than Karn. *"King of the Jungle, Bones. Stop worrying and start fighting! Everyone already ran off, other than the guy with the makeup. And he's so focused on his work that he doesn't realize there's a fight. Just go all out."*

Bones nodded, calling forth his necromantic light as a twisting and clinking mass of purple chains streaked towards him. Unknowable color flooded straight into Pennington's eyes as apocalyptic visions tap-danced through his mind, each echoing step further eroding his sanity.

He let out a choked gasp, his hair turning brittle and white, falling off his head and shattering like glass on the floor. His face withered instantaneously and he let out a long groan, the decorative leatherbound book tumbling to the ground from weak and brittle fingers.

The orb rolled from Pennington the Necromancer's limp fingers, plopping onto the ground, the energy inside fading and vanishing as Bones absorbed it for himself.

Bones stood before him, his magic not yet released. "Leave this place. Get out of here and leave all these people alone." For the first time in many years, his words came out strong and confident. If it weren't for the circumstances, he would have temporarily paused, utterly shocked at the sound of his voice.

Unfortunately for Bones, Pennington the Necromancer wasn't interested in his character development. Frothing at the mouth with fear, he hurled himself into the Sun Beam River in his desperation to escape. The rushing river carried his body chaotically downstream, dashing him viciously against the dam. Only his faint trickle of necromantic energy kept him alive, re-forging his broken and dislocated limbs. Eventually, he managed to fit through the spillway.

Soon, he was nothing more than a tiny, glimmering purple speck of light far off in the distance.

"Bones, great news, I was right! We found a monster by the river and recruited him to join our circus. This guy says he wants to be our strongman!"

Bones turned and found Karn walking back with a grinning Pennington the Zombie, their arms clasped in brotherly admiration around each other's shoulders. Though there was a significant height difference, Pennington the Zombie's lower arms were very conveniently placed for friendships with shorter individuals. Of the two, Pennington was clearly the worse for wear, but he didn't seem to mind.

"We're cool now," Karn explained. "He turned back to normal after I beat him up. Said the other guy was controlling him with that orb."

Pennington the Zombie nodded, his four eyes blinking in confusion. To Bones's surprise, he now had a very articulate and scholarly voice, a sharp contrast to his hulking, terrifying body. Indeed, Pennington's multiple limbs distracted from the fact that he also had multiple brains. Though he'd been animated without a soul, he had a mind of his own through sheer cerebral volume. If it weren't for the terrifying form his necromancer had given him, he would have fit excellently among the Islington student body—it was a truly unfortunate case of nature vs. suture. "Yes. The orb had such a terrible effect on me. I could hardly hear myself think. I—"

He suddenly broke off, his body seizing up. Purple mist emanated from his body and Bones's eyes widened as he realized what was happening. With his necromancer uninterested in keeping him alive any longer, Pennington the Zombie was losing the life force that animated him.

But that was where Bones could step in.

He placed his hand on Pennington's chest. Bones's magic wound its way through Pennington's body, granting new strength to dead flesh and rotting organs and repairing the significant damage done by Karn's fists.

"That should do it," Bones said. "I've given you enough energy to go off on your own now."

Pennington the Zombie blinked as his multi-brain mind returned to consciousness. He glanced down at his body, his already impressive muscles now enhanced by necromantic might far greater than anything he'd felt before. "This is unbelievable. It feels like an entirely different body. Same mind, though. I'm still Pennington. At least, I think I am. I received some conflicting information. I'm Pennington, aren't I?"

Karn and Bones glanced at each other. Having just met both the Penningtons, they had no real way to answer that question. Pennington the Necromancer certainly seemed like the kind of guy who would necromantically enslave his brother.

"You know, you can be whoever you want to be," Karn replied. "I know you were born yesterday, but it's never too late to start living your best life!"

"I think I'm Pennington, therefore, I am Pennington!' Pennington declared. Unfortunately for poor Pennington, his triumphant grin never left his eyes. His four eyes twinkled with excitement and enthusiasm, but his cheeks had not been stitched for grinning and no matter how happy he was, all he could do was bare his sharpened teeth and twisted, mottled tongue.

"Well, this is great," Karn declared. But his smile faded as he glanced around. "Wait a second. Where did everyone go? I was going to tell them to watch our circus in exchange for saving them!"

Bones stared at the wooden gate leading back to campus. "If I had to guess, they probably took cover."

Pennington's four eyes were downcast. "You know, the scholars of Islington are known for their calm and reason. I'm sure if you two explain what happened, they'll see you for the innocent entertainers you are. However, I was used to intimidate and terrify them, so perhaps it would be for the best if we went our separate ways."

"Well, I don't know about that, either," Bones hastily replied. From what he could tell, Pennington seemed like a cool guy, and at the moment, their circus only had four people, including him. With so few employees, he didn't think he could afford a twenty-five percent attrition rate.

A cough echoed from the work table.

It was a masterful, attention-getting cough, somehow indubitably polite yet also bizarrely carrying a way to gather everyone's focus while maintaining plausible deniability.

A voice oily enough to singlehandedly start a bonfire called out to them. "Ah. My terrifying yet undeniably effective saviors. Perhaps I can help you smooth things over with the Islington campus. I promise it will only cost you a tiny, little bit…"

Chapter Seventeen

Bones stared at the man, his eyes widening with recognition as he saw past the bizarre disguise. Unfortunately, Bones mostly remembered Sir Francis Baskerville for trying to steal his soul and fleeing in terror after he'd failed. Social niceties like the demon's name and title escaped him at the moment.

Sir Francis smiled, nervously licking his thin lips with a forked, serpentine tongue. "Ah. It seems like you recognize me. You know, you seemed like a kind, thoughtful, and considerate man the first time I met you…"

"Um. You're…Frank. Frank Baskerville."

Sir Francis was unsure of where to even begin correcting Bones. In the end, he settled for saying his full name with an equal amount of grievance on every syllable. "That's *Sir Francis Baskerville* to you. But don't take it personally. It's *Sir Francis* to everyone. *Sir Professor Francis Baskerville* when in Islington. Keep the order of the titles in mind. I was a knight before I was a professor."

As he spoke, he pulled back his long, black cloak, revealing his fine, red clothes with all their decorative ruffles. He patted himself down, maintaining shocking dignity for a man who'd been brainwashed just moments before.

"Wait. You're a professor here?" Bones was extremely surprised to hear that. Islington University was known for its science. He hadn't known they'd had a magical curriculum. "You know, Sofia was talking to me about finding a magic professor. I know this might be a weird question, but do you know if someone could accidentally kill a bunch of people with their magical power without knowing it?'

Sir Francis's forehead wrinkled as he barely suppressed a shiver at the thought of Bones's magic. "Without knowing it, huh? I mean…accidents do happen, I suppose, but you would probably find out what happened eventually. I suggest you practice your magic a little more, just to be safe. And just so you know, I don't teach literal magic here. I teach economics."

Sofia and Patches had said the same thing about practicing his magic.

It seemed like there was no easy way out, no magic word that would tell Bones he would always be safe to be around or that he was innocent of what had happened back at his family manor. He would simply have to work hard every day to feel confident in himself.

"So, um, what happened to you, Sir Francis? Did Angelo get you?" Bones asked.

Sir Francis gnashed his sharp, black teeth. "Well. Have you ever heard the saying that world leaders hellbent on world domination aren't very focused on good local governance?"

"Um…no. I haven't heard that saying before," Bones replied.

"That's because I just made it up myself. Pretty catchy, isn't it? It explains everything that's going wrong with this barony," Sir Francis replied, growing increasingly animated by the moment. His clawed, black fingers seemed to sketch out charts and graphs in the air as his words tumbled faster and faster in a stampede of circumlocution. "Look at the declining roads, the ever-increasing number of bandits, why, even esteemed professors like myself are being kidnapped. Angelo's ambitions do not extend to taking care of his people, and worst of all, it's been horrible for my businesses, absolutely horrible. There's nothing I hate more than a slow decline. When things are going great, I have many investments in many companies. When things suddenly plummet to rock bottom, that's the perfect time to sign the desperate to long and exploitative contracts. But a slow and steady decline…why, there's nothing worse. All these fools seem to think that they are just one lucky break from prosperity again, no matter how many downward graphs I show them."

"Oh. Um. Yes. I see," Bones replied, not seeing at all. He nodded in a manner identical to most of Professor Baskerville's other beleaguered students. "So, uh, what does this have to do with how you got caught?"

"Ah. Sorry about that. I'm in professor mode right now, you see. But I suppose you aren't my usual captive audience. I'll do my best to make it brief. In short, I was busy manipulating circumstances from afar, sending my associate Charlotte to help Karn recover his body in time. If either the students or that artist turned into Baron Angelo, that might have spelled disaster for the realm. But since I was so farsighted, I didn't see what was right in front of me. Before I realized, that two-bit necromancer you just dealt with had seen through my disguise and slapped me with a pair of chains from that abominable control orb."

Karn grinned. He wasn't surprised Sir Francis knew who he was. *Everyone* was supposed to know who he was. "Wow. So *you* were the one who helped find my body?"

"Of course. Why, you owe your very existence to me. Or, well, perhaps not your existence, but at least your fleshly existence. Who do you think sent the transportation?" Sir Francis smugly replied. "And those services will continue if you allow me to join this circus troupe you were just talking about."

"Wait. You want to join us?" Bones asked.

"Why, of course! A talented group of performers like yourselves…it would be the honor of my life to work by your side. I mean, I already have had a successful stint as a professor. I'm sure I can apply my prodigious talents to clowning around." Sir Francis's voice grew ever oilier with every syllable. Bones, Karn, and even Pennington were utterly captivated, their minds moving on a smooth and frictionless ride towards giving Sir Francis exactly what he wanted.

"Well, I must say, this man was a good professor," Pennington added. "He did his best to protect the students from Pe—ah, from the necromancer who created me." Having declared himself Pennington, the zombie was determined to accomplish great deeds both physical and intellectual from here on out, thereby leaving his creator in the dustbin of history.

"Why, yes," said Sir Francis, "I'm certain that as your circus grows, you will have an increasing need for my expertise and services. I mean, the taxes alone are a nightmare.

Do you know how difficult it is without the tallyman coming to tell you precisely how much you owe? And you already know about my skills in acquiring transportation. And then there comes the hidden parts of entrepreneurship. Why, I could summon legions of paid recommenders to travel the realm singing your praises. Hire audience members who can stand in the crowd and glare at those who don't cheer fast enough. Perhaps if a critique grows a bit too mouthy, a nice assassination will be just what is needed. There's no limit to the skullduggery I could come up with."

At that moment, Sir Francis's approval rate was at its peak, but he waggled his clawed finger a bit too much as he spoke and the pasty makeup he'd caked on to hide his scales began to peel.

Karn's eyes widened, the previously pleased caveman belatedly taking note that the thing in front of them wasn't quite human.

The wind howled, blowing back Sir Francis's tall beehive wig and revealing his horns. He hurriedly put it back in its place, but he was a beat too slow for Karn, who had entered a state of constant vigilance.

"Bones…this *thing*. It's a demon! Their kind has preyed on us since the dawn of humanity." Much like magic-users, demons were very rare, but Karn's immortality meant that he had a very large set of experiences to draw on.

Sir Francis glowered at Karn, but not too much.

He couldn't believe that between Bones, Karn, and Pennington, there were three of these almighty freaks now, but that was just what he needed at a time like this. "You know, I'll kindly overlook your discrimination for now and state that I'm not looking for a contract. I'm simply hoping for a gentleman's agreement."

"What kind of agreement?" Karn replied, his eyes narrowing. "You don't look like much of a gentleman to me."

"Like I said, I wish to join your troupe. I will work for free—no need for payment at all." Working for free went directly against what Sir Francis taught his economics students, but these were dire times.

"What do you get out of it?"

"Simply put, safety. I rather like having my mind free of those chains. Baron Angelo and his pet necromancers are an unfortunate thorn in my side, and with your troupe, there will be safety in numbers. Why, to show my value, I'll give you three a free sample of what having a man like me around could do for you." He pointed at Pennington. "I've already come up with the perfect defense for this young man. His black reputation is no fault of his own. It was because of that nefarious control orb. If it comes to a court of law, I've already come up with two airtight legal defenses: temporary insanity to start things off, and if that doesn't work, I'll end my argument with an accusation of child neglect. Why, what would you do without my silver tongue?" At the end of his speech, Sir Francis nervously licked his lips, revealing a tongue that was forked rather than silver.

Karn remained unconvinced. Sir Francis didn't know his audience. He used too many obscure words for Karn's liking, and the caveman was getting more irritated with every syllable. "How many souls have you captured over the years? I say if you want to join our circus, you need to first let them go."

Sir Francis indignantly threw up his hands. "Why...this is pure stereotyping! I'm just a humble economics professor trying to share my business knowledge. The only thing I've been capturing is my students' attention!"

That blatantly false statement ripped Bones out of the reverie created by Sir Francis's marketing skills. "Wait. You said you had a lot of souls the last time we spoke. Back then, your experience was a selling point...and now that I'm thinking about it, I can sense the number of souls bound to you right now."

Sir Francis froze mid-retort. His highly analytical mind promptly conducted a cost-benefit analysis, which he considered a significantly more advanced version of the pros and cons lists used by everyday idiots. In the end, Sir Francis decided that while he'd spent a great deal of time collecting his beloved portfolio of souls, it wouldn't do him any good if he was enslaved again. "Ah. Well. What I mean to say is that my experience in captivity taught me just how badly I was treating others. I had already intended to dismiss my portfolio as soon as I was freed. I had simply forgotten to in all the chaos. Heh. Silly me."

His hands glowed, generating a pillar of sickly-yellow flame. The flames burnt bright, then faded, replaced by sheaths of contracts that blossomed onto the demon's scaly hands. Sir Francis gave them one last longing look, then he pulled a long peacock quill from his pocket. "Allow me to sign some autographs. There's quite a bit I need to get through. Hopefully, this doesn't give me carpal tunnel."

"Give you what?" Bones asked. He hadn't taken Islington University's highly popular speculative medicine course, Ailments of the Future.

But Sir Francis didn't hear him. He had already begun signing, scribbling his peacock quill across the contracts with furious speed. In the past, Sir Francis had rarely freed anyone from soul servitude, and so to mark the occasion, he finished every signature with a wide, dashing flourish, bringing back his arm as if it were a wing.

But that gesture quickly became tiring, so he moved on to a simple yet effective scrawl.

Forty contracts later, he was no longer writing in cursive, and twenty contracts after that, he kept only the "Sir" while adding his initials, signing as "Sir F.B."

That was about as far as he was willing to simplify it, but as he continued working and as his wrist continued aching, he thought he would have to drop his beloved title. Thankfully, the last contract came before the last of his dignity crumbled.

Soon, Sir Francis was surrounded by trembling papers slowly tearing themselves into confetti.

As the contracts were destroyed, all of Sir Francis's victims were summoned at once to regain their freedom. It was as if the world itself began to shriek as a menagerie of freed souls paraded themselves before the troupe—demons with fanciful crowns of horns, ghosts that looked like little more than white sheets, and women with long, unkempt hair and obscured faces. Next came mewling spectral cats, chittering ghostly spiders, and eerily hooting ectoplasmic owls that all skittered off into the distance. The greatest portion, of course, were the freed human souls. There was a whole host of them from over a century of collecting. Some were dressed in the same kind of fanciful outfits as Sir Francis, whereas more modern members of the nobility were dressed in modern wear. Plenty were serfs with simple cloaks and tunics, but all had shocked and joyous expressions on their faces.

Forcing a grin onto his scaly face, Sir Francis waved them goodbye, then winced and clutched the wrist of his battered hand. "You are free now…through my infinite generosity and *significant* physical sacrifice…"

Many of the souls wanted to tell off Sir Francis for his sheer shamelessness, but they thought better of it. After all, talking with the demon was how they'd landed themselves in such trouble in the first place.

But though most of the souls fled, a single one remained.

The grass beside the river rustled and then a familiar carriage burst into existence. This time, it was pulled by two muscular lionesses, their faces filled with almost jarring expressions of admiration and worship as they stared adoringly at the tall, spectral figure in the cab.

"Oh. It's you, Sir Francis. I was wondering what had happened. You haven't given me a job since you made me take that lot to the cave."

"Well, Charlotte, that lot is right in front of us," Sir Francis said. "Thanks to their generous request, you are now free! Our contract has been terminated."

Charlotte stared down at them from the carriage cab, her veiled face turning first from Sir Francis and then to Bones, Karn, and Pennington, whom she observed with somewhat more curiosity, having never seen him before.

"So I'm free now?" she asked. Bones expected her to jump, cheer, and celebrate, but she just shrugged. "Well, that's nice. My friends and I had a good time carrying you around, so if you need anything else, just give me a shout!"

"Wait!" Sir Francis cried, quickly recognizing the problems with free will. "Wait! Please! I was hoping you would join this group and give them transportation. You seemed to like them the last time we spoke about it."

"Well, I mean, that could be fun…" Charlotte mused. Though she had immense charms, allowing her to befriend almost any animal in existence, Charlotte herself was also easily swayed—which was how she'd fallen into her transportation services contract with Sir Francis in the first place.

She glanced down at the lionesses, who let out a long purr and kneaded her body against Charlotte's leg. Like most of Charlotte's outdoor companions, they liked it when she had a job, as it meant seeing her more often.

"I mean, it should be all right," Charlotte said. "And, Bones, I apologize for leaving you without a word before. My old contract forbade me from talking to outside clients." Sir Francis had claimed that their non-disclosure clause had been because he hadn't wanted his plans leaking. In reality, like most employers who discouraged conversations about wages and working conditions, he simply hadn't wanted Charlotte to know how badly she'd been ripped off.

"That's great!" Bones exclaimed.

"Well, something does give me pause…" Charlotte admitted. Her voice trailed off disapprovingly as she stared at Karn. Though the coachwoman's face was obscured by a black veil, Bones could imagine her eyes narrowing. Belatedly, he realized that it probably wasn't a good idea to have a man in animal skins around when trying to appeal to an animal lover. He gulped nervously. "Um, you know, we're planning to get some new circus uniforms soon. Uh, I mean, perhaps you could benefit as well. You know, an even scarier cloak or something like that…"

Charlotte didn't respond, but the lionesses did.

They gently nudged themselves from their stirrups before frolicking in front of Karn like they were housecats.

"Wow. I've never seen my friends befriend someone else so quickly before," Charlotte said.

"Oh, it happens all the time." Karn grinned. "These animals can recognize a fellow apex predator. Though normally, I have to give them a thorough beating first. Looks like your friends are smarter than the rest."

He knelt and began petting them awkwardly. Just like with humans, Karn had spent most of his life killing rather than befriending animals, but long after the rest of the world had developed civilization, he was finally in his civilized era.

"I suppose if my friends want to join, I better get with the times. I'll call the rest of them later. Let them know that we've gone legitimate. We're not working for a demon anymore— we're joining a circus instead!"

The wooden gate creaked as Sofia tentatively poked her head outside.

After having been sent away, she'd heard about the dramatic necromantic duel from the fleeing students. But now, Karn and Achille were standing there with the spectral coachwoman, the four-armed zombie they'd fought, and strangest of all, an Islington professor.

"Achille?" she called. "Just what is going on?"

Bones didn't even know where to begin. "Um…well, I guess with the addition of another trio, we're a troupe now?"

His explanation only triggered more questions.

"How did any of this happen? Are we safe now? Everyone else has taken cover in the buildings. Professor Roman said he saw Pennington flying through the sky like a shooting star!"

"No, he jumped into the river," Bones said.

"*I* am Pennington," Pennington insisted.

"*What?*"

Sir Francis smiled. "Well, this is what you lot need me for. As a respected member of the Islington staff, I will be able to smooth *everything* over."

Chapter Eighteen

With Sofia by their side, the newly formed troupe pushed their way back into the courtyard. Charlotte drifted dreamily through the air, floating a full two feet off the ground. It was only her contract with Sir Francis that had compelled her to disguise her ghostly nature. The cloak flapped ominously beneath her, making it clear that she was no longer touching the ground.

But for once, Sofia had bigger concerns than investigating the supernatural. She eyed the heavily made-up Sir Francis before discreetly nudging Bones. "Achille…how do you know Professor Baskerville?"

"Oh. He, um, showed up outside our cottage. The same day we met Karn, actually, just much earlier in the day."

"What? An Islington professor came to visit us and you didn't tell me?"

"Um, well, he was definitely looking for me at the time…"

"Yes, yes," Sir Francis agreed, his ears twitching as he eavesdropped on their conversation. "I most definitely did not visit your cottage under my capacity as a professor. I'm sure that visiting our students' homes is likely a violation of some human resource agreement or another."

"So what exactly *were* you doing there?" Sofia asked.

"Erm…well…let's just call it 'extracurricular activities'…"

Bones knew that there was no chance of Sofia dropping her line of inquiry. "Basically, Sir Francis is a demon."

Sofia was even more shocked. "What? A *demon* came to visit us and you didn't tell me?"

"I did tell you! You just didn't believe in them!"

"I wish I still didn't." Sofia groaned. "Life was a lot more peaceful before I opened my mind."

She eyed Sir Francis cautiously, her common-sense dislike of demons battling with her respect for Islington's professors. In the end, she settled on polite silence.

Though Sofia had only recently come to believe in the supernatural, she was increasingly realizing that her beloved Achille, far from being a naïve baby bird, was actually a very responsible and reliable figure in his own right. He had handled an entire second world without any assistance from her. If Achille had accepted this demon, perhaps she should too.

After walking past the stone garden, they found themselves inside a mostly empty courtyard. Pale and frightened faces pressed themselves against seemingly every window, staring at the group with a mixture of fear and fascination. As a general rule of thumb, students didn't attend Islington without a great deal of intellectual curiosity. But having already been scared half to death by Pennington the Necromancer's power trip, the student body, as well as the vast majority of professors, was determined to avoid the fate of the cat.

Only two men were brave enough to stay in the courtyard.

The first was Archibald Roman, Professor of Physics.

Professor Roman was an uncommonly dignified-looking man—it seemed like his face was permanently set in a serious and thoughtful expression. He was almost completely bald, with only the faint hint of shortly cropped red hair on each side of his head. His eyes were hidden by square spectacles with tinted lenses. Ever since a childhood accident during which he'd tried playing with a stove, he'd had an extreme sensitivity to bright light.

Roman had remained outside because despite his austere appearance, he was completely and utterly foolhardy. The strange chills around Bones, the blazing heat around Sir Francis, Pennington's bizarre body, Karn's glowing stitches, and Charlotte's eerie resemblance to a grim reaper…he found every single one of those things to be fascinating quirks and eccentricities.

The man beside him could not have been more different. Octavius Arial, the famed creator of the post office and Professor of Psychology.

Professor Arial was a thin and spindly man with a drooping mustache and an even more drooping frown. He nervously twined his fingers into knots as he stared at the approaching troupe, occasionally taking the time to play with the golden badge on his chest, which displayed a human brain beside a magnifying glass. The man was almost impossibly pale-skinned, even paler than Bones, and he carried a massive, black umbrella in his right hand, so wide that it seemed almost like a mobile roof.

Professor Arial did not want to be outside, but after the success of his post office project, he had been cajoled into doing all of Islington University's administrative work. At this point, his diligence was more or less the only thing keeping the school afloat. After being forced to work outside at zombiepoint, Professor Arial wanted nothing more than to take a nap in his beloved office. He was here simply because he knew the school's insurance policy required multiple witnesses to any reported incident. As terrified as Professor Arial was, he was even more terrified of Islington University's potential insolvency.

Bones stared at the two professors and raised his hand in an ineffective gesture. "We, um, come in peace?"

"We're, uh, entertainers," Karn agreed. "And while he might not have experience with it, Pennington's arms can be used to help people."

"I'm Pennington now," Pennington helpfully added.

Sir Francis stepped forward. "Ah. Allow me to explain what happened."

"P-Professor Baskerville," Arial stammered. "I…um… Well, it's good to hear you talking again. You seemed under the weather recently."

"Ah, yes. I was fighting a severe case of brainwashing."

"'Brainwashing'?" Professor Arial asked.

"Yes. That Yesse was a real bad egg. With all his necromancy advertisements, Baron Angelo wasn't just looking for men to join his dark trade. He wanted henchmen who displayed the dark triad."

Despite himself, Professor Arial giggled. He did enjoy a good psychology joke. "Well…I'm glad you're free."

"Again, I must stress that it's all thanks to these good people," Sir Francis declared, waving his hand generously at the rest of the troupe. "They were my saviors. It was a close fight, but they sent that brat Yesse Pennington packing. As for Pennington the Zombie over here, he had the same grievous affliction I did. He is more than willing to make amends."

"Very much so," Pennington agreed. "What better than a man with four arms to help make up for all the damage done? Though I have to ask, aren't you guys worried about Baron Angelo himself coming? I mean, you disposed of his henchman."

Bones nodded. He didn't know much about politics, but common sense dictated that Angelo would be upset about Yesse's overthrow.

"We should just find Angelo and kick his ass ahead of time. Back in my day, pre-emptive strikes were the premier military strategy." Karn grinned.

The professors winced at the open treason.

Sir Francis wanted to criticize Karn for his caveman's understanding of politics, but even his blackened and shriveled heart realized that would be unfair. "Unfortunately, Karn, politics has become much stupider since your time. Common men like us can't go after nobles even if they did something wrong. What we need is to get *other* nobles on their side. Have the students write their fathers, telling them what Angelo's man did. Angelo might be one of the duke's favorites, but there are students with relatives of even higher stature. I'm sure he will try to evade responsibility, to disavow his servant, but over time, we will erode his political support."

Professor Roman nodded eagerly. He was much more experienced with letter-writing campaigns than military campaigns.

But Professor Arial was still nervous. "Well, it would be nice for justice to be served, but our *real* problem is the funding. The school is broke. And I doubt Angelo will pay us anymore after we get rid of his education advisor. Perhaps one of these nobles will fund us in his stead, but it will take a long time for the money to be delivered and there's plenty of desperate bandits roaming the roads."

"Ah, thankfully, I have secured the school an immediate cash infusion. You see, I've joined a circus recently! Of course, I'll still be available for remote work and lectures."

Professor Arial blinked. "I'm sorry? Your plan to make money for the school is that you individually joined a circus? Your salary might not fund a single day of operations."

Sir Francis laughed merrily. "No, of course not. You see, the circus is looking for products we can provide. They've come to Islington looking for costumes just like the ones in our drama department."

Bones paused. "Wait. I don't think I told you about that."

Sir Francis chuckled. "Oh, Bones. I know you wanted me to know about that. Why else would you talk about it in your home? You know I have eyes and ears everywhere."

"Um…no, I didn't know that."

"Well, you should have! And anyway, I know just the costumes we need," Sir Francis said, speaking with so much confidence, he swept everyone up in the excitement.

Injecting himself into a transaction and skimming off the top was one of the demon's most successful business practices. As the self-proclaimed Islington University bursar *and* the self-proclaimed business manager of the troupe, Sir Francis found himself in a rare position, negotiating on both sides of the deal.

Normally, he couldn't have dreamed up a better scam than this, but for once, he was in the unique position of wanting both organizations to succeed instead of simply trying to enrich himself. Sir Francis needed Bones and the troupe for safety and he loved teaching on its own merits. The ability to grade his students on whether or not they'd listened to him closely enough was beyond magnificent.

"You see, Professor Arial, this particular circus requires specialized products. As a fire-eater, Karn must wear a costume that does not burn. Pennington needs sturdy fabric that can stretch with his massive muscles. Charlotte's dear animals must have outfits that are adorable and durable in equal measure. And why, with Bones around, our costumes must keep everyone warm in all conditions while remaining lightweight enough for performances. Only Islington's department can design such wonderous costumes."

The rest of the troupe couldn't help but agree. Not even the exceedingly responsible Sofia had thought of all these minor details.

"And don't forget about the tent! Why, with the help of the physics and engineering departments, I'm sure we can design a tent that is a true marvel. Some grand device that can fold up perfectly for traveling. Of course, we will need the hands of Rustling to build these marvels, but surely, the school can be paid for their part in creating such wondrous designs."

"Yes. A very big tent," Karn agreed. "But not so big that I can't see my fans."

"I have many friends who will want to perform with us," Charlotte chimed in. "So we need something even bigger than what the Great Circus had."

"So let me get this straight," Sofia asked, stepping in at the perfect time. She was far inferior to Sir Francis in business sense, but she at least had some idea of what was going on. "Islington will provide the designs and Rustling will make them. And we will pay both parties a fair amount?"

"Yes, exactly," Sir Francis replied. "A triple win. The school gets a cash infusion, the Rustling economy is stimulated by your work, and we get our costumes. Why, with me here, everyone is winning at world historical levels. Now all that's left is for Charlotte to take us to Rustling. A tailor will take our measurements and then both sides will work together to create the perfect designs."

"I like the sound of that. Follow me back to the carriage."

As the troupe walked back towards the river, Bones peeled off to draw a picture of the backflipping cat over the tent, pinning it on the school noticeboard. The professors had no idea what it was but didn't comment. Bones had saved the university from both slavery and insolvency, and after their sordid experience with Pennington the Necromancer, this felt like a much less sinister inexplicable symbol.

Meanwhile, Sofia whispered to Charlotte. "Wait. Now that you're free from your contract, can you tell us how you teleport?"

Charlotte gazed back down at her and her veil dipped in a way that made it clear she was winking. "Trade secret still, sorry. And besides, with such a short distance to cross, we should just do a normal trip." She reached into the pocket of her black cloak and pulled out a wondrous horn the likes of which nobody had ever seen before. The glimmering, rainbow-colored instrument was a mess of fur, scales, and feathers, constructed in a dogged effort to make every animal feel included.

When she raised the horn to her lips and blew, the whole troupe felt a strange tug that resonated throughout their bodies. The horn's primal command reminded some deep part of them that at the end of the day, they too were animals.

After just a few minutes, the grass growing around the school rustled, and two horses emerged, galloping towards the carriage.

On the surface, they looked much like horses Bones had seen before, but Charlotte's were bigger and more powerful, better cared for in a way that was obvious even to Bones's uninitiated eyes. Their carefully groomed coats gleamed in the sun and their manes were even more elegant than normal, trailing fashionably to the side of their heads almost like noblewomen's braids.

The horses stopped just beneath the eastern archway, staring at the group hesitantly, flicking their tails from side to side. Bones and Pennington were obviously terrifying, but Sir Francis also had a strange, discomfiting smell to him. The horses got the feeling that they would burst into flame if they stepped too close.

But with Charlotte there, they couldn't resist.

"Oh, come on over!" she cooed. "They won't hurt you. Everything will be fine."

She smiled gently as she placed the horses in the harness and the troupe loaded themselves into the spacious carriage.

Meanwhile, Professor Arial got to work, rounding up the required departments and putting them to work creating new designs. Not only that, he spoke with the wealthiest students on campus, playing up their already rightful grievance at Pennington's actions. The rich kids wrote very angry letters to their fathers, explaining just what had happened and mentioning Baron Angelo's name many times.

But Sir Francis had misread Baron Angelo, missing a key part of the baron's retraining platform: his focus on short-term financial speculation. Sir Francis had erroneously believed that the baron was simply planning on borrowing money and not paying people back, a proven financial strategy for individuals with friends in high places.

In reality, it was because Baron Angelo thought he was finally ready for his necromantic conquest.

He just wanted to squeeze as much money out of the system as possible before embarking on his childhood dream of becoming the Deathless Prince. If Angelo had known what was happening, he would have struck at Islington University immediately to snuff out any survivors who might inform the other nobles of his schemes.

Of course, the only man who wanted to tell Angelo what had happened was currently old and shriveled, barely kept alive by his necromantic magic as the river violently carried him out to sea. It would take a good deal of time before Pennington returned to his master.

Meanwhile, blissfully unaware of their impending confrontation, Bones and his troupe set out for their costumes.

Chapter Nineteen

With Pennington defeated and the campus convinced of their safety again, Islington University, once eerily quiet even with the sun high in the sky, returned to its usual comforting hustle and bustle. As the carriage rode off, the troupe heard the more passionate students arguing vigorously about this or that theory as the lazier ones argued with even greater vigor that Pennington forcing them to work at his necromantic assembly line merited a several-day extension on their projects and papers.

As the carriage pulled past Professor Arial's absurd post office, the horses swerving around the legs with peerless accuracy, Sir Francis turned to Sofia. "So, you grew up in Rustling, is that correct?" His voice was seemingly casual, but in reality, Sir Francis was trying to gather information on yet another scheme to save Islington's dwindling fortunes.

"Yes, I am," Sofia replied, her fear of demons battling with her desire to respect an Islington professor.

"What are the people like?" Sir Francis replied, leaning in with keen interest.

Sofia paused.

She suddenly felt *much* too hot, the heat blazing so abruptly that she felt lightheaded. This was not due to any romantic attraction to the demon—it was a literal overabundance of heat.

"Pennington, do you mind switching spaces with me?"

"Sure."

Sofia slid over and abruptly felt better again. Now that she was equidistant between Achille and Sir Francis, the necromancer's chilling aura perfectly canceled Sir Francis's internal demonic fire. "Ah. That's better. Sorry about that."

"No offense taken at all," Sir Francis lied. "So…how are the people in Rustling?"

"The town has supported Islington from the shadows for a long time. The people living there have a lot of technical skills—you know, tailoring, blacksmithing, glasswork. I'm glad I attended Islington, but I'm equally glad it was a correspondence course. The snobbery could be a bit much at times."

"I see. Technical skills, eh? So, you would say most people in Rustling work a trade?"

"Well, there're also farmers and chefs. And since we're so close to the Sun Beam River, we farm rice instead of the usual grain. It's not as common in the barony, but there're plenty of foreign scholars who prefer it."

"Ah, yes, the farmers." Sir Francis chuckled. "You know, just a few weeks ago, before that two-bit necromancer's little power trip, the students were talking about trying to farm their own rice to save money."

Sofia raised an eyebrow and suppressed a chuckle. "Really?"

"Yes, they said that Islington was near the river as well. Of course, that all fell apart when they realized only one in every hundred of them had ever worked a day in the fields before."

This talk of rice made Karn hungry. After rediscovering his love for eating, he was eager to rediscover it again. "How is the cooking at Islington?"

"Terrible." Sir Francis scoffed. "The cafeteria is just miserable. For a while, the school required students to take turns cooking for each other, and the brats were about as abominable at it as you would imagine. There was a solid spectrum from inedible to poisonous. Half the students just order food delivered from Rustling and the other half order it from even more far-flung locations."

"Rustling has good food, huh? Well, I can't wait to try it when we get there."

"Do you even need to eat?" Sir Francis asked. "My information told me that you were immortal."

"Well, if I don't, I'll miss it. And Bones has bought me food before."

"Need and want are two very different things," Sir Francis replied. "Think about it, Karn. If we get costumes and a tent, that will be a big investment. I'm not sure our little company can afford to splurge on benefits like food."

"Well, I mean, we can afford to pay…" Bones interjected.

"Can you?" Sir Francis asked. "What revenues has this little circus generated so far?"

Bones had a reasonable vocabulary, but he'd never heard that word before. It didn't naturally come up when he was stuck in the cottage. "What are revenues?"

"Money. The amount of money you earn!" Sir Francis hissed. He glanced furtively around the carriage, scowling. The road was quiet, without a spirit to be seen, but Sir Francis nervously adjusted his disguise wig as he continued searching for any eavesdroppers.

"Um, is everything all right?" Bones asked.

"Well, I must team up with you for safety reasons, but I admit, I do fear the mockery of other demons. I can just imagine that hornless freak Platinumspoon cackling once he finds out I've teamed up with a business lackwit. It's enough to make me hope he manifests in this barony so that Angelo can get him first."

"It's not all bad," Bones replied. "We might not have made money yet, but we did get to stay at the inn when we performed."

"Yeah, and we got food too," Karn added.

"Room and board. With no earnings," Sir Francis replied. "At this rate, your troupe is little more than a group of dancing hobos. Which, I suppose, is better than murder hobos, but not by much. Until our troupe becomes solvent, we must remain a low overhead business, and that means using our competitive advantages. Karn, Charlotte, and Pennington must all go on a hunger strike until the circus becomes profitable."

Charlotte heard her name and briefly glanced back from the cab. "What are you talking about?"

"Oh, nothing. Just business talk," Sir Francis replied.

"All right," Charlotte replied, turning back around again. She looked forward to joining the circus but was rather disappointed to find out that Sir Francis would still go on his long tirades about business. The only business Charlotte found interesting was monkey business.

"I will say, though, Bones…I might make a tycoon out of you yet." Sir Francis cackled. "Free undead workers…your powers are brilliant. There's nothing like it!"

"I guess it's a wonder more failing businesses don't turn to the dark arts," Bones muttered.

"Oh, they try," Sir Francis replied. If he'd still had his contracts, he would have waved them. There'd been plenty of saved businesses and damned souls back in his heyday. "I'm telling you, Bones…if you had a single mean bone in your body, you could dominate the world."

"I don't know about that. Dominating the world doesn't sound like a good way to make friends."

"You can *force* them to be your friends. With me by your side, I could get you a stack of Mandatory Friendship contracts in moments. Everyone will be forced to watch your circus!"

"That doesn't sound like a very good basis for friendship," Bones dubiously replied. "And besides, even if I took over the world, I don't think I would be able to run it. It sounds…complicated. Even getting these costumes sounds like a huge headache."

Sir Francis groaned. "Oh, the incorruptible ones are always the most boring. But just you wait, kid. With me by your side, you'll understand the dark magic of business soon enough."

As the carriage rounded the crossroads, the troupe found themselves on a thin and narrow road, the beaten path maintained only by the footsteps of Rustling's villagers as they made their way to Islington to sell their wares.

Halfway along the narrow road, they passed by the discomfiting site of a burnt and blackened clearing littered with stray arrows and discarded weapons.

"What do you think happened here?" Sofia whispered, fearing for her family.

"Seems like some kind of fight," Karn said. "Do you think it was the baron you guys are always talking about?"

"A fight between two bandit gangs, most likely," Sir Francis replied. His eyes narrowed as he saw a shield marked with a familiar coat of arms: a roaring lion standing above a sword. "That shield was taken from Baron Angelo's storehouse. That's his mark. If I had to guess, these brigands were once his soldiers." The demon sneered. "Talk about excellent leadership. At this rate, the feudal system is becoming more of a futile system. Infuriating a bunch of violent, armed men by refusing to pay them… Great idea, Angelo! That's never led to instability at all!"

But if there were bandits, they didn't dare attack the carriage. The terrifying aura emanating from within was enough to paralyze beast or man.

The horses brought them directly to the town of Rustling. Most of the town had been obscured by a hastily constructed barricade of sloped mud and dirt, with a swinging wooden fence in the middle. Only the tallest rice plants poked out over the top of the roughshod wall.

Sofia frowned. "That wasn't there when I grew up."

A voice suddenly cried out to them—reedy and scratchy on the surface, yet strong and determined underneath. "Halt! Halt! Who goes there—stop your carriage at once!"

Beside Bones, Sofia jolted in surprise, but he had no time to ask her what was happening, as a dozen guardsmen suddenly stepped out from behind the barricade. The villagers were dirty and unkempt, with mud and dirt splattered all over their faces and haircuts so bad that it seemed like the village barber must have been kidnapped.

They wore slapdash armor that was little more than wooden planks awkwardly bundled together and their weapons were similarly improvised. Some carried knives and pitchforks, while others had slings or bows, but the crude weapons looked like they were meant for hunting rabbits, not fighting humans. Two of them had spears, but even then, they looked like little more than daggers loosely tied to sticks.

Although the village guard were all armed with shoddy gear, their eyes were keen and alert. They had a level of preparedness that could only come from actually having been attacked before.

As Charlotte pulled the carriage to a halt, Sir Francis cried out. "We're from the university!"

That did not help matters.

The Rustling villagers had seen the posters advertising necromancy plastered all over campus and Pennington's and Karn's blatantly zombie-like appearances did very little to assuage their doubts.

One of the men broke off from the pack. "Stay still. I'll inspect you." Due to the speaker's strangely weak voice, Bones immediately knew it was the man who had shouted at them earlier. He was about six feet tall, with a fierce expression on his face that Bones found strangely familiar. His hair was thin and frayed, a strange mixture of red and white strands that alternated on his head almost like a zebra's stripes.

"Keep your hands up. We've been dealing with bandits recently and we've heard rumors of worse," he said. But when he looked into the carriage, he stammered in surprise. "W-Wait. Grandma? What are you doing here?"

Chapter Twenty

Despite the circumstances, Sir Francis never passed up an opportunity for flattery. It was one of the most statistically successful methods of emotional manipulation and in-group ingratiation. "'Grandma'? Why, Sofia, you look far too young to be a grandma."

Sofia ignored him. She had bigger concerns, like why her hometown had suddenly become militarized.

"William, what's going on?" Sofia asked. "I saw that burned-down field earlier too. Did something happen?"

William stared back at her, his face slowly recovering from his shock. "Like I said, bandits. And there were rumors of darker things from Islington. A large monster was seen shambling around the campus. It's…"

He abruptly trailed off as he saw a large monster that fit that very description sitting inside the carriage. As William slowly scanned the group, he wasn't sure what he was most shocked by: the presence of his grandma or the group that surrounded her. William, like all members of Sofia's family, had their matriarch's courage and aversion to the supernatural, but this was all a *bit* too much.

Considering the eldritch context, he was rightfully suspicious of Sofia as well.

William thought quickly, improvising a security question on the fly. "Grandma, what happened to me when I was five?"

Sofia blinked, but her confusion lasted only for a moment. "Ah. You got sick with a horrific case of pneumonia. And I suppose it's good to be suspicious, William. We've dealt with bandits and darker things too."

One of those darker things chose that moment to pipe up. Sir Francis had only joined Islington University as a cover, but the more he'd taught, the more he'd realized his passion for it. "Your security is weak, my boy. If it were me, I could have guessed that just from listening to your voice. You need to ask more difficult questions. Childhood nicknames and the like."

Sir Francis's generous advice further convinced William that the troupe weren't infiltrators. Truth be told, Pennington alone looked like he removed any need for subterfuge.

"Trust me, William," said Sofia. "We're just here to buy food and supplies from the village. Bones is starting a circus and these are his fellow performers. If anything happens when we're here, this crew should be able to deal with your bandit problem. I can vouch for Achille and Karn especially."

"Oh. So, this is Achille, huh?" William asked, eyeing him. The pale-faced figure in the carriage certainly fit his grandmother's description of Achille—he was, indeed, a strange young man with a fondness for circuses. Like Sofia, William was able to ignore the necromantic chill surrounding Bones's body, but he still felt it. "Well, if it's you two, come into town, then. And, you're right. Looking at your group, I doubt any bandits are going to want to mess with them. I'm almost hoping they attack right now."

Normally, letting in a group of monsters to protect oneself from other monsters was one of the riskiest gambits in civilization history, a surefire way to end up stuck with the greater of two evils—but rarely were those monsters led by the decision maker's grandma.

He turned and nodded at the men manning the barricade. "This should be good. Open the fence."

The guards remained unsure, but William had led them through worse, so they acquiesced.

It wasn't nearly as dramatic as a castle drawbridge, but with a creaky swing, the center wooden planks on either side of the piled-up mud swung open and Charlotte guided her horses through the beaten path leading into Rustling.

Haphazardly strewn huts made of thatched straw dotted the dirt between the two fields of golden rice, waiting for harvest. Unlike the centrally planned Golden Fields, it seemed like the villagers had just built their homes wherever they felt like it. Aside from the square flooded rice fields by the Sun Beam River in the background, there was no hint of central planning.

Fresh, green grass grew across the town and instead of actual roads, there were simply natural divots created by years and years of people treading along the same path.

A few of the homes had roughshod signs planted outside of them, along with a few rickety work sheds built from carved-up wooden planks. All told, Rustling was very small and simple—the major reason why Sofia had left and sought a home elsewhere after her husband had passed away. She'd felt like they could take care of things without her. There just wasn't much to take care of.

Of course, that had changed with the introduction of some very dangerous-looking individuals. As the remaining guards watched them warily, William nodded. "I'll escort them through the town, make sure nothing happens."

Two of the guards glanced at each other, then nodded and followed him. In truth, none of the three guardsmen could do anything to stop the guests if they went rogue. Pennington literally had more muscles than all of them put together. But these were farmers who had volunteered as guards to protect against bandit attacks—the sort of decision that automatically selected for exceptionally brave and dutiful individuals.

Sir Francis waved a clawed hand at the guards. "Farmers leaving their fields to take up arms… That's a leading indicator of societal collapse if I've ever seen one. When did you set up that barricade?"

"Three months ago," William hesitantly replied. "Right after the first attack happened. That was how the field burned. The next time the bandits came, they argued about whether or not to charge the wall before turning on each other."

"I see," Sir Francis replied. "I'll talk to the Islington students when I return. Perhaps they can send reinforcements."

"The Islington students will help us the gate?" William asked incredulously.

"Not personally. I meant that perhaps they could help design some additional contraptions or perhaps coax their fathers into summoning guards."

"I'm not sure we'd be able to pay for that."

"Oh, I'm sure we can arrange something. Perhaps a reduced sales price on rice," Sir Francis replied, waving his hand dismissively. "I seem to be the only man in Islington who understands the benefits of economic integration. No wonder they hired me as a professor."

Charlotte gently pulled back the reins and her horses pulled to a halt in the center of town, in a patch of muddy dirt about thirty feet away from the cluster of homes. The troupe disembarked, with Karn vaulting eagerly out of the carriage. "Ha! Time for my tent! And don't forget about the costumes, either!"

The caveman's mighty leap brought him flying straight over the baffled Islington guards.

Not to be outdone in the drama department, Sir Francis vanished in a puff of smoke and brimstone, reappearing outside the carriage one step ahead of Karn. Under normal circumstances, Sir Francis hated drawing attention to himself. He preferred ruling from the shadows, but there was just something about Karn that got under his reptilian skin and he refused to be outdone by some classless caveman.

Afraid of losing his newfound friends, Pennington leaped from the carriage as well, flying so high, he wound up grabbing on to a tree with his four mighty arms, swinging through the branches like an ape to catch up with them.

The few villagers outside hurried back inside. Despite the troupe's bizarre appearance, the presence of trusted townsfolk like William, Sofia, and the other guards helped maintain calm, but the addition of bizarre behavior pushed it over the edge.

"Good grief…scaring everyone for no reason like that. I'll make them apologize later," Sofia muttered.

"Do you think they even know where they're going?" William asked.

"Well, uh, with Sir Francis there, I'm sure they can find the tailor…" Bones replied. "He seems to be an avid shopper."

Charlotte chuckled as she fed her horses apples. "Wait for me here, if you don't mind."

Then she turned to Bones, her smile evident in her voice despite her hidden face. "With dramatic entrances like that, people are going to come to our circus very early. The more I think about it, the more excited I get. I'm sure my friends will enjoy performing."

"Honestly, this whole thing is coming together better than I could have imagined," Bones admitted.

"Of course it is." Sofia scoffed. "It's because you always anticipated failure…you never once believed in yourself. Much like William over there. He could also learn from putting himself out there."

William groaned as he heard her deliberately carrying whisper.

"I know you heard that, William. Any luck finding a wife yet?"

"Oh, w-well, I mean…" William stammered.

The men accompanying him chortled—this a familiar refrain among everyone in the town.

Though William was a strong and strapping man now, famed for his courage and leadership abilities, he had been very sickly in his youth. Until adulthood, he'd been weak, frail, and unfortunately prone to projectile vomiting at inappropriate times. Like most people, he hadn't quite escaped his childhood insecurities and he'd fumbled an unfortunate number of interested women—women who, contrary to William's expectations, thought of him as the town hero rather than as Vomit Boy.

"You're too in your own head. Remember when you thought Jolene just needed help with her garden every day?" one of the guards said.

"I could have sworn I saw Bernice checking you out the other day too," the other chuckled.

At this point, William wished it really had been bandits who'd come to attack him. At least his friends wouldn't have betrayed him to ally with the invaders.

Furiously trying to change the topic, William hurriedly pointed to a building at the far-east corner of the town, yet another combination of straw hut and wooden workshop, this one decorated with a simple wooden sign displaying a pair of shears.

"Ah, Grandma, we need to be careful when we talk to Bernard. He can provide the costumes you're looking for…but you remember how superstitious he is."

Sofia smiled. She knew just what William was doing but figured she'd embarrassed him enough. "Oh, I better save poor Bernard right away. I remember when he was a kid, he was always running around waving that alleged demon-slaying sword of his. It would break his heart if he found out it didn't actually work."

They hurried after Karn, Pennington, and Sir Francis, who, to William's and Sofia's pleasant surprise, had indeed managed to locate the tailor's shop without their help.

Karn shrugged at his animal skins, grinning. "It would be nice to get something new."

Before, Sofia had viewed Karn's immortality as impossible. But now that she'd accepted it, she couldn't believe he'd lived for so long with such a miserable standard of living. "I still can't believe you never thought to get new clothes."

"Well, I mean, these worked fine."

Sir Francis snickered. "Talk about thrifting."

"I'm pretty sure in Karn's time, it was called 'scavenging.'" Sofia chuckled. "Though speaking of which, Achille, you're well on your way to becoming the next Karn. Getting a new circus troupe outfit is the perfect opportunity for you to finally update your wardrobe," she said, eyeing his tattered, black rags.

Bones sighed. The worn-out black cloth was just too comfortable and familiar. It fit around his body in a way that not even a master tailor's new clothes could. "I just wish I could get something that felt like it was worn in. That's the problem with new clothes. You can't get them used."

"I know exactly what you mean," Charlotte agreed. "There's just something right about this old cloak."

Sir Francis once again furtively eyed his surroundings, hoping that his demonic rivals weren't here snickering at the poor company he kept. Satisfied with his privacy, the demon swaggered to the front of the group. "Well, as the most fashionable among us, allow me to take the lead."

Sir Francis confidently knocked on the tailor's door. "I've scientifically studied the art of knocking. Two quick and brisk raps, that's the optimum to communicate both politeness and urgency."

A voice called from inside. "Coming!"

The call was followed by scuffling footsteps and Sir Francis grinned. "See? He was entranced by my knock."

"I think he was just entranced by the prospect of business," Sofia replied.

The thatched straw door swung open and the tailor peered out.

Bernard was a thin, elderly man with fraying, gray hair who wore a matching set of indigo tunic and pants made from cloth so fine, it seemed to glow. There was some light fraying and wear around the edges, plus a patched hole at the knee, but the imperfections had been repaired near perfectly, the fixes themselves an indicator of his skill. He had a beaten-up monocle on his left eye and he was slightly hunchbacked, the result of many years craning over a table.

Before Sir Francis could speak, William made a hasty introduction. "Bernard. It's good to see you. This group might look strange, but they are from Islington and promise to do good business."

"I see…" Bernard cautiously replied. As he scanned the group, his brow furrowed so deeply that he could have planted seeds in it. He found Sir Francis particularly troubling. Despite Sir Francis's disguise, near-human monsters like himself had provided the evolutionary basis for the uncanny valley effect.

But Bernard when saw Sofia, his tense shoulders settled and his face burst into a sudden grin.

"Oh! Sofia! What are you doing here?"

"This unique crowd would like to get some costumes from you. They will require some special cloth from Islington, but we wanted everyone to get their measurements done first. Plus, we wanted to get your creativity started early—I'm sure you'll come up with some beautiful costume ideas." Sofia turned to the group and smiled. "Just so everyone knows, we grew up next door, or what passes for it in Rustling. I was about ten years older, so I helped look after him as a child."

Bernard laughed. "Oh, I was a real demon child. My parents mostly just dumped me off on you when I became too unbearable."

But Bernard soon discovered the difference between a metaphorical demon child and a literal demon adult when Sir Francis's wig shifted to the side again, revealing a coiled horn that was a *bit* too sharp to explain as a mere birth defect. The demon grabbed the beehive and snarled. "It was perfectly fitted before…the strain of working *must* have done something to my horn growth."

"Those horns…" Bernard stammered. "What… What was that?"

Sir Francis eyed Bernard, conducting an instant psychological profile of the tailor.

Judging from his clothes, Bernard displayed a great deal of pride, wearing his wares to greet prospective customers. As Sir Francis glanced over the man's shoulder, into Bernard's simple straw house, the demon also noticed the thin sheen of sweat on the tailor's forehead.

Bernard's bed was in the left corner and the entrance to his workshop was on the right.

But Sir Francis's eyes instantly found a small stack of red talismans stacked one on top of the other, just by the window. On a small desk right next to his workshop stood a gleaming gold figurine depicting a cat with a coin in its mouth.

Bernard thought that those items would ward off ill fortune while bringing good luck. Unfortunately, he was misguided. All they managed to do was advertise his superstitious nature to Sir Francis.

"Oh, of course, these horns are fake." Sir Francis chuckled, shifting his wig to hide the horns again. "They're props. I'm a method actor."

"A what?"

"A method actor. I go around in costume and behave like a demon to get into character. It's a very prestigious school of acting, which is exactly why I went to this very prestigious store. My previous tailor moved, and you are the only one whom I believe can match his quality. Not only that, but we don't just want a few costumes. Islington plans on commissioning an entire tent as well, not to mention items for the animals that will be performing in our show. Why, you stand to make a fortune working for us!"

At the end of his already highly appealing speech, Sir Francis smiled a smile so charming, it broke past the realm of charisma, encroaching upon minor mind control.

"Oh. Well. That's very nice to hear. Yes, I'd like to think that the quality of my work is unparalleled. I've worked for princes, you know," Bernard boasted, his fear temporarily quelled by Sir Francis's flattery. "There're plenty of Islington nobles who can attest to the quality of my work. Come on in."

Chapter Twenty-One

Bernard led them into his home, smiling apologetically as he gestured at their surroundings. "Pardon the mess. Normally, I tidy up for scheduled appointments, but I'm more than happy to get to work right away."

Bones glanced through the very clean dining table, freshly made bed, and elegant flower arrangements. If this qualified as a mess, Bernard likely would have considered Bones's room an apocalypse.

A simple, wooden door connected Bernard's home to his workshop, a simple and unassuming building made from wooden planks instead of straw. The air smelled faintly of undyed wool—grassy, earthy, and surprisingly sweet. A single narrow window let in a slanted beam of sunlight, revealing a well-used worktable covered in nicks and scratches.

The walls were lined with rough wooden shelves, each crammed with neatly organized cloth—full bolts of wool and linen, plus swatches of finer material salvaged from noble garments from all around the world. A few half-finished projects hung from pegs: a patched cloak, a tunic with its hem undone, and a pair of trousers awaiting new knees.

"So, what exactly are you looking for?" Bernard asked. "You said you were actors?"

"Circus performers, actually," Sir Francis replied. "My part requires some acting, but the others have different roles."

"I see," Bernard replied. "So, circus costumes…"

His eyes scanned the troupe again, this time lingering on Pennington and his unusual body. Despite his superstitious nature, Bernard chose not to comment. As far as he was concerned, a paying customer was always right, even if they had the wrong number of arms. For the sake of his sanity, Bernard chose to view Pennington as some kind of conjoined twin. Having spent his life working for students from Islington, the scientific explanation was far more comforting than a supernatural one. "You said Islington will provide the cloth?"

"Yes. All we need now are our measurements taken," Sir Francis primly replied. "Though I am interested in discussing additional business opportunities after we're done here."

"Very well. Step up and I'll take your measurements and we can work together as I sketch out some designs. But first, what are the colors of your circus?"

"Colors?" Bones asked.

"Yes, colors," Bernard replied. He met Bones's eyes and promptly regretted it. Thankfully, the presence of his childhood babysitter, Sofia, plus the promise of enormous amounts of gold, managed to keep Bernard from fleeing. "The colors of the tent and uniform. Performing troupes often make sure everything matches."

"The Great Clown uses red and gold, for example," Sofia helpfully added.

"I like red," Karn suggested. "I feel like it brings out the color of my hair. And gold is great too. It looks like a fire. Maybe we can copy them."

"Copying the Great Clown would be a tall act to follow," Bernard politely replied. "Though if you'd like, I can accomplish that."

"Well, I wouldn't go with red and gold. Even a small shift—scarlet and goldenrod—can help us avoid any legal liabilities," Sir Francis interjected.

"Wouldn't it be better to do something very different?" Sofia asked. "I mean, the Great Clown is still performing."

"I'm not sure he is after what happened…" Bones muttered. "I might have scared the laughs right out of him."

"Oh, come off it Bones." Sofia groaned. "Besides, he definitely wouldn't be performing if you'd let the bandits kill him."

"I suppose there's something to be said for not inadvertently promoting a rival," Sir Francis conceded.

"Oh, I know what we can do!" Karn exclaimed. "Bones…the flowers you made at the end of our first show. We should go with those colors. I'd hardly ever seen them before!"

"Now that's a good idea." Sofia smiled.

"And just what colors are those?" Bernard asked.

"Well, uh, do you mind if I demonstrate?" Bones asked. "I can use those flowers on your table."

"Um…sure," Bernard hesitantly replied. He had no idea what was going on.

Bones gestured, and then one of the flowers on the table blossomed outwards, its formerly white petals shifting and transforming into a mix of vibrant violet, majestic magenta, and boundless blue.

Bernard was immediately taken aback—not just by the clear act of magic done right in front of him, but by the sheer uniqueness of the colors. He placed his pride in his work as a tailor over his superstitious fears. "Wow. I have never seen such beauty before. I will have to work very hard to acquire the proper dyes."

"Oh, I'm sure the Islington chemistry department will be able to help with that as well," Sir Francis replied. "With your guidance, I'm sure we will arrive at the best possible combination of theory and practice."

With the colors settled, it was time for Bernard to stump the troupe with his next question. "And what is the name of your circus? I can monogram everything at the hem." He pointed at a gleaming, black cloak with *S.U.V.* engraved in silver on the cuff.

"Oh. Uh. Name, huh?" Bones sighed. "Maybe we should just stick to performing in taverns…avoid the complicated questions."

Karn, meanwhile, had returned to a familiar well. "Well, why don't we set our ambitions clear from the start? If the Great Clown has the Great Circus, we need to be the Greater Circus!"

"I like the sound of that," Sir Francis agreed. "Perhaps after a few years, we can become the Greatest Circus ourselves while setting up smaller Greater Circus franchises around the nation."

"Uh…I don't know about that…" Bones muttered. "I mean. The colors are one thing. But ruining someone else's circus and then calling ours 'the Greater Circus' seems a bit too spiteful for me."

"It's because you have no killer instinct, Bones!" Sir Francis exclaimed. "Destroying your enemies and stealing their ideas is a key business practice!"

It fell to Pennington to come up with a smart idea. He had all those brains for a reason.

"We should call it 'the Second Chance Circus,'" Pennington proposed. "Everyone here is on their Second Chance. Well, except for Bones, I guess."

"I like that," Sofia agreed. "It's sweet. We should put it to a vote. According to my political science class, we're all going to follow democracy one day. We might as well get ahead of the times."

"'The Second Chance Circus' sounds good," Charlotte said.

"Well, I think we should stick with the ambitious idea," Sir Francis countered. "I mean, what would our smaller franchises be named? 'The Third Chance Circus' doesn't have the same ring to it… Why, the very name would suggest our circus employs a bunch of layabouts and sad sacks."

"'Second Chance' sounds nice, but I do like the sound of 'the Greatest Circus.' What do you think. Bones?" Karn asked.

"I think 'Second Chance' is best." Bones smiled. "You might not know it, Pennington, but this feels like it's my second chance too. It took me forever just to leave my cottage and start making friends. It's like you said, Karn. It's never too late to start living your best life."

"I said it with more exclamation," Karn replied. "*It's never too late to start living your best life!* That's how you're supposed to say it. But you know what? That makes me like the 'Second Chance' name more."

Pre-empting the perils of additional democracy, Sir Francis lifted a ruffled sleeve that hadn't been popular for over a century. "Fine, we'll go with the more popular name, but we must avoid total tyranny of the majority and mob rule. Save for adhering to the circus colors, I propose we allow total individualism in our costume designs. I'm attached to my old-school, classy, classical look, though a hat that fits more snugly around my horns would be nice."

Bernard nodded and jotted down a quick note. "Well, I suppose we can start with you, then."

"Excellent, excellent." A toothy grin split Sir Francis's face. "I will be our fortuneteller, so whatever props and toys you think I might need, jot them down as well. I'm sure the smith or glassworker can get our orders together."

A murmur passed through the rest of the Second Chance troupe.

"What?"

"A fortuneteller?"

"What even is that?"

"Oh, don't you worry." Sir Francis cooed. "I've been through enough villages to know what they want. And, like I said, just make sure my outfit is in my current style, simply in the circus colors."

"Yes, I understand," Bernard affirmed. The tailor was rather glad he could get the most difficult customer out of the way first.

"And I already know my measurements," Sir Francis smugly replied. "After all, I'm a man of culture and taste." He began reciting in rapid-fire succession, his voice growing increasingly prouder as he moved onto ever more obscure details. "Height. Six feet and two point two inches precisely. Six feet and six point six inches when including horns. Weight, 187.1 pounds precisely. Collar, 16.2 inches. Chest, 43.2

inches. Waist. 32.7 inches. Inseam, 33.1 inches. Outseam, 42.4 inches. Sleeve length, 26.2 inches. Ankle opening, 8.4 inches."

The list just went on and on. Bones hadn't even known most of these body parts had existed.

"Do you mind if I check?" the tailor asked.

"Why, certainly." Sir Francis swaggered up to him. "I love being the star of the show."

Bernard quickly picked up a few pieces of sewing tape from his desk, swiftly and efficiently gathering Sir Francis's measurements with the flexible pieces of cloth while muttering under his breath. "Well. Everything is mostly accurate. Though I will say, I think your chest has shrunk by about a quarter of an inch and your waist increased by about an inch."

Sir Francis snarled, swiping the tape away from him with a clawed hand. "Don't you dare use your temporary numbers! Do you know how difficult it is to maintain proper fitness procedure while enslaved by a control orb?"

"Um…n-no, I don't know how d-difficult that is at all…" Bernard stammered.

"Oh, that's not why." Charlotte giggled. "It's because you're always making me carry you around! A good walk would do you some good, Sir Francis."

"Silence!" Sir Francis cried. Unfortunately, he was unable to silence Charlotte now that he no longer owned her immortal soul.

"Oh, don't *silence* me, Sir Francis. You know, now that I think about it, our prior arrangement might have been a bit of a toxic relationship. There was quite the power imbalance there, with you owning my immortal soul and all."

"Your what?" Bernard asked.

"Never mind," Sofia interjected. "This group is, um…very into getting into character. They're all playing around in their costumes. Cosplaying, if you will."

Bernard nodded, anchoring his mind again to the promise of large quantities of gold. "Well. Um. Sofia…what role do you play?"

"Oh, I'm just along for the ride." Sofia laughed. "I don't need an outfit."

"No way," Bones interjected, shaking his head. "She's…uh, she's going to be our announcer. She'll tell everyone about us and all that. She'll be our master of ceremonies, just like the Great Clown was at his circus."

"Oh, well, that sounds nice." Sofia smiled. "I think I could do a good job of wrangling you lot."

"The master of ceremonies…" Bernard nodded. "I'll design something appropriately classy." He quickly gathered Sofia's measurements, then sketched the beginnings of a costume, a tall hat with a fanciful coat and dashing cane.

"Who's next?"

"I am," Karn excitedly replied, practically bounding forward. While he'd clung to his animal skins for millennia, he figured it was about time to reject tradition and embrace modernity.

Bernard's forehead wrinkled as he studied the strange man. "What kind of performance do you do?" he asked. "Um, are you perhaps some kind of zombie imitator?"

"Everybody says that." Karn groaned.

"Well, perhaps that means you're an excellent zombie imitator," Bernard replied. His attempt at polite flattery failed completely.

"I'm no zombie," Karn sharply replied. "I'm a fire-eater! You ever see a zombie eat fire?"

"I, um…suppose not," Bernard nervously replied. In truth, he'd never seen a zombie at all before, and while he feared he just had, he didn't want to think about it too deeply.

Sir Francis interjected here. "He will need something with fire-resistant properties. The Islington chemistry department will help design the cloth. I'm sure you will be able to work with the material."

Bernard nodded, quickly measuring Karn and jotting down notes about his unusual figure. Karn was not very tall and the outfit would have to fit around his pronounced potbelly. However, the strangest thing about the stitched-up man was his bizarrely coiled muscles, wound so tightly, they seemed almost springs. "Any thoughts on your design?" he asked.

"I want to look like a living flame," Karn replied.

Unsure of where to begin with such an abstract design, Bernard settled for jotting down a few additional notes.

"Mind if I go next?" Charlotte asked. She drifted forward, the long, black cloak shuffling and swishing around her.

"Um…what is it that you do?" Bernard asked.

"I'm the animal trainer. And I have the perfect costume idea in mind. The lone ranger who finally found her pack. The more I think about this circus, the happier I am to be a part of it."

"I could do something nice for that," Bernard replied, grinning. Unlike Karn's more abstract suggestion, Charlotte's design was much more in line with the costumes he made for the Islington drama department. He sketched out the beginnings of some leather armor, including a few details he usually used for their romantic productions.

"I would like to keep my face hidden, however. Ideally a veil, but perhaps some kind of fancy mask. And a belt to hold my horn would be nice. It can be a bit tricky fumbling for it in my robes."

Bernard stepped forward, licking his lips nervously. He wasn't sure if Charlotte wore the cloak and veil for some religious purpose or, considering the strange characteristics of her peers, if she was just hiding some horribly twisted visage.

As a result, he tried measuring her with the cloak flapping around her, but it was simply too large for him to figure out the actual size of her body.

"Um…if you don't mind…uh…could you take that off?" Bernard asked. "Just to get you fitted for new clothes. It's all right if you can't. I can, uh, make an estimation."

"Very well," Charlotte replied.

She pulled off her cloak, letting it drop to the ground along with the veil that had hidden her face.

Beneath it, Charlotte wore sturdy ranger's gear. Due to her love of animals, she'd opted for a lightweight piece of chain armor rather than the traditional leather breastplate. The sturdy metal loops gleamed over a purple cloth tunic. Unable to find reliable footwear that didn't use animal products, she'd gone barefoot in life. Thanks to her now spiritual nature, her body below the waist simply trailed off into an ectoplasmic tail.

Under normal circumstances, the highly superstitious Bernard would have been aghast to see her floating in the air, but he, like everyone else, couldn't help but stare at Charlotte's face.

Charlotte's appearance matched her voice—regal and aristocratic.

She looked like a storybook princess, with shoulder-length brown hair that curled down to her shoulders; piercing-blue eyes; a slightly hooked aristocratic nose; and cherubic cheeks. Her skin was exceedingly pale, partially from being a spirit, but mostly from wearing a veil over her face all the time.

Three narrow scars ran across her right cheek, only adding to her beauty as if drawn by a particularly creative makeup artist.

Though Charlotte's reputation would have suggested they'd come from some exotic animal, they were actually the result of an exceptionally grumpy local tomcat from her childhood, the animal she'd put by far the most effort into befriending.

After Charlotte's face reveal, the entire workshop went quiet. Even Sir Francis, who had seen her several times before, couldn't help but gulp and nervously lick his lips with his thin, forked tongue.

"Wow. I would not keep a face like that hidden," Karn marveled. Human beauty had advanced significantly over the years.

Charlotte scoffed. "I'm tired of the constant ogling. Can I just get measured and move on? And make sure you don't read my height aloud. I'm a little sensitive about being so tall. Under no conditions should anyone be comparing me to an ostrich right now."

Of course, nobody had any reason to think that, but now that Charlotte had mentioned it, they couldn't help but ponder the similarities.

"W-Well, y-yes, of course," Bernard stammered, hurriedly picking up his sewing tape again.

As Charlotte drifted back to the troupe, picking up her cloak again, Bones couldn't help but ask her how ghostly clothing worked. This was the first time he'd heard of a spirit changing clothes before. "How does that stay on you? Come to think of it…how did the tape stay on?"

"Oh, most spirits can turn solid at will," Charlotte replied. "Including things we're touching. It's why we don't change clothes all that much; things just don't get dirty. See?" She touched the wall once, making solid contact. Then she phased her hand through the wall the second time.

She noticed Bones opening his mouth to ask how it worked, but she hurriedly shook her head. "I have no idea, and I don't want to think about it too much. I'm afraid if I get into my head and stop believing in myself, I'll crash right into a wall."

Pennington walked up next, his massive body barely fitting beside Bernard's table.

"What's your role?" Bernard asked, nervously eyeing the massive man. It wasn't just that Pennington was over seven feet tall—he was also almost as wide.

"I am Pennington," Pennington explained, eager to affirm his identity.

"Um…is that…?"

"Ah. I understand. You meant my role in the circus, not in the greater tapestry of life. I'm the strongman," Pennington explained, flexing his ample muscles.

"Great," Bernard replied. "Well. I guess we'll want to be showing off some of these muscles, then. Perhaps a sleeveless shirt would be best."

"That sounds like an excellent idea," Pennington agreed.

But despite the simplified costume, the measuring process took longer than expected. The stitched-on muscles, especially around his bulging chest, gave him proportions closer to a puffed-up bullfrog than an actual human.

"A bit of a bodybuilder, aren't you?" Bernard muttered.

"You could say that," Pennington replied. For Bernard's sake, he decided not to pedantically explain that actually, someone else had built his body for him.

The tailor nodded. "Well, next, then, please."

"I think I'm the last one," Bones said.

Bernard eyed the boy suspiciously. On the surface, he was the most normal-looking of them all, but up close, he somehow seemed even eerier than Sir Francis. As Bones stepped closer, Bernard felt a cold hand grasp his spine and he whirled around, lashing out with his arm.

But of course, nothing was there.

He whirled back to Bones, the paranoid expression on his face slowly fading into embarrassment. "Who…? What…? Oh. Um. Sorry about that. I just thought…"

He shivered, then gulped and shook his head.

Sofia nudged Sir Francis forward, the demon's internal heat creating a miniature internal weather front that helped keep Bernard warm.

Reinvigorated, Bernard began taking Bones's measurements while making a mental note to buy a few more protective talismans. It felt like the ones he had weren't working.

"So, what's your role?"

"I'm the magician," Bones explained. "You know. Tricks with making flowers bloom and things like that."

Bernard brightened. He had finally found an explanation that would allow him to get a good night's sleep. "A magician. Well, I suppose that explains everything that's happened here. It's all just tricks and illusions. You're excellent, my boy. You really had me fooled. So, something fancy for you? Perhaps a cloak with stars and a plumed hat."

"I would like that," Bones replied.

As Bernard finished with his measurements and sketching out his design, the whole troupe smiled. Despite any number of human advancements, matching outfits remained the foremost technology for bringing a team together.

Chapter Twenty-Two

As the rest of the troupe prepared to leave, Sir Francis stepped forward, coughing politely and putting on his smoothest deal-making voice. "Master Tailor Bernard…in addition to these costumes, I have a business proposal."

"What kind of business proposal?" Bernard asked. "You mentioned a tent? That's not my line of work, but I can provide an introduction to the town seamstress."

"Oh, I would talk to her—and to the city's other experts. Tell me: do you take on apprentices often?"

"Um…well, I plan on passing the store to my son. But otherwise, no. Rustling is a very isolated town. We have a rich clientele in Islington, but other than that, there's not much reason to come here."

"That's where I have a proposal. A partnership between Islington and Rustling. We will hire you and the other experts as professors. Obviously, we will pay you a very handsome wage. Does that sound like the thing you might be interested in?"

"I wouldn't say *no* to a handsome wage," Bernard replied.

"Excellent, excellent." Sir Francis grinned. "Do you mind gathering your other colleagues for a meeting? It would be easier to talk to all of you at the same time. Say…tomorrow evening? I would be honored to bring in catered food for everyone."

"That means he'll send me to bring the food back." Charlotte groaned.

"Well, we do have a very excellent cook at Rustling. Sofia's third son," Bernard said. "Perhaps we can see what he can do."

"Lewis's cooking is very delicious." Sofia smiled.

"Is that so?" Sir Francis asked. "Invite him along with the artisans. Perhaps Islington could start a culinary program as well. Our current cafeteria is so putrid, it needs both a deep cleaning *and* an exorcism."

After the troupe had left Bernard's workshop, Sofia turned to Sir Francis, tilting her head quizzically. "That was a very kind offer. Are you really going to reform Islington?"

"Why, of course I am. Practical courses on campus? It's a brilliant idea, one that only I could have come up with. Sure, we have to pay the professor, but the students? Why, they will have to pay *us* tuition, and for their lessons, they'll have to do work around the school! We'll have them paying us to work for us. And I thought claiming immortal souls was an exploitable market inefficiency!"

Sofia sighed. She had only just met Sir Francis, but it didn't take long to understand his personality. "Well, even if it was for suspicious reasons, it could still lead to a good result." Despite Sofia's great respect for Islington's teachings, she knew firsthand that it took different kinds of skills and intelligence to make the world go round. When people were starving, cooks and farmers were much more important than biologists who could tell them precisely *how* they were starving.

Suddenly, two excited voices called out.

"Great-Granny Sofia!"

"Wait, it's Great-Granny Sofia!"

Two youths sprinted towards the troupe, bright smiles on their faces as they shared a bushel of grapes. Like the rest of Sofia's family, they observed the troupe's bizarre appearances and simply decided to ignore it, having been taught from a young age that it was rude to comment on other people's physical appearances or clothing choices.

One was a thin boy with bright-red hair, the other a girl with long, brown hair that trailed down to her waist. Both of them wore sturdy tunics of blue and gold cloth emblazoned with a gleaming crest: a shield in front of a castle, the Bonaparte family crest.

As Sofia ran up to her grandchildren, Bones smiled. He was glad that *someone* was using his old childhood clothes.

The two young children hugged her. They were so small, they only went up to her waist.

"We didn't know you would be here; you usually write!" the girl squeaked.

"Are you still working for Achy Heel?" the boy asked.

Sofia laughed. "It's Achille. And he's over there."

She turned and nodded at him.

The two children waved at him awkwardly and Bones returned their wave with equal awkwardness. Due to his isolation, he didn't have much experience with kids. Cottages made of gingerbread tended to attract wayward children, but ones made of regular stone lacked that special appeal.

"What are you guys doing here?" the boy asked.

"Well, Achille and his other friends have decided to start a circus."

The proclamation was greeted with world-record excitement. They barraged Sofia with questions, the girl speaking first, then the boy, rapidly alternating yet somehow maintaining the good manners not to talk over each other.

"A circus, really?"

"Just like the Great Clown's?"

"He was here a few months ago, you know!"

"Yeah, I think Mom wrote you about it!'"

"Do you think you'll put on a show here?"

"Well, we plan to," Sofia replied.

"We definitely should," Sir Francis agreed. "Nothing will be better for my grand economic integration than a show to bring both cities together!"

"Ha, I like the sound of that," Karn agreed. "More people mean a bigger audience."

"Well, considering the sheer number of family members I have here, I'm sure I could rouse up enough of a crowd to please even you, Karn."

"Excellent! I knew that inventing filial piety would pay off one day."

But to Sofia's surprise, the two children grew a little hesitant.

"Well, my dad is going to be busy with harvest season," the boy whispered.

"Mine too…the rice is getting pretty golden," the girl sighed.

"Maybe we could help them," Bones suggested. He'd been on a real roll of helping people lately. "Speaking of which, I promised a friend of mine a favor. Could someone point me to the town noticeboard?"

The girl with brown hair smiled. "I'll take you!"

They walked off, allowing Bones to avoid a heinous display of classism from Sir Francis.

"Harvest? Why would we help them with their harvest? We're entertainers; we shouldn't *help* them!"

"I mean, we have the ability," Sofia replied. "Karn and Pennington alone…"

"It's the principle of it all! There is a distinction between skilled and unskilled labor!"

Pennington, Charlotte, and Karn had no idea what Sir Francis and Sofia were talking about. Despite Pennington's four brains, all six of their combined brains still had zero days of economic education. They just wanted more people to watch the show.

"Wait, we can get more people at the show if we help them out?" Karn asked.

"Of course," Sofia replied. "I say that part of entertaining is making sure that people are free to be entertained. A business needs to meet its customers where they're at. And these people need help."

Sir Francis snarled in disgust. "'Customers'? Well, they might pay for a show, but will they pay us for working the field? This is utter nonsense. I won't have any part of it!"

"I think this sounds fine," Karn said. "Perhaps these people will show further appreciation by giving me food. Pennington, come harvest the fields with me. You've got the build for it too. People can't be entertained if they're hungry!"

Unfortunately for Karn and Pennington, they didn't know what they were doing. Sofia hastily ran after them before they waded into the wet fields, explaining that everything had to first be drained. There were still a few more days before harvest season started.

"Perhaps my friends could just lap up all the water," Charlotte proposed.

"They have a drainage system for that," Sofia replied.

By then, Bones had returned from pinning up his drawing. "Where did everyone go?"

Sir Francis snarled. "The economically illiterate buffoon brigade is helping the village with their harvest. Helping people work so that you can entertain them…what is this nonsense? At this rate, people all around the world will be clamoring for our show to play in their town."

"Well, that sounds pretty good to me," Bones admitted. "The more fans, the better."

"Bah! Under your leadership, we're not so much of a business as we are an entertaining charity!" Sir Francis screeched.

"I don't know what's so bad about charity," Bones replied. "I mean…I would rather be rich in experiences than rich in wealth."

Sir Francis covered his face with a scaly hand. "Of course you think that. You grew up rich in wealth. But fine, go labor in the fields like some common man. The continued development of the economic sciences will prove you wrong, my boy. Geniuses like me are never appreciated in their time!"

Like everyone else, Bones had no idea what Sir Francis was talking about. "But, Sir Francis. If you go help in the fields, you'll be appreciated right now."

Sir Francis prepared to scowl, but instead, he was suddenly struck by a bolt of inspiration. He'd always considered himself more of an ideas guy than an actual worker, and once again, he'd stumbled open an ingenious scheme.

He bent over, his fingers closing around one of the grape seeds that Sofia's grandchildren had spat out. "Bones…get over here. With your magic, we can just make all the plants bloom, and then we can go back to what we were meant to do: sitting back and enjoying lives of luxury!"

Bones paused. "Huh. I didn't think about that…"

"Of course you didn't. That's what you have a business mastermind like me for. We should call everyone back and celebrate my genius!"

"Um, well, I should probably try it out first. I don't want to be put on the spot. There might be, well, different rules with making food with necromantic energy…"

Sir Francis hastily handed the seed over. "I don't want this thing sprouting on me. It might ruin my skin."

Bones closed his hand around the seed and concentrated, pouring his magic into it. Just like with the barest flower stems, the seed bloomed instantly, empowered by Bones's magic, accelerating into full growth in mere moments.

The vine had burst outwards from his hand, stretching off at least a dozen feet into the distance. The heart-shaped leaves were twined with the same mysterious dark-blue color as before. The grapes were massive, the bushels bigger than pineapples. The swirling purple and blue patterns mesmerized Bones the longer he stared at them, as if the grapes were begging to be eaten.

"Wow. This looks amazing."

"Well, I came up with this idea, so I should get to try the first one," Sir Francis said. He took one of the largest grapes and popped it into his mouth.

As soon as Sir Francis had taken a bite, Bones knew that something had gone wrong. The grape crunched in an utterly disturbing manner, as if the skin were made of bone rather than whatever fruit skins were made of.

With a shriek of disgust, Sir Francis spat the fruit out, his forked tongue swirling wildly in his mouth, like some kind of tortured snake. "My tongue! It feels like my tongue is molding! This fruit tastes like death itself!"

The inside of the fruit had the same beautiful swirl as the outside: blue on green, granting the fruit an exotic and paradise-like feel. Unfortunately, it seemed only natural that a fruit grown with necromantic energy would taste like death itself.

Bones sighed. "Well, I guess it's like putting paint and glitter on food. It might look shiny, but it won't be very good."

As Sir Francis staggered off for water, he raised a clawed hand, incinerating the vine with his demonic flame. "There…" He gasped. "That's my good deed for the day. Even peasants deserve to eat gruel instead of this."

Bones sighed. He supposed that despite Jack Pillary's utopian art, a life of necromantic luxury was a bit too good to be true.

Of course, if he found the Rustling cemetery, he could raise a force of zombies to harvest the rice for them. He had a feeling people wouldn't like that, though. People generally preferred their ancestors' remains respected rather than desecrated.

"Well, I guess we'll just have to help them the good, old-fashioned way."

Bones walked up to the rest of the troupe, who were in the middle of receiving an explanation on agriculture from Sofia.

"So first off, I deeply appreciate all of you wanting to help." She smiled. "It'll help the town and I'm sure that even more people will come to our show. However, the rice isn't quite ready yet, and even when it is, it takes seven days for the water to drain from the fields."

"What?" Pennington grunted. His knowledge of farming was so low that for a brief moment, he sounded just like the brutish zombie minion he was built to be.

"Seven days?!" Charlotte exclaimed. "But I was hoping we could put on the show immediately."

"I didn't even know the water could drain from the fields to begin with," Karn muttered.

"Why doesn't the rice just suck the water up?" Bones asked. "It probably needs a lot of water to grow, right?"

"Well, actually, the water is there because it kills weeds. Rice can grow in flooded plains, but most plants can't. I've told you this many times before."

"You guys didn't know that?" the boy with red hair asked.

"Shut it, kid," Karn grumbled, not realizing he was telling off one of his countless descendants. "Farming wasn't even invented in my time. Show some compassion!"

Bones had to admit that Karn's excuse for not understanding how rice paddies worked was much better than his excuse of just not paying attention when Sofia had told him. The rest of the troupe had equally superior excuses.

"I was a weapon made to kill," Pennington said. "However, I will store that information away for the future."

"I ran away to live in the woods," Charlotte added.

"As you're waiting for the fields to drain, we should rehearse," Sofia declared. "And once we find out when everything will be finished, Charlotte can use her friends to send invitations across the realm. Of course, most people won't make the trip, but we can be certain that the people who do will be devoted circus fans."

As the troupe walked off to prepare, Bones smiled shakily and took a deep breath. Costumes being made, invitations eventually getting sent out—it all felt extremely real.

To his surprise, he didn't feel quite as nervous as he'd thought he would. It was still there, though, and a hidden part of him knew that things would be different once he actually got up on stage.

But for now, he was much more focused on practicing than dreading the trouble ahead of him. After all, Karn and Sofia were right. Things had gotten a lot better after he'd left the cottage.

He wasn't ready yet, but he knew how to get better.

"Patches."

"*Yes?*" the doll sleepily replied.

"If it's a big tent with a lot of people, I won't just be able to point. It'll have to be like the old days, commanding magic with my mind. I'll have to direct it carefully…make sure nothing bad happens."

Patches shifted in the bag. Though he couldn't see her, Bones figured she was nodding.

"*Yes, flowers across the whole tent will be difficult, but I'm sure you can manage it. If you're worried, just make sure Karn is nearby. It will be hard to control the flow of your necromantic energy for such great distances… but I'm sure you can manage it. You gave me the miracle of life, after all. Though, speaking of which, that's enough life for one day."*

The presence in his mind faded with a gentle yawn as Patches went back to sleep.

Chapter Twenty-Three

The days fell into a familiar pattern for Bones and the newly named Second Chance troupe as they waited not just for their costumes to be finished, but for the harvest to begin.

Their mornings began in the Islington dormitories, where Sir Francis had managed to wrangle individual rooms for all of them.

In the afternoons, they conducted their rehearsals by the river, obscured from any prying eyes that wanted to try to catch a sneak peek. Despite their supernatural talent for their roles, all the performers remained diligent, save for Sir Francis, who claimed he already had the perfect show in mind. Instead of practicing, he loafed around Islington and Rustling, striking up conversations with random strangers while slowly catching up on the vast amounts of economics homework he still had to grade.

Under normal conditions, Bones might have considered questioning the exceptionally lazy demon, but he was far too busy with his own practice.

Just as Patches had promised, finely controlling his magic across long distances was more difficult than he'd thought it would be. Despite his tremendous amounts of magic, Bones was used to releasing it in powerful bursts.

A controlled trickle was the exact opposite.

Each day, as he stared out at the rushing river, Bones imagined row after row of visitors eagerly anticipating his performance, attempting to visualize beforehand how daunting the show might be. Then he would make the grass and plants around the river bloom, challenging himself to direct his necromantic energy across great distances or unusual angles, maintaining a steady flow at all times.

At the inn, he'd managed to turn his excited spurt of energy into an advantage, but this time, he didn't want anything unpredictable to happen, so he practiced and practiced.

To his surprise, Bones enjoyed the work far more than he would have imagined.

In the past, his fears about his magic had kept him from practicing, but now he was surrounded by friends who could both support him and keep him in check.

He felt safe pushing himself to be his very best.

In the evenings, the troupe spent time in both Islington and Rustling, bringing the two long-separated groups together. Naturally, as respected individuals from their respective towns, Sofia and Sir Francis took the lead. Bones and the rest of the troupe, each uniquely unsuited for diplomacy in their own unique way, mostly stayed silent and listened.

For Bones, the strangest thing about spending time in Rustling was meeting Sofia's family. Because of his fears, he'd only ever glimpsed them from afar when they came to visit, and now he was seeing all of them at once.

Sofia had so many descendants that he could hardly tell them apart—she had seven children and each of those children had inherited her love of family. William was her only grandchild who didn't have at least three children of his own yet.

With so many people at once, Bones was only able to gather a few small and essential pieces of information. All of them had heard of Bones, though of course, they called him "Achille." Every single one of them adored their family matriarch, and several of them had some extremely disturbing similarities to Karn.

The combination of concentrating harder than he'd ever had in his entire life—for both magical and social reasons— left Bones exhausted by the time he crawled into bed each night.

His sleep was peaceful and dreamless, without any need for Patches to intervene.

And so, the days passed quickly for Bones, but in a very different way than how they'd darted by in the past.

When Bones had lived in the cottage, the days themselves had felt slow in the moment. Every minute sitting around doing nothing had felt like a painstaking eternity. But the time had passed all the same, and before long, he'd built up twenty years of isolation. When he looked back, it was all just a boring, nondescript blur without a single good memory to latch on to.

Now, joyful and exciting things happened every day, with the promise of more when he awoke the next morning. It had taken him almost twenty years, but he was finally living his life again.

On the morning of the fifteenth day, after the rice had matured and just before the fields finally drained for harvest time, two newly minted Islington professors found the troupe in the courtyard.

Bernard had a freshly pinned gold badge showing a suit and a dress on his indigo tunic. He stood next to a lady with tangled gray hair that looked a little like a bird's nest. The same badge had been pinned onto her chest.

Roana was the only one remaining of Rustling's seamstresses. The others, seeking higher wages, had moved to Avaron Heights. For reasons nobody could quite understand, the capital had a seemingly insatiable need for them.

While seamstresses and tailors had distinctions, the longtime friends thought their fields were close enough that they might as well work alongside each other, particularly because Islington University simply didn't have enough separate buildings on campus.

"Hello." Bernard waved. The hesitance and fear in his voice had lessened significantly since their first meeting. At this point, the troupe was known for their friendliness and generosity, known more for the content of their characters than the rather horrifying contents of their bodies. "Your outfits will be finished in a week's time."

"The tent as well," Roana chirped. "It would have been done faster, but the engineering and physics departments made a mistake with their design. The smiths and I had to work hastily to make sure the whole thing didn't collapse."

"I'm glad there wasn't a collapse during the show," Bones nervously replied.

"It was honestly to be expected, considering the wonderous design," Roana said. "I'm just glad it's working now."

"Yes, everything was very fanciful," Bernard said. "Though most of it will be up to your expectations. The only thing we struggled with was the fire-proof cloth."

Bernard eyed Karn nervously. He had no idea how the caveman would react. This failure was entirely the fault of the chemistry department, but the professor and students were too afraid to show up themselves. Bernard and Roana had much more experience dealing with annoying customers—including, at times, the very same professors and students.

But Karn was no annoying customer. While he had high standards for everyone, his highest standards were for himself. "Ah, well, I figured it might have been too good to be true. I'll just have to make sure I don't burn myself. The most important thing is my costume design."

"Oh, don't you worry." Bernard smiled. "You will look just like a living flame."

"Excellent!" Karn exclaimed.

"Well, now that we know when the show is happening, it's time to send out some invites," Sofia declared.

"I can't wait," Charlotte merrily replied. She drew the multi-colored horn from her belt and blew. Bones felt the same soul-shivering stirring from before as the grass and trees rustled all around them. Birds flocked to their location, some walking out of the grass before taking flight and others drifting down from the tall green trees around Rustling.

Birds of prey, along with birds that were prey, unified as one before Charlotte.

Sofia's eyes narrowed. "You don't see eagles walking on the ground too much… It seems like appearing from cover is a requirement."

"We'll figure it out eventually," Bones said. "Pennington, you're really smart. Do you understand how this works?"

"Absolutely not," Pennington replied. "Frankly, this is the first time I've been allowed to pay attention to birds.

Charlotte smirked beneath her veil as she pulled a goose quill from her cloak, quickly scribbling notes on a parchment. "Where exactly are we hosting the show?" Charlotte asked.

The troupe glanced at each other. They hadn't thought about it yet, but thankfully, they had Sofia as the master of ceremonies. "The Islington University courtyard," she replied. "It's the only place big enough to hold everything."

Charlotte nodded, but Bones took that moment to interject.

"Uh, actually, do you mind adding two additional notes? I ran into an invisibility spirit looking for his wife and promised to leave some notes wherever I went so they could find each other."

"Oh, how romantic," Charlotte replied. She smiled as Bones described the flipping cat insignia. The cat she drew was far more anatomically correct than Bones's. "I'll just send it around with all the notes; maybe she'll catch a glance. What's the other thing?"

"I patronized an artist before coming here. Jack Pillary. He lives at the site of the One Day War, at Karn's former tomb. Can you send him a note to come as well? And let people know that we'll be selling his works."

Charlotte continued scribbling away with her quill, her spectral wrist thankfully protecting her from the maladies Sir Francis had suffered during his excessive writing.

Meanwhile, Sofia muttered irritably to herself. "Oh, *Jack* was patronizing, all right."

"What was that?" Bones asked.

"Never mind." Sofia chuckled.

Despite her personal disapproval of Jack, Sofia was impressed by Achille having the business sense to invite him and display his wares. Perhaps Sir Francis was a better influence than she'd thought. Achille was almost excessively kindhearted—he needed some demonic counsel to survive in this cutthroat world.

As the invitations flew away, Bones had never been happier, but two crises would strike him at the peak of his joy.

Far from Islington, Pennington the Necromancer had finally managed to fish himself out of the Sun Beam River, a difficult task, considering that his arms and legs had snapped like twigs upon his excessively violent encounter with the riverbed.

Still, thanks to his magic, Pennington knew he would be back on his feet before long.

The drenched necromancer was far more concerned about his career prospects than his immediate health. He was faced with a perilous conundrum that haunted all ambitious employees through time and space—how to deliver bad news to his boss while making it abundantly clear that the situation wasn't his fault.

Pennington was well aware that Baron Angelo viewed people in two distinct categories.

Most individuals with such black-and-white thinking classified people into friends and enemies, with nobody in between.

Angelo used those same categories of friends and enemies, but, as a necromancer, he took it a step further. All friends were useful to him alive and all enemies were better off dead. Most people fell in the unfortunate second category. After all, zombies were stronger, more resilient, and most importantly, far more obedient.

Thus far, Pennington's generational talent as a yes man had kept him in the alive category, but this was his most difficult challenge thus far. His return to his master was deeply delayed by his requirements for both transportation and the perfect excuse, thereby pushing Angelo's assault on Islington even further into the future.

But that evening, Bones would suffer a much more immediate crisis. William informed Sofia that the fields had finally drained, and the next day, Bones performed manual labor for the first time in many years.

Chapter Twenty-Four

It was the day before the Second Chance troupe's performance, and everyone was eager to finish the harvest in time.

Bones groaned as he stumbled across the drained field, his feet ill-adjusted to the damp clay terrain. He carried a scythe in one hand and a wooden bucket in the other, filling it up with the stalks he'd painstakingly harvested. The rest of the troupe, save for Sofia, was deep in the fields. Sofia was with another group, working with her younger family members to separate the grains from the stalks.

A bald man with a burnt-red beard gently laid a hand on him. "Kid…are you all right?"

Bones turned and shakily nodded. Even if his vision hadn't been blurry, he would have struggled to recognize the villager. "I'm… I'm fine," he replied. "Just want to do my part. I survived all the other days. I can do this too…"

As Bones turned back to tall stalks, the man eyed him cautiously. Normally, a boy with stark-white skin and tattered, black rags emerging from the golden crops with a sickle in his hands would have been terrifying enough, even without the shifting shadows and creeping chills. But at this point, the Rustling villagers were far more worried about Bones hurting himself.

To his sorrow, Bones was exceptionally ill-suited for farm work. Splinters from his scythe's wooden handle seemed predestined to pierce his palm and the sun was an even deadlier adversary, searing his skin and drenching his body with sweat.

Here, his necromantic energy was more curse than boon.

Though the steady trickle of necromantic energy restored his aching muscles and forced the splinters out of his hands, it didn't do anything for the keenly felt pain.

If anything, repeatedly restoring Bones to full strength had created a cycle of hell-like torment, allowing him to continue working despite how difficult it felt. To make matters worse, his magic refused to acknowledge that Bones could tan, repeatedly healing his skin back to its original pallor, allowing him to experience blistering sunburns time and time again, even after the days of work that had come before this.

But the longer Bones worked, the more his magically restored muscles grew.

By now, he found that he was able to bear the pain long past the point he previously would have thought was unbearable.

To his pleasant surprise, Bones felt a strange joy working in the fields with everyone else despite his torment. This was just like digging out the well outside Sofia's and his cottage. There was a strange joy in hard work, even if he could have accomplished the task through magic alone.

Bones muttered under his breath. "You know what, Patches? Just like working on my magic, this is more fun than I thought it would be."

"*I don't know about that...*" Patches sleepily replied, stirring when Bones had called her name. "*This seems a lot harder than using your magic. If farming is so great, why don't nobles do it?*"

"Well, I mean, I can see why it would be tough to do this for a living. A serf's life would get way more complicated if they ever got injured. But that's why I'm here to help them out. This just feels worth doing, even if I'm doing it very badly." Bones winced in pain, dropping his scythe again as more splinters buried their way into his hands. "It seems like my magic is chipping away the wood and making it splinter faster." He groaned.

Patches chuckled lazily. "*You keep stabbing yourself like that, maybe you'll be in patches yourself.*"

Bones snickered but picked the scythe back up again, continuing to harvest his row. "After doing all this hard work, I feel like I understand Sofia's way of thinking better. Now I know what she meant when she said that other people have it way tougher. I can't believe they have to do this backbreaking work every single day. It feels like just one day's work should be worth fifty gold pieces!"

On the other hand, Patches did *not* understand Sofia's way of thinking. The stuffed animal was more or less the most pampered being in history. Every aspect of her existence was cared for by Bones. Even eating took virtually no effort, and her biggest life complaint was her owner waking her up with bad dreams. "*I can't tell what's worse... thinking hard or working hard. Bones, summarize the lesson you learned today and tell me about it later. I'm going back to bed.*"

"Ah, Bones, fancy seeing you here," hissed a reptilian voice.

Bones turned and found Sir Francis pushing himself through the golden crops. "What are you doing here, Sir Francis?"

"Well, from the looks of it, you're learning the lesson of a hard day's work. It's a valuable perspective, one that the Islington students and professors should enjoy as well."

The crops rustled again as Professor Roman led a large group of students with a huge grin on his face. Just the walk here had left the elderly professor sweating, yet he was beyond eager to indulge his intellectual curiosity. In this case, his love of learning extended to learning just how bad he was at farmwork. "Doing a hard day's work of our own free will— what could be better?"

The same could not be said for the very frustrated students.

"I regret saying anything… Sir Professor Baskerville is even worse than Pennington!" a gaunt student sighed.

"You can't even tell a joke in front of Sir Professor Baskerville," a lady with long, curly hair covered her face in her hands.

"Well, I mean, maybe we can prove him wrong. This can't be too hard, can it?" a pale-faced nobleman hopefully asked.

Much like Bones, who still wore his classic black rags, none of the students were properly dressed for fieldwork. Bones recognized the Plumage Barony scholars from outside Karn's tomb by their distinctively eccentric costumes. In mere moments, they found themselves snared by the rice plants like birds caught in traps.

As the students waded deeper into the rice fields, the Rustling farmers stepped away for safety reasons. None of them had wanted to give these underqualified harvesters scythes, but Sir Francis happened to have a very large collection of his own.

"Oh, you don't you worry." Sir Francis chuckled, waving a clawed hand. "If we damage any crops, Islington University will pay for it. We are on an official school field trip."

"Nice to see you guys here," Bones said, panting and wiping sweat off his forehead. Despite his speech to Patches earlier, part of him was glad for an excuse to take a break.

"We're trying to bring both cities together and that means establishing an understanding. This lot claims that Rustling has overcharged them for goods and services over the years, so I'm here to show them that the work is more difficult than they think."

One of the Plumage Scholars gasped for air, his coat drenched in the hot sun as he bent down to pick up his dropped scythe. "All right. Sir Professor Baskerville. We get the idea now. It is harder than we thought…"

Sir Francis chuckled. "Keep at it for a bit. Hard work builds character."

Watching the scholars struggle more than he did made Bones feel quite a bit better. Just a few moments ago, he'd been worried that he was the worst farmer in human history. Now, he realized he wasn't even the worst farmer of his generation.

Normally, he would have thanked Sir Francis, but he couldn't help but remember what the demon had said just a few weeks ago. "Wait, I thought you said it was bad for us to work in the field on principle. Now you're dragging the students into it too?"

Sir Francis didn't even hesitate before replying—if anything, acknowledging his hypocrisy only made him grin even wider. He'd only been lecturing students for a short time, but he'd been talking out of both sides of his mouth his entire life. "Oh, that was just for me… It's one of my favorite things about being a professor. Sating my sadism and pretending it's for a good cause!"

Before Bones could reply, the rice plants rustled as another familiar figure pushed his way through.

"Bones, what do you make of this stick?" Karn asked.

"Um…it's fine, I guess," Bones replied. "I mean, a stick is just a stick, right?"

"For our biggest show yet? It can't be *just a stick*." Karn groaned. He tossed his stick aside, shaking his head and muttering under his breath as he continued searching.

Unlike the rest of the harvesters, Karn did not carry a scythe. His hands alone had the strength and precision to rip the shoots off without damaging the plants. Under normal circumstances, he would have been the most effective worker, but he was so easily distracted by random sticks on the ground that his net performance was roughly equal to Bones's.

It'd fallen on Pennington and Charlotte to defend the troupe's harvesting honor. With four arms, Pennington simply worked faster than the rest, and while none of Charlotte's animals were disciplined enough to harvest without eating, she was just perfectly suited to wielding a scythe, drifting above the crops to strike at the perfect angle.

By the end, all the fields had been reaped, and the sun was setting off in the distance, its glow lighting up the entire Sun

Beam River, causing the waters to shine beautifully with their signature golden hue.

"So that's why they call it that…" Bones smiled, wiping more sweat off his forehead. "That was a nice day of work…but I'm going to need to get a change of clothes."

He walked out of the fields, carrying his bucket of harvested stalks to where Sofia and some of her great-grandchildren were separating the grains.

Sofia chuckled when she saw Bones walking up to her, and her smile only grew as the Islington students staggered in behind him, their characters thoroughly built after a day of exhausting work. "Achille. I've been telling you! You need to wear white when you work outside. Black absorbs all light; it just heats you faster."

Bones had no idea what she was talking about. Sofia had explained it to him before, but the concept had gone in one ear and out the other. However, the Islington University students groaned like they'd made an obvious mistake, so Bones nodded along with them so as to not seem unintelligent.

Suddenly, Sir Francis's voice echoed from the fields. "Attention! Attention!" The demon had a naturally carrying voice and due to his reputation as an Islington professor, everyone turned and paid attention. "At the conclusion of our harvest season, I'm excited to present our newly minted professor: Chef Professor Rogerson. An unusual title, to be sure, but he considers himself a Chef first and a Professor Second."

"'Rogerson'?" Bones asked Sofia. "Is that one of your kids?"

Sofia nodded. "Lewis, my third son. I'm glad to hear that he's working at Islington now too. He always wanted to start a culinary school; he just never quite had the money for it."

"He has brought food for us at the edge of the fields," Sir Francis declared. "Make sure we all approach in an orderly manner."

Chef Professor Rogerson was a rotund man with a large, round nose, green eyes, and very thick eyebrows. He had an apron slung over his stomach and he wheeled forward two carts all by himself, pushing one with each muscular arm.

The carts carried cauldrons of bubbling soup—chicken, rice, and carrots warmly floating on the surface, plus platters piled high with freshly baked bread stuffed with cheese, herbs, and meats.

Behind him, other villagers pushed a cart stacked high with what looked like balls of rice.

"Those are my favorites," Sofia said. "The rice balls are an Islington signature. If I remember right, someone from Golden Fields taught them the recipe centuries ago after learning it from Gon the Gut. They're stuffed with meat inside. It's delicious."

Sofia wasn't the only one who was excited.

An appreciative murmur rose from the steadily growing line of hungry workers. As the best chef in the village, Lewis always fed everyone after the harvest, but just a look told everyone that the ingredients were a much higher quality than usual.

Sir Francis chuckled, a wide grin on his face as he walked up to Sofia and Bones. "I was delighted to discover that Rogerson was even better than my usual cooks. And now that

I've provided him with elite ingredients, things will be all the better."

Professor Roman stumbled out of the field, sweat pouring from his brow. His bucket had barely any stalks inside. "Whew. Well. That was enough work for the next decade! And it seems like I was late finishing too!"

"Don't worry, Professor. I can handle that for you." Sofia laughed.

Roman placed the bucket in front of Sofia, then turned to Sir Francis and smiled. "Well. That was awfully generous of you. Not only finding us a new professor, but even providing the catering for today's meal. I suppose there's no better way to show his skills."

"What do you mean, 'generous'?" Sir Francis asked. "I billed Islington! This is a company expenditure, now that he's a professor. And besides, we were all here because we were teaching the students about an honest day's work."

Professor Roman paused. Even for the exceptionally scatterbrained professor, this seemed like a logical stretch. "Um…well, I mean, the school is very short on funding. Are you sure that was a good idea? I don't know what Professor Arial will say about this…" However, Roman's furtive glances at the food made it very clear where his heart truly lay.

"Oh, what do you think our endowment is for?" Sir Francis asked. "It's to tide us over during tough times like these!"

Before Professor Roman could ask how Sir Francis had gained access to the university endowment, Sir Francis waved his hand. "Here. I'll bring you to the front of the line."

Before long, they were all enjoying plates of food.

The Second Chance troupe sat together in a rough circle, grinning as they dug in.

Charlotte drifted along with them. Even though she couldn't eat, it was nice to feel included.

Bones bit into the rice balls, and they were just as good as Sofia had promised—perfectly chewy and, in his case, filled with delicious fish. He drank from a small cup of chicken and rice soup and his smile grew even wider. "Oh…this is so good…"

"Well, don't get me wrong… I don't mind cooking, but if our circus makes it big, we should get a professional chef," Sofia added.

"Perhaps your son can train one. We can get him on a discount, perhaps even pay him in experience rather than gold. I mean, he'll just be a student," Sir Francis replied.

Karn dual-wielded rice balls, eagerly jamming them into his mouth, with a whole stack of stuffed bread for backup. "Oh, this is great! Man! People keep coming up with better and better foods! Can't wait to see what they'll come up with another hundred years from now."

Like most good meals, it took a while for everyone to finish eating, with plenty of second and even third helpings.

Even after everyone had finished their meals, the Islington students mingled with the villagers like never before. The two sides had built a new bond forged by a hard day's work.

Sofia turned to the troupe and smiled. "Well, Karn. This might be a good time for a bit of a preview. Everyone's still here; it seems like the perfect opportunity."

"Oh, I like the sound of that."

Karn stood and dashed to the pile of debris he'd removed from the ground, picking the finest stick he'd gathered. Then he swaggered up to Chef Professor Rogerson, who was in the middle of cleaning up his empty carts.

"Mind if I borrow your fire?"

Ignoring Rogerson's very reasonable surprise, Karn stuck the stick into the fire, igniting it.

Then he turned to everyone, waving the stick above his head.

"Everyone, listen up!"

All eyes turned to Karn. With their stress and worry about the harvest alleviated, the villagers were eager to be entertained, especially because Karn was one of the people who'd helped them finish their work.

But instead of performing, Karn froze, experiencing the rare and heretofore undiagnosed phenomenon of reverse stage fright. After all the build-up around the tent and costumes, Karn didn't want to do low-production-value performances anymore. "Well, everyone…just wanted to tell you all to come to our show tomorrow!"

A confused murmur passed through the crowd. Thanks to the notices plastered through town and the dogged advertising campaign by Sofia's great-grandchildren, everyone had already known about the show. Considering Karn's attitude, they had expected a preview, but they shrugged and thought little more of it.

As for Karn, he irritably tossed his stick to the ground, but before it landed, Lewis Rogerson darted out and caught it. He was a big man, but like a hippo, he could move very quickly when food was threatened. "No need to give up such a great stick," he declared. "It seems to be burning very well. I can use it to make meat skewers later."

Karn smiled. "Ah. I see you're a man of taste—that was the best stick I'd found. I'm glad you can use it because I won't be needing one until the show."

With that, Karn swaggered right back to the group.

"What was that?" Sofia asked.

"Karn…I didn't know you could get nervous…" Bones muttered.

"I didn't get nervous," Karn replied. He shrugged disdainfully and bared his teeth in frustration. "It just didn't feel worth doing is all."

"What? You had no problem in the inn," Sofia replied.

"That was an inn! This is an outt! It doesn't feel right to do a show outside, but tomorrow, everyone here will know enough excitement for a lifetime." With that, Karn stomped off, eager to find the Plumage scholars who had visited his tomb. The utterly exhausted nobles were already dreaming of a good night's sleep, but eager to establish his historical legacy, Karn wound up forcing them into making the anthropological discovery of their lives.

But as Karn regaled the scholars, little did know how true his words would be.

Tomorrow, all the performers and all the guests would receive enough excitement for a lifetime.

Chapter Twenty-Five

The night before the show, Bones was so tired that it felt like he'd simply traveled through time, hitting the bed one moment and waking up seconds later.

The next morning, he blinked in surprise as he found himself inside his room in the Islington University barracks. His once-exhausted mind and body had recovered, the twin miracles of necromantic energy and deep sleep working together to bring Bones back to peak condition.

Bones was possibly the only student in Islington history who'd received a boarding upgrade by moving into the dormitory. The Islington dorm room was much bigger than his bedroom back in the cottage. A wooden bed with a functional mattress sat next to a wooden nightstand. Large, beige curtains covered up the room's only window, holding back the sunlight and granting a reprieve to Bones's constantly battered skin. A work table sat on the other side of the room, but otherwise, the room was shockingly clean and empty, almost as if nobody lived there.

Despite the improved accommodations, Bones had spent almost no time in his room since arriving at Islington. It was just too much fun being with everyone else.

A lazy yawn drifted into his mind.

Patches—hiding under Bones's bed in the dormitory—remained inside the bag, which provided the perfect amount of shade. *"You're awake?"*

"Yeah. What's up, Patches?"

"You've been sleeping peacefully lately. No abrupt spikes of your energy. It seems like you haven't thought about the family home in a while."

"Um, no, I haven't," Bones replied, blinking in surprise. It was a strangely wistful realization. The image of the burning manor had haunted him for the last twenty years, but now, it was only a dull pain in the back of his mind. "Well, I mean, it's not like I moved on or anything. I've just been so busy with everything that I haven't been able to think about it."

"It's because you finally got out of the cottage, just like Sofia told you to. She was right! You couldn't let that moment haunt you forever, Bones... and besides, I still don't think it was your fault, even if you felt your magical energy drifting through the air."

Bones for a moment, then firmly nodded his head. "You know what? Let's figure out what it was, after this show. We can go by the family manor. Other than Sofia, everyone in the troupe has experience with magic, and maybe her science can help too. We'll figure out the mystery ourselves. Find out what really happened to my family."

Patches was silent for a long time.

"You all right?" Bones asked.

"It's just... well... you've grown, Bones," Patches replied. *"You're ready to face whatever happened head-on."*

Bones smiled as he got out of bed. He'd thought he'd grown as well, but it felt much better hearing it from someone else. "I just need to—" As he pulled back the curtains, Bones broke off, blinking furiously as harsh light flooded through the window. "Wait, what? It's almost noon! Patches, why didn't you wake me up?"

"How would I know it was noon? I'm stuck inside a bag!"

Bones couldn't really argue against that alibi. He hurriedly got dressed, scooping up his bag and bolting out the door.

"So, you're finally awake. It's about time."

Bones turned and found Sir Francis leaning against the wall with his arms crossed, carefully posed for maximum coolness. The demon was dressed in his typically overly ruffled clothes, but today, they were the circus's otherworldly colors: violet, magenta, and dark blue. Through hard work, diligent effort, and significant cooperation from the Islington University chemistry department, Bernard had managed to dye the cloth the precise shades that Bones had asked for. "Everyone else has been setting up the tent all morning."

"I can't believe it! I was just too tired… I better get there now," Bones replied, hurrying down the hall.

"I would have been there too if I hadn't been waiting for you," Sir Francis shamelessly lied.

As Bones hurried out of the building and into the courtyard, he found an entire flock of birds, with feathers of every color and size ranging from eagle to hummingbird, slowly pulling apart a large tent.

"My. Bones…your taste is better than I thought," Sir Francis said, grinning and baring his fanged teeth as he made his way out of the dormitory. "The colors truly promise a unique circus experience. It's far better than what I had in mind. Why, the townsfolk from either city can't get enough of this tent."

Indeed, the others stared, cheering and gasping in equal measure as the marvelous tent grew and grew.

Bones was unable to reply. Despite his earlier feelings of growth, his words still caught in his throat. As the tent kept on expanding, it felt like his self-doubts were expanding with it. This tent was about three times larger than the Great Clown's tent and it made him feel like he had three times as much of a burden to live up to.

But once again, Bones managed to push away his anxiety. "I'll wait until I'm on stage to freak out," he muttered.

Unfortunately, as soon as he conquered that fear, another fear appeared before him.

The flap of the tent opened and Sofia walked out, a canyon-like scowl on her face. "Achille, why are you late?"

Sofia was already dressed, with a violet tunic and pants decorated with a magenta sash and gloves. A dramatic cape—navy blue with a very high collar lined on the inside with magenta satin—flowed behind her, cutting off just above her high-heeled navy-blue boots. Bernard had suggested a longer cape, but Sofia didn't want her movements hampered.

On top of her brown-and-gray hair, Sofia wore a tall top hat with a similar scheme to the cape, navy blue with a magenta band. She'd carefully tucked three violet-dyed quills from Islington in the band to emphasize her connection to the school.

Charlotte and Karn poked their heads out of the tent behind her. Charlotte and Karn had also gotten dressed, and the uniforms they wore were the perfect complement to the judgmental looks they had on their faces.

"It's not like you to be late, Bones," Charlotte said. "Should I find a rooster to sleep by your bedside?"

"What are you doing, Bones?" Karn groaned. "We're only ever going to get one first show!"

Charlotte had on a navy-blue hooded cloak with a magenta veil completely obscuring her face. Underneath the heavy garment was a violet blouse with magenta trousers with blue, curly, pointed felt shoes. She had on violet fingerless gloves with a decorative bow slung along her back.

She pointed at it and though her face was covered, Bones could tell she was smirking. "Bernard said it hinted at me being a ranger…but it's just for decoration. I don't think it can loose arrows, and even if it could, I wouldn't know how."

"So why are you wearing it?"

"Well, he wanted us each to have props and I didn't want a riding crop or whip. To me, the true skill of taming animals is not needing to threaten them."

Karn's outfit had far fewer decorations than Charlotte's, but he seemed several times more satisfied. "What do you think, Bones? Pretty amazing, isn't it?"

"Well, that's one way to put it," Bones hesitantly replied.

Karn had on a body-fitting navy-blue jumpsuit with magenta and violet flames running up his body. The caveman carried two brightly glowing torches in his hands, effortlessly twirling them as he spoke.

"Unfortunately, they couldn't quite figure out how to make a flame-resistant cloth, so I asked them for the next-best thing. Putting a cool flame design on it. Unfortunately, the dyes they used to make the flame design are very flammable, so I need to make sure I don't make a mistake. That's why I'm getting some extra practice in."

Unfortunately, he got a little too close to Bones and the torches promptly guttered out as he threw them into the air.

"Oh, come on!" Karn grumbled.

He was so irritated he forgot to catch them on the way down again. They burst into splinters on the ground, and the wooden shards precisely landed in the shape of someone falling and snapping their leg in two.

Karn looked down at it and raised an eyebrow. "Wow, I didn't know splinter art was one of your skills, Bones."

Bones groaned. "This the definition of a bad omen. There's no way you can argue otherwise."

Without any way to argue against him, Sofia elected not to argue at all. "Achille, sweep that crap off the ground and then come inside to get dressed. And make sure you help us set up the chairs. You've overslept for long enough, and don't forget, you invited Jack Pillary to come. You'll want to be dressed up before he meets you."

Bones nodded and hurriedly stepped into the tent. Sir Francis, eager to avoid work, hustled in alongside him.

The first thing he saw was the very wide stage, built by a carpenter from Rustling. It took up the entire back fifth of the tent. A wooden pathway separated the audience section, creating a runway that extended to the end of the tent. The sheer size of the stage, plus the runway, was meant to ensure that Charlotte's companions had plenty of room to perform. Like the tent itself, it had been designed to fold up in on itself, with collapsible wooden pieces.

The stage was draped with several brightly decorated curtains in the circus's colors, but there was also a set of black curtains in the middle held by a metal rack.

"I wish the stage were in the middle," Bones said, nodding back at the center of the tent. "I feel like it could have given everyone a better view."

Sir Francis scoffed. "You see that black curtain at the back?"

"Yeah."

"It's backstage. There's a place for us to sit down, rest, relax… If we were in the middle of the audience, everyone would be looking at us the whole time. What if you want to scratch your butt when Karn is performing? Do you want everyone to see that?"

Bones supposed he didn't want that.

At the back table, a single outfit remained. Bones immediately noticed that Pennington's wasn't there.

Sir Francis, practicing his emotional reading in preparation for the night's show, noticed Bones's noticing. "If you're thinking of Pennington, he picked his up already."

"Well, just didn't want him to be left out is all."

Bones smiled as he gazed upon his uniform, a carefully tailored coat with matching trousers—navy blue and magenta pinstripes. A large, violet cape was attached to the back, decorated with magenta stars and moons. Beside it were many small pouches of seeds, handpicked for his act.

There was something about the uniform that just felt right.

"And that's what backstage is for," Sir Francis said. "Go in and change. You'll be delighted at the feel of the clothes. I ordered the students to design a new cloth that felt like an old cloth."

As Bones stepped behind the curtain and got dressed, he was overjoyed to learn that Sir Francis was right. The outfit

fit perfectly snugly on his body while remaining soft and comfortable. He grabbed several pouches of seeds, stuffing them into his pocket. Then he took several more, just in case he ran out. Even after that, he was still nervous, his past bad dreams leaving him frightened of losing the seeds through some unknown hole in his pants.

As he stuffed his pockets to the brim with pouches, he realized there was a prop already hidden there.

He pulled it out, his eyes widening.

A magical wand, carved from handsome oak…

But as he held the wand for a beat longer, he realized that it didn't contain any magical power.

He poked his head back out from behind the curtain. "Sir Francis…this is my prop, right?"

"I suppose so. Make sure you wave it around a great deal. I have a prop of my own too. The circus guests love their genre conventions."

With his outfit securely in place and Jack Pillary still nowhere to be found, Bones got to work arranging the chairs around their wooden stage. Despite the ill omen, his feet seemed unlikely to snap anytime soon, and Bones soon forgot about it entirely. Hard work was an excellent tonic for excessive worries.

As Bones continued arranging the chairs, Sir Francis lazily followed him around. Having no worries about his upcoming performance, he felt no need to work hard—until he eventually got bored. When Pennington hustled by, stacks of torches in his four arms, Sir Francis waved him to a halt.

Pennington's outfit was simple, all sown from a single piece like Karn's.

However, while Karn's covered his arms and legs, Pennington's had been cut short at the shoulder and knees, all the better to show his bulging muscles and four arms. The simple, navy-blue uniform had magenta and violet stripes running down the side, and the four-armed zombie also wore a huge, gleaming belt with a decorative violet plate that proclaimed him the strongest being in the world.

"Give me one of those," Sir Francis said, deftly plucking it off the pile. "Bones, get over here."

Bones set down a chair and then walked over to Sir Francis. "Do you need something?"

"Oh, I was thinking more that you needed me. You see, with demon fire, the torch won't gutter out so easily."

He snapped his fingers above the torch, which crackled and then burst into bright-yellow flame, one that remained strong despite Bones's presence. "Ah. There we go," he said. "Nice and strong despite your terrifying presence. Though I suppose the color is a little off."

"Very off," Pennington replied, wrinkling his nose in disgust. "And it smells horrendous. Just one whiff will send our fans scurrying away. It makes me glad I have the normal number of noses."

"Oh, Pennington should have stitched your nostrils shut," Sir Francis replied. "You zombies don't need to eat or breathe, anyway, after all."

"No, *I* am Pennington," Pennington insisted.

"Oh, after tonight, you will be the most famous Pennington in all the land," Sir Francis replied. "But light a torch normally and hand it to me. I'll just have to concoct the perfect blend."

After Pennington had handed him a normal torch, Sir Francis narrowed his eyes as he carefully held them together, mixing the flames like a chemist precisely calibrating their beakers. Though it took a while, he eventually created a handsome orange glow.

"Very nice." Pennington said, the flames reflected in his four admiring eyes.

"Well, place the torches down there, would you?" Sir Francis asked. "I'll handle this all myself. I need to make sure that the fire is up to my perfect standards, after all."

"It seems like even you're starting to have fun, Sir Francis." Bones smiled.

"'Fun'? Bah." Sir Francis scoffed. "I figure the more people stick together, the easier it will be for me to hide in the pack. Don't get the wrong idea, kid."

Soon, the entire tent was lit in a bright-orange glow, mostly comforting with only the slightest amount of uncanny eeriness.

The shadows abruptly shifted as Bones heard a faint rustling from the flap of the tent and then a voice hesitantly called inside. "Tycho? Um... Tycho, are you here?"

Chapter Twenty-Six

Bones turned his head from side to side, but there was nobody. The voice wasn't Tycho's—which could only mean one thing.

"Um, excuse me," he asked. "Are you Tycho's wife, Ophelia?"

"Yes!" the voice exclaimed. "I'm Ophelia! Did Tycho tell you about me?"

Bones laughed. "I didn't realize you were also an invisibility spirit. Tycho didn't mention that. I guess he wasn't just an invisible 'wife guy.' He was also an 'invisible wife' guy."

Ophelia giggled. "Well, that sounds just like my Tycho, all right. It sounds like you know him. Is he here? I saw a bird pinning a pamphlet on a noticeboard. I thought he might be inside, but normally, he might have answered me by now." Her voice wilted with almost exaggerated disappointment. "You know, it's tough, as two invisibility spirits who can't read, getting forced into a long-distance relationship. We really have a hard time reconnecting."

"Well, you were supposed to go to…" Bones broke off, glancing at the very large tent that had gone up behind him. The invites that Charlotte had sent out hadn't explained where the Great Clown's tent was. They'd just depicted the tent and the cat. Not only that, they had explicitly advertised the Second Chance Circus instead. It was easy to see how the mistake had been made. "Yes. Apologies. He asked me to deliver a message to you, but I made a mistake."

"What kind of mistake?"

"Well, you see, there're two tents, but I can fetch him. Make sure you stay here," Bones hurriedly added, remembering what Tycho had said about staying in one place.

"Charlotte!" Bones called.

Charlotte drifted over to them, looking not nearly as frightening in her brightly colored ranger outfit. "Yes?"

"Can you send a bird to Golden Fields and write a note telling the invisibility spirit in the tent that he should come to Islington? Maybe draw a school or something... He, uh, can't read."

"Golden Fields, huh? Where I picked up you and Karn?" Bones nodded.

"Oh, well, it shouldn't be too far to visit there again," Charlotte replied. "I've got a pretty good idea of where that is by now. I'll go bring him myself!"

She pulled out her horn and moments later, her carriage rattled into existence, pulled by lithe and graceful snow leopards with sleek coats of spotted white fur and chilling, blue eyes that looked like glaciers.

But as she vaulted into her usual seat, the animals hesitated, eyeing her new outfit suspiciously.

"Oh, come off it." Charlotte groaned. "It's me!"

Bones could have sworn he saw the proud cats chuckling as they pulled her away.

"Wow," Ophelia muttered. "Your circus has some pretty talented performers."

"It's a recent development. We were pretty low production value a few weeks ago. But if you and Tycho stay, you'll be in for a real treat."

"Oh, we shall. The good thing about being a spirit is you don't have to worry about seating."

Bones had just begun congratulating himself on solving one problem when Sofia called out to him from the other side of the courtyard. "Bones! Get over here! Pillary is here to see you!"

As Bones walked back around the courtyard, again passing by the outside of the enormous tent, he couldn't help but feel like a very important person. Everyone wanted his attention before the show—which was exactly what happened to most nobles who sponsored events.

The key difference was that Bones did not like the attention.

Unfortunately, as soon as he saw Jack, he realized that he was going to get a lot more of it.

"I have to say," Sofia muttered, approaching Bones as he walked up, "his work is top-notch and he's looking a lot healthier than he did before. Perhaps you saw something in him that I didn't."

Like most people, the necromantic artist had benefited from a significantly relaxed work schedule.

His skin was no longer pale, his arms had regained some vague amount of muscle definition, and most importantly, it no longer looked like he was expending life force just to stay on his feet.

Behind him, Jack pulled an ordinary wooden cart carrying extraordinary wares—marble sculptures of Bones, Karn, and Sofia, the detail so incredibly fine, it looked like they'd been frozen in stone. Beneath it were two canvases of blood-splatter paintings. Just like before, Bones couldn't make heads or tails of them. One of them might have depicted some kind of giant, red spider.

"Ah, my wondrous patron!" Jack cried, beaming from ear to ear. "As you see, I have created some works in honor of your sponsorship. I purchased the materials using your generous upfront payment. Consider them a gift from me to you. If you have some kind of laborer, perhaps they could offload them for me. And, of course, you will receive a portion of proceeds should these wonderful blood-splatter paintings sell."

"Where's Karn?" Bones asked, glancing around. As far as he could tell, the caveman was no longer working on setup. "He would love this statue."

"He's watching from the clock tower," Sofia said, pointing. "He says that the statue's beauty is best admired from afar."

"One more thing." Smiling, Jack reached into his cart and handed over a cloth bag filled with parchment. "A sheath of posters, printed on fine parchment and drawn in a new signature Jack Pillary style by my own hand. I'm sure they will delight the fans. I remember purchasing a poster from the Great Clown during my youth in Avaron Heights."

Bones was a little hesitant. Thus far, Jack Pillary's art had landed with mixed results. But when he opened the bag and leafed through the posters, he was pleasantly surprised.

The posters were drawn in swirling brushstrokes of black ink, the dramatic spirals coalescing into images that were abstract yet still recognizable. Bones was doing magic, mysterious clouds of energy rising high above him. Karn was caught in mid-flip of an acrobatics performance, and Sofia dramatically posed with a cane and top hat, clearly acting as master of ceremonies.

Of course, their acts weren't entirely accurate, but these were reasonable suppositions, given what Jack had seen of them. Bones was very magical, Karn was very powerful, and Sofia had the sheer force of personality to keep them in line.

"These are delightful," Bones said.

"Yes, it's a new art style I'm developing. I find the intersection of the black swirls to be particularly beautiful. I considered using my blood-drip painting for the posters, but when I first tried advertising your show, my invitations were unfortunately mistaken for ransom notes."

"Oh, yeah. We wouldn't want that," Bones hurriedly agreed.

Jack gazed up at the tent. "The next round of posters will be in the circus colors. I went with black ink to be safe. And, of course, I speculated a little on your acts."

"No, this is wonderful," Bones said. "I'm sure people will appreciate it. I—"

Before Bones could finish his sentence, Sir Francis burst out from the tent. His keen eyes had spotted the gleam of finery, even from beneath the flap. Moments later, a disappointed snarl stretched across his face as his keen ego felt insulted. "What is this nonsense, Bones? Why isn't there a statue for me? And am I really going to be missing from these first-edition posters?"

Jack Pillary was completely taken aback by Sir Francis's presence. "Ah. I'm sorry, sir. I, um, wasn't aware you were part of this establishment. They only had three people when I met them."

Sir Francis knew it was an innocent mistake, but demons never cared about innocence. "Pennington! Charlotte!" he cried. "Look at this snobbery! There must have been some early joiner benefits we didn't know about. We latecomers *must* unite before any other nonsense occurs. Perhaps we can visit a magistrate and force them to acknowledge us as equal founders!"

Sir Francis's grievances went unanswered.

Charlotte was off looking for Tycho and Pennington was inside the tent getting actual work done. He had never been gladder of his four arms. For some reason, all the other troupe members were outside and there were still many chairs that had to be placed.

"Ah, there's no need for that," Jack replied. "I'll be creating statues of all your members soon. I can't wait to enjoy the show!" Jack tilted his head to the side, observing Sir Francis with careful reverence. "Why, I'll have to do my best just to capture your fine figure and style. That's a Bellini-style tunic, is it not?"

Jack's comments successfully mollified Sir Francis's demonic temper. "Very few men can recognize my fine fashion. It is in the Bellini style, though I have to admit it's a modern replica."

Identifying an opportunity for a sale, Jack brought out his blood-splatter paintings. "Well, you see, I made those statues as a gift, but my true passion lies in these necromantic blood paintings. I went for a bit of a royal theme this time. I call the one on the left 'The Eight-Legged Queen,' and the one on the right, 'The Crimson King.'"

Jack had launched into a lengthy speech about his painstakingly difficult drip painting process, each word captivating Sir Francis further. The demon's eyes widened with every mention of blood splatters and necromantic flows, tilting his head and squinting eagerly to try to identify the captivating patterns Jack had described.

In the end, Sir Francis seemed even more excited than when he'd been when he'd lurched out to grab Bones's soul.

"How much for it?" Sir Francis asked. "A blood-splatter painting sounds *truly* novel. Platinumspoon can't possibly have something like this!"

"Well, I put my life's blood into it," Jack replied. "It's an original Jack Pillary painted with original Jack Pillary body fluids. I won't sell it for any less than seventy gold pieces."

Bones was utterly shocked. Seventy gold pieces were more than he'd paid Jack for a year of patronage. According to Sofia, it was worth several years of a regular man's labor, but of course, Sir Francis was no ordinary man.

Having exploited the common laborer with over a century of corrupt bargains and comically exploitative contracts, Sir Francis was undoubtedly a parasite on the local economy. However, Jack, having schmoozed with the obscenely wealthy his entire life, had evolved into an economic hyperparasite, an expert at siphoning excess money off of individuals with far too much of it.

"I'll take it!" Sir Francis exclaimed. "Why, perhaps I should take both! That way, Platinumspoon will *never* be able to get his hands on one." The demon abruptly whirled on Bones. "Bones! You don't think you will ever make necromantic art like this, do you?"

"Um…no, I don't think I will…" Bones replied. "I mean, I don't even understand this work."

"Well, then, perhaps I should buy both and destroy one of them," Sir Francis mused. "And in our sales contract, we must agree to a right-of-first-offer clause on any future works."

Bones's and Sofia's eyes met, and Bones fought off a laugh as he realized that *this* was what Sofia had thought of him in the first place when he'd initially offered to patronize Pillary. Bones was almost offended—he might have been a sucker, but he wasn't a sucker for clout.

Meanwhile, Jack Pillary began marveling inwardly at the idea of self-destructing art. It seemed like another excellent exclusivity tool. Perhaps if he honed his blood manipulation further, he could make the ink escape from the painting after purchase.

"Allow me to return to my quarters," Sir Francis loudly declared. "I have a hundred and forty gold pieces in my vault."

Jack Pillary knew better than to offer a buy one, get one off discount. Customers like Sir Francis gained a significant amount of utility simply from loudly declaring that they had a hundred and forty gold pieces in their vault.

But as Sir Francis turned to leave, a horrified murmur passed through the crowd—and not because of the demon's wasteful spending.

A horde of undead clowns sprinted across the courtyard, moving with such vigor that their limbs kept falling off, forcing them to awkwardly stagger back for self-replantation.

Despite the confusion and genuine terror, however, nobody fled.

The Second Chance troupe's kindness had partially desensitized Islington and Rustling to the frightening appearances of alleged monsters. Moreover, due to their costumes, the townsfolk thought that these clowns were just part of the show, a logical assumption drawn from faulty first principles.

Bones's eyes widened as he stared at their very familiar and very horrifying faces, chittering, needle-like teeth, haphazardly stitched-on cheeks, and void-like black eyes.

"Oh, I remember you guys," Bones said. "You were at the Great Clown's performance. Um…sorry about what happened at the end there. Are you here to try out for our show instead?"

The clowns stared blankly back at him until their leader pushed himself to the front of the troupe.

He was much bigger than the rest of them, with an exceptionally wide, almost triangular body. His red cap with a rusty old bell looked like it had been melded into his scalp.

Over the years, most of the head clown's chest had sunk into his stomach, largely due to sitting and watching other shows instead of performing. Despite his decrepit body, the clown had carefully patched and mended his clothes over the years. All of the clowns were great sticklers for precision, the kind of people who grew irritated when others referred to 'north' as 'up.'

Bones had to strain to hear the head clown speak over his clashing teeth and creaking bones. "No…my performance days are over… I'm here for a very different reason…" He raised a quill and a piece of parchment, holding them aloft with pasty bloodless hands. "We are here to give you a review…"

"I'm sorry? A review of *what*?" Bones guilelessly asked.

"We're starting a pamphlet that reviews performers throughout the realm. We call it *Undying Jest*. We just started working on our first issue when we heard that there was a new circus, one that seeks to rival the Great Circus itself!"

"Oh… Um… I mean… I wouldn't say we're trying to rival the Great Clown."

The head clown tried to cluck his tongue disapprovingly but accidentally stabbed it with one of his teeth. He cursed in pain, hiding his mouth with his hand to classily fix his dental malfunction. When he'd finished, he muttered under his breath as he scribbled a note on his parchment. "Unambitious…"

"Is that a pro or a con?" Bones hopefully asked.

"It's a pro," Sir Francis interjected, his eyes narrowing as he abruptly returned to the conversation. "A classless lot like you…I doubt you've ever heard of *humility*." Under normal circumstances, he would have left to purchase the blood paintings right away, but he felt like protecting Bones would result in greater net reputational benefits.

The head clown turned to Sir Francis. As their eyes met, they instantly recognized each other as rival snobs.

"What would *you* know about humility?" the head clown asked. "I mean, just look at your face, caked with all that hideous makeup. It's so much tackier than mine. Meanwhile, I'm speaking quietly to you, even though I'm angry at your false accusations. *That*, to me, shows humility and class." The head clown's soft voice had much more to do with his messed-up teeth than civility, but he was still going to use it to his advantage.

Sir Francis scowled. "Heh. For *you* to try to speak to me about class. My class extends far past mere behavior. For instance, what do you know about fine art? Look at these paintings that I've just purchased. Original Jack Pillarys!"

The head clown's eyes widened so abruptly that his makeup cracked, the shards of congealed paint falling from his face and revealing the hideously graying flesh beneath. He had no idea who Jack was, but Sir Francis spoke with so much confidence that he found himself caught in the craze. "Oh. Wow. An original Jack Pillary. Two of them!"

"Not just an original Jack Pillary—I even have Jack Pillary himself here!" Sir Francis explained, pointing at Jack. As the avant-garde clowns chittered in amazement, Sir Francis went for the kill. "Impressed now, aren't you? Tell me," he asked, pointing at 'The Eight-Legged Queen' painting. "Do you know what lands the Crimson King has conquered?"

Jack, who hadn't even thought of that himself, made a mental note for his next painting. As for Sir Francis's mistake, Jack stayed silent. Though he badly wanted to correct the demon, Jack knew how the game was played. Some moves were best left unmade.

The Undying Jest clowns, meanwhile, were forced to concede to Sir Francis's superior taste in art. "Well. We didn't realize that this circus employed a man of such highbrow tastes. We will make note of it in our pamphlet."

With that, the clowns walked into the tent, seating themselves.

The rest of the villagers and students had already gathered outside the tent, but they remained hesitant, caught between their natural aversion to zombie clowns and their desire to get the show started.

Things grew worse moments later as a horde of spirits swept themselves into the tent, unbound by human conventions for lines and seating arrangements.

Some had been attracted to Bones's necromantic energy, but instead of fleeing, they were captivated by the circus. Others had seen Bones's necromantic blooms, and after whispering about his magic to their other spirits friends, they'd built up the courage to attend. Still more had simply seen Charlotte's announcements around the realm, taking full advantage of their low transportation costs for a night of entertainment.

A fraid of ghosts peeled off of the line, waving and pointing at Bones.

"Hey, it's you!"

"Our savior!"

"Thanks our heads back!"

Bones was very glad they explained who they were. Considering they'd dashed off right after he'd helped them, it was virtually impossible to recognize them with their heads in place.

"This is just marvelous! We were looking for a place to celebrate our reneckings and found those fliers. Turns out we were saved by the circus master himself!"

"We tried to find other ghosts for you to heal, but we didn't run into any!"

Bones would have been happy to help anyone they'd found, but all things considered, he was glad that they hadn't run into anyone else who'd been unjustly beheaded.

As more and more spirits drifted inside, the once-excited townsfolk grew increasingly hesitant. They couldn't see the spirits, but the sheer density was enough to frighten even the most diehard of skeptics.

It fell on Sofia's family members to cut through the hesitance as they pushed their way into the tent. While not all of Sofia's family had the same strict aversion to the supernatural as their family matriarch, they were significantly more afraid of Sofia than they were of anything else.

Emboldened, the rest of the crowd streamed in shortly afterward, quickly filling out the rest of the seats, so many people that Bones couldn't even pick out anyone he recognized.

Bones and Sir Francis hustled back to the tent, not wanting to be late, but before they entered, Charlotte's carriage swept into the side of the tent and the spectral coachwoman disembarked, smiling beneath her veil as the crowd *ooh*ed and *aah*ed at her ghostly-white snow leopards.

Ophelia's ecstatic cry echoed across the courtyard. "Tycho! You're here!"

Tycho's dignified voice echoed from within the carriage. "Thank you, Bones, my friend, for your work reuniting us. And better yet, I've brought some friends with me!"

More spirits drifted inside, eager to see a real show after their sore disappointment in encountering an abandoned tent.

"Ah, my lovely Ophelia." Tycho beamed. "It's time to…"

He trailed off. There was no truly classy way to say what he wanted to say. "Um. Bones. We will…ah, take advantage of our invisibility for a bit…and join the show after."

And so, everyone on the guest list had arrived, but little did the troupe know that they were on someone else's enemies list.

But for now, blissfully unaware of impending danger, Sofia cleared her throat and prepared to speak. Not only had she raised a very large family, she'd raised Achille shortly after, and the boy was a consummate master of zoning out. As a result, she effortlessly projected her voice through the crowd, promptly earning a positive mark from the Undying Jest pamphlet. "Come one, come all to the Second Chance Circus! Welcome to our show!"

Chapter Twenty-Seven

A cheer rose from the audience as they stared up at the stage with rapt attention and excitement. Their own tightly packed body heat was complemented by the presence of a near-equal number of spirits and the chilling aura around their bodies. In turn, Bones's far more dramatic chill was counteracted by Sir Francis's many demonic torches. The bizarre circumstances blended perfectly, as if drinking a dozen different poisons had somehow created an elixir of immortality. The audience enjoyed an absolutely *ideal* temperature, one that not even the faraway miracle of air conditioning could rival.

There was only one slight problem.

The heat slowly melted off the clowns' makeup, revealing their blackened flesh beneath. Despite Sofia's charisma, the audience members sitting next to them couldn't help but nudge themselves away, giving them a slight berth—which was just how the Undying Jest clowns liked it.

Due to Sofia and Sir Francis's community unification scheme, the citizens of Islington and Rustling, common serf and wealthy noble, all sat together under the tent, an overly egalitarian seating arrangement that lost them points with the Undying Jest pamphlet.

The zombie clowns might have terrified the villagers, but they themselves were equally repulsed by the serfs. Having been supported throughout their entire lives by wealthy patrons, they didn't understand the purpose of the common rabble.

But Sofia continued speaking with the same crowd-pleasing charisma as the Great Clown and her first choice of performer had similar swagger. When she called Sir Francis the Fortuneteller to the stage, fear of zombies and fear of the poor alike were instantly forgotten.

"Welcome to the stage our first performer, Sir Francis the Fortuneteller, a man whose wisdom has guided hundreds of souls over the years!" For the sake of a family-friendly performance, Sofia neglected to explain exactly *where* he'd guided those souls.

Sir Francis appeared on stage in a puff of smoke and brimstone, not even bothering to walk through the black curtain.

As the crowd gasped at the seeming display of illusion, Sir Francis scanned the audience and smirked. In a way, working in a circus was very similar to approaching hapless strangers and promising to fulfill their wildest dreams. It was all about putting on a dramatic show and feigning utter confidence.

"So many guests, with so many bright fortunes." He smiled, projecting his charismatic voice through the tent. "One of you will have the tale of your life told tonight on this very stage. Allow me to commune with the divine spirits and discover just whom they want to bless with their gift of prophecy."

He fell silent.

Karn and Bones, poking their heads through the black curtain to enjoy the show themselves, frowned in confusion.

"Bones, what's going on? I don't see anything," Karn muttered. "Like nothing-nothing. Not spirit-nothing."

"Yeah, I don't feel any magic, either…" Bones whispered.

Sir Francis was simply scanning the crowd for the easiest mark. Karn and Bones, easy marks themselves, were still looking for spirits when Sir Francis pointed at William. "You! Right there between those two redheaded men. Come onto the stage. The spirits have chosen to read your future tonight!"

William stood up and walked onto center stage, the crowd cheering for him as he pushed his way through. As he climbed onto the stage, Sir Francis noticed a subtle buckling in his right leg and smiled to himself.

Sir Francis shook William's hand warmly as he stepped onto the stage. "William…ah…Rogerson, is it?"

A small impressed murmur passed through the crowd, but it only came from the exceptionally easily impressed. At this point, everyone knew William. Indeed, his eyes narrowed suspiciously. "Oh, come off that act. Grandma Sofia told you my name!"

"Yes, but she didn't tell me that you were hit just beneath the knee by a bandit during the last attack. Why, you kept that from her to stop her from worrying."

Sofia, who had been watching Sir Francis calmly, let out a surprised cry. "Wait… What?"

William stammered. "I… What…? How…?"

In lieu of answering, Francis pulled out a gleaming crystal orb from his pocket. He knew that other fortunetellers used a whole ball, but Sir Francis greatly disliked carrying heavy objects and he was too cheap to pay for a table. "The spirits told me just how brave you are, William. You are the kind of man who takes on the pains and burdens of others. You will never let your family or community down. And now, allow me to glimpse into your future!"

Sir Francis waved his hands in appropriately mystical patterns, muttering nonsensical yet dramatically pronounced spells richly spiced with Es and Ts. The demon figured they were the most popular letters in the language for a reason. "Ah. Yes. The orb says you shall achieve satisfaction and happiness."

"Oh. That sounds pretty good." William smiled. "Though I mean… I'm pretty happy right now…"

"Yes, and that happiness shall be with you for the rest of your life," Sir Francis replied.

William seemed satisfied with the basic prediction, but a voice called out from the crowd. "Wait. What do you mean by satisfaction? Is William going to be rich?"

Sir Francis paused. "Ah. Allow me to consult the orb to see just how wealthy William will be."

As he muttered more nonsensical spells, he cursed that unwelcome interloper in the audience. For the circus's next performance, Sir Francis decided to ensure that nobody could ask any unnecessary questions, perhaps with some rabble about how the spirits were shy.

Indeed, Sir Francis's prediction of William's satisfaction had been based entirely on his psychological studies of hedonic adaptation, an effect whereby people returned to a stable level of happiness despite extremely good or extremely poor life effects. Since William was such a happy man, it had stood to reason that he'd be happy in the future.

Predicting his future wealth was very different. Through common sense, Sir Francis knew that social advancement was *extremely* difficult, especially for a serf. But through reading the crowd, he could tell that people were rooting for William and wanted him to succeed.

Considering the social downside of a bad prediction, Sir Francis figured that he might as well go all-in.

"Yes!" Sir Francis cried, his eyes widening. "Brave William will be rich beyond his wildest dreams! Not only that, he shall be blessed with a great and wonderful romance. He will find a wife here on campus at Islington University!"

A new murmur passed through the crowd.

"Someone will marry William?"

"Who might it be?"

"Tell us! Tell us!"

Completely unable to answer that question and completely unwilling to shoulder the consequences of playing failed matchmaker to Sofia's grandson, Sir Francis discreetly cracked the orb with his nail. The splintering sound cut straight through the audience's excitement.

Sir Francis cried out in fake shock, hastily adding a few more guttural spells and increasing his frantic hand motions before letting out a long and windy sigh. "Oh, William, the orb has shattered. Your future was simply too bright! Still, I'll be excited to witness your triumphant life over the years. Don't forget, no prediction can *ever* be as good as the real thing."

With that, Sir Francis sauntered back behind the black backstage curtain, leaving a shocked audience behind him. The demon's utter confidence enthralled not just the crowd, but even Sofia.

Instead of calling out the next performer, she poked her head behind the curtain. "How could you possibly have known that?"

"Which part?" Sir Francis asked.

"Well. Start with him finding a wife on campus."

Sir Francis chuckled. "Oh. It's simple. Rustling is a small town. Islington is much bigger. He's just single because of the small sample size. Not only that, I spent the entire session singing his high praises to the audience. I'm sure he'll do very well here. There's got to be a woman who is tired of dating these nerdy scholars."

"Wait. So you just made all that up?"

"Well, there were no spirits, but I can use my eyes. Your William is a very handsome man, and besides, I wanted to benefit someone we knew with our audience participation segment," Sir Francis replied, mollifying Sofia.

Bones, meanwhile, was overthinking as always. "What if there's someone from Rustling who secretly loves him? Someone who has yearned for him since childhood?"

Sir Francis groaned. "Do you know anyone from Rustling? Why would you even care about them? And if there's a woman from Rustling who secretly yearns for him, well, she'll probably try to make her move tonight. So, it'll still be on Islington's campus!"

"Wait. The ball does nothing?" Karn asked, sorely disappointed. "It doesn't have any powers?"

"It's called the power of observation, you caveman. Here, you can have it." Sir Francis tossed the broken ball right at him.

"But wait. What about the part where he becomes rich?" Sofia asked.

"That's up to us. You see, we're going to have to work hard to prove me right. If the circus succeeds, he'll think I was a genius when he gets his inheritance. And if the circus fails, well, it's not like he'll know where to find me. Now let's get to work making my prediction true. Bring on the next act."

Chapter Twenty-Eight

The crowd murmured, eager to see more after Sir Francis's mystical act. Everyone was captivated, save for a few women who hurriedly left the show, determined to be the first one to make a move on William.

Unfortunately, the follow-up was delayed on account of the master of ceremonies popping backstage to discuss her grandson's future. Right as the zombie clowns of Undying Jest were about to write down a negative note about professionalism, Sofia popped right back onto the stage.

"Apologies, apologies. I did not expect there to be a prophecy about my grandson tonight." She laughed. "If you'll forgive me, I was just clearing out the finer details."

Just like the best lies, the best bit of showmanship had a bit of truth to it, and the audience laughed along with her.

"Now, feast your eyes on our next act, the strongest strongman all in the realms, the one and only Pennington!"

Pennington swaggered onto the stage, carrying four massive weights, one in each hand. With hardly any effort at all, he lifted them high above his head. Islington's physics and engineering students hastily muttered to themselves as they calculated the sheer mass Pennington carried.

However, as Pennington continued his act, switching to ever-heavier weights and ever-larger barbells, he couldn't help but notice that the crowd wasn't as impressed by him as they were with Sir Francis.

The weights he lifted were exceedingly impressive—his inhuman shape much less so. A giant zombie with four arms and all those bulging muscles simply looked like they were *supposed* to be able to lift all those objects.

Pennington noted this but was not discouraged. With four eyes, he was very good at seeing things from other people's point of view.

He finished his act, hauling the weights off the stage to polite applause.

"They're not as impressed as I'd like them to be. Next time, maybe I should do a riddling competition instead," Pennington noted.

"Well, now there's an idea," Karn agreed. "People can see your muscles—your hidden backup brains, not so much."

Sir Francis scratched his chin. "Perhaps you could be a mental strongman, not just a physical one. Then again, if you were a political strongman, you could simply force them to cheer your name."

After her previous mistake, Sofia was eager to keep the show moving. "Now, prepare to be utterly delighted by the ranger who knows the secret paths of the world, who has befriended animals from all around the globe: Charlotte!"

As Charlotte stepped onto the stage, the visitors stood up from their seats, chattering with excitement.

"Did you see the birds earlier? They all worked together to pull the tent apart. I'd never seen anything like it!"

"That's nothing! They rode to Rustling using zebras once—striped horses, I swear!"

"You were already in the tent, but she rode here on white leopards!"

Pennington took in their excited cheers and began theorizing advanced performance tactics he could use to earn such vigorous praise.

As for Charlotte, she grinned widely beneath her veil, bringing the glimmering rainbow from her belt and blowing a long, echoing note. The soul-piercing sound had already made Bones's spine tremor back in the courtyard, but indoors, inside a tent carefully constructed to maximize acoustics, he almost wanted to dash out onto the stage himself.

The crowd was even more captivated. Only the sheer density of the people inside the tent prevented a stampede and more than a few visitors awkwardly stumbled and fell onto the ground, blushing as they were helped back up by their neighbors. A few of the spirits phased through the tent's canvas walls before sheepishly returning indoors.

A sudden cacophony of padded footsteps and eager hooting echoed through the tent as a troop of monkeys burst through the flaps of the tent, scrambling onto the wooden stage on all fours. They all had intelligent amber eyes and coarse, brown fur, with long, swaying tails. Despite Charlotte's eagerness, there wasn't enough in the troupe budget for individualized outfits for every single animal. Instead, the monkeys wore brightly colored ribbons tied around their foreheads.

Excited laughter burst through the crowd as the monkeys leaped onto the stage in a cascading waterfall of cartwheels before launching into a miraculous show that would have put even the Great Clown's acrobats to shame, a never-ending ballet of flips and somersaults.

Just when the crowd thought the performance was about to end, the monkeys joined together, forming into the shape of a tree with their bodies, holding each other's hands and feet, intertwining their tails together for balance.

Bones and Karn poked out of the curtain, completely stunned.

"This is amazing!"

"It's even better than during practice."

Sir Francis cursed. "It was a major missed business opportunity not to have her doing this before…"

As the crowd gazed at the monkey-created tree, Charlotte turned back to the curtain.

"Karn, will you toss me that pack? The gray one."

Karn grabbed a sturdy gray pack stuffed to the brim with ripened bananas and tossed it to her.

Charlotte pulled out a banana for each monkey as she slowly climbed up the tree. Every so often, one of the monkeys would sneak in and grab an extra, and as each of the monkeys began eating, the tree quickly lost its structural integrity.

The whole thing tumbled towards the ground.

Deliberately choosing not to fly, Charlotte fell with an exaggerated cry of shock before flipping and catching herself at the last moment and landing on her feet. "I learned that one from a particularly big cat." She giggled.

The audience began applauding, but Charlotte waved them off. "The show is far from over!" she cried. "You're all going to meet the cat I was telling you about, but first, make sure you keep clear from the runway. There's not going to be much space for stragglers."

An enormous stampede echoed from outside the tent, thumping footsteps loud enough to create a miniature earthquake. The people sitting at the edge of the rows ducked back, scooching away their chairs and pressing in as the sounds grew louder and louder.

"Hang on." Charlotte smirked. "They've got a lot of energy. Let them get a few laps outside first."

The crashing footfalls built and built and the crowd's anticipation built along with them.

"Her showmanship is great." Karn grinned. "It makes me want to be even more flashy with my show."

Sir Francis scoffed. "Oh, she always was like this. Riding around in that giant cloak and pretending to be a grim reaper, she scared people half to death."

The flap burst open and then three elephants swaggered down the wooden walkway, trumpeting loudly and wagging their tails like dogs to show off the ribbons that'd been tied to them. They built up speed and then charged, scaring the monkeys straight off the stage. They hooted and hollered in mock fear, still eating their bananas as they danced right out of the tent.

The elephants turned to the crowd and for a moment, everything grew still, the entire tent eagerly anticipating their performance.

But then a massive roar echoed from outside.

The elephants trembled, turning stock-still, and then a lion with a ribbon tied around its forearm burst through the flap.

The crowd cried out in fear and shock, ducking back even farther than they had for the elephants. One of the zombie clowns was so frightened, he accidentally left his left leg behind.

Charlotte winced, belatedly realizing that letting a predator run loose—even a well-trained one—would naturally spook the audience. She hastily cried out. "Have no fear! This is the cat I was talking about. David is a friend of mine!"

David the lion chased off the elephants, who stampeded back whence they'd come. They stopped just before leaving the flap, standing side by side with their bodies outside the crowded tent but their heads still poking in.

Interlocking their trunks, they bowed together as the crowd cheered and applauded.

The zombie clowns chittered endlessly amongst themselves, utterly overwhelmed by the sheer display of skill. At this point, there was no discussion regarding whether or not Charlotte was good. They were merely wondering if Undying Jest should add a sixth star to their rating system. However, most of the clowns, stodgy traditionalists that they were, were sticklers for tradition, even traditions they'd invented solely upon entering the tent.

Once again, the Second Chance troupe was themselves captivated by Charlotte's show.

"Amazing…"

"How did you teach them to do that?"

"You should have kept the elephants on stage longer…"

"Unfortunately, the bow was the only thing I could teach them," Charlotte admitted. "I figured it would be for the best if I truncated their show. And unfortunately, David isn't much better. I was just going to have him run around for a bit."

At that, Pennington came to a realization. He poked his head out of backstage and muttered a quick request.

"Oh, he'll love that." Charlotte laughed. "David is lazier than any housecat."

Pennington returned to the stage and picked David up off the ground, cradling the cat in his four arms as if David really were a housecat as he carried him out of the stage.

The crowd cheered and applauded, getting up to their feet as Pennington walked out of the tent. Technically, the lion was lighter than the weights he was carrying, but the unusual image was utterly delightful.

When he finished, Pennington returned to the stage with a wide grin on his face. "If I am to be a physical strongman, I suppose we need to find innovative objects for me to be strong with."

Bones chuckled and nudged his pack. "Patches, that's like a bigger version of us."

Despite the ruckus of the circus, Patches had still managed to stay asleep, but Bones thought he felt a very satisfied twitch from inside the bag.

"But wait!" Charlotte cried. "There's more!"

"Not from you!" Karn protested. "I still need to go!"

Charlotte groaned. "What? But I was saving all the good stuff for later!"

Sofia just stared at her. "What? Lions and elephants were *the build-up?*" But then she shook her head. "Look. You should hold back a bit, Charlotte. Build some interest for a second show. You might be having fun now, but think about how fun another show would be."

"Huh. Guess I can't argue with that." Charlotte had hoped to give her attention-loving zebras the grand finale. Thankfully, she knew how to make up for their disappointment: copious apples and carrots, plus the promise of a future show all to themselves.

With that, Karn, an expert at making things about himself, leaped onto the stage. "Enough talk about ordinary animals. It's time to see a dragon in human form!"

Chapter Twenty-Nine

Karn's self-introduction was enough without anything from Sofia. He stood at the center of the stage, silently observing the crowd.

"What is he doing?" Bones asked.

"Probably just copying me…" Sir Francis muttered.

Karn, as the fourth act, felt like he had a great deal to live up to. Not only that, he wanted to integrate aspects from other performers into his act, to ensure that he was considered the greatest performer of all time.

"You!" Karn pointed out a short girl from Islington, sitting in the very front row.

Sofia shot him a curious glance. "You sure? She looks like she's only twelve years old!"

"Oh, I'm sure," Karn replied.

The girl was short, nervous, and thin, with very pale skin and a slightly crooked neck from a lifetime spent poring over books indoors. She wore a pair of silver, wire-frame spectacles that perched slightly askew on her crooked nose. A child prodigy, she'd been sent to Islington because her parents couldn't figure out what else to do with her.

She gulped loudly as she got onto the stage.

"What's your name?" Karn asked.

"L-Lydia," she stammered.

Understandably, she was very nervous. Being asked to volunteer in a fortunetelling act was interesting and exciting. Being asked to perform in a fire-eating act was potentially fatal.

"Fetch me two torches." Karn smiled, gesturing broadly across the tent. "Any two will do. Pick the ones you like the most."

As Lydia left the stage right after getting onto it, Sofia turned to Karn and muttered. "What? Why did you do that? Don't we have torches in the back?"

"Everyone cheered when Sir Francis did some audience participation. I thought I should get in on it myself."

"And why did you ask the smallest girl in the entire tent to grab your torches?"

"The other day, Sir Francis told me that the main performer should pick someone shorter than them, and she was the only person shorter than me whom I could see. It's a good thing she was in the front row." Indeed, Lydia was one of the few people in the stadium shorter than Karn. Her rabbit-like diet was unfortunately comparable to caveman nutrition standards.

Thankfully, Lydia brought the torches up to the stage with no problem, though she handled the flames with very particular care. "To be clear, I'm giving these to you, right? I don't have to do anything?"

"Huh? Yeah," Karn replied, taking the flames. "What, did you think I was going to make you eat fire?"

That was exactly what Lydia had been worried about, but she didn't want to give Karn any ideas. "Can I sit back down now?"

"Of course."

As she scurried away, Karn took the flames and smiled, blissfully oblivious to the sheer pointlessness of his newly-created audience participation segment. Karn raised the flames above his head, the long shadows they cast flickering and dancing behind him.

A shocked murmur passed through the crowd as they marveled at how the shadows seemed to move entirely of their own accord. Bones's eyes widened with appreciation as he realized that Karn had managed to turn the suspicious aura around him into a benefit, transforming the grasping shadows into a delight of their own.

"Yes, yes." Karn grinned. Like everyone else who had performed so far, he had no problem projecting his voice. His years of shouting battle cries had given him excellent lung capacity. "These torches are very impressive, but I have brought my own flames as well, and they are just as excited to perform."

He pointed proudly at the flames on his jumpsuit, creating another stir through the crowd.

"What is he talking about?"

"Is he going to strip naked for us?"

"He knows that's cloth, right? Or... *is* it cloth?"

Karn did not hear any of the crowd's doubts. Even if it weren't for Karn's near-invincibility to doubters and haters, Sir Francis's demon fire crackled far louder than normal flame. The caveman-turned-fire eater began to dance, carefully calibrating his speed at the very edge of ordinary human visibility. The flames on his uniform seemed to crawl off the fabric, mixing with the burning torches in his hands.

"Wow..." Sofia muttered. "He was able to turn moving very fast to his benefit too."

Karn abruptly skid to a halt, stopping dramatically at the center of the stage.

He glanced down at his jumpsuit with feigned frustration and disbelief. "Ah. It seems like the fires are feeling lazy today. They won't shake off no matter what. I guess that's a good thing. Nobody wants to see me naked."

As the crowd laughed, Karn slowly, deliberately, and painstakingly brought the torch in his right hand up to his mouth. To place an additional emphasis on showmanship, he even deigned to look fearful. Unfortunately for Karn, after thousands of years of invincibility, he had no idea what fear looked like. To most, his expression looked like a mixture of seventy percent nausea and thirty percent constipation. The people sitting in the front-row splash zone feared he might vomit over them. When Karn heard the confused muttering, he realized he had to get on with it, and in a single swift motion, he gulped the flame down.

The crowd gasped, utterly shocked.

Karn pulled the doused torch from his mouth, letting out a long puff of pitch-black smoke. Then he began to dance again, this time, moving much slower as he twirled the remaining torch. Belatedly, Karn realized that he'd already come up with a far livelier audience participation gimmick, so he began pointing out people in the crowd.

"You! Toss me that torch!"

"Now you!"

"You! Just make sure to get it on the stage—anywhere close and I can catch it!"

This time, there were far more torches than the inn, but Karn managed to catch and juggle them without any problem, tossing them higher and higher into the sky to give himself time to gather more, a feat of strength and dexterity that captivated all in the crowd.

The tent gradually grew darker and the stage continually shone brighter, Karn's glowing magical stitches burning bright in the demon fire light.

With one final toss, Karn threw all the torches high in the air, giving him time to turn backstage. Once again trying to integrate elements of other shows, Karn wanted his own backstage props.

"Bones…toss a chair over to me."

"What?"

"Just grab one of the chairs we have backstage. I need it for the show. Quickly! The torches aren't going to be in the air forever."

Sir Francis promptly found a chair and sat on it. "This one's mine. Don't throw it out."

Karn grumbled with frustration, catching all the torches and throwing them in the air again to give himself more time. "Hurry up!"

Bones grabbed a nearby chair and pushed it over to Karn, who grinned as he turned back to the crowd.

"Tell me, what is a burning chair but a collection of burning sticks stuck together?"

Nobody in the audience was able to argue with his impeccable logic and reasoning.

He caught one of the torches and lit the chair on fire, then fell into a deep bow in front of the burning chair as the remaining torches landed around him in a glowing circle.

The crowd, undeniably confused yet even more undeniably impressed, burst into cheers and applause.

"Wait. Um. So why did he need the chair again?" Charlotte muttered.

"No idea, but I'm glad I didn't give him mine," Sir Francis replied. Then the demon's eyes widened. "Wait. Bones. Hurry on stage and put it out with your necromantic chill. If my demon fire gets onto the stage, the whole thing will go up in flame!"

As Bones hurried onto the stage, Karn shook his head. "Ah, no worries. For my final act, I will put out this burning chair by sitting on it!"

He sat on the chair and the flames transferred onto his body, just like they had when Bones had first met him. Soon, an aura of brightly glowing burning flames formed around Karn's body as the audience watched in stunned delight.

Karn waved his hand, gesturing like a king. Just like before, the flames seemed to shift and crackle to his call.

Unfortunately for Karn, burning chairs had exceptionally poor structural integrity. With a deafening crash, he fell hard on his butt, hitting the ground with an echoing jolt. The fire disappeared and he lost both his literal and literary aura.

The audience burst into laughter, charitably believing this was a deliberate end to the act.

Karn groaned, getting back to his feet, but his confidence remained unshaken. "Well. That's what the next show is for. Maybe we can pay the engineering department to make an unburnable chair."

He swaggered backstage to yet another round of applause, grinning from ear to ear. "All right, Bones. You're up next. Close it out just like you did at the inn and make us proud!"

"Right…" Bones gulped.

He walked onto the stage, staring out into the crowd.

Just as he'd feared, his nervousness had abruptly returned after seeing everyone in the audience.

There were more people here than he'd ever met in his life, more people here than he could have possibly imagined. Based on their fashions and styles, there were even people from outside of Islington and Rustling. Logically, Bones knew that Charlotte had sent invitations all around the nation, but for some reason, the sight of the diverse costumes had a particularly damaging effect on his confidence. He saw the zombie clowns raising their quills and winced as he imagined the damaging reviews about the show's poor ending.

Things got worse as Bones kept staring. He could have sworn he saw a flash of bristly, red hair. Bones's eyes widened and he re-focused on the back of the tent, trying to get a closer look, but the tent was so tightly packed that whomever he'd seen had vanished among the crowd again.

Red hair alone didn't mean much—most of the barony had red hair—but there was something about that bristly hairstyle that reminded Bones of the Great Clown.

Bones was here with his own circus now, and the audience was evidently delighted by their acts.

All Bones had to do was send them off, but the thought of the Great Clown's mastery filled him with a frightening sense of inferiority. He felt rather foolish. The pockets of his trousers were stuffed to the brim with seeds. Perhaps he'd grabbed too many of them.

The flap at the back of the tent suddenly burst open.

"Oh, thank the gods," Bones muttered. "A bandit attack. Just what I needed to calm down."

But it wasn't bandits.

It was the baron who created the socioeconomic conditions that created the bandits.

Chapter Thirty

The first zombie to push their way through the flap was Pennington the Former Necromancer, now tragically reduced to Pennington the Other Zombie. Infuriated by his poor work performance, Baron Angelo had demoted him straight off the mortal coil.

Pennington had never been particularly well-liked, but seeing him transformed into a zombie hit awfully close to home. The students standing closest to the flap promptly began screaming at the tops of their lungs.

The flaps around the tent burst open and more zombies streamed in, marching from every entrance in rigid, single-file formation. The mindless warriors far outnumbered the visitors and performers. Zombies could not breed, but they could stitch together more zombies in Angelo's factories buried beneath Avaron Heights. Over the years, he'd collected corpse after corpse as he'd devised ever more plausibly deniable ways to kill his own subjects.

Angelo's troops were dressed in mottled-green uniforms decorated by a snake fang insignia, the sigil of a deliberately unidentifiable army. The scheming baron was so well-versed in advanced backstabbing theory that he'd developed false flag operations in a time when most people still called flags "banners." Considering the sheer numbers of this attack and his famed interest in the dark arts, Angelo had almost no presumption of innocence, but he simply couldn't help himself. One of the baron's *very* few hobbies included designing creative outfits for new false enemies to frame for his crimes, the primary reason why seamstresses were in such demand at Avaron Heights. Though Angelo had taught his zombies to stitch limbs, they still struggled with complicated things like crests and colors.

The zombies themselves were a patchwork, mishmash bunch, rotting flesh with plenty of exposed bones. They wore moldy, leather breaches with matching tattered tunics. Rusty helmets clunked over their misshapen heads, the visors pulled back to reveal their empty, staring eyes. Swollen and bloated hands artlessly carried crooked maces and caved-in shields, the tatterdemalion gear little more than raw bludgeoning tools. Drustan had always complained about the army's insufficient budget for weapons, but Baron Angelo had known all along that the soldiers lacked sufficient motivation.

Just a glance was enough for everyone to see that these were nothing more than undead killing machines, created without minds of their own and driven solely by Angelo's necromantic control orb.

The zombies shouted out basic commands, their tombstone teeth clattering with every word. "Surrender! Drop everything! Surrender now!"

Previously a mere inconvenience, the overcrowded tent quickly became an outright hazard, the fear and chaos of the crowd erupting into a dangerous stampede despite William and his men's attempts to maintain order. The zombie clowns burst from their chairs, bemoaning that the constant attacks during shows were a sign that nobody respected the arts anymore. Most of the spirits fled as well and the ones who stayed only added to the panic, screeching out eldritch battle cries as they ineffectively tried to frighten the zombies away.

But while zombie attacks were best outright avoided, the Second Chance troupe's tent was, statistically speaking, one of the safest places to be during an unavoidable zombie attack.

Karn burst from behind the curtain, ripping torches from the walls as Charlotte brought her horn to her lips.

Sir Francis immediately calculated the optimal way to keep himself safe while pretending to help. "Bones! It's Angelo's army. I'll keep Sofia safe backstage!" he cried, pulling her behind the curtain. "I have a demonic spell that can get us out of this, though I warn you, it has a very long charge-up time!"

But not even Sir Francis was faster than Pennington, powered by the sheer hatred of a disgruntled employee. He surged forth, pulverizing his former master with an existence-erasing punch. Bits of bone and flesh tumbled uselessly to the floor, the faint cloud of necromantic magic that had empowered the zombie's body fading away into oblivion.

Bones tightly clutched the seeds in his hands, pouring his necromantic energy into the vines, urging the plants to grow, all of his practice coming to the surface as he guided the vines with the utmost precision of an exceptionally gentle man. Massive, viridian tendrils shimmering with a kaleidoscope of eerie colors twisted through the crowd, ensnaring the zombies and enveloping the guests in protective thickets. With the tent so packed, Bones was keenly aware of the dangers of his necromantic aura. Channeling his magic through a medium was the most he was willing to risk for now, and even then, the space was so cramped, he could only create so many vines.

Karn threw himself into the crowd, shoving zombies aside in a furious effort to keep all his newfound admirers safe. Dual-wielding blazing torches, Karn jammed his signature weapons violently into the horde of zombies, striking them with so much force that he ripped straight through their gear. Due to his love of flame, Karn had inadvertently turned himself into an expert at anti-undead operations.

Moments later, Pennington joined him, the Second Chance troupe's heavy hitters standing back-to-back as they pushed their way through the ever-growing zombie swarm. He'd already discovered the zombies' other weakness, the fact they couldn't function without their heads. Despite Pennington the Necromancer's constant condescension, Pennington the Zombie was in fact very good at pattern recognition. He struck with precise uppercuts, aiming carefully beneath their helmets and sending a rain of skulls flying through the air with his four muscular arms.

Charlotte streaked through the audience, taking full advantage of her spectral form to pull the zombie army's eyes away from her bestial reinforcements making their way into the tent.

A horde of mice streaked across the floor, tripping and undercutting zombies with ribbons in their paws and mouths. Thunderous footsteps echoed as the elephants stampeded back inside. Their ruthless charge immediately proved that though they were poor at tricks, they were very adept at fighting.

Wisely, Charlotte kept the predator animals she'd summoned—wolves, panthers, snakes, and of course, David the lion—outside the tent to avoid increasing the panic even further. Instead of bursting inside, they focused on thinning out the zombie horde from the outside. Many of the additional zombie reinforcements that made their way back into the tent were missing limbs. Others were simply missing entirely.

With the troupe establishing a strong defensive foundation, William and his fellow guards were finally able to create some semblance of order. Hearing the screeching and scrabbling outside the tent, they did their best to keep people from fleeing outside and falling into far greater danger. Instead of the weapons they'd unfortunately left at home, they used the chairs as shields and barriers, doing their best to protect everyone from the seemingly never-ending horde.

But despite the troupe's bravery, skill, and strength, the sheer numbers and zombie-wave tactics were overwhelming. For every zombie that fell, it felt like two replaced them. Even worse, the zombies fought without any regard for the bystanders, and every time the troupe stepped in to save someone, they were hurt in their place.

Whenever a guest was run over, Bones redirected his energy to heal them, but that only allowed the zombie army to tear through more of his vines and continue their advance.

The slow and steady push left the troupe trapped around the stage along with all their audience members, a swarm of overpacked and terrified bodies.

Karn's reckless flame seemed to dim and one of Pennington's arms went flying through the air. Charlotte cried out in terror as a dozen zombies leaped on top of one of the elephants.

Things were bad enough that Sofia tried to join in on the fight.

She picked up the remains of Sir Francis's replica crystal ball, hurling it into a zombie's head. Any normal man would have been disfigured by the explosion of glass, but it only managed to enrage the horde even further.

Bones in particular was completely unused to sustained fighting. "What's happening?" he asked, continuing to direct his necromantic vines. He'd stuffed so many seeds in his pocket that he could thankfully keep creating them all night. "Why aren't we winning?"

"I've tried calling for more numbers, but it's too dangerous outside. More and more of my friends are getting scared and leaving."

Pennington suddenly went flying through the air, tossed back by a horde of zombies. He smashed onto the stage beside Bones and Charlotte, hitting the ground with a loud groan. Two of his four eyes spun wildly, but he smacked himself in the temples and got back up again, concussing himself on purpose to switch to a backup brain faster. His destroyed arm burbled and regenerated, his body empowered by Bones's necromantic magic.

The four-eyed zombie turned to Bones, his sudden healing a reminder of the young man's necromantic superiority. "Bones! Any chance you can just drain these guys' life force away? I'm not sure how much longer we can hold them off without people getting hurt!"

"We need some kind of distraction!" Bones shouted, trying his best to be heard through the swarm. "My magic will drive everyone insane!"

Before Pennington could reply, the tent ripped, whirling high into the air as the sheer number of bodies inside reached a critical mass. For a brief moment, the physics and engineering students felt a spurt of pride as the tent collapsed in on itself, miniaturizing into storage mode as it flew through the air, leaving only the wooden stage and the flowing backstage curtain.

Unfortunately, their spurt of professional pride was very short-lived, as everyone saw what had been waiting for them outside. The entire Islington courtyard was surrounded, all four exit arcs teeming with an apocalyptic number of zombies.

"Bones!" Karn roared. "Your magic is the only way we get out of this! I'll be the distraction!"

Twirling his torches, the caveman lit his entire body on fire.

The zombies hurriedly tried to snuff him out, throwing their bodies on top of him, but Karn was relentless, fighting back to the surface time and time again, even scrambling across the top of the enemy army in a grotesque parody of crowd surfing.

"Everyone! Look at me!" Karn shouted, leaping into the air with all his might.

Almost nobody could hear him, but they nonetheless stared at the blazing caveman's abrupt ascent. No matter how terrifying the enemy army was, it was simply human nature to react with surprise when a second sun suddenly appeared in the sky.

Karn hurtled higher and higher into the air, glowing like an angel of salvation as the real source of salvation did his work.

Bones fully released the aura of necromantic energy around his body, using his magic to the fullest for the first time in his life, covering the entire range of the courtyard.

The nimbus of indescribably terrifying color burst forth, irradiating the endlessly staring eyes of the soulless zombie horde. Under normal circumstances, the mindless flesh automatons wouldn't have felt any fear, but the sheer eldritch nature of Bones's magic tickled a primal instinct buried deep within their decaying brain stems.

They paused for only a moment—their last moment.

With a collective, shocked gasp, they staggered and sank to the ground, lifeless, as Bones drained away the necromantic life force that empowered them. The entire horde fell, body after body, extending from the very center of the Islington courtyard, back out past the archway, and even to the war camp that Baron Angelo had set up outside of the Islington gates.

A cheer rose from among the audience members, but Bones's eyes widened as he felt the thrum of much greater necromantic energy off in the distance. He could tell that Baron Angelo was coming, along with zombies much more powerful than the ones that'd just fallen.

"If Angelo came himself, it means he won't let anyone live to tell the tale," Sir Francis hissed, poking his head out from his safe space behind the backstage curtain.

"Everyone needs to get out of here," Bones shouted. "Something's coming! Hide in the river!"

Bones's voice was not nearly as carrying as the other troupe members, but thankfully, they emulated his message. The crowd quickly evacuated through the western gate, fleeing the courtyard and heading back to the river, the head clown of Undying Jest making a good note on his parchment about audience safety.

Before long, everyone was gone, save for Jack Pillary.

"What are you doing here?" Bones asked.

The man's face was pale, but his eyes were wide and manic. "I will paint this final battle in my own blood, this grand confrontation between you and your final foe. Such is my duty as your artist!"

An impossibly handsome man walked through the eastern arch.

Baron Angelo was very confident in his appearance. He groomed himself every day, using body manipulation magic before a focus group of forcibly summoned women's souls, contractually bound to answer truthfully. His red hair, flecked with gray, had a precisely calibrated number of curls and the point of his goatee looked sharp enough to draw blood.

He was dressed for battle, with gleaming, black armor engraved with the skull-and-crossbones insignia he used as his personal sigil. None of his yes men had dared to tell him that it looked like he was wearing the armor version of a pirate flag.

Angelo's face was still, so carefully controlled, he looked a little like his statue. Over the years, he'd endeavored to eliminate all emotion from his mind. Every feeling save for the will to power was folly, suitable only for the weak-willed cattle he ruled.

His right hand carried a very much non-decorative grimoire filled with countless spells he'd studied over the years. In his left was a gleaming orb filled with dense clouds of gray magic, as if he'd captured a piece of an ever-storming sky.

Angelo was surrounded by terrifyingly familiar faces, faces that Bones hadn't seen for almost twenty years. Their bodies had been damaged by shrapnel and flame but stitched back together with the same magical threads that glowed brightly on Karn's face.

Gabriel Bonaparte, a burly man with a prominent mustache and a scar beneath his chin, and Annabella Bonaparte, a woman with bouncy hair and a slightly crooked nose. Behind them were the men who had served alongside Gabriel at war: Marvin, Clyde, and Leo, all with weapons drawn. There were servants not only from the family manor, but even the serfs and peasants who had tended their land for miles around. Shambling along with them were glowing skeletons—the reanimated remains of the bodies Gabriel had once so painstakingly reinterred in the family cemetery. Most were humans; the last was a two-headed wolf.

Their eyes glowed with pale-gray fog and their faces were empty and broken. Angelo thought *he* lacked emotion, but these zombies truly did. Bones had reanimated them alongside their souls, but they were now metaphorically soulless after nineteen years of imprisonment and slavery.

"Angelo. Angelo. Angelo."

Their voices echoed through the courtyard, familiar to Bones yet twisted and hollow, forced to mutter the name of the man who'd enslaved them.

Angelo sneered at the shock on Bones's face. "You should have stayed in that cottage, boy. Nothing good can come from magic as wild and untamable as yours. Just look at what you did to your own parents."

But beneath Angelo's confident words was a quaver of fear, an emotion he had tried desperately to forget since that day almost twenty years ago. He'd tried claiming Bones for himself with one of his control orbs, only for the device to shatter in his hand. And now, the boy had crushed the zombie forces created at his own factories, forcing Angelo to strike instead with his stolen army.

Still, he thought that the sight of the boy's parents would cripple his mind. In Angelo's estimation, Bones was sentimental and weak. He had some passing talent, but he was utterly inexperienced in the art of war. Angelo resolved to crush Bones where he stood, establishing himself once and for all as the Deathless Prince.

Yet Bones was stronger and wiser than he had been when he'd been a child. He knew that it was never too late to start living life. He thought not of some dusty old prophecy, but of getting his family back.

All conventions would have dictated a magical duel for the ages, a final clash between the two rival necromancers.

But Bones was not alone.

The entire troupe burst into action, each and every member launching their own plan to get the control orb out of Angelo's hand.

Chapter Thirty-One

Karn, first to join the troupe, was also first to act. Unlike the others, who took time coming up with their respective intelligent schemes, he simply put his head down and charged, his body still aflame.

The zombies quickly surrounded Angelo in a defensive phalanx. As Karn barreled right into them, his fire guttered and died. The same frigid cold in Bones's body also ran through the zombies he'd reanimated. Not only that, their muscles had been empowered by his magic, allowing them to stand, albeit briefly, against Karn, who found himself pushed back by countless clammy hands.

Karn snarled, shoving the zombies aside in his desperation to reach Angelo. Though Karn was able to shatter their limbs and gain a temporary advantage, the necromantic energy powering these zombies was just as strong as what coursed through Bones's own body. Not only were they instantly healed of any injury, but the sheer speed and explosiveness of the regeneration blasted Karn backward, the regrown limbs hitting him with such force that Karn skidded back across the courtyard, howling in frustration. "Bones…I can tell this is your family, but did you have to do such a good job with this?"

As Karn launched himself back into the fray, Angelo was forced to order the zombies to protect him instead of charging. The baron suddenly found himself in an unprecedented military situation where his hostages were also his bodyguards. "Stay here and protect me. I'll deal with them with my spells."

Angelo flipped open his grimoire, the pages glowing as he gestured at Karn, uttering a necromantic spell under his breath. A nimbus gray storm cloud of magic swirled around his palm, crackling with power, but before the baron could strike, Tycho and Ophelia swirled around him.

They too had stayed to assist Bones, but of course, nobody had noticed their courage.

The two invisibility spirits screeched at the top of their lungs, shattering Angelo's concentration. He cursed and flipped the pages of his tome again, switching to an exorcism spell, only to be caught by a spray of crimson blood that landed right in his eyes. After his ill-fated battle with Karn and Bones, Jack Pillary had refocused his combat style to emphasize annoying and inconvenient attacks.

As Angelo furiously rubbed at his face, Charlotte blew her horn, signaling for her animals to strike. The beasts circled Angelo and his forces, but their bodies trembled and their tails were tucked back in fear. Bones's magic enveloped the reanimated corpses, and the terrifying aura was far too much for her friends to deal with.

With no other choice, Charlotte decided to strike herself, flying high before hurling her prop bow at Angelo's head as hard as she could.

The zombified body of Bones's mother, displaying absurd power and recklessness she'd never had in life, leaped into the air, catching and shattering the bow before landing so hard that her legs crumpled beneath her.

As Annabella's wounds slowly generated, Patches, furious at seeing her former owner treated this way, burst from Bones's bag. Calling forth virtually all of her necromantic energy at once, her body abruptly swelled in size, the countless stitches on her body stretching and growing. In the blink of an eye, she suddenly became a towering and terrifying figure, seven feet tall with horrifying rays of light bursting from within her body, as if she'd swallowed a twisted sun.

The gleaming light seemed to stun even the horde of zombies, particularly the ones directly from Bones's household. They gazed at Patches, their bodies still and unmoving, but the stuffed cat had badly overexerted herself. Her energy was spent in an instant, and her body shrank as she tumbled face-first onto the floor.

"Oops… sorry about that, Bones. Fighting is more tiring than I thought…" Her voice trailed off as she sank back into unconsciousness.

By then, Angelo had wiped the blood from his eyes, just in time to see Pennington pulling out his defunct control orb, which he'd salvaged as a souvenir. The four-armed zombie made a grand show of fine-tuning it, muttering loudly about calibrating necromantic frequencies.

Of course, Pennington did not know any necromancy, so it had no chance of working. However, it looked convincing enough that Angelo split his forces. "You four, get him!"

Bones's father, two peasants, and the shambling two-headed wolf lunged for Pennington. It was a group that never would have worked together in life, but Angelo viewed all the zombies as simple interchangeable tools. The zombies, their bodies empowered by Bones's magic, sprinted forth, their absurd strength enough to end Pennington's bluff, forcing him into a sudden fight. He managed to drive the zombies back, but due to their endless regeneration, he soon found himself surrounded and swept aside, forced into an endless cycle of mutual regeneration.

Sir Francis vanished from behind the black curtain, reappearing beside Angelo in a puff of brimstone and a burst of smoke. "Ah…Baron Angelo…you remember me, don't you? It's your good friend, Sir Francis!"

Still protected by his zombies, Angelo snickered. The last time the two had met, the demon had barely escaped his grasp, fleeing in terror. "Ah, Francis. Have you realized there's nothing to be done? My zombie army will defeat these rebels and I will capture that little boy and use him as a power source…"

"Yes… Y-Yes…" Sir Francis stammered, his voice inflicted with genuine fear. "I have seen the error of my ways. I see that you will be the rightful winner and I simply wish to collaborate with you. You see, I have some information to provide you." Sir Francis licked his lips nervously as he launched into a long speech, half-lecture and half-confession. "This troupe might have powerful undead forces, but there is an ordinary woman among them. The maid Sofia. She has no magical abilities, and I'm sure she will try to sneak up on you while you are solely focusing on supernatural foes. And not only that, the Islington professors and student body have fled behind the river. With their scientific and technical knowledge, no doubt they are preparing some kind of grand weapon, perhaps some kind of long-range cannon. And there may be reinforcements coming, you see. Many of the students wrote their wealthy fathers during Pennington's original seizure of power. By now, some may have arrived, so if I were you, I would carefully watch your flank."

Baron Angelo listened carefully as Sir Francis continued informing up a storm, but he was equally careful to watch the orb in his hand, holding it out of Sir Francis's clawed grasp. Having met Sir Francis years ago, Angelo suspected the demon of cowardice and treachery in equal measure.

But all of Sir Francis's talking was simply a distraction for the real ambush.

As Angelo turned to watch Sofia sneaking up on him, he let out an abrupt howl of pain and shock as his skin withered and shriveled, his bones decayed and snapped, and his organs rapidly began to fail. His handsome appearance vanished, leaving him with straggly, white hair; bleeding, red eyes; and a crone-like hunched back. His gleaming, black armor, suddenly too heavy for him to wear, began crumpling his body, piercing his skin and grinding his bones to dust.

Pure, unmitigated terror coursed through Baron Angelo's soul as just a single taste of Bones's magic demonstrated the vast gulf between them.

Bones had taken the longest to strike, but not out of fear. His training with Patches firm in his mind, Bones had carefully calibrated his magic to strike Angelo alone, while leaving his family and their people safe.

Angelo collapsed to the ground, uttering a restoration spell with a decrepit voice. The orb glowed and the zombies around him withered and fell as he drew from their life energy to heal himself. Angelo's skin seemed to slough off his body as new flesh burbled from within, forcibly returning him to his usual young state.

Bones let out a frightened cry as he abruptly shifted his magic, pouring his strength back into the weakened zombies. He knew it was beyond foolish to heal nominal enemies, but he could feel their souls still in their bodies, battered and abused as they were. He had no idea what would happen if he let them die again and he had no interest in finding out.

But that was the moment that Angelo had been waiting for.

Baron Angelo sneered, the prophecy of the Deathless Prince still first on his mind. The boy would never be able to lead invincible undead troops with such pathetic compassion for his servants. He drew more power from the zombies, a coil of black runes bursting from his hands as he struck Bones dead in the chest with an aging curse.

Bones gasped and let out a choked cough, spitting out bile. He staggered as the runes furiously grasped at him. Despite the pain, Bones felt a distant dismay in the back of his mind when he realized how quickly his hair was receding. It seemed to be coming awfully early in the aging process.

Angelo's lips twisted into a hateful snarl as he struck Bones with all the necromantic knowledge he'd acquired over the years.

Bones writhed in pain and torment, afflicted by poisons and diseases he did not understand. His blood boiled, thick bile smothered his throat, and his brain twisted like it was going to fold in on itself.

His necromantic magic flared, his body instinctively working to undo the damage, but Bones refused to relinquish his hold on his family and their people, continuing to empower them even at the expense of his own body, and so he slowly and steadily grew weaker.

Angelo's hateful snarl curled into a sneer of triumph. Even with him parasitically siphoning their necromantic energy, the zombies had enough strength and regeneration to hold off the rest of the troupe. All he had to do was bring Bones down.

Karn was blasted back by another whirl of regenerated limbs. Sir Francis, his treachery revealed, was sent flying away by a vicious backhanded strike, whizzing straight through a building. Pennington, even with four arms and four brains, was forced into a vicious stalemate, unable to think or fight past his foes.

But despite the circumstances, the rest of the troupe kept trying to force their way to Angelo, doing everything they could to claim the orb, no matter how useless their actions seemed. With resolve that nobody—especially not himself— could have predicted, Sir Francis returned to the fray in a puff of brimstone, his hands glowing with demonic flame.

But Angelo was just too well-protected, standing alongside not just Bones's family and household, but all the serfs who had worked their land. With a cruel gesture, he summoned freezing water directly into Bones's lungs, the shocking chill mixing with the earlier heat to ravage Bones's body.

Bones let out a weak gasp and fell forward, hastily catching himself with his hands, turning the fall into an awkward front flip. It was the meagerest of tumbles, far more awkward than the ones he'd been praised for as a kid, which themselves hadn't been very good.

But when they saw it, Bones's parents and their servants briefly paused, giving the rest of the troupe a chance to burst forward.

Angelo cursed, redirecting his forces so that the serfs would protect him instead, but Bones saw the buried recognition in his family's eyes, glimmering beneath the dark-gray fog.

They'd stopped earlier too, when they'd seen Patches. Bones had thought it had been out of fear, but perhaps it had been something else.

Perhaps beneath everything, they remembered a small hint of the young boy and his circus dream.

Suddenly glad that he'd packed so many, Bones pulled more seeds from his pocket. With a wave of his prop wand, he imbued them with the gentle magic he'd practiced with Patches, the twisting vines snaking through Angelo and his zombie army and granting each of the zombies a vibrant and eerie bouquet.

The serfs didn't recognize what was happening, so they continued fighting, but Angelo flinched. The sight of the highly realistic wand had convinced him that the flowers were a feint meant to disguise some sort of twisted, eldritch subterfuge.

Bones's parents and the household froze entirely, staring at the flowers that had grown in front of them. Back when Bones had been a child, he had never used his magic for tricks like these, but deep beneath their mental control, the zombies recognized the intent behind his action and paused.

Unwilling to use his magic on Angelo, for fear of him weakening his family again, Bones launched himself forward, sprinting hard with the muscles he'd gained from working in the field. He still wasn't very fast, but at the sight of his earnest sprint, the peasants briefly stopped fighting. When they saw Bones, they only felt a bare hint of recognition, nothing like the strong sense of community that had held the Bonaparte household together, but the sight of a noble risking their life for them was unlike anything they'd seen before.

With Bones suddenly appearing in front of him, Angelo snarled, activating yet another spell. His muscles burst outward, swelling into prominence as he flooded his body with chemicals. He swung a vicious fist at Bones, but Bones ducked low, temporarily ignoring the orb and going for his knees just as his father had taught him.

He crumpled Angelo's knees, slamming the now much-bigger man to the ground. The sheer force of the impact caused the swirling, gray orb to fall from Angelo's hands. With a desperate cry, Angelo lunged for it, but Bones grabbed him with both hands, jerking him back. Without any more orders, the zombies around the courtyard fell still as the two necromancers rolled inelegantly around the dirt, fighting and struggling for the control orb.

Physically, Angelo was much bigger and stronger, his enhanced body easily enough to crush Bones's limbs. But after working in the fields, Bones was *just* strong enough to hold on, and his magic was far superior. Every time his limbs were shattered, they simply grew back again. Little by little, Angelo's body withered away as Bones drew away not just his life force, but his very essence as a necromancer.

In the end, Bones found himself holding a withered and broken man, his hair dissolved to ash, his body gaunt and skeletal, his bones poking straight through his dried and tattered skin. All of Angelo's magic had abandoned him, without even a single spark remaining. Only the look of disbelief in Angelo's eyes and the piteous, shallow gasps for air told Bones that the man was anything more than a mummy.

The fight was over.

Just in case it made a difference, Bones pulled the grimoire from Angelo's withered hands, throwing it to Karn. "Burn it."

"No…" Angelo reached pitifully for the grimoire, a broken and defeated man, his mind wracked by fear and despair that he'd never felt before. The mere thought of trying to move seemed to unravel his muscles.

But for Bones, this had never been about Angelo.

He got back to his feet and picked up the orb, drawing away its energy and nullifying its nefarious controlling magic. The glow in the zombies' eyes slowly vanished as the light of consciousness returned. Though they were still undead, they were recognizably human, their faces slowly morphing from frozen despair into disbelief and then joy.

Bones's family and their people were finally free.

Chapter Thirty-Two

Slowly and steadily, Bones's natural necromantic healing scourged away Angelo's curses. Bones's face, once pale and withered, alternatively red hot and freezing cold, was restored to its former pallor. He walked over to Patches, picking her up off the ground and smiling. "Thanks, Patches. That might have taken a lot of effort, but you showed me exactly how to win."

Patches's voice was faint after her overexertion. *"Well, in a way, I saved you and Annabella. Two owners rescued in a day... Pretty good for a lazy cat."*

Annabella Bonaparte's eyes widened as she saw Bones smiling with Patches. She had thought of her son playing with his favorite stuffed animal countless times throughout her years of servitude, longing to see him in that small part of her mind that had still been her own.

A chorus of familiar voices called his name. The genuine emotion could not have been more different than the murmurings for Angelo.

"Achille..."

"Achille?"

"Achille!"

Despite Sofia's best efforts, Bones hadn't even thought of himself as Achille for a very long time, but to hear everyone from back then call him by that name felt special.

He tried to speak but couldn't.

Surrounded by all these familiar faces, he was simply overwhelmed with emotion. The guilt he'd felt over the last nineteen years, the fear that he'd somehow destroyed his own family, was gone, replaced instead by an overwhelming sense of grief at the realization of what had happened to them.

Warm tears trickled down Bones's face.

During Angelo's original attack, none of the now-zombies had understood the supernatural. But at this point, they were excessively familiar with it. Though they weren't necromancers themselves, they understood what had happened. Bones had brought them back to life after the original attack, only for them to fall under Angelo's sway.

But now, Bones had finally freed them.

Gabriel and Annabella Bonaparte, standing at the front of the group, didn't know where to begin, either, but they knew they were happy. It took a long time before they managed to speak.

"Achille...you've grown," Gabriel said. The real version of Bones's father was much kinder than the dream one. The voice of his father spurred Bones to reply.

"I'd like to think so," Bones said. "I got a lot of help from Sofia. And my new friends."

Gabriel stared at the troupe. Despite their odd appearances, he remembered them fighting loyally by Bones's side.

"You have good and loyal people around you. Men like the soldiers who fought alongside me." Behind him, the warriors of the Bonaparte household nodded, their eyes filled with respect and admiration for Bones's martial victory, unconventional as it had been.

"Yeah. We ended up starting a circus. A real one. And we had a huge show. With a big tent, and, uh, a lot of fans…" Bones trailed off. Of course, all around him were simply the fallen zombies from Angelo's original army, with no fans to be found. "They're, um, off in the distance, behind the river. We made sure they took cover. You know, audience safety and all that… And the tent…uh, well, it got blown away. But it's real. You can go back and ask them if you want. They might be scared of you, though."

Bones really wanted his parents to understand that his show was a success. A clamor rose from the Second Chance troupe, Sir Francis loudest of all. Nobody wanted to interfere with Bones's emotional reunion, but they were eager to convince his parents that he was a legitimate businessperson.

Annabella chuckled. "I'm sure it's real, Achille. You were always a terrible liar."

"Well, um…that's good. I'm glad you guys believe me," Bones said. "Maybe you can watch a show sometime. I, uh…"

He trailed off yet again.

New worries blossomed in Bones's mind as he promptly began to overthink his joy at this reunion.

In fairness to Bones, nobody would have been able to process his sudden shift in fortune. In the morning, his biggest concern had been putting on a good show, but his life had been utterly upended after this battle, and even a good utter upending was still an utter upending.

He was happy to see everyone again, to have freed them from Angelo, but he also knew that he couldn't go back to how things had been before. Bones didn't know if any of these people wanted to be zombies or not, nor did he know what that meant for his future. Was he expected to return to the family lands and administer them? Just as importantly, who was going to bring Angelo before the king to charge for his crimes?

And what of the serfs they'd freed? Many of them stood behind the Bonaparte household, dazed and confused. Others had already begun sneaking away, fearful that Bones would steal back their newfound freedom.

Bones's parents cut through his worries. They knew that even as a hero, their son was still an overthinker.

"Yes. We would like to go to a show sometime." Gabriel smiled. It was a wonderful feeling to have emerged from nineteen years of torment, only to realize that all their son's wildest dreams had come true. "Are you thinking of traveling performances?"

"That was the plan," Bones replied.

"Well, then," Gabriel stated, "we will happily take care of things here, at least for now. The way I see it, we owe you about twenty years of caretaking. We will have to return to our manor and lands, fix things up, make recompense for people who were injured alongside us."

"And that's not all," Annabella added. "We must make our case before the king."

On the cobblestones, Angelo finally stirred, angry tears falling from his eyes as he desperately tried to push himself back to his feet.

As he gazed down at his withered hands, Angelo felt guilt for the first time in his life.

Angelo had broken almost every unwritten rule of life and despite the significant leeway granted to the nobility, he had broken most of the written ones too. But he regretted none of his deceptions and manipulations, none of his heinous crimes, none of his countless murders and human experimentation sessions. He'd never believed in any moral code—he'd only believed in himself. Yet despite that self-belief, all of his efforts had come to nothing.

His dream of conquering the world with invincible, undead troops had been shattered in his very own barony, leaving him stripped of his youth and magic alike.

Angelo had let his past self down, and he had to make it up to his future self somehow.

In a rather shocking demonstration of willpower, he managed to force himself back to his feet, but even a simple step was impossible. His feet creaked and shattered, all ten of his toes dislocating themselves at once as he crashed back onto the ground, his legs snapping like twigs.

Karn let out an excited cry. "Wow, Bones! The splinter prophecy was real! This guy broke his legs—both of them! It's a double prophecy!"

Annabella Bonaparte swooped forward. Like her son, she had always been on the shy and quiet side, but she was fierce beneath. Here, she put her necromantic strength to good use, grabbing the withered and battered Angelo as he tried crawling away.

"We will tell the king what happened here," Annabella said. "We never liked doing it, but your father and I know how to play the political game. We'll explain everything that happened."

Sofia's eyes widened as she internally noted that the dead did indeed tell tales.

Before Gabriel and the household could leave, one of the zombies broke off, kneeling before Bones and grinning—it was the two-headed wolf he'd used to pet as a child. The creature, ancient yet noble, went up to about Bones's chest. His body consisted almost entirely of brightly glowing necromantic energy shaped to make up for the many missing parts of its corpse. Old and withered bones held together the magical sparks, helped by a few stubborn bristles of fur. He looked about eighty percent spirit and only twenty percent skeleton.

Gabriel frowned. "You know, I never figured out why there was a two-headed wolf with us."

"You grabbed the wrong remains for the cemetery," Bones said. "Some very incorrect remains."

Gabriel laughed embarrassedly. "Huh. I suppose I'll have to track down what really happened to that ancestor. Another thing to do when I get back to the manor."

The wolf nudged Bones again with both its heads.

"You want to come with me?" Bones asked.

Unlike Patches, the two-headed wolf could not speak, but after having so many orders barked at him by Angelo, he could loosely understand what Bones was saying. He only had one tail, but he wagged it enough for both heads.

"Well, I'd like you to come with us too. Do you have a name?" Bones asked as Charlotte squealed with delight.

The wolf shook his heads.

If Bones remembered correctly, the two heads had almost always acted as one, but he thought he might as well ask to be sure. "Do you guys want a separate name for each head? Or just one?"

The heads looked at each other, then nodded together to confirm they preferred to be named collectively.

Bones breathed a sigh of relief. Coming up with two names would have been even more difficult. "How about 'Heads'?" he asked.

The wolf wrinkled his two faces in a surprisingly human display of consternation.

Patches's disdain resonated in everyone's mind. *"Bones, what are you talking about? Heads? That's a terrible name!"*

"I mean, it was the first thing that came to mind! You know, Bones, Patches, Heads. There's kind of a plural-objects theme."

"You might as well call them 'Brains.'" Sir Francis scoffed.

"Or worse, 'Legs.'" Sofia chuckled. "He's still got four of them."

"Or 'Fangs,'" Karn said. Then he paused. "You know, Fangs would actually be a pretty cool name for a wolf."

The twin-headed wolf wagged his tail. "Well, Fangs it is, then." Bones smiled.

With that, the Bonapartes and their household turned to leave, there were also plenty of zombies remaining. The peasants were scared, confused, and afraid, fearful that they had simply traded one all-powerful master for another.

Though they knew who Bones and his family were by reputation, they'd never met their lords before death and almost twenty decades of servitude had left them rightfully suspicious of the nobility.

Bones called his parents back, hoping for guidance, but they shook their heads before passing through the archway. "Achille, we will manage the home and set things right, but technically, we died. By the law of the land, you are the lord now. You have accomplished your duty by saving us and them, but you must decide what to do next."

Bones had no ruling experience, but his travels had taught him that the peasants' lives had already been very difficult, no matter who their lord was. Their lives as zombies were undoubtedly worse. It seemed undeniably cruel to order them back to their lands.

"If the king offers us any recompense for what the baron did, it shall be split evenly with you and your descendants. But otherwise, you're all free to go. Please, go on and live your lives."

For obvious reasons, the newly freed zombies did not need to be told twice. They hurried away from the courtyard, joining those who had already vanished earlier.

"Releasing a bunch of near-invincible zombies might cause problems," Sir Francis commented.

Bones nodded as he watched them leave. "It could. But they'll be a lot happier than all of Angelo's troops who were running around with deadly weapons and empty stomachs. I'm hoping that especially after what happened to them, they'll want to live their lives peacefully, just like we are right now. But if something happens… Well, I guess I'll have to take responsibility and deal with it."

Bones did not like fighting, and he suspected he never would. But after today, he'd realized just how important it could be.

"Well, there's no need for such a serious tone." Sir Francis nervously chuckled. "I'd say that most people just want to live and let live with their lives. Of course, those people are usually dominated by people like me who want wealth and power, but I suppose with your magic protecting them, they'll be able to protect themselves better than most."

"I wouldn't worry too much about the zombies leaving. They're probably just glad to be free, like I was," Pennington interjected. "You should be a lot more worried about the zombies still in the courtyard."

The zombies reanimated by Bones were off living their unlives, but the army created at Angelo's factory was still strewn across the courtyard.

Karn eyed the hideous mountains of rotting flesh. "What are we going to do with them, Bones?"

"Their souls are gone. I can't bring them back as they were. But these people, well… They were probably other people's families. It…" Bones's words caught in his throat. He was far from Angelo's only victim. "We should try to find out who they were. Get their remains back home if we can."

"That will be difficult," Sofia said. "But at Islington, it won't be completely impossible."

A voice called out from beyond the western gate. "Indeed, you're at a place very adept at researching and cataloging."

Professor Roman strode back through the archway, leading the rest of the audience.

At first, they were wary and timid, staring at the defeated zombies with very well-justified fear that they might spring back up again, but soon, they were all cheering for the Second Chance troupe. The show had gone above and beyond all their expectations. Not only had the performers put on the show of their lives, they'd also saved everyone's lives.

Sofia nudged Bones. "Send them off," she whispered.

"Oh, right."

Bones gulped, strangely still feeling nervous despite everything that had happened. Fortunately, after his heroics, the audience members were very inclined to listen to him, even if it was a struggle to hear his soft voice. "Well, thanks for enjoying our show. We have a memento for everyone to take home!"

Even after the fight, Bones still had plenty of necromantic energy. And due to his overpacking, he also had more seeds. He pulled them out of his pocket, then waved his wand in a dramatic arc.

Vines grew once more through the courtyard, twining through the audience and leaving each guest with a souvenir bouquet.

"Please, tell everyone you know about the Second Chance Circus! Hopefully, the next show won't be quite as chaotic, but we can promise that it'll always be a performance that you will never forget."

Chapter Thirty-Three

But even though the show had ended, there was still the very important matter of cleaning up. Charlotte summoned her birds to track down the tent as everyone else got to work clearing the bodies out of the courtyard. The Rustling natives, by virtue of having worked their whole lives, did the lion's share of the work, but the Islington students did their best to assist them. Everyone ignored the putrid scent the best they could.

Professor Roman mused excitedly to himself. Identifying the bodies and contacting their family members was completely outside his area of training, but he struggled to think of anyone else who could fulfill such an important task. "Well, we don't even know how long Angelo has been amassing bodies. I suppose we'll all just have to study forensics for a year. It seems more learnable than necromancy."

William was much more practical. "We probably won't be able to find everyone, even if we do our best. But we should create a memorial to honor those who were lost."

In a grand irony, some of the students were even considering learning embalming to maintain the corpses until their families could be found.

The troupe got to work alongside the audience members, with Bones dismissing the idea of animating the zombies and having them walk into the school. It felt like the audience had had enough of zombies for one day and though Bones did not know who Angelo's nameless soldiers were, he felt like they at least deserved to be carried after the terror that had happened to them. Even Fangs got into the mix, pulling bodies on a makeshift wooden sled created by planks from the destroyed gate to Islington. In a way, it seemed fitting for an undead wolf to herd corpses.

Only a single group refused to do any manual labor, sitting in the corner and chittering irritably to themselves.

By the fifth dirty look, Bones decided to see what the fuss was all about, and he walked up to the gathered zombie clowns of Undying Jest. The clown's foggy eyes narrowed as he walked towards him. Having seen just the devastating effects of Bones's magic, they were genuinely afraid.

The massive, triangular-shaped lead clown pushed himself to the front again. Despite his fears, he considered himself a bold truth-teller who wouldn't be cowed, no matter how powerful or frightening the target of his unfortunate truth. Throughout the wild battle between Angelo and Bones, the Undying Jest clowns had been single-mindedly focused on providing the Second Chance troupe with an inaugural rating from the *Undying Jest* pamphlet, even peeking out past the gate to occasionally watch the fight. "Excuse me. There was a bit of commotion before the show, but judging by your statue and your position as the final performer, is it safe to assume that you are the proprietor of this establishment?"

Bones had no idea how to answer that question.

"Um…what do you mean?"

"You are responsible for the acts? Do you receive most of the show's profits?"

"Uh…I don't think we discussed payments are going to be divided," Bones replied. He knew that Sofia and Sir Francis had collected several sacks of gold, but he'd been so focused on his upcoming performance that he hadn't thought about it at all. "I mean, I think we would probably all share it. These are my friends. I don't think I'm their boss or anything like that…"

The head clown chittered, his decayed eyebrows jolting upwards with such force that they got lodged in his forehead. "You mean to say that you don't own this circus? You have some kind of non-traditional ownership method?"

"Um, I guess?" Bones replied. He felt very uncomfortable answering economics-related questions, but Sir Francis was nowhere to be found. Not even his proud horns were visible above the sheer quantity of people hustling through the courtyard.

"Are you at least responsible for the acts?"

"Um. I mean… People kind of just make up their own acts."

At this, all of the Undying Jest clowns leaped back at once, so shocked that their eyes fell from their sockets and plopped onto the ground. The triangle-shaped head clown stumbled so far back that he left his foot behind him. He stumbled around trying to grab it but was unable to see it without his eyes.

"Uh…let me help you guys out," Bones said.

With a wave of his hand, necromantic energy bound the clown's eyes back into their sockets, while also returning the head clown's foot.

As one, they scowled at Bones, muttering angrily to each other.

"More inappropriate magic use. I mean, I appreciate my eyeballs, but it's the principle of it all. What of the magician's code?"

"He probably could have passed off that necromantic duel as the result of special effects, but collapsing the entire army was just a bit too much. He couldn't resist showing off!"

"Look at what he did to the poor baron! Upending the social order in the middle of his show. It's almost like he doesn't understand the point of bread and circuses!"

Bones had no idea what the Undying Jest clowns were going on about. "I'm sorry, what do you mean?"

The lead crown leaned forward, his voice stern and flinty. "Well. We thank you for inviting us to your show."

Bones hadn't invited them at all, but he was too polite to say so. He merely nodded.

The clown handed him a piece of parchment. "We regret to inform you that your final rating is negative one star. And trust me, after your stunt with the eyeballs, you're lucky it hasn't dropped to a negative two."

"I'm sorry?" Bones asked.

"A negative one. We understand that it doesn't fit on the traditional zero to five star scale, but we felt like it was worth breaking tradition. Your show is a total scam. All of those tricks are pure falsehoods."

Bones stared at the clowns, unable to even begin processing their line of thinking. They seemed even more stubborn than Sofia! How could they possibly think that their magic had been mere falsehoods? He supposed that Sir Francis technically hadn't used magical powers, but the demon still possessed them.

But as the head clown continued speaking, Bones grew even more confused. "It seems like all your performers simply get by with magical strength. There is no *craftsmanship* involved, no sleight of hand or optical illusions. And to make matters worse, you exposed yourselves by saving your audience members, thereby losing your chance to become truly legendary."

The other clowns chittered in agreement.

"Yes. Yes. Such a shame. People would have whispered about your troupe until the end of the time."

"You had the chance to go down in tragic history."

"Dying to the baron at the peak of your show would have been a story for the ages, the stuff of circus myth and legend."

Bones couldn't help but ask. "Wait. How would anyone have whispered about us if Angelo killed every single person in the audience?"

The clowns chittered and sighed. "Well, that was why we took cover first. We knew you needed witnesses to your tragic end. After we spread our rumors, imagine what the first person to stumble upon this ruined school and the burnt-down tent would have thought to themselves. Now *that* would have been true art."

Bones was still getting the hang of socializing, but the clowns viewed things from such a fundamentally different viewpoint that it felt impossible to relate to them. He didn't even bother mentioning that Sir Francis's act involved trickery, which by their definition was honesty. "Let me get this straight. You are giving me a negative one-star review because we saved everyone's lives, thereby revealing our magical powers. And you're also mad that I cured your blindness."

"Exactly!" the head clown eagerly exclaimed, glad that Bones was finally understanding things. "Saving us from Angelo was appreciated, and so was restoring our vision during the review process. Our negative one-star rating has nothing to do with you as a person. We are solely evaluating you as a performer, and we *must* stick to our reviewers' code."

The clowns glanced at each other, chittering sympathetically.

"Yes, pursuing true greatness is very difficult."

"Performers must sacrifice themselves to the art."

"Well, we trust we won't see you again. We have no interest in a crude, lowbrow show such as this."

With that, the zombie clowns left, leaving an utterly confused Bones in their wake. Part of him wished that Fangs would have come over and bitten them, but the wolf was busy working.

"Ah, I wouldn't worry about them," a confident voice called. "I've dealt with them before. Their comments are bad enough when they claim to be your fans. They're just a bunch of decaying dicks. Well, maybe they *have* a bunch of decaying dicks. It would explain why they're so mad all the time."

Boners turned and found a very large man with a very excited smile gazing down at him. He had red hair parted on either side, so frizzy, it looked like a bonfire. His simple, red tunic strained against his ample stomach and his gleaming, gold pants were caked with mud and dirt from the hasty evacuation.

"Wow. It's… I-It's you…" Bones stammered. "I… What? Were you at the show?"

The Great Clown nodded. "Yes, a little bird told me about the circus. An actual little bird, mind you, a fascinating touch. I know I'm known for my metaphorical stories, so best to clear that up."

"Wow…why did you come?"

"I'd been feeling terrified and frightened, and I thought your show might pick me up."

"W-Well, a lot of terrifying and frightening stuff happened…" Bones stammered. "But, um…I think we got rid of a terrifying threat at least?"

The Great Clown nodded, only a slight tremor coursing through his body. For obvious and unfortunate reasons, the Second Chance troupe's inaugural performance hadn't exactly alleviated the Great Clown's fear of necromancy, but learning that Bones was a definitive force for good had certainly helped. "Well, just knowing there's an excellent show out there makes me want to get the crew back together again as soon as possible. Speaking of which, I better leave for Golden Fields now to pick up our tent. A word of advice: you never know when creativity strikes, so strike while the fire is hot, and don't be afraid to follow your impulses!"

With that, the Great Clown left, walking through the western gate.

He returned moments later. "Oh. Right. That leads right back to the river. And here I was hoping for a dramatic exit."

"You can leave through any of the other three."

"Just my luck." The Great Clown laughed.

As he watched the Great Clown walk away, Bones tossed the parchment from the Undying Jest clowns aside. The Great Clown's words mattered much more than some slip of paper.

Bones and the Second Chance troupe worked in the courtyard for the rest of the day, and when night fell, the citizens of Islington and Rustling left side by side, happily chattering among each other and resolving to spread word of the Second Chance Circus far and wide. Sofia smiled. She would have forced her family members to endorse the show, anyway, but recommendations always felt more genuine when people truly believed them.

"So, Bones…where to next?" Karn asked as the troupe regrouped beside Charlotte's carriage. "There should be time for a few good performances before your parents get everything settled, right? Hopefully, there will be more show and less fighting. Technically, I'm retired from violence, but I make an exception for self-defense."

"Um, well, do you guys have any ideas?" Bones asked.

"I have no idea where anything is," Karn replied.

"Me, neither," Pennington added.

"I don't care where we go." Charlotte shrugged. "I have friends all around the world!"

"I'm happy with whatever you decide," Sir Francis said. "I need to make myself scarce in Islington for a while, anyway. This cataloging project sounds like it will cost the school a great deal of money and I don't want to be responsible for replenishing it."

"You should decide for yourself, Achille! You run a necromantic circus. Be more whimsical!" Sofia laughed.

Fangs barked affirmatively and Patches let out an agreeable mental meow.

Bones thought back to the Great Clown and his comment about not being afraid to follow his impulses. "Well, I was thinking about the Great Clown and his joke about Gon the Gut… Let's head east. See what's going on there."

"I don't see why not," Charlotte replied. She pulled out her horn and blew, and the troupe piled into the carriage, now pulled by a pair of antelopes with proud, black horns.

And from that day on, Bones swept through the world, invincible with his undead troupe at his back.

THE END